DESSA'S CROSSING

A Novel and Other Stories

Atanas Radenski

Paperback ISBN-13: 979-8-9985181-0-2
Ebook ISBN-13: 979-8-9985181-1-9

The book is cataloged in WorldCat (OCLC no. 1564328155).
Names: Radenski, Atanas, author
Title: Dessa's Crossing: A Novel and Other Stories
Subjects: Fiction | Families | Commitment (Psychology) | Duty | Search and rescue operations
Classification: PG1038.28.A26 D47 2025

Cover image: "The Lawrence Tree," painting by Georgia O'Keeffe, 1929 (public domain)

Literary consultant: Bruce McAlister
Developmental Editor: Emily Ohanjanians
Line Editors: Melissa Prideaux, Angela Bojinov
Copy Editor: Ellen Tarlin

Published in the United States of America.

TO MY READERS

It took me two years to write this book, but then three more years to revise it four times, learning how to make it better. We writers, "are all apprentices in a craft where no one ever becomes a master," as Ernest Hemingway put it. I wholeheartedly agree with him: writing is a perpetual learning process that continues even after the book is completed.

To me, reviews are essential in this process, helping me understand what works and what does not. I read every single review that I receive, with appreciation and respect for the opinions you offer. Please leave an honest review or rating on Amazon, or Goodreads, or both.

There is one more thing I need to ask of you: please share information about this book with friends, acquaintances, and social network connections who might be interested in taking a look. You might also suggest it to your local bookstore and library.

Thank you with all my heart. Happy reading!

For Roumi and the kids

DESSA'S CROSSING:
A NOVEL

CHAPTER ONE

Dessa never wanted Penelope to die—she only wanted to leave her.

Yet here she was—dead.

Dessa searched Penelope's empty eyes.

The hate had vanished from them now, and the love was gone too—yet her last words, "You'll be mine forever!" still echoed in Dessa's mind.

She stood up, stared at her bloody hands, and her knees gave way.

But she was a rescuer, a warrior—and on the search-and-rescue battlefield, she'd seen it all. Climbers, nearly frozen—brought back to life. Hikers, vanished without a trace—never found. Children, injured in ravines—saved. Bodies, bloated in rivers and lakes—recovered. Every time, she managed to quell her emotions, focusing on the rescue itself. There was time for feelings once the mission was done.

Now, too, she needed to stay cool, stay calm. Keep it together—like she had at Wallace Falls, on Baring Mountain, in Devil's Cave. Even Penelope's death—her ex's death—shouldn't throw her off-balance. It mustn't. It wouldn't.

She closed her eyes, drawing in a deep breath and holding it for a few heartbeats before exhaling steadily. She focused on the tip of her nose and inhaled again.

After a dozen breaths, her body softened. She glanced at her hands, now trembling less. She wiped them across her pants and dialed 9-1-1, but the call didn't go through.

Of course. She was in Europe—she needed to dial 1-1-2.

When the call connected, she reported what had

happened, and emergency services said they would be there as soon as they could.

Hanging up, she stared at the door. Penelope had locked it and hurled the key out the window. Dessa was trapped here —with Penelope's body—unless someone helped her get out.

She dialed Fred, but her call went straight to voicemail. Fred was sleeping downstairs and might hear her if she shouted—though she didn't want to risk waking Archie next door.

She had no choice but to rappel out of the locked room.

After rummaging through her climbing gear, she pulled out a rope and secured it to the bed frame. With one last tug to test its hold, she climbed over the windowsill, swung outside, and rappelled down the wall to a downstairs window. She knocked on the glass, and Fred stirred, rising from the couch in the dark.

He opened the window and gazed at her. "Dessa!"

The rope bit into her hands.

"The moonlight around your head... You look like a saint."

"I'm no saint."

Fred's eyes widened. "Is that blood?"

"Yes, it is. Now back up."

She swung onto the windowsill, landing in a squat, and jumped into the room.

"I need to clean up."

Fred stood at the window, staring into the night. "Why haven't the cops arrived yet?"

Dessa stirred in her chair, her throat raw. "Zarena is a tiny village," she murmured. Deep in the Balkan Mountains, they were far from the services they'd taken for granted in Washington State. "There's no law enforcement here. The police have to drive all the way up the mountain from the county seat."

Fred left his post at the window and sat opposite her. "You haven't had your tea."

"I tried… I couldn't swallow."

She bowed her head.

"Do you want anything else?"

She raised her eyes to meet his, her chin quivering. "I want to reverse time and handle everything differently." She let out a sob. "I'm a rescuer, not a murderer."

"No… You're not a murderer."

But wasn't she?

Police sirens wailed in the distance, their shrill tone slicing through the silence. She glanced at Fred, and he offered a reassuring smile.

She swallowed her tears.

Who would have thought, after the way they'd met a year ago—when she'd hoisted him off a cliff face and carried him to safety—that Fred would be her only support in this surreal moment?

CHAPTER TWO

One Year Earlier, Washington State

"You can't get lost if you don't plan on going back." Fred hitched his fingers on the straps of his pack.

He abandoned the trail, threading along the forested ridge, dry twigs crackling under his boots. He paused by a cedar tree, roots clinging to the shallow soil at the cliff's edge. A gnarled branch jutted out—over the abyss.

This was the spot.

Settling himself on the ground, he took off his backpack and fished out a bottle of Courvoisier and a dark chocolate bar. He unsealed the bottle and took a swig, the cognac warming him with its velvety smoothness.

He bit into the chocolate bar and took another swig.

Fred smirked at the absurdity of it all: if he got too drunk, he might stumble off the cliff and ruin his plans to hang himself. Talk about wasted effort. He staggered to his feet, deciding to hang the rope on the branch while he was still semi-sober.

From his pack, he pulled out the rope and his phone. He'd had the foresight to download instructions for a hangman's knot and was reading them now. Uncoiling the rope, he threw one end over the branch and tried to tie the knot, but he kept messing it up.

Tying a noose sure wasn't easy if you'd never hanged

yourself before.

When the noose was finally ready, he turned it in his hands, inspected it, and put it around his neck. It fit just right, neither too loose nor too tight.

He raised his phone, took a selfie, and stared at the screen. His nose didn't strike him as too crooked, and his graying goatee wasn't too ugly. In fact, just a couple of days ago, his shrink insisted he was still a looker for his age, slender and wiry as he was. Now, even though no one was watching, he straightened his back and shoulders. He didn't want to die looking unpresentable.

He shoved the phone into his pocket and crouched with the noose still around his neck, reaching for the bottle. "Cheers," he muttered, taking a huge swig. He stared at the now half-empty Courvoisier bottle before kneeling to stash it in his pack, as if he could finish it in the afterlife. Rising again, he donned his pack and peered over the edge.

The rocky crests of the North Cascades stretched to the east, with Glacier Peak's ice-covered slopes rising over the ridges from the distant Pacific Northwest. Fred was glad he had chosen to end his life here, amid the mountains he loved, rather than overdosing on pills in bed.

Standing at the edge—the wind whispering through the branches, memories flooding his mind—Fred closed his eyes, and his life flashed before him.

He saw himself as a baby boy, spending evenings snoozing in a vegetable basket at his parents' Paris bistro. As a horrified toddler, certain his father was murdering his mother when in fact they were making love in the quiet kitchen when business was slow. As a confused teenager, unable to see women as anything but mother-like angels or purely sexual objects.

As an apprentice, making the best cassoulet in town.

A cash-strapped immigrant, working night shifts in Seattle cafeterias. A popular cook at the Grumpy Chef across from Boeing. A junior menu consultant at Boeing by day and a graduate student by night. Finally, a full-time instructor in culinary arts at Puget College.

And then he saw... Eva.

Eva Joy, the visual art student who, gods know why, had taken his Pastries course. The very Eva Joy who had been his wife for a quarter-century now.

He opened his eyes, glanced once more at the blue horizon, and tightened the noose. It was time. Standing straight, squaring his shoulders, and lifting his chin, he sang.

"Little skylark, lovely little skylark, I will pluck your neck, little lark... O-o-o-oh! And your head, and your beak, and your neck! A-a-a-ah!"

Singing, he leaped into the abyss.

A burning pain cut through his neck, an invisible whip cracking above his head. His derriere slammed into the cliff. He tumbled down the smooth, steep face. The branch, still tethered to the rope, rattled behind him like a rambunctious puppy. Spread-eagled, he slid through a patch of bushes and hit a small ledge, bending his knees. The branch shot by him and pulled the rope taut. He staggered but managed to grab a crack in the rock, keeping his balance.

Standing upright on the ledge and clinging to the cliff with his hands, he looked around. Miraculously, he had come to a stop in the middle of the cliff face, a hundred feet below the edge. Another hundred feet farther down, the cliff base was littered with sharp-edged rocks.

The branch was dangling below him, pulling on the noose—pulling him down.

His stomach churned, and his legs trembled. He could fall and die at any moment now—but he didn't want to! Not anymore!

Now he wanted to live.

He unclenched his fingers from the crack and snatched

his phone from his pocket. His hand shook as he dialed 9-1-1. A woman answered the call right away.

"I fell!" he yelled. "Mount Pilchuck! Send help."

The connection was poor, and he could only catch part of the reply. "Mountain Search and Rescue... hold on... if necessary... at night... four or five hours, no more..."

"Four or five hours!?" His chin quivered like a child's as he spoke. "I'm hanging off a cliff with a noose around my neck! A huge branch is pulling me down! If it doesn't choke me, it'll pull me into the abyss! Send a helicopter—" But then, his phone battery died.

A disquieting silence fell around him.

The helicopter roared into view after an hour. Fred's heart leapt with hope—only to crash as the aircraft rumbled past him, thundering away along the jagged south ridge.

Oh, No! Why couldn't they spot him, standing on this ledge smack in the middle of the cliff?! Hugging the rock tight, the branch still tugging on his neck!

He waved his arm, screaming. His neck was swollen and throbbing, and he was unsure whether to lament or congratulate himself for making a terrible noose that hadn't choked him to death yet.

He waved and screamed again.

And—voilà!—the helicopter returned, circled, then hovered a hundred feet above him. An orange-clad figure appeared in the open door of the aircraft. The figure swooped down, swirling around in the rotor wash, and landed beside him on the narrow ledge. The rescuer, a petite person with a girlish figure, smiled at him.

He must've died, he thought, and this was a little flame-colored angel coming to take him to heaven.

"I'm Dessa Sinich," shouted the woman through the wind and engine noise. "I'll get you out of here, but we have to hurry because this ledge is rather precarious."

She unzipped her pocket, pulled out a Swiss Army knife, and cut the rope hanging around his neck. The branch tumbled down the cliff and shattered on the rocks below.

"So far, so good," his angel said. "Now let's take off your backpack... carefully, carefully... that's it." She placed the pack on the ledge behind her.

She wound a strap around his chest, under his arms, and clipped it to the rescue hook. "This is to prevent you from sliding out of the chest strap." She attached another strap between his legs. "One last check, and we're ready to be hoisted up!"

"Can we take my backpack?... My car keys are in there!"

"Of course." She hoisted his pack onto her shoulders. "Now get ready to play pinball—except we'll be the ball."

"I'm scared!"

"Scared? What could possibly go wrong?"

"We could fall and die!"

She gave him a quick smile. "I wouldn't let you die even if you wanted to."

She spoke into her radio and waved at a man sitting at the helicopter door. The hoist cable grew taut as they reeled them in. In a couple of seconds, Fred hung below her, and she wrapped her legs around his torso. They spun together, hurtling toward the cliff—but she pushed off the rock face with her arms. They swung back toward the cliff, but she pushed them away once more.

He filled his lungs with air. His savior looked tiny, but she was tougher than rock. *Phew!* He exhaled.

The man at the door helped him and his rescuer inside and pointed to a seat. Fred slumped over and closed his eyes. The man pulled the door shut, and the next moment they were flying up and away from the cliff. Farther and farther away.

His last bit of strength vanished, and he drifted off.

Eva appeared before him... sitting at his desk, completely naked.

"Let me have some Courvoisier." Eva winked at him. "With every sip, I'll tell you about one of my lovers."

"No, don't! You're making me feel sick." A surge of bile rose in his throat. "I'm going to throw up!"

"In the bag!"

He opened his eyes. That voice didn't belong to Eva—it was his rescuer's. She pushed his head forward, pressed a paper bag to his mouth, and he vomited.

"Please, hang on. We'll be landing at the hospital in a couple of minutes."

He wanted to nod but couldn't. Instead, he just closed his eyes again.

CHAPTER THREE

As Dessa stepped out of the helicopter onto the rooftop helipad, Fred lunged for the door.

"Wait!" she barked, but he was already stumbling out, landing in a heap at the feet of a startled deputy. Two orderlies rushed forward, hoisting Fred onto a gurney.

The deputy shook his head. "That's one way to make an entrance."

"He fell a hundred feet down a cliff. By some miracle, he survived—and without any visible injuries."

"God must've intervened."

"No. He's drunk."

Not just drunk—wasted. He had thrown up all over the helicopter, and she'd have to clean it.

She and the deputy watched the orderlies as they rolled Fred away.

"Drunk people survive because they don't resist the fall. They roll down cliffs like balls of play dough. The sober ones die."

Behind her, the helicopter droned louder. It was time to fly back to the search-and-rescue base, wrap up the mission, and go home.

Dessa strode toward the aircraft, jumped inside, and took her seat by the side door. The helicopter lifted a yard above the roof—then wobbled. The engine roared to full power, and she gripped the edge of her seat, her fingers vibrating with the fuselage. The tail rotor wailed like a circular saw, the main blades chopped through the air, and the helicopter rose like a startled bird.

Helicopter pilots don't just fly—they beat the air into submission.

The aircraft turned toward the SAR base.

"Sorry for the rough ride, guys." The pilot steadied the helicopter with a practiced hand. "I'm hungry."

The flight helmets muffled the engine noise, and the pilot's voice resounded in Dessa's headset.

She nodded in understanding. He was a great pilot—and she knew there was more to it than just an empty stomach. His wife was away visiting her sister in New York, leaving him lonely and anxious, with no one to talk to in his wifeless kitchen.

"Do you want me to order you a pizza?" the copilot asked.

"Thanks, I still have some from the one you bought me yesterday."

"Then should I play you a song?" the crew chief piped up from the back.

The crew chief was a big man who sat at the side door during hoists, his long legs dangling in the air. His name was Joe—but people called him Big Joe.

"Alexa, play 'Leftover Chicken, Leftover Ham'," Big Joe shouted.

The pilot's phone streamed the song into the crew's headsets. The three men hummed and traded jokes as Dessa watched the cityscape fade away. The forested hills around the base came into view, peppered with farms and rural homes. She lived in one of those homes with Penelope and Archie—and as they flew over the ridge, Dessa spotted it.

They descended—but in the middle of the helipad stood a donkey, so still it seemed tethered by invisible chains. The helicopter swooped down with a rumble and hovered thirty feet above it. The donkey looked up with a placid gaze, bent its legs, lay down, and lowered its head. Its ears drooped.

"It must've run away from the donkey farm," Big Joe said.

They waited, still hovering above the animal.

Dessa pursed her lips. "It won't budge."

"Looks like it's lying down for the night." The pilot ascended and orbited.

There was no one at the base to round up the donkey. Dessa suggested calling the sheriff, but the pilot opposed it.

"If we do, we'll become the laughingstock of the whole county. Just imagine the headlines... 'Pilot calls for help, ass needs saving.'"

Big Joe and the copilot agreed.

The pilot turned to her. "I wonder if Penelope could drive down and chase away the animal?"

Dessa called Penelope, laughing as she told her about the donkey. But when she asked if Penelope could come help, Penelope hung up mid-sentence. This left her uncertain whether Penelope was actually going to come—but then she spotted Penelope's Toyota leaving the garage and heading into the forest.

Ten long minutes later, the Toyota arrived at the helipad.

She watched Penelope slip out and walk to the donkey, toting a paper bag. As Penelope got closer, the donkey bared its teeth, as if to say, "Do you want a kick in the face?" It looked as if Penelope bared her teeth back at the animal.

Penelope stopped three feet from the animal and pulled a carrot from the bag. The donkey rose, approached her, and took a bite. Penelope took a couple of steps back and offered the carrot again while pulling out another carrot. The donkey took another bite and followed her, chewing. Bite after bite, Penelope led the donkey away.

The pilot descended to the liberated helipad.

Penelope glanced at the landing helicopter over her shoulder, her cheeks puffed up like a hamster's. Without waiting for Dessa, Penelope got into the Toyota and headed back home. The donkey followed along the road, accompanied by the fading sounds of the helicopter's engine. The rotors stopped turning, and everybody spilled out onto the pad.

The pilot turned to Dessa. "Penelope didn't seem happy about coming down here."

"I interrupted her teleconference." She glanced away. "She's been so busy at work lately, so stressed out."

The pilot nodded. "I wanted to thank her for driving down here and helping us out."

"I'll tell her when I get home. It'll make her happy."

An hour later, the helicopter sat in the hangar, gleaming under the lights. It was spotless now, scrubbed of dust, vomit, and the memory of near-death.

Everyone had left, except for Dessa. Not ready to go home, she wandered into the team lounge and noticed a poster of Albatross, Jules Verne's helicopter, crumpled on the couch by someone's careless behind. Rolling it up, she left it on the table.

After brewing a cup of tea, its faint chamomile scent filling the air, she curled up and sipped from her mug. Her gaze settled on the familiar pictures on the opposite wall: a photo of the helicopter team hung in a wooden frame beside a poster of the entire mountain rescue unit.

It took her a few seconds to spot her own tiny figure, lost among the other mountain rescuers.

She picked up a pencil and drew a long mustache on her own face—thin, like Dali's. It was barely visible, and nobody would notice it, anyway. Only she would know.

She looked at the photo of the helicopter team, where the pilots and Big Joe stood, surrounded by a few flight medics and rescue techs.

She was there among them, the sole woman on the team.

Flexing her muscles, she patted her biceps.

She had to take fitness tests alongside the men to qualify for missions, always passing them because she trained hard. She trained like a professional, even though, like everyone else on the team, she was an unpaid volunteer.

Well, everyone except for the two pilots and Big Joe.

She sipped her tea and stared at them: three men in sheriff's uniforms, standing by the helicopter, helmets under arms. They looked very dignified.

Then she laughed. The donkey! And these three manly professionals had been too afraid to call the sheriff for help. It was a priceless memory! She laughed again.

Still amused, she thought of the drunk guy stuck on the cliff with a noose around his neck.

He'd had a funny accent... French?

Yes... He sounded and looked French.

We may die, he had said.

Yes, hell, they both could very well have died.

Her smile faded.

They could have gotten smashed against the rock wall. The helicopter could have lost lift, tumbled down, and crashed into them. Or the hoist cable could have gotten tangled in a tree, forcing the crew in the cabin to cut it and fly off.

The crew had a procedure for such emergencies, and the pilots and Big Joe would review it aloud before each mission as she listened.

She didn't doubt they'd cut the cable by the book if they had to. They'd just do their job, and she would drop to the ground like a stone.

But she understood: on every mission, she did her job too, which was to rescue strangers in desperate need of assistance. Rescue strangers—like the Frenchman she'd saved today.

And right now, she didn't expect anything in return. Except for the adventure, of course. The camaraderie as well. Here, she felt valued and respected, and that was enough.

She raised her eyes toward the helicopter team photo,

glanced at the three men in sheriff's uniforms, and for just a moment, imagined herself in a sheriff's uniform, standing next to them with a shiny helmet under her arm.

The night descended upon the hills, and it was high time for Dessa to leave the base.

Each mission was like shore leave for her, a chance to escape and feel alive. Too bad this one was over.

After locking the hangar door, she hopped on her bike, turned on the headlamp, and rode off.

As she entered the forest, a burly silhouette dashed out of the trees and stopped in the middle of the road. Her heart pounding, she swerved and rolled into a ditch.

As she stood up, she felt a stabbing pain in her ankle. She squinted at the silhouette. It was the donkey!

Limping, she tried to push her bike past the donkey, only to hear a *thwip, thwip* as the rim hit the brake with each turn of the bent front wheel.

She needed to call Penelope again, this time to ask for a ride home.

CHAPTER FOUR

Dessa needed a balaclava for the winter missions—a woolen cap to cover her head and neck. Frostbite gnawing at her nose and ears during last January's Stevens Pass avalanche rescue still haunted her. She'd sworn she wouldn't let it happen again. But she couldn't knit one herself, and the idea of asking Penelope for the money made her stomach tighten.

At least a bivy—a lightweight, zipped sleeping shell to use instead of a tent—was something she could make on her own. Kneeling on the bare floor by the fireplace, she cut thin pieces of Gore-Tex, biting her lip whenever the template refused to line up.

She straightened her back, adjusted the bandage wrapped around her ankle, and glanced at the far end of the living room. There, sunk in a plush recliner, Penelope was typing on her laptop as Chewbacca, their dog, lay by her feet. Archie marched in a circle in the middle of the room, just as he had been doing for the last hour, clutching a plastic fork in his left hand and a ketchup bottle cap in his right.

She looked at her watch. *Already dinnertime!* The boy must be hungry.

She rose and walked to the kitchen counter.

"Who wants burritos tonight?"

Penelope stared at her. "We can't eat Mexican food every night."

Dessa lowered her gaze to the counter. If Mexicans could eat Mexican food three times a day, why couldn't she, Archie, and Penelope eat it once a day?

"I'll order pizza," Penelope said, wrapping it up. "You can

pick it up while I finish writing my report."

Dessa gave Chewbacca his food and sat at the table with her plate.

"How is your bivy bag going?" Penelope asked, mid-chew.

"Not easy. But it's coming along."

She gave Penelope a small smile. "Maybe I'll also need a balaclava for the winter missions—"

"Ah, a balaclava. Of course," Penelope said. "Money isn't the issue here. I earn plenty to provide for all three of us. I can order one for you, no question."

Dessa drank her water, watching Archie nibble on his pizza.

As a volunteer, she earned no income from the search-and-rescue work. Perhaps she should start offering guitar lessons again on the side, like she did when she still lived with her parents. Even small earnings would be her own money.

"Listen, rescue missions are dangerous," Penelope said. "Last winter, you got frostbite. This winter, you could freeze to death. The helicopter's no better—it can kill you anytime, even on a perfect summer day. Yesterday proves it: I had to save you from the donkey! And somehow, you still managed to injure your ankle and wreck the bike!"

Dessa stiffened. Yesterday's mission had been her most challenging yet. The most challenging, yes—and she'd done so well. But all Penelope could talk about was the donkey, her injured ankle, and the bent wheel.

She looked at Penelope, and Penelope stared back at her.

"Don't you think it's time for you to drop the rescue missions?"

What? Drop rescue missions?

No way! Dessa wanted to shout.

She'd rather end up with a noose, like the Frenchman

yesterday, than give them up.

She wanted to shout—but couldn't. All she could do was watch as Penelope served herself another slice of pizza.

"I'm always anxious when you go out on a mission—and so are your parents. You'd make everyone happy if you left SAR. Taking care of Archie and our home is more than enough. I'll keep earning the money, and you can still roam the mountains —just for fun."

Penelope picked a mushroom from Archie's plate, laid it on her own pizza, and took a bite. Then she grabbed another and tossed it into her mouth. "I spoke to your father about it, and he supports the idea."

"You did what?" Dessa nearly choked. "You spoke with my dad?"

"Yes, we had a good conversation."

Dessa pushed her plate away.

This was new: Penelope nudging her to leave SAR, even recruiting her father to help. So far, they'd gotten along fine—Penelope, Archie, and herself. Not without problems, but fine enough. But this?

This threw everything off balance.

Then again, it was bound to happen. Bound to happen because she couldn't bring herself to say "No" to Penelope. She hadn't been able to since moving in with her four years ago.

"Yes, you'd make everyone happy if you dropped the rescue missions," Penelope said. "Take time and think about it. It needn't happen overnight."

Dessa wanted a warm balaclava—but got an offer of gilded shackles instead.

She sat mum, watching Penelope finish her pizza and wipe her mouth with a napkin. Penelope rose, leaned over her, and kissed her—once, and then again, this time longer.

Dessa lowered her head and didn't kiss Penelope back.

A moment later, she stood. Dinner was over, and clearing the table was *her* task—as always.

◆ ◆ ◆

"Afghan hounds can't climb trees." The vet's words echoed in Dessa's mind as she watched Penelope brush Chewbacca on the couch, his reddish-brown tresses glinting under the light.

It was only a month ago that she had accompanied Penelope to the shelter to adopt the Afghan hound. She had stood aside as Penelope entered Chewbacca's cage and approached him. Chewbacca crouched, turning his head between Penelope and the vet, his coat trembling as he shivered.

"His owners abandoned him when they sold their house and moved away," the vet told Dessa. "Neighbors found him barely conscious, stuck on a weeping willow branch. Nobody knows how he got there—Afghan hounds can't climb trees."

She and the vet fell silent as Penelope crouched by the frightened animal and began petting him with long strokes. Still trembling, the Afghan turned his head to Penelope, breathing fast with his mouth open.

Penelope continued stroking the animal, moving her hand toward his head. She reached the hound's skull and petted him behind the ears, using both hands. Chewbacca sprang and stuck his snout between Penelope's legs while she massaged his head. Tears flowed from his almond eyes, and Penelope wiped them away, continuing to massage and murmur to him.

Dessa had no doubt—Chewbacca fell in love with Penelope right then and there.

They had taken Chewbacca home and bathed him. Every night since, Penelope brushed his coat until it gleamed, tangle-free.

Every night, Dessa watched the same ritual unfold:

Penelope stood by Chewbacca's crate, leash in hand, testing the hound's patience.

Tonight was no different. She coaxed Chewbacca into the crate, shut the door, and stood glaring at him for a moment while he panted inside, his tail wagging.

Penelope nudged the crate door open, but as soon as the hound tried to stick his paw out, she snapped it shut. Again and again, she opened and closed the door, each time slower than before, until the dog froze in the middle of the crate. Only his tail twitched in anticipation. At last, Penelope left the door open, her gaze locked on the dog. "Good boy! Let's go out for a stroll."

Chewbacca padded out, docile as a lamb, and stood still while Penelope clipped the leash on him. Dessa rushed to him, knelt, and hugged him around the neck, her eyes closed.

As Chewbacca and Penelope left, Dessa stood motionless, her gaze fixed on her feet for a few seconds.

She lived in a cage just like Chewbacca, only hers was invisible. The door to her cage was always open, but she couldn't leave.

She was bound by a promise, trapped by a choice.

"Can you flush the toilet for me?"

Dessa turned, her toothbrush still in her mouth. Archie stood in the doorway, his pajamas rumpled, his timid voice barely above a whisper. Poor kid. He must've been waiting there— , working up the courage to ask.

"Um... Can you check with your mother first? If she's fine with it, I'll flush. If not, we might get scolded."

Penelope wanted Archie to face his fear of flushing—and blamed Dessa for enabling his phobia by flushing for him.

"I can't check with Mother. She's using the other bathroom."

Archie looked up.

"Would you flush for me?"

Dessa thought about it. *What would Philip do?*

Philip, her beloved brother. Philip—her fraternal twin. Philip—Archie's father.

Philip, who had been in Heaven for four years.

Philip was a good-hearted dad. He'd flush the toilet for Archie. So, she would flush, too.

"Okay. I'll flush for you today, but only if you promise to try by yourself tomorrow."

She turned around and waited for Archie to relieve himself. She pushed the lever—and the water whooshed and gurgled down the toilet. Archie looked at the swirling flow, covered his ears with his hands, and dashed to his room, screaming.

Everyone went to bed. Chewbacca whimpered in the darkness, then quieted down. Soon, people and animals were sleeping. Only Dessa was awake, counting sheep, while Penelope breathed next to her.

At dawn, Penelope woke up and reached for Dessa.

Penelope didn't seem to notice Dessa was unaroused again—Penelope never did. Dessa let Penelope twist her body until Penelope squeaked in pleasure and went to the shower, leaving her alone at last.

Dessa dozed off and had a dream.

She was trapped in a desolate pit, sad and lonely. She wanted to climb out and stretched her arms toward the walls, but they were cold and slick, offering no grip. She looked up, unable to see an exit, and yelled for help, but her cries echoed back to her, unanswered.

The dream began to dissolve, yet the pit walls lingered in her formless haze of sleep.

CHAPTER FIVE

Three Months Later

After days of autumn rain, a pristine Saturday dawned. Flooded rivers and muddy trails didn't stop hikers eager to get back into the mountains, and Dessa knew the risks all too well—drownings, slips, and sprains often led to rescue calls. Yet the clear weather made it a good day for her and her SAR colleagues to practice climber rescue techniques on the cliffs near Index, Washington.

In the final exercise, she rappelled down with the stretcher-bound Jesse—a Boeing engineer, fellow SAR volunteer, and trusted friend—and helped him free himself from the straps and ropes.

It had been a long day, and it was time to wrap up and stop for Mexican food with the guys en route back to the base before going home.

The others bantered with her and Jesse, joking about their contrasting sizes—she was petite, while Jesse was stout. As usual, calm Jesse kept quiet, but Dessa joined in the banter, ensuring she responded with a witty retort to each joke.

Just as they laughed, Dessa and the others received a call from the sheriff for a rescue mission. A thirteen-year-old boy named Lucas was stranded in a rock niche above Wallace Falls, roughly ten miles northeast of their current location.

Oh well, the Mexican food would have to wait.

Dessa and the rest of the group loaded all the gear into the two search-and-rescue Suburbans and drove to the falls in silence.

Lucas threw a pinecone and watched it tumble into the river's choppy current, flipping and twisting like a minnow trying to break free before vanishing over the falls.

He tried to imagine where it landed. He'd heard a woman drowned here once, swept over by the same current—but that had been a long time ago.

He turned back and noticed two girls whispering and giggling, their eyes darting his way. He smirked, grabbed another pinecone, and hurled it harder.

Up the meadow, his father sat in his fishing chair, nibbling on a sandwich and staring at his phone. Lucas eyed the girls again and decided to cool off in the river.

He took off his sneakers and waded into the river. The bedrock was polished smooth by the water and slippery. Yet he continued wading inward, balancing with his arms outstretched. The fast water caressed his knees, and his calves softened. He turned his head toward the girls, gave them a nonchalant smile, and took another step forward. That's when he slipped on the slick rock, staggered, waved his arms, and fell into the river. The current grabbed him, sweeping him toward the waterfall.

Was he going to die now? This couldn't be real... it couldn't be happening to him. He gasped for air and choked, his heartbeat pounding in his ears—but Bobby Pendragon's voice came to him from the watery abyss: "Traveler, relax! Just ride down feet-first and try to stay away from the middle of the river."

Lucas did as the voice instructed. He raised his legs toward the surface and drifted along, riding the current with his head and arms held up as if on an invisible sled. His feet bumped into an underwater stone. He twisted his body left, bounced off like a springboard, and landed on a ledge above the rushing water.

Pressing his back against the wet rock, he hugged his knees. The river barreled over the falls' edge right under his nose, sweeping over his feet. He tried to stand but hit his head on the stone above.

He looked around, coughing and spitting out drops of water. He was trapped in a tiny alcove, just feet from the thundering falls.

True, he was alive, but he had no idea how to get out of this trap.

He cried.

Moments later he noticed his father running back and forth along the opposite riverbank. He was still holding the sandwich and phone, scanning the river. Lucas yelled, but the roar of the river drowned out his voice.

After a few long seconds, his father finally spotted him on the rock.

"Lucas, I'm here! I'm with you! Everything will be fine! Hang in there!"

His father looked around as if wondering where to leave his sandwich—and tossed it into the river, the waterfall swallowing it in an instant. Lucas watched him grip his phone with both hands and dial a number—hoping it was not his mother's, but 9-1-1.

With only an hour until sundown, the pilot sped the helicopter to Wallace Falls, assisted as usual by the copilot and crew chief, Big Joe. Clifton and Greg, two volunteers, sat in the back, ready to deploy.

The pilot circled the falls, hovered for a minute over the river, and surveyed the cliff above it. The overhang jutted into the air like a jagged lip, making it impossible to lower a line to the stranded boy.

"We can't hoist anyone here," he declared.

He made a broad turn, climbed above the ridge, descended to an inclined meadow, and hovered again, this time only a few feet above the ground—low enough for Clifton and Greg to toss their packs and leap to the grass.

The rescue mission wouldn't end before nightfall, so the pilot had to deliver—before it became too dark to fly—a load of camping gear and drop it off at the meadow.

He gained altitude and sped back to the base.

Clifton didn't mind working with Greg on rescue missions—even though the two couldn't be more different. Greg, a slim Seattle man who made his living as an apartment manager, had joined the helicopter rescue team only a year ago. Clifton, an intrepid Air Force vet, had grown tired of Oregon's Mount Hood and moved to Washington to see something new.

Clifton led Greg from the rumbling helicopter across the meadow, down the hill, and to the cliff—all in less than fifteen minutes. He paused high above the stranded boy—unable to see him in his rock niche—but determined to somehow reach him, get him in a harness, and wait with him for ground rescuers to extract him to safety. With this goal in mind, he rappelled down the cliff and over its edge, secured by Greg with a belay rope.

Before long, Clifton hung below the overhang, above the churning water. He waved to the boy and began swinging toward him. As he swung, his weight-bearing rope rubbed against the edge of the overhang, raining down nylon flakes onto his face. He looked up and eased into another swing—curious to see what would happen—and the rope snapped. He plummeted and splashed into the white water, and the current grabbed him, pulling him toward the falls.

He refused to let himself be swept over the edge. Flexing every muscle in his body, he pulled himself up along the belay rope, out of the water, and climbed back to Greg.

Now, he and Greg had no choice but to stay put, wait for the ground team to arrive, and assist them with the rescue.

A state park volunteer waited for Dessa and the rest of the team at the trailhead. His first words sounded grim: "The river's too swollen to cross safely where the boy is trapped."

The volunteer said that a hiking trail wound along the river to a meadow above the waterfall, with the boy trapped across the water in a rock niche. The current in front of the boy —constricted by the cliff—ran deep and turbulent.

Jesse glanced around at the others. "Let's talk about options with the SAR deputy."

Dessa and the group gathered around the radio and discussed rescue strategies with the SAR coordinator deputy. They eventually organized into three teams: liaison, rescue, and support, positioned to collaborate for the mission's success. In the end, the deputy appointed Jesse as the mission field leader to coordinate the on-site rescue efforts.

As the teams formed, Dessa had to decide which one to join.

The liaison team role was to stand by the radio in the parking lot, greet firefighters summoned from the nearby town of Gold Bar, and wait for additional rescuers from more remote areas. Dessa didn't find this team appealing—it sounded like busywork, far from the action.

The support team had to hike up the trail to the meadow above the waterfall. They were to establish visual and voice contact with the boy and act as intermediaries between him and the other two teams. To Dessa, this team's role seemed modest at best.

Jesse was set to lead the rescue team up a forest road ending a mile above the waterfall. They would attempt to ford the flooded river and bushwhack along the opposite bank to reach the boy.

Wherever Jesse went, there was sure to be action—it was obvious. She had to join the rescue team. She hurried after him to one of the Suburbans.

Dessa loved driving a Suburban—feeling its power in her hands as she steered through mountain roads. But Jesse was field leader today, and that meant he drove. She settled into the seat next to him, the park volunteer close to her right and the others in the back.

The volunteer jingled the keys to the forest gates. "You've already had a whole busy day of training. I can drive if you feel tired."

"Don't worry about it." A smirk touched Jesse's lips. "I have a Dessa next to me."

"Having a Dessa is like having a Swiss Army knife," Grace said. "Multi-talented, will probably fit in your pocket—and will definitely cut you if you don't respect it."

"Good Lord," Marco chimed in. "This needs to be made into a plaque and hung in the hangar and every other building on the base!"

"No need, Marco," Dessa responded. "It's pretty self-evident. But if we do proceed, might I also suggest plaques on all SAR vehicles?"

"Plaques on the vehicles too? Perfect!" Jesse started the Suburban, the team's laughter mixing with the engine's rumble.

Dessa laughed along with the rest of the team. Only the volunteer remained silent besides her, staring straight ahead.

As Jesse drove off, she leaned back in her seat, her arms falling limp at her sides. She needed to relax—this drive and the swollen river crossing were just the beginning.

Jesse stepped out of the Suburban, his boots crunching on gravel as he faced the river. It was calm enough here to cross, but the deeper currents and rocks downstream wouldn't forgive a mishap. The weight of every life—his team and the boy's—pressed on him tonight.

The park volunteer stood beside him, hands in his pockets, shoulders slightly hunched as he faced the rippling water.

"I can drive the Suburban back to the parking lot," the volunteer said. "I'm supposed to be there, meeting and greeting visitors."

"Okay... but wait for us to cross first. We'd need the Suburban if anything goes wrong."

Jesse waded into the river, pulling an orange rope behind him. Once he reached the east bank, he tied the rope to the trunk of a fir tree.

Four men followed him in pairs, gripping the safety rope. This way, if someone slipped and fell into the river, he could still hold on to the rope while his partner helped him back to his feet.

Marco and Grace stepped into the river, their movements cautious against the current. After a few unsteady strides, they paused as the water pushed hard against them and retreated to the bank. Jesse watched as they exchanged a few words with Dessa, all three still on the opposite side, before climbing into the Suburban with the park volunteer.

Dessa braved the crossing alone.

"Marco and Grace were humbled by the current," Dessa said, glancing toward the departing Suburban. "I told them to go back and assist the coordination team—no shame in that."

Jesse gave her an approving nod.

He took the slope to the cliff above the waterfall, with the others following. All were wet, but bushwhacking kept them warm. With their headlamps on, they reached Clifton and Greg, and Jesse queried the pair about the situation at the falls.

Next, he radioed the support team waiting in the dark on the other side of the river. They reported that thirty men and women had assembled there, including the firefighters who had hiked up the trail with their ladder. They carried it wherever they went.

"A good climber could rappel down to the rock ledge—upstream from the overhang—scramble along the river to the niche, reach the boy, secure him with a harness, and lead him out." Jesse paused. "The team above could pull both of them up the cliffside."

It took him and the rest of the group an hour and a half to plan the details. They discussed and rejected four different rope systems—until Dessa proposed a system he liked because it ensured that if the climber or the boy fell in the water, the fallen one would not drag the other into the falls.

Jesse reviewed the plan of action with the group. "The support team will lower the fire ladder with ropes across the river."

"Lower it like a London bridge over the Thames," the park volunteer chimed in over the radio.

Sure, Jesse thought, *just like the Thames River.*

"If they succeed, a solo climber will descend the cliff on the upstream side of the overhang, toward the ladder."

"Holding onto the rock and secured with ropes," Dessa continued his words, "she will step onto the ladder, and from there, like from a springboard, reach the niche where Lucas is huddled."

He glanced at Dessa. Did she just say *she*?

Yes, she did. Dessa wanted to descend to the river and extract the boy herself. She could make it, he thought. She was just as skilled as anyone on the team, and she'd do whatever it took to succeed. She'd take all the risks the river had to offer. But that was exactly his concern with her. She'd never abort a rescue, even when it was necessary for her own safety. She was known for that. She'd strive to take care of the subject and forget about herself.

So far, she'd always succeeded, always ending up happy, enjoying her place as a key member of the SAR family. But what if she failed tonight? What if she slipped in the river? What if she perished in the waterfall? Personally, he'd be better off protecting her and doing the rescue himself.

Dessa looked him in the eyes. "It ought to be me. I'm the lightest one."

Her gaze told him what he knew well: he was a big man, the heaviest in the group.

"Lightweight is good," Dessa continued. "Less risk of overturning the ladder in the river. Easier to pull up together with the boy. Easy on the ropes."

Right is right, he thought.

"You can do it next time when I'm not around," Dessa added—and it seemed to him she gave him a tiny wink.

He decided to take a chance on her. "I hope you'll always be around," he said, winking back.

The pull of his lips hadn't faded when the radio crackled. "The boy seems to be freezing. We can see him shivering, and he looks exhausted. We're concerned he might lose his balance and fall into the river."

"Understood." Jesse glanced at Dessa. "We have to work as fast as we can, but without compromising safety."

Everyone set about tying the ropes, headlamps bobbing around the fir trunks and branches.

It took them two hours to set up the rope system down the cliff and lower the rope-secured ladder from the opposite bank. At last, they were done thirty minutes before midnight

With everything in place, it was Dessa's turn to act.

The cliff loomed steep and shadowy as Dessa descended, the river's roar below sharpening her thoughts. On the opposite bank, the support team's headlamps flickered like fireflies, but Jesse and the rescue team were far above, out of

sight. She knew all they could do was wait for her up there in the dark, striking up conversations to help pass the time.

She reached a rock shelf above the current, scrambled down onto the ladder just a couple of yards from the falls' edge, and did a split over the rough water. The ladder wobbled beneath her left foot, its metal rungs slick with water spray. Her right foot found purchase next to Lucas, who let go of the rock and shifted toward her. It took her a while to get the boy into a harness and clip him to a rope. At last, she led him over the tip of the ladder and up onto the rock shelf.

The rescuers above began pulling the ropes up, and she let out a grunt of relief. Soon enough, she scrambled over the cliff edge with Lucas. She stood up, taking the pose of a proud eagle, her legs spread, arms pointing to the horizon, and her face turned to the night sky.

That was her moment of glory. She closed her eyes and found herself—only for an instant—in that desolate pit of her dream three months ago. Unlike in the dream, this time she spotted stars flickering above. She was about to climb up toward the stars when the rescue crowd exulted, and she opened her eyes just in time to see Jesse rushing toward her, his arms open for an embrace.

As soon as Jesse let her go, she hugged the boy, Lucas. He shivered in the cold night, his shorts and T-shirt still wet, and his bare arms and legs prickling with a million goosebumps in the light of her headlamp. She rummaged in her backpack, found a dry pair of socks, and handed them to him. Three other rescuers gave the boy their spare pairs, and he pulled them on top of each other in place of shoes. Dessa gave him her jacket. He put it on, crossed his arms over his chest, clenched his fists to warm up, and looked at her with a shy hint of a smile. He was a sweet boy, indeed.

They all headed up the slope. When they reached the meadow, they found the air-dropped load of sleeping bags, pads, and food.

"We'll camp here tonight." Dessa spread out a sleeping

pad for Lucas. "In the morning, the helicopter will haul us out of here."

The boy nodded, his face softening as he huddled into the sleeping bag. The team moved quietly around them, setting up camp under the sprawling sky.

Dessa woke up hungry and thirsty an hour before sunrise. She pulled her arms out of the sleeping bag and stretched them out. Her hands touched the grass; it was cold and damp from the dew.

She huddled in the bag and lay motionless for a few minutes, staring wide-eyed at the starry sky, gazing at the familiar constellations, and whispering their names. It seemed they whispered her name back, too.

She caught footsteps at the edge of the meadow—rose halfway—and spotted a man's shadow emerging from the forest.

The man stopped and leaned forward as if to arrange something on the grass.

He stepped back into the forest and wandered among the trees with his headlamp on. He would bend down, pick something up, and stand up again. Finally, he turned off his light, returned to the meadow, and knelt.

She tried to figure out who the man was and what he was doing but couldn't.

She slipped out of the sleeping bag, stretched, tiptoed in the darkness, and stopped by the kneeling man. He raised his face to her.

It was Clifton, and he was building a campfire from dry twigs and branches.

"It's cozy to light a fire at dawn." Clifton glanced toward the sleeping camp. "I always do it when I spend the night outside."

As the flames crackled, Dessa turned to him. "I wanted to

ask you... Yesterday, when your rope broke, how did you get out of the river? ... Because if it were me, I would've drowned."

"Ah, my plunge... It wasn't a problem for me. I don't drown. I was born under a lucky star."

"Lucky star?"

"Yes, Jupiter. That's why nothing bad ever happens to me. Just as my mother promised when I was little."

She looked at him, then gazed at Jupiter low in the east. A planet, but brighter than all the stars.

The wind blew onto her face, and the treetops rustled.

She turned to Clifton again. "I heard you were in the helicopter that crashed on Mount Hood."

"Well, I was. We hovered fine over the glacier, but the wind gusted just as we were hoisting up the litter with an injured climber. The Hawk lost lift—but the pilot managed to fly away from the ground rescuers underneath.

"I had to follow the emergency procedure and cut the hoist cable. I guess you know the injured climber fell to his death."

She nodded.

"Yeah... It was a tough call." Clifton stared at his hands. "Sacrifice the subject trying to save the crew."

She thought about it. Would she ever be able to sacrifice someone to save herself? She didn't know. A tough call, indeed.

"We crash-landed on the mountain anyway," Clifton continued. "The helicopter rolled down the slope eight times, and we bounced around like we were in a ten-ton centrifuge. Then it came to a stop on a rocky edge, belly up."

Clifton poked the logs to keep them burning, sending embers in the air.

"My colleagues were injured—but I was unscathed."

Clifton looked her in the eye. "I'm afraid of nothing. I was born under a lucky star."

She looked at Clifton. Did he truly believe that?

Hell, he did!

Her throat constricted as if something truly

unfortunate were about to happen to him.

Dessa stood by the sleeping boy, eyeing the glimmer of dawn on the eastern horizon—and the stars melting in the twilight. Clifton's fire flickered at the meadow's edge. The makeshift camp stirred as her fellow rescuers prepared to leave.

Jesse approached and stopped by her. She understood what he wanted without words. She knelt and placed her palm on Lucas's forehead.

She looked up at Jesse, trying to read his face.

"I feel bad having to wake him up."

Jesse said nothing.

She tapped Lucas's shoulder. She shook it. No response. She shook the boy's shoulder again, even squeezed it a little. Lucas moved, rubbed his eyes, and rose from his sleeping bag —"Rabbit! Rabbit! Rabbit!"—and she pulled back just in time to avoid their heads colliding.

A soft chuckle escaped her. Archie had the same superstition. Without fail, he shouted "Rabbit! Rabbit! Rabbit!" immediately upon waking every first of the month—believing it would bring him good luck for the entire month.

"That works if you shout it upon waking on the first day of the month—but today is already the second."

"I thought it was still the first."

"It's actually better this way. Today is the first day of your second life, and you'll be lucky for the rest of it."

She winked at him, and he beamed at her in return.

Dessa shielded her eyes as the helicopter flew in, shattering the morning calm. Its blades scattered dew and bent the grass below. An AirTEP rescue platform dangled beneath it, open like a wild rose in bloom. When the aircraft hovered twenty yards above the inclined meadow, she retreated to the forest edge with the others, watching Big Joe slide back the side door and step onto the landing skid. The helicopter dropped lower, and the platform settled onto the grass.

Big Joe spoke with her on the radio. She was to escort Lucas by air and hand him over to his parents. After that, the helicopter would evacuate the others.

She took Lucas's hand, and they stepped onto the platform, crushing the grass that peered through the square holes of the bottom net.

She secured Lucas and herself with safety straps and waved up to Big Joe. The helicopter soared, cleaving the morning air, with the platform trailing behind, pushed back by the air current. She spotted the waterfall through the net beneath her feet and the winding river serpentining through the greenery of the forest. The morning sun, rising over the rocky ridges, shone in her eyes.

The helicopter approached the parking lot, now nearly deserted. It seemed that everyone from the support team had already departed. Only the two Suburbans and SAR's own food truck waited by the picnic area. A man and a woman stood next to a black sedan, their faces raised to the sky. Lucas's parents, she guessed.

The helicopter hovered for a few seconds, then descended. Below, Marco and Grace approached the swinging platform, grabbed it by the side, and held it steady until it lay on the ground.

Dessa unclipped Lucas, helped him step out, and watched him walk toward his parents, his head hung. They rushed toward him with their arms outstretched for a hug—but before he hugged them both, he turned to Dessa and locked his eyes with hers for a moment.

Subject rating—10 out of 10, she thought. Would rescue again.

Hands on her hips, Dessa turned to Marco and Grace.

"We've got a new cook," Grace said.

"He's good," Marco added.

Dessa gave them a nod and headed for the food truck. The aroma of coffee and hot food wafted out of the open door.

She stepped inside.

"Good morning." The cook gave a slight bow. "I'm Fred, and you're Dessa, right?"

The Frenchman! The one who tried to hang himself but fell down the cliff instead. The one she rescued three months ago.

He wore a turquoise apron over a denim shirt and a matching kitchen cap. The cap had a navy-blue inscription embroidered on the front: *SAR Volunteer*.

"I sewed it myself." Fred pointed to his cap.

She gazed at him, speechless.

"Just wanted to be among people and useful," Fred added.

She nodded. SAR had helped him stay alive, and he was here now to help SAR in return.

His kitchen cap looked much better than the noose he wore around his neck three months ago.

"Now, let's grab the bull by the horns—tell me what you'd like for breakfast."

She gave him a faint smile.

"What's on the menu?"

"Beverages include water, soda, apple juice... I've also got tea and coffee. For the main dish, you have a choice of *gratin de lasagne* or burrito. Ah! I also have chips and salsa if you eat that kind of thing."

So, Fred had cooked French lasagna but also had her favorite Mexican food.

She glanced at the cooking area behind him. A new butcher block with multicolored knives stood by the stove. Fresh, unfamiliar kitchen towels hung above the sink.

He'd renewed the kitchen, she thought. He'd renewed himself, too.

A small mirror hung on the cabinet door across from her, and she glanced at it. Her eyes were already as round as ping-pong balls. They got like that whenever she was fatigued and sleepy.

"May I have both lasagna and a burrito? I'm famished."

Outside, the helicopter roared again, and the others began to enter the food truck.

Dessa sat with everyone else at the picnic tables. They ate and chattered, at times bursting into cheers and laughter.

Fred came out of the truck with a trash bag and cleaned up, pausing now and then to chat with her and the team.

She was the last one to finish her meal, now doing nothing but watching her teammates leave the tables one by one and trudge to the two Suburbans. Everybody had to return to the base, where their own cars had been waiting for them since yesterday.

"Thank you for the food, Fred." She stood up, looking toward the humming Suburbans. "Everything was delicious."

After a couple of steps, she glanced back at him.

Fred gave her a soft smile. "See you soon."

She was glad he had recovered so well.

"See you soon," she replied.

CHAPTER SIX

Fred spent the afternoon at Roam & Brew, lounging on a loveseat and reading *The Soul of a Chef,* a book he'd discovered shelved among the board games in the corner.

He skimmed the last page, closed the book, and took a sip of his espresso. The drink was now as cold as the rain outside, its bitterness sharp against his palate. He pushed the cup aside. It was time to go home and cook himself a dinner worth eating. Tossing the book back onto the shelf, he stood, grabbed his jacket, and headed for the bathroom.

As he washed his hands, he looked in the mirror and splashed cold water on his face.

He wished his face looked younger and fresher.

His face, however, was like a garment that he could never change, no matter how much he wanted to. With the passing years, the garment grew old and worn. His problem was that the man who was behind it remained young.

He left the bathroom and walked past two girls curled up together on the love seat. They glanced at him, whispered to each other, and giggled. He shrugged and headed for the exit—and noticed Dessa sitting at a tall table by the window.

She was unwrapping a sandwich. Her pack lay on an empty chair; her bike leaned against the wall—a common sight here.

He approached her. "Hey!"

"Oh, hey."

"Didn't expect to see you here."

"I'm in town to give guitar lessons to a set of twins."

"Guitar lessons?"

"Well, yes. I have to pay for my egg sandwich somehow."

Dessa pulled a beat-up water bottle from her pack and took a drink.

A group of seniors poured into the coffee shop and lingered by him, shaking their umbrellas and laughing. They headed to the counter and began examining the pastries.

"What did the twins learn today?"

"*Row, row, row your boat gently down the stream,*" Dessa hummed.

"*Merrily, merrily, merrily, merrily, life is but a dream,*" he continued. "I didn't know it was arranged for guitar."

"It sounds good on two guitars." She pulled her pack from the chair and dropped it under the table. "Would you like to sit down?"

"I would but let me get myself something to drink."

He returned to her table with a bottle of Perrier water and an empty glass and sat opposite her. "*Mon eau minérale préférée.*"

Dessa didn't seem impressed. "You speak French without an accent."

"Of course. I was born and raised in Paris." He poured himself a glass. "And you? What languages do you speak?"

"I was born in Sofia, so I speak Bulgarian."

He nodded and waited for her to continue.

"When I was nine, my father got a job as a professor at the University of Oslo. My mother, my twin brother Philip, and I all went with him. Within two years, Philip and I learned Norwegian."

He watched her as she turned her bottle in her hands, her gaze distant for a moment. She took a sip and continued.

"The first year in Oslo, my brother and I looked strange. We went to school in green sweaters knitted by our grandma. My hair was crazily frizzy, and Philip's cane was just a sanded twig with a rubber tip at the bottom. Kids at school avoided us, leaving us isolated and alone. It was hard for us, but we didn't tell our parents."

Fred remembered the loneliness that tortured him when he'd moved to a new school at ten. Fortunately, Dessa hadn't been in Oslo by herself.

"You and your brother stuck together, didn't you?"

"Yes, we were inseparable. Always together. Wearing the same colors. Reading the same books. Listening to the same songs. Going to the same movies. Sleeping in the same room. We were like two peas in a pod."

"But Philip needed a cane, and you didn't." He looked at Dessa. "I wonder..."

"Philip had a leg injury, but it didn't last forever." She turned her battered water bottle in her hands. "No big deal, really..."

A wet sparrow landed on the ledge outside, tilted its head, and looked Fred in the eye, as if to say, "It sounds like a big deal, stupid, but you don't need to know everything. Not right now, anyway." The sparrow glanced at Dessa and flew away.

"After Oslo, we lived for two years in Paris," Dessa continued, "and we learned French."

Ah!... That's why she wasn't impressed by his French.

"But then my father got a permanent appointment in California. That was nineteen years ago." Dessa looked at him. "Now English feels like a native language to me.

He watched her as she took a bite of her sandwich.

"You speak English without an accent. I would've never guessed your first language was Bulgarian," he said.

"Actually, my first language wasn't Bulgarian."

"I'm confused."

Dessa finished her sandwich and washed it down with water.

"My brother Philip and I spoke *twin talk* first."

Oh, he got it. He'd heard of it.

Twin talk, a secret language that some twins developed.

"Our parents hired a Turkish babysitter. She knew only Turkish, so she spoke Turkish to Philip and me all day long;

our parents talked to us in Bulgarian in the evenings and on weekends."

Dessa tapped on the table.

"In a few months, Philip and I ended up speaking in a language of twisted Turkish and Bulgarian words, a twin talk that only we could understand. *That* was our first language."

"Can you say something in twin talk?"

"I can't. It's all gone now. Doctors told our parents that Philip and I wouldn't develop normally unless they separated us. So, they did. Our parents sent Philip to our grandma in Varna, on the Black Sea, and kept me in Sofia. We were separated until we forgot our twin talk and learned Bulgarian. Philip came back, and we were happy again."

Dessa gazed out the window, and he followed her eyes. A wet sidewalk sign that read, "You may have ninety-nine problems, but our coffee isn't one," stood above a puddle that reflected its glossy letters.

"Countries and languages mix together in my dreams." Dessa glanced at him. "Last night, I dreamt I was in our Norwegian house. I walked out the door and found myself in Paris's Bois de Boulogne. Um... my sister-in-law, Penelope, says that I talk in my sleep and mix English with Bulgarian and Norwegian with French."

"Your sister-in-law? She knows what you do in your sleep?"

"Well, Penelope is only formally my sister-in-law."

"What do you mean?"

"Um..." She licked her lips. "We actually live together. We're partners."

"You and your sister-in-law are partners?!"

"Yes... partners since a year after Philip passed away."

Dessa and her sister-in-law had become romantically involved, Fred thought... but why not? They weren't blood relatives, after all.

He'd once had a Facebook friend who died in a motorcycle accident. The man's older brother dated and then married his widowed sister-in-law. The couple's in-laws supported the marriage because the older brother was going to help raise the kids and keep the family business running.

Fred glanced at Dessa, trying to put on a compassionate face.

"Philip had acute leukemia. Penelope couldn't take it and developed depression. She was both sad and irritable and talked about suicide. She couldn't care for Philip, so I moved in to do it for her."

"That was a tough decision, I guess."

"It wasn't that tough... I was going through a lot back then... the loss of a relationship... a toxic work environment... and trying to change jobs and move someplace far away. Moving in to care for Philip was an escape from my problems. In a way, it made my life meaningful again."

Dessa breathed out.

"Three months later, Philip, already on his deathbed, asked me to help Penelope raise their son, Archie, after he was gone."

"Your brother asked you to help his wife raise their son?"

"Yes, he did. 'I beg you... help Penny raise Archie after I'm gone,' he said. I still remember his words as if it were yesterday."

"And you agreed?"

"I didn't just agree. I promised him." Dessa rubbed her neck as if it were sore. "I gave him my word."

"So, you stayed with Penelope and Archie after the funeral?"

"Yes... but I only meant it to be temporary at the time."

Dessa paused, her face softening in the light of the bronze chandelier.

"Archie is autistic... Mildly autistic. His autistic traits are harmless. He runs in circles for hours, holding a pencil and a spoon. He has phobias, but nothing too bad—noise, bugs, the outdoors."

Dessa looked at Fred. "I actually find Archie's fear of

flushing the toilet kind of sweet."

Fred gave her time to find the words.

"My brother looked much like me, and Archie accepted me as a foster parent."

"Did Penelope accept you as a substitute spouse?"

"You could say that."

"So, Penelope's happy with the setup."

"Yes, she is."

Dessa stared at her hands.

"My parents are happy, too."

She pursed her lips.

"Especially my father. He loves Penelope."

Fred watched her fold and unfold her napkin in silence.

"My father says Penelope was his best grad student ever... the smartest one he'd ever had. He wished Penelope was his daughter, he says.

"Back then, when Penelope was still a student, my father used to bring her home for dinner, and that's how Philip, my mom, and I got to know her."

Dessa's voice lacked enthusiasm. "Philip passed away, but my parents are happy with the new setup."

She looked at Fred. "As a matter of fact, they're happy in general. They have a good life. They own a nice house near LA. They travel to Europe whenever they want. My father flies my mother to Catalina Island on weekends."

"Your father flies?"

"Yes. He bought a secondhand Piper. A thirty-year-old one."

A thirty-year-old Piper was too old, Fred thought. Too much wear and tear. Dated avionics, no GPS—unless her father had the plane retrofitted—but that would be too expensive.

"My father is flying my mother here for Thanksgiving. I asked them to fly commercially, but he won't listen."

That Piper couldn't be a safe plane to fly. Not all the way from California to Washington. Not in late fall.

A coffee grinder roared to life in the back, filling the

room with a buzz, and Fred cast an irritated glance at the counter.

Dessa finished her water and stowed the empty bottle back in her pack. “And you? How have *you* been?”

“So far, so good. I’m getting divorced. Now I live in a trailer. It’s small but has a pretty good kitchen, so I’m happy.”

“You live in a trailer?”

“Yes, I do. I left the family house entirely to my wife and rented an old trailer parked in someone’s backyard.”

He hesitated for a moment, then continued, trying to speak matter-of-factly.

“My wife can now paint all she wants, undisturbed by my presence.”

“Your wife is an artist?”

“Yes, in her own way. She paints young men she finds online—on Cougar Life—naked, and posts the portraits on Facebook.”

He pulled out his phone, tap-tapped on the screen, and turned it to Dessa. “Like this boy here.”

Dessa stared, wide-eyed, at the screen.

“He’s wearing my favorite bathrobe.” His voice hardened. “The last time, she brought two boys together, so there were no bathrobes left for me.”

The same day, he’d put that noose around his neck—the day he met Dessa.

“But why do they do this?… Your wife and her young boyfriends?”

“Well, because she’s a mature woman and enjoys coaching them—and they enjoy pleasing her. It’s all about sex. They’re obsessed with it.”

Dessa looked away from Fred. “My boyfriend, Tucker…”

“Oh, you have a boyfriend too?”

She turned back to him.

“That was back in high school.”

“Ah.”

“So, my boyfriend Tucker didn’t want to have sex. I

thought it was me and felt awkward, so I encouraged him to date other girls and try it first with them."

"And he... did he try it with them?"

"No, he didn't. He told me he didn't want to have sex before marriage, neither with me nor with anyone else."

"*Oh mon Dieu*... why?"

"Tucker was afraid Jesus wouldn't like it if he slept with girls... Both he and his parents were really religious."

"I see."

"But they were good people. They had a restaurant, and on their way to work every morning, they stopped by the church. They were hardworking, honest people."

Fred sipped his Perrier and gazed through the window at the darkening street. The lights of a bus glistened on the wet pavement. A solitary streetlamp flickered on the sidewalk.

He decided to change the subject.

"Is it fun being on the helicopter rescue team?"

Dessa livened up. She gave him an account of the team's last training. She opened Facebook and showed him a few helicopter pictures. In the end, they added each other as friends.

He invited her to visit him someday in his trailer. "For French desserts, served on real porcelain," he added—and she agreed.

He longed to give her the attention she needed to feel more confident—not just to grow confident but to gain a new lease on life.

They said goodbye to each other, and Dessa pushed her bike out the door. She waved at him through the window, and he waved back.

It was already too late for him to cook dinner. He walked to the counter, bought himself an egg sandwich, returned to the table, and ate.

He stayed in the coffee shop, alone, watching people go by.

CHAPTER SEVEN

Dessa never expected a personal call from the sheriff's office. When it came a few days ago, her first thought was that something bad had happened—maybe like in one of those dreams where she'd be kicked off the helicopter team, or worse, out of SAR entirely.

The officer wanted to talk with her about the Wallace Falls mission.

But why? she wondered. True, that rescue wasn't a walk in the park. She could have drowned, the boy could have died. But she didn't make any mistakes... did she? It all ended well, and more missions followed in the fall, why revisit it?

"Your outstanding performance in the Wallace Falls mission is recognized with the Citizen Medal of Valor," the officer said. "You acted quickly, using your expertise and judgment to rescue a distraught victim from a perilous position in the falls."

It was not a bad dream after all! Her heart raced.

"It is extremely unlikely that the boy would have survived without your skill and bravery that night."

Her voice shook as she thanked him, adding, "I couldn't have done it without my outstanding colleagues."

"That's right," he said. "Yet, it was you who took the biggest risk. It was you, the volunteer, acting at the level of a dedicated professional."

She smiled long after that conversation was over. *A dedicated professional*—those words sounded terribly good to her.

Dessa was having breakfast with Penelope and Archie.

"How was your mission last night?" Penelope broke the silence.

"We had to carry an injured hiker all the way down the trail, and that took us a long time." Dessa looked at Penelope, who—chewing with her jaw clenching at each bite—didn't ask for any details.

Sipping her tea, Dessa glanced through the window. Past seven, still barely dawn. The kitchen lamp, hanging low, glowed on the porcelain edges. Archie nibbled on his peanut butter toast while Chewbacca, sprawled on the living room beanbag, watched him, nostrils flaring.

What slowed the SAR team down even more last night was Marco, whose leg had been hit by a rock. They had to carry him, too. If Penelope knew about it, she'd remind Dessa of the dangers of rescue missions and pester her, again, to leave SAR.

The mission was tiring, but fortunately, the food truck awaited their return at the deployment point. Their new cook, Fred, was quite the entertainer. He served them a menu of what he initially called Greek moussaka, Turkish ayran, and Romanian cabbage rolls, which he had precooked at home. When she told him that all those were, in fact, Bulgarian, he chuckled and admitted he knew that and cooked them just for that reason.

Archie drained his milk in one go and thumped the mug on the table. Dessa looked at him, lost in thought for a moment, and reached over to pour him more.

Last night, Fred had also offered them Serbian plum brandy he had discovered in a Russian store. Three brandy bottles, he said, stood long forgotten and dusty behind a shiny row of vodka, so he pitied them and bought one.

She smiled to herself, leaning back in her chair. The chair squeaked, startling her. She sprang up, hands spreading in uncertainty, moved the chair an inch, and sat down again.

"What are you smiling about?"

"Um... Fred—you know, the new cook—served us plum brandy last night," she said. "But we're not allowed to drink on missions. Only Jesse took a polite sip, not to offend poor Fred."

"Poor Fred? Were you late because of *poor Fred* last night?"

Dessa swirled the tea in her glass.

"Fred's funny, and I like funny people. But he's just a friend. Nothing more. You have no reason to be jealous."

"What's that supposed to mean?" Penelope's voice dropped to a low growl. "I'm not jealous. Not of an old man."

Jealousy had always been Penelope's way, though—so far—Dessa never gave her any reason.

She shrugged and finished her peanut butter toast.

Penelope, done with breakfast, transitioned to the living room. Archie went to the front window and peered out. The lights of the front-yard Halloween dragon flickered on his face.

Dessa zipped Archie's snack into his backpack and set about making Penelope a bento lunch box.

Twenty minutes later, Dessa latched the box—salmon and rice, cucumbers, seaweed, and mochi for dessert—and took it to the living room, where she found Penelope tapping on her laptop.

"I packed you a bento box for lunch."

"Ah, no. Today, I'm having lunch with folks from China Air."

Dessa hesitated, her fingers clenching on the box.

"Didn't you have lunch with China Air last week?"

"No, last week, it was with Delta."

Dessa watched as Penelope flipped the laptop shut, stood, and stretched. Then, looking Penelope in the eye, she said, "Tonight, I'll be at the town hall for the awards ceremony.

Remember?"

"Ah, yes... I haven't forgotten... your Wallace Falls adventure. Your Medal of Valor."

Penelope slipped her hands into her pockets and stared at the bento box for a while. "You're lucky you didn't kill yourself over that dumb kid," she remarked. "Although he still ruined our weekend." She stowed the laptop in her bag. "I'm sorry, but I won't be able to attend. I'm taking Chewbacca to an obedience training tonight."

Dessa bowed her head. Her Medal of Valor didn't matter to Penelope—Chewbacca's training session did.

She tried not to feel too disappointed, though—Penelope's disregard for her SAR work was to be expected, considering how badly she wanted Dessa to quit search-and-rescue altogether.

But wait! What if she wouldn't leave SAR? What if, someday, she left Penelope instead?

She smirked, and for a few seconds, her disappointment faded.

◆ ◆ ◆

"That boy... why didn't he simply hop off his rock? I mean, you just tell him to jump. You use a teleportation cannon to fire a portal underneath him and transport him to safety, like where his father was," Archie said.

Dessa knew Archie loved activating portals in his favorite game, where he guided troubled travelers to safety. The line between virtual and real often blurred for him, and she found their conversations about it amusing.

But this time, she didn't respond. All she could do right now was stand before Penelope without uttering a word. She was getting a Medal of Valor, but Penelope was refusing to attend.

"Archie, you're going to be late for school," Penelope snapped. "Go get dressed!"

"I am dressed."

"You can't go to school dressed as a deer. Put on normal clothes."

"But Mother..." The blue lights of a police car flashed outside, and he fell silent.

The lights flickered on the living room walls, and Archie, startled, dashed to his room.

Nothing unusual, Dessa thought. The boy was autistic and didn't like bright lights or loud noises.

The lights went off, and there was silence for a few seconds. Dessa didn't mind.

Penelope stretched her hand to Dessa's head, stroked her hair, and squinted as she spoke.

"I'm sure the award ceremony will go well tonight, even without me." Penelope searched her face. "There will be other awardees, won't there? You won't be lonely."

"It's not that I would be lonely." Her voice sounded flat and dull, like it came from a synthesizer. "The real problem is —"

"My not coming isn't the end of the world," Penelope cut her off, tightening her jaw.

"No, it's not the end of the world." Dessa bowed her head and stared at her hands.

The real problem was Penelope never appreciated what Dessa achieved on her own. But how could she tell Penelope that without hurting her ego or making things awkward? She never had before.

She was committed to taking care of Penelope, not embarrassing her. So, whenever they had a conflict, she'd end up telling Penelope it was her own fault, not Penelope's. She'd apologize to keep Penelope's ego intact.

This time, however, was different. She was going to be awarded a Medal of Valor, and Penelope refused to attend. Maybe it was time to stop pretending and be honest. She should tell Penelope that she was wrong and should be there for her.

She turned to Penelope, but before she could say anything, someone rang the bell, and Penelope trotted to the front door.

A deputy stood outside by his cruiser, talking with Penelope on the porch. Dessa watched from the window, wondering what had brought the man here.

When Penelope returned to the living room, she called Archie. No response. Dessa followed her to Archie's room, where Penelope checked under the bed and rummaged through his closet. She found him buried under a pile of clothes and pulled him out, standing him next to Dessa.

"Archie, did you call 9-1-1 yesterday?"

"I don't remember."

"You called and told the operator there was something like a fire-breathing dragon in our front yard. You also told her there was thick smoke coming from our neighbor's house."

"There was smoke, really. The neighbor had lit her fireplace. I explained everything to the police when they arrived."

"Why do you do such things?" Penelope raised her voice. "They could fine us!"

"I was lonely," Archie said. "I wanted to talk to someone."

Dessa turned to the window, her eyes glazing over the blurred shape of their Halloween dragon, until the school bus drove by.

"Archie just missed his bus," she said. "I guess I'll have to give him a ride to school."

Archie tugged on his hoodie, grabbed his backpack, and slid his hand into Dessa's. She led him into the garage, where her truck waited. SAR gear stuffed in the passenger footwell: a mission-ready backpack, a rain poncho, a helmet, an old tarp, an ice ax, and ropes. A pair of sneakers and a change of clothes lay on the seat. She tossed all gear into the back, under the truck cap, clearing a space for Archie, who climbed into the cab, fastened his seat belt, and buried his face in his phone.

She started the engine and headed for the school. A melancholy song played on the radio, and she hummed along for a few seconds.

"Archie, do you want to come with me to the award ceremony tonight?"

The boy didn't answer, lost in his phone.

"Archie, you ought to respond when people talk to you."

He turned to her and fixed his amber eyes on her. "Does Chewbacca yawn?"

That was out of the blue—but she was used to it.

"Yes, of course he yawns. Haven't you seen him?"

The boy said nothing. He focused on his phone again, tapping on the screen. He played a clip and turned toward her, laughing—and she realized she couldn't stay mad at him for too long.

"Oh, no, no, no!" she said, deadpan. "The yawning pup again. We've already seen it ninety-nine times."

She winked at him. "Exactly ninety-nine times, I'm sure."

Archie snorted and played another clip. She flicked her eyes at his phone: a giant gray cat sang in a measured cadence, pausing between each line as if savoring the words: "Oh, no, no, no... Oh, no, no, no... Oh, no, no, no..."

She glanced at Archie, and he looked back at her. They giggled together and, watching the road ahead, the two sang along with the gray cat, swaying back and forth.

At the end of the clip, she meowed in full voice. Archie burst into laughter, and she laughed with him.

Her smile faded as she gripped the steering wheel tighter. Could she ever think about leaving Penelope? Leaving Penelope would mean leaving Archie—but abandoning her innocent nephew would certainly pain her. On the other hand, staying with Penelope would only bring her more pain. Hurt her more and more as time went on.

She ran her fingers through her hair. She had to find a way out of this deadlock—but right now, she could see none.

CHAPTER EIGHT

The last time Dessa saw both sets of parents together, they'd stood by Philip's casket in hushed grief. Today, they were supposed to reunite for something more cheerful—Thanksgiving dinner.

Her father had insisted on flying his small Piper instead of taking a commercial flight like Penelope's parents. The trip seemed to be going well until her mother called from Portland. "The engine had a bit of a power hiccup," she said, her voice light but strained. "We're waiting on repairs and should arrive tomorrow. Don't worry about us—we'll be fine."

Dessa tried not to picture the tiny plane against the November sky, its engine sputtering.

Meanwhile, with Penelope still at work, Dessa had to pick up Penelope's parents at Sea-Tac, navigating heavy traffic for more than an hour to get them home.

They were already having an early dinner together—she, Archie, Penelope, and Penelope's parents—when her phone buzzed with a rescue mission call from the sheriff's office.

"Someone is stuck on Baring Mountain." She rose from the table. "I have to go."

Penelope stared at her, fork suspended mid-air, her expression unreadable. "Your mom and dad are landing at Harvey Field tomorrow. Remember?"

Harvey Field was their neighborhood airport.

"I remember. Please meet them for me if I'm late."

At the door, she turned back, her gaze lingering on the table. "I'll see you all later." She walked out, masking her excitement for the mission.

It had all begun five hours ago when Sheldon Bird climbed the alpine route to Baring Mountain alone while his friends readied themselves for a kegger in town. A paratrooper veteran still in excellent shape, he'd started late but made good time, reaching that beast of a summit an hour before sunset.

At the edge of the mountain's 3,500-foot-high north face, he planted his feet and surveyed the horizon. A week ago, his niece Virgie had stood here too, her parachute pre-packed with care—by him. But something had gone wrong, and she'd fallen 800 feet to her death. He'd gone over it again and again—had he missed something?

The memory burned, but it couldn't deter him. He donned his helmet over his balaclava, tightened his pack's chest and leg straps, and steadied himself. This jump wasn't just for him; it was for Virgie. Her memory demanded it—and maybe, so did his guilt.

Ready to go, Sheldon remained still for a couple of minutes. The North Cascades' bluish ridges stretched as far as he could see. Above them rose dormant volcanoes covered with glaciers—the caps of Mount Baker to the north and Mount Adams to the south, and between them the bell of Mount Rainier and the cone of Glacier Peak. Far to the west, like a gray spot in the sky, hung the silhouette of Mount Olympus. The mountains were snow white and beautiful.

He widened his shoulders and jumped off, flying into the abyss. He opened his parachute—but the moment after, he hit the rock face, bounced, and dangled helplessly about a hundred feet below the edge. The harness straps clawed into his thighs.

Panting, he looked up at his parachute lines and groaned. The ropes were caught on a rock chimney.

He held his breath and moved a bit, then shifted again. The tangled ropes above stayed attached to the outcropping.

It was a good thing he had brought his satellite beacon today. Before hitting the trail, he set the device to tracking mode and stowed it at the top of his pack. As he hiked, the beacon broadcast his location to the Globalstar satellite network every few minutes, which sent his coordinates to a ground data center. The data center posted his location on a web map for his friends to see.

His beacon was meant to be a lifesaver in the absence of cell coverage.

Before jumping, he'd taken the beacon out of his pack and clipped it to the parachute's chest strap. Now he was glad he had, because the device was easy to reach. He gripped it in his left hand and used his right hand to lift the flap and press the red SOS button.

After a minute, the *message sent* light flashed green, and he had never seen anything so beautiful. Instead of posting it on the web map, the network would forward his SOS to an emergency call center. They would pinpoint him at Baring Mountain—and summon the rescuers.

The frosty air was already nipping at his nose. He'd done the right thing dressing in layers of thermal underwear under his jumpsuit.

He hung, resting motionless on the ropes. As the minutes crawled by, his legs went numb. Dizzy and getting cold sweats, he realized just in time that impaired blood circulation and reduced oxygen flow to his brain were about to throw him into orthostatic shock. If he didn't move, he would faint and die.

He loaded his leg muscles by pushing against the rock wall every so often to keep his circulation going, and—thank God— he felt better, the numbness in his legs fading and his head clearing.

◆ ◆ ◆

Dessa was the first rescuer to arrive at the Baring

Mountain trailhead on Blackout Wednesday evening. She parked her truck and checked her gear, glancing at the empty lot. With the Thanksgiving holiday tomorrow, she wondered how many sober volunteers would show up—or if she'd be climbing this mountain alone.

An hour later, two art teachers arrived in a Volkswagen Beetle, its dim headlights flickering as they rolled into the lot. She unfolded a map on the hood of her truck and discussed the climbing route with them. When a third man, a rescue newbie, showed up another hour later, she decided it was time to move and led the team up the slope, their headlamps cutting through the pitch-black night.

They carried everything they might need for the rescue on their backs, loaded like donkeys. She let the group catch their breath at the ridge before continuing with the long traverse that led to the base of a steep gully. Once there, they pulled out their ice axes and climbed to the saddle below the summit. The wind had cleared much of the snow at the saddle—just as she had expected—and they scrambled up the rock to the summit in haste.

At 2 a.m., she dropped her backpack where Sheldon had stood a few hours earlier. Standing beside his footprints, she called out into the darkness and heard him answer in a hoarse voice from somewhere below the edge.

So, he was conscious and not seriously injured, and she couldn't ask for more.

Now she had to get her team to work. Extracting the man from the rock wall would be no easy task. The north face of Baring Mountain was dangerous—it took climbers ten years to finally conquer it, but not before the wall claimed a life. The rock here was unstable and prone to crumbling; the weather was whimsical and uncertain. As if to confirm her thoughts, the wind picked up, shifting directions, and a fog rose from the dark valley.

Working near the edge, she and her teammates rigged a

rope system farther to Sheldon's left so that a possible rockfall during the descent wouldn't harm him.

With the ropes secured around several trees, she rappelled down, the lonesome beam of her headlamp cutting through the fog. She discovered an obscure side ledge and, step by step, hugging the rock, neared Sheldon.

"Why didn't you send the helicopter, damn it," the man wheezed.

The helicopter? It was too late in the day to fly—that's why. Flying into the mountains as daylight faded would bring lousy visibility, forcing the pilots to play a guessing game with jagged terrain. Topping it off with a night rescue from the air? It would be like diving into a cocktail of deadly risks.

Sheldon cursed. "Do you want me to die here?!" He cursed again.

A rock crumbled under her leg and thundered down the mountain, but she managed to keep her balance and step to the other side of the ledge. Danger lurked here, and she had every reason to turn back, climb up for safety, and wait for daylight. But this man, no matter how rude, needed her right now, and she could do nothing else but take care of him. Take care while forgetting about herself—just as she had done for years with her brother Philip when he was injured and walked with a cane. As she had when Philip, by then Penelope's husband, was dying from leukemia—and as she had, more recently, with the widowed Penelope.

She attached a rope to Sheldon's parachute harness without a word, moved aside, and her teammates above pulled him over the edge to safety. Without wasting time, they pulled her out too. As she held onto the ropes, she imagined, with a faint sense of relief, that she was emerging from the desolate pit of her dream—and her grip tightened as the ledge disappeared below her.

Her team collected the ropes and equipment and spent the rest of the night on the summit with Sheldon. Concerned that he might suffer from suspension trauma after hanging in his harness for so long, they kept him warm with their own gear. To stay warm themselves, they walked, jumped, and even danced. At dawn, a helicopter arrived to fly Sheldon to a valley town, while she and the three men shouldered their heavy backpacks and made their way back down the snowy route off the mountain.

After the sleepless night, walking downhill fully loaded was harder than going uphill.

Back at the trailhead, her teammates gave her high-fives. She jumped into her truck and rushed to Harvey Field, hoping to be on time for her parents' landing.

CHAPTER NINE

Dessa was only two miles from Harvey Field when she spotted her father's Piper descending, its wings tilting with exacting adjustments, as if even the wind had to yield to his control. She hurried to park and headed toward the tie-down area. From a distance, she could see her parents talking to Penelope, her dad's arm resting on Penelope's shoulder.

Dessa's mom noticed her first and ran, arms open for an embrace. Dessa hugged her, and they kissed each other.

Dessa walked to her dad.

"Hi, Dad. Good to see you made it here."

"Good to see you made it too, Pumpkin. I hear you've been entertaining yourself with some risky missions."

She didn't want to talk about missions right now and said nothing. Her dad stared at her for a few seconds and chuckled. "Got a kiss for the old man, too?"

She gave her father a light kiss on the cheek. Penelope stepped to her, and she gave Penelope a light kiss too—and meant to pull back, but Penelope embraced her and held her tight.

At last, the courtesies were over, and they headed to the house.

Back home, Dessa napped for an hour, waking to the muffled sound of voices drifting from the living room. She stretched, still groggy, and shuffled toward the voices, yawning. Everyone was there—her parents, Penelope, and

Penelope's parents—sitting and chatting around the table.

Everyone except Archie.

She looked around and spotted him through the open door of his room, lying in bed with his phone in hand.

"We were waiting for you!" her father called.

A plum brandy bottle stood next to his half-full glass. Her father loved plum brandy, and Penelope had bought the bottle for him. The others—Penelope, Dessa's mom, and Penelope's parents, Tim and Betty—were all drinking strawberry lemonade. She stepped to the table and poured herself a glass from the jug.

Her father topped off his brandy and rose.

"Now that we're finally all together, let's clink glasses," he boomed. "Let's clink glasses for good health. *Nazdrave*!"

Everyone clinked glasses with her father and drank.

Everyone, except for Archie.

"Won't Archie knock a glass with me?" he asked.

Her father's technical English was good, but his colloquial English was less so.

She shrugged. "Ask his mother."

"He will, why not," Penelope said. "Archie, put your phone down and come here!"

Archie lapsed into silence.

"Enough videos! Get out of bed," Penelope said, raising her voice. "I'm talking to you!!!"

"Don't yell at him," Tim said. "Try with kindness." He gave his daughter a timid smile. "Try with kindness and kindness alone."

Dessa knew from Penelope herself that Penelope's parents had never denied her anything and never forced her to do anything, except once they'd tried to make little Penelope eat chili instead of pizza. Penelope had told them she'd rather starve to death, locked herself in her room, and refused to eat the whole day. They'd given up and let her eat all the pizza she wanted, but she still starved for another day.

Penelope had had everything her way ever since.

Now Dessa watched her own dad turn to Penelope. “Shall I try with kindness, and kindness alone?” Without waiting for an answer, he added, “Watch me now!”

He got up and stepped close to Archie’s room. Speaking through the open door, he glanced back at the others.

“Archie, if you get out of bed and come to the table to knock glasses with me, I’ll take you on a trip to Bulgaria this summer.”

Archie showed up at the door.

“Is Bulgaria in Asia?”

“No, it’s not in Asia.”

“Is it in Europe?”

“Yes, it’s in Europe.”

“Then I won’t come!”

“Why?”

“Because there are giant hornets in Asia and Europe. If you get stung by one of those, your lungs get paralyzed and you die in fifteen minutes.”

“Archie, you mustn’t believe everything on YouTube!”

“Why? The guy has two million followers.”

The boy turned on his heel and disappeared back into his room.

There was nothing wrong with Archie enjoying YouTube, Dessa thought, watching her dad amble back toward his chair. Nothing wrong, especially if the boy could out-argue her dad—a famous scholar—with ease.

Dessa sipped her strawberry lemonade, half-listening as the conversation drifted around her.

“Will you go to Bulgaria again this summer?” Tim asked her father.

“We’ll go...” Her father leaned back in his chair, swirling his brandy. “We emigrants are like storks... Every summer, we return to our native swamp.”

Her mom twirled her empty glass, reached for the jug, poured herself more lemonade, drank, and looked at Tim and Betty. "Would you like to go to Bulgaria together? Maybe this summer? Our village house in the Balkan Mountains is a little wonder. We sleep ten hours a night there, and we always wake up happy."

"Our village house is old, but it smells good," her father said, grinning. "It smells like bathed fairies in the bedrooms."

Bathed fairies? Oh, come on... Her father loved to embarrass her sometimes by talking this way.

"The capital, Sofia, doesn't smell like fairies," her mom said. "And our condo there is not large. Still, it will do for a few days before we go to the mountains. By the way, the neighborhood is full of restaurants and cafés. I think you'll like it."

"Yes, yes, you'll like it," her father went on. "Restaurants and cafés... and the best bridal fashion store in the Balkans, bridal gowns, veils... the works."

Dessa stared at her father. Bridal gowns, veils... What was he implying? Same-sex marriages weren't legal in Bulgaria, but her dad wasn't a homophobe—unlike many of his countrymen. A pang of irritation flickered—was he hinting at something, or just being his usual self, saying whatever came to mind?

"Yes, plenty of restaurants and cafés," her father continued. "We will have a good time... Bulgaria is a small but merry country."

"Interesting idea," Tim said, stirring in his chair. "Very interesting... We've never been to a country like Bulgaria. Thank you from the heart. We'll think about it."

Her father sipped his brandy and nodded. "Yes, yes, think... Everyone should think. Because Dessa hasn't been there for ten years, it's about time she went back."

She said nothing, only grabbed a handful of almonds and shoved them into her mouth.

High time to go to Bulgaria? Really?

Actually, what she needed now was Thanksgiving dinner. Maybe some food would stop her father's endless provocations—or at least keep her too busy eating to care.

"Who cooked the turkey?" Dessa's father asked, turning to her.

"Don't know," she said, filling a plate for Archie. "Penelope ordered it online and had it delivered by Instacart."

The Thanksgiving dinner looked fine to her: turkey, cranberry sauce, sweet potatoes—the usual.

She piled food on her plate.

The dinner would have been the same, she thought, even if she hadn't gone on a mission and cooked it herself.

"Aren't you going to say a prayer?" Betty asked Tim.

"I'd rather have Penny say a prayer. It's her table."

Penelope grabbed Dessa's hand and turned to Dessa's father, who reached out his hand to her.

Everyone held hands, and Penelope said a prayer, concluding with "Let's eat."

They ate and talked and ate some more. An hour later, everyone leaned back in their chairs.

It was time for pie, Dessa thought, but no pie was on the table.

She glanced at Penelope. Penelope nodded, rose from her chair, and headed to the kitchen. When she returned, she carried a bottle of champagne instead of pie.

Champagne? Dessa had no idea there was champagne in the house.

Penelope opened the bottle and poured everyone a glass, standing with her own glass in hand.

"I am thankful to our dear parents for coming to our home today. It's beautiful, all of us coming together.

"Peter and Tanya," Penelope said, nodding to Dessa's parents, "flying a small Piper all the way from California.

"Mom and Dad—enduring a bumpy flight from Honolulu.

"And Dessa—coming back home safe from a dangerous night-long rescue."

Penelope put her hand on Dessa's father's shoulder.

"Peter, you told me a while ago, 'You are Dessa's sister-in-law. Can't you stop her from going on all those risky SAR missions?'"

Penelope slipped her hand in her jacket pocket.

"Well… I couldn't convince her to leave SAR as her sister-in-law…"

Dessa watched Penelope pull out a small black box.

"… but I hope to succeed as her spouse…"

Penelope opened the box, revealing an engagement ring.

"… if she'll have me," Penelope finished while sliding the ring on Dessa's finger.

"Oh, Penny—" Dessa began, but Penelope leaned in and kissed her.

For a few seconds, all she knew was that Penelope's lips were glued to hers, and she couldn't breathe.

Her father clapped, and everyone else followed suit.

Penelope let her go at last—but she was unable to move or speak, as if caught in a bad dream. Everyone else moved around her, talking and cheering.

She watched as Penelope's father rose and shook Penelope's hand. "Congratulations, Daughter."

Penelope turned to Dessa's father, and they shook hands too.

Dessa licked her lips and glanced around, her eyes searching for help in vain.

"Well done, Penny," Dessa heard her father say.

"I couldn't have done it without your support," Penelope said.

Dessa's mother came and gave her a hug.

Tim and Betty hugged her next. As they let her go, a throb ran through her finger. She looked down and found

Archie holding her hand, the one with the ring, as tightly as he could. She stared at him, pursing her lips, and he let her hand go.

Penelope and the whole parental body had a toast, and they all made their way into the kitchen to help themselves to pie, leaving her alone.

She pushed aside her glass, still full of champagne, stood up, and walked out of the house.

Dessa walked fast, going nowhere.

Just walking away.

"Dessa!" her mother called from the darkness behind her, her voice cutting through the night. "Where are you going?"

"I need to exercise a bit, Mom!" she called back without turning around. "I need to be by myself," she whispered.

The night was cloudy and cold, yet the ring burned on her finger, hot and heavy.

She had dreamed of leaving Penelope, but instead, she found herself engaged to her. Engaged to be married in the not-so-distant future.

She strode along the road, watching her breath wisp out.

When she remained with Penelope after her brother's death, she hadn't planned to stay for too long. But one thing led to another, and a year later, Penelope told her she loved her. Dessa was her everything, Penelope said, and Penelope's eyes showed it.

Back then, Penelope had seemed so insecure after losing her spouse, and Dessa couldn't bring herself to reject her. She said she loved her too.

Dessa slowed down. "But it wasn't true!" she whispered. "It wasn't true."

It was true, though, that she found making love to Penelope interesting, even enjoyable at times.

However, Penelope's earlier kindness, a comforting constant in the courtship days, had been fleeting and fizzled out quickly—and so had Dessa's desire. Yet, Penelope still wanted to have sex with her, without noticing she didn't enjoy it anymore.

Once, Dessa hoped they could just do things together—sit in front of the fireplace and listen to music, read the same book, stream a movie and talk about it. Also camp and hike in the mountains.

Her hopes, however, had been in vain. They never materialized. Apart from sex, all Penelope cared about was her work. Penelope seemed to think intimacy consisted of doing laundry together and sharing the same bed.

Without passion, without closeness, why would Dessa want to marry Penelope?

Besides, Penelope had asked Dessa to leave SAR, but Dessa loved SAR.

She loved SAR, not Penelope.

She stopped by an abandoned house—broken windows, peeling paint, and a missing front door—and stared at the ring. It was big on her small hand, heavy like a shackle. She pulled it off and threw it at the house. The ring bounced off the siding and fell into the weeds.

For a while, she remained motionless.

Stepping to the house, she stood at the threshold and gazed inside with unseeing eyes. A minute passed in silence —and then she heard her dead brother Philip's voice from the darkness: *I beg you... help Penny raise Archie after I'm gone.*

"I will. I promise," Dessa heard herself saying.

That was right; four years ago, she had promised to help. But now Penelope wanted Dessa to marry her and support her for life. Dessa's father wanted it too.

Was she ready to marry Penelope?

Oh God, no!

No...

Oh, how she wished she could roll back her deeds from

the last four years and set a new course. She would just remain a dedicated aunt to Archie, taking good care of him without tying herself romantically to Penelope.

However, it was too late now. She'd already assumed the part of Penelope's substitute spouse and Archie's substitute parent. Now she had to either marry Penelope or break up with her.

If she married Penelope, she'd be sacrificing her entire life for the promise she'd made to Philip.

But could she break up with Penelope right now?

Why not? After all, nobody had asked her if she wanted to marry—and that alone was reason enough to refuse.

She imagined going back to the house, looking Penelope in the eye, and saying, "No!"

Penelope wasn't going to bow, kiss her hand, and say, "Respecting your decision. Grateful for our valued connection, no matter." Penelope would lash out with hurtful words instead. Penelope would blame Dessa for causing her and Archie emotional pain.

Worse, Penelope could grow desperate and turn violent toward Dessa—and even Archie.

"Penelope has a dark side," Philip had told Dessa once. "Sometimes she can be toxic. Yet, like most people, I put up with it for my kid's sake—and stay in the marriage."

Dessa knew firsthand how toxic Penelope could be —manipulative and controlling, jealous and possessive. But Dessa too, like her brother, could choose to stay in the relationship—for just a little longer. Because currently, she was only engaged; she wasn't married yet. She wasn't going to tie the knot tomorrow. Penelope and parents would need time to organize the big event. It could take months, more likely a year. So, she had time and could give Penelope the opportunity to become a better person. If Penelope failed to change, Dessa could still say "No" to the marriage when the time came.

The important thing was that right now, she had to neither marry Penelope nor separate from her. She could just postpone.

Postponing her decision and giving Penelope a chance would be good for Archie—Archie and everyone else—everyone but herself. Yet, she was willing to do it.

She turned on her phone's flashlight, and the ring glistened in the weeds. Picking it up, she slid it back on her finger before walking back onto the road and heading home, searching for stars in the cloudy sky.

Her face was wet, and for a moment, she thought it was tears. But it couldn't be, she told herself. It must have been raindrops—raindrops falling from the sky.

CHAPTER TEN

Fred had already lit the outside grill and was adjusting its vents when Dessa pulled up on her bike. He glanced up and smiled —still humming a tune under his breath—but she didn't smile back; she only lowered her head and stared at the flames. Her silence unsettled him—Dessa was usually the first to flash a grin. But today, deep creases ran from the sides of her nose to the drooping corners of her lips. He'd never seen her like this before.

A moment later, Dessa stared at the moisture-laden clouds swamping the skies as the light from the fire dimmed across her face. He ushered her into the trailer and settled opposite her at the table, his eyes fixed on her.

A few seconds passed.

"Are you okay?" He leaned forward.

"I'm fine. About 40 percent fine."

"What's wrong?"

Dessa only dropped her chin to her chest.

Fred knew—just like anyone in SAR—that Dessa had no steady income. Fellow rescuers often invited her to dinner at restaurants or their homes, and nobody seemed surprised when he, now a SAR cook, began asking Dessa to his trailer.

The first time Dessa visited him, a month after their impromptu rendezvous at Roam & Brew, he treated her to a café noisette in a delicate Belles Saisons cup and saucer. It turned out—much to his delight—that she'd never tried café noisette before and didn't even know what it was. An espresso with just a kiss of hot milk, he explained to her then.

A couple of days before Christmas, he baked dark-chocolate cookies for her, which she devoured. In the quiet of January, she stopped in for an afternoon chat, helping herself to his signature lemon lavender cake topped with edible flowers.

Dessa seemed to enjoy her visits more each time.

And why wouldn't she?

He was a French chef—he knew food—and she liked to eat well.

Besides, he was an immigrant like Dessa herself. An outlander who could understand her better than the Americans. An elderly confidant she could trust with her private thoughts.

Fred's eyes returned to Dessa, hunched over the table—so strong in the mountains, yet seeming so vulnerable now.

"What's wrong?" he repeated.

Dessa remained silent.

"Slushaĭ... Az... tvoĭ... friend," he stammered in broken Bulgarian.

She looked at him, tipping her head to the side.

"For six weeks now, I've been studying Bulgarian at U-Dub."

A shallow breath escaped Dessa's lips.

"Listen, I am your friend," he repeated, now in English. "You can tell me anything."

Dessa's shoulders rose, steadied for a moment, and fell, trembling.

"If you tell me about it, you will feel better."

Dessa took a napkin and unfolded it on the table. "Can you give me a pen?" she whispered.

She sketched what looked to him like a schoolgirl sprinting across a street to the sidewalk, hands extended for an embrace, a car behind her, and a boy flying in the air above the car hood. A hunched woman stood on the sidewalk with a black dot for a mouth—a mouth open in a scream.

"That's my brother." Dessa pointed at the flying boy. "He was hit by a car twenty-five years ago today."

And the girl was Dessa herself, Fred surmised. Dessa, running for a joyful hug toward that older lady, still unaware of what was going on behind her.

"I've been thinking... no matter how I live my life, I'll never forget the thud, the screech of brakes, my grandma's scream."

Her chin quivered.

"I can't forget my brother lying on the pavement like a broken puppet, his limbs all twisted and his blood spilling on the asphalt... That memory still stabs at my heart."

She stared at the peeled trout fillets, all bloody-pinkish, that he had soaked with marinade in a glass tray earlier. He sprang and moved the bloody tray from the table to the kitchen nook across the aisle.

Returning to the table, he looked at the napkin with Dessa's sketch.

"I suppose... you might feel guilty because the car struck your brother but not you," he said in a low voice. "You were healthy while he had to walk with a cane."

Dessa shook her head. "I feel guilty because I'm the reason for the accident. I led Philip into the car's path."

Fred exhaled and leaned forward, softening his gaze.

Dessa stole a quick glance at him. "It was Grandma's birthday, and she waited for us on the street to take us out for ice cream. The last bell rang, and I stormed out of the classroom, shouting 'Catch me! Catch me!' Philip followed me, and we ran down the hallway and across the schoolyard. I saw the car coming, but I knew I could cross just fine before it, so I did.

"I did, but Philip *didn't*."

"But Philip's injury was temporary, right?" That's what Dessa had told him at their Roam & Brew rendezvous. "Doctors fixed him, right?"

"Not until we arrived in California five years later. Philip couldn't walk by himself until then. He used a cane, but I still had to support him walking to school, climbing stairs, going back home, visiting the restroom, and taking a bath. I had to fix him dinner and make his bed."

"You were the only one to do all that?"

"Yes, but I wanted to."

"You did?!"

"I certainly did. My dad was trying to make it big as a mathematician, but he didn't get paid much back in Bulgaria. Like, he couldn't buy Philip a real cane, so he made one from a willow twig. My mother was his assistant, and they worked hard every day, even on weekends. So, I wanted to take care of Philip. That was my job."

"I wonder—if you don't mind me asking—didn't your grandma help, too? Fix Philip's dinner and keep him company sometimes, so you could go out with friends?"

"No... Grandma couldn't." Dessa ran a hand through her hair. "She passed away a month after the accident. She thought it was all her fault."

"Oh... That's too bad."

"You have no idea."

Perhaps he did... He closed his eyes and saw little Dessa, creases on her face—just like today—taking care of her brother, staying home, and losing all her friends.

"So, your childhood was unhappy..."

"Not really... Taking care of Philip for my parents made me happy. I was only eight, but I was like another adult in the family. My parents appreciated what I did and respected me for it. And it worked out in the end. My dad beefed up his résumé, got jobs in Oslo and Paris, and brought us all to California."

Dessa had grown up taking care of her brother, Fred thought, always putting him first and not thinking about herself. And now, Dessa continued doing the same by looking after her brother's widow, who had curiously become Dessa's fiancée.

Her latest role didn't seem to bring Dessa joy though.

"Your fiancée... what's her name again? Penelope? Did you tell Penelope that you're only 40 percent fine today?"

"No. We're not talking at the moment."

"How come?"

"I told her I wanted to apply to grad school." Dessa frowned. "I told her... since we are going to be married... I could become a special ed teacher. Have a job and help Archie, too.

"My colleague Jesse—you know him, he's in SAR—gave me the idea. I liked it and was so happy... but Penelope wasn't."

Dessa furrowed her brow.

"She snapped at me and tried to pick a fight. I stayed silent, and she stopped talking to me."

"All that must've been tough."

"It was." Dessa bit her lip. "I couldn't sleep all night."

Fred hoped she'd open up and talk more about herself —and feel better. Yet she remained quiet, her eyes darting aimlessly. He lowered his gaze, but not too low, still able to see her fidgeting with her hair.

A few seconds later, she continued: "I couldn't sleep all night, and then something horrible happened to me an hour ago."

She paused, raising her eyes to him.

"At first, everything was normal. I was just biking here... At one point, I stopped at a traffic light. As I waited, I looked up into the sky."

She went on in a whisper, and he leaned closer to hear her.

"And then unexpectedly, in a flash, the sky ceased to be sky. It turned into a lead plate... a cold plate that pressed me down with all its might and crushed me... crushed me into a tiny speck of dust."

She looked at him, her eyes unseeing, and bowed her head.

"I suddenly realized that I'm nothing but a speck of dust, crushed by the infinity of time and space... not even dust but plain nothing."

"That thought hit me out of the blue, hit me like lightning... pierced through my heart and overwhelmed me completely. For the first time in my life, I understood so clearly that I was nothing... nothing in the boundless universe."

Dessa wiped her eyes.

"Have you..." She looked at him. "Have you ever had a crisis like mine... feeling worthless and lost in the cosmos?"

"Who, me?" He gave a friendly smirk. "A few times, yes."

He glanced out the window.

"It first happened to me when I was nine years old. I was suffering from constipation—and as I was sitting hopeless on the toilet, it struck me out of nowhere that my death was inevitable."

Dessa stared at him.

"Seriously... I was horrified, and everything blackened before my eyes. Back then, my life seemed pointless... My mother, however, gave me a laxative, and I forgot about death in no time. I was carefree again."

"I've had other crises, of course. The last one was just before I tried to hang myself."

He stroked his goatee, his voice quiet but steady.

"My wife was unfaithful—in fact, promiscuous—and I grew old and useless in my own eyes."

Dessa glanced at him and lowered her gaze to the napkin.

"You know, whenever I begin pondering the meaning of life, it turns out, sooner or later, that what I actually need isn't some deep philosophical sense but something quite specific and practical."

"Like a laxative," she said.

"Yeah, like a laxative. Or in my case a divorce, even if it wasn't what I wanted."

He leaned in again. "In your case, a good full-time job and your own apartment perhaps."

He watched Dessa nod, her face softening.

"Believe me, you can live without knowing the meaning as long as everything else in your life is in order."

He leaned back. "But you must take care of yourself.

Nobody else will."

He rose.

"Now I'm going to grill the trout. Would you like to join me?"

They stepped outside. Fred placed the trout fillets on the grill while Dessa stood close beside him, watching. Feeling warm, he tried to convince himself the heat came solely from the grill.

"Last Saturday, you got to the summit really late."

He had followed her hike on her satellite beacon web map.

"It was okay. Clifton and I spent the night up there watching the stars."

"Clifton was there, too?... Um... Weren't you cold sleeping in the snow?"

"Well, no, we slept in our bivy bags." Dessa laughed. "There was no moon, the sky was pitch black, and the stars were fabulous."

She shifted from foot to foot as she spoke, her legs slightly apart and her hands in her pockets.

Fred flipped a corner of a fillet. "I guess you had a good time with Clifton."

"Yes, we did! We had a great time together."

He wished he could be in Clifton's place, but he knew he was too old to sleep on snowy summits.

"Let's go inside and eat before the trout gets cold," he said, glad to share a meal with her—if not the stars.

"Allow me to present the menu." Fred outstretched his arm. "We'll start with a simple but elegant salad of cherry tomatoes and sliced fennel. Here is the trout... It comes with Dijon potato cubes, roasted with mustard and garlic. I know you don't drink, so I've got strawberry lemonade for you and Sauvignon Blanc for me. Both pair well with fish. Ah—we'll have petits fours for dessert and a cheese platter at the end."

He started serving. In a couple of minutes, he had covered the table with plates, bowls, and glasses.

"I'll leave the petits fours and the cheese on the counter for the moment." He sat down. "Now, bon appétit."

They ate in silence for a while.

"Fennel is popular in California." Dessa poked a cherry tomato with her fork. "As soon as we settled there, my mother began to put fennel in every salad. She loved it. But my brother and I came to hate it."

Dessa forked the last tomato into her mouth. All the fennel slices were still in her bowl.

"You like trout, don't you?" Fred asked.

"Oh, I do." She took a big bite. "Your trout is delicious."

He watched her gorge on another piece.

"Would you like to see the recipe?"

She didn't respond, busy eating.

"It's my own."

"Uh-huh," she said, chewing. "Let me see it."

He pulled out the recipe—a sheet in his crooked handwriting—from the overhead cabinet. "Here it is."

She read aloud, *"Pŭstŭrva à la Dessa Sinich..."*

She looked at him, grinning. "You named the dish after me?"

"Yes, I named it after you."

"Retsepta za dvama ot Fred Perin..." Her voice pitched up. "It's in Bulgarian! Whoa!"

He gave her a crisp nod. Trout à la Dessa Sinich. A recipe for two by Fred Perin.

He didn't have to tell her Google had translated it all for him; he'd only copied it by hand. Writing in Cyrillic by hand was tough enough for him.

"It should be *trout*, not *truut*." She squinted at the text. "Um... Never mind. It's funny."

He watched her eyes dance as she read aloud, following the words written by his hand. Her face was soft, her lips succulent. The creases around her nose melted away.

She lifted her head and smiled at him.

"It's funny... You're a funny man."

She paused.

"I like funny people."

Warmth radiated through his body.

"And I like young people."

He hesitated for a moment.

"I don't want to be old. I'd rather die."

"You know what? You needn't die. Simply stop thinking about age. Don't think about age; just live. That's what young people do."

"Don't think about age, just live," he repeated.

But why not? He was going to give it a try.

He piled the utensils in the sink and stepped to the kitchen counter. A gust of wind splattered the first raindrops against the window. He took the petits fours and the cheese from the counter and brought them to the table. They ate and drank in silence.

The day was short, and it was getting dark.

"It's time for me to go," Dessa announced.

"But it's raining outside."

"It doesn't matter. I won't think about the rain. I'll just bike."

Dessa walked out, and he followed her outside. She mounted her bike, waved him goodbye, and he watched her until she disappeared behind the curtain of rain.

When he got back inside, he was soaked, but it didn't really matter, and he didn't think much about it.

CHAPTER ELEVEN

End of March, California

"The mule tripped and fell into the canyon, dragging the rider down the ravine." Tanya stared at her phone. "It broke her bones… her shins… and her left ankle… her right wrist… her left shoulder… and a few ribs."

Seated at the kitchen table, she glanced at Peter, who stood at the door, still in his pajamas.

Peter raised an eyebrow. "What happened to the mule?" Without waiting for her answer, he yawned, stepped into the kitchen, poured himself a cup of coffee, and sat next to her.

"Listen, mules are the safest way to go into the canyon. No one's ever died on a mule ride."

It had been four months since their visit to Dessa and Penelope, but Tanya hadn't had a single worry-free day since. She worried about the economy, school shootings, the security of their bank accounts, inflation, climate change, and more. Today, she worried about the couple's forthcoming mule trip into the Grand Canyon.

She and Peter were to fly their Piper to the Grand Canyon Airport, spend the night at Bright Angel Lodge on the canyon rim, and in the morning, take a mule ride down the steep trail to the Colorado River. They would stay overnight in a Phantom Ranch cabin at the bottom of the abyss and get on the mules at dawn for the long return to the rim.

She worried more about the old Piper with Peter at the controls than the mule ride, but she didn't mention it; it might hurt his ego.

"Actually, it says here a man died. Not some tourist but a professional muleteer."

"Is that why you couldn't sleep?"

"No. It's not that."

"Then what is it?" Peter put his coffee on the table. "Inflation again? School shootings? Or the goldfish?"

What she worried about all the time, though she almost never dared to tell her husband, was their daughter, Dessa.

"I'm afraid Dessa's helicopter will crash."

"I worry about that too. And not just the helicopter but about everything she is exposed to by SAR—cliffs, waterfalls, avalanches, all that."

Tanya rested her wrists on the table's edge. Her right hand twitched.

"You know that Penny's trying to convince her to leave SAR," Peter continued. "I believe Penny will try much harder once they get married. Dessa will leave sooner or later."

"Yes... I know... Penny is trying... and Dessa will leave. But that's what I'm worried about too."

"Worried? Worried about what?"

"Worried about Dessa leaving SAR."

"Really?"

"Yes, really..." she said. "You might've noticed how much she loves SAR. This is where she finds herself. This is where she is happy. If she leaves SAR, Penny, you, and I might be happy—but she wouldn't be."

She rocked back and forth a couple of times. "That's what I am worried about."

Peter smirked, and she hurried to continue before he could say anything.

"I'm worried Dessa wasn't thrilled by Penny's proposal. She walked out right after Penny slid that ring onto her finger." Tanya's voice trembled. "Perhaps she wouldn't enjoy her marriage, either. I think she should've never stayed with Penny because—"

"Dessa did the right thing by staying with Penny and Archie," Peter cut her off and slurped his coffee. "Penny and Archie were already used to Philip, so they didn't have to adapt to Dessa—and she gave them comfort right away when they needed it most."

Dessa and Philip, even though twins, weren't the same person, Tanya thought. A mother and child weren't just used to their spouse and parent—there were way deeper feelings and connections at play. But while Peter's take on family relationships was a bit reductive, she couldn't blame him. He was born and raised in Zarena, his mountain village in the Balkans, where for centuries, folks had emphasized sticking together and having each other's backs when things got tough. Peter, like his ancestors, had a strong sense of duty and obligation to take care of his own during hard times. In that regard, Dessa was like him.

"Imagine Penny remarried an American man," Peter said. "A stepfather Archie neither knows nor loves would be a disaster. Clueless about our ways, the man would be a turn-off for you and me too." He smirked. "Picture it: you nod, and he thinks yes; you shake your head, and he thinks no... It would take us years to teach him that nodding and shaking heads mean the opposite in our culture."

Her husband, a professor, was lecturing her again. He didn't need to. She knew well enough that Dessa, being Archie's aunt, already had a strong bond and love for him. Yet, she had faith that there were other good people out there for Penelope to marry, and for Dessa, too.

Peter banged his cup on the table.

"In contrast, when Dessa marries Penny, the disruption for all of us will be nearly nil."

If Dessa married Penelope, Tanya echoed in her mind, the disruptions would be nearly nil. Just as they were a quarter of a century ago, when Dessa devoted herself to the injured Philip so that Peter could continue his research full throttle, keeping Tanya as a full-time assistant by his side. The disruptions for Peter were minimal, and he published papers, gave talks, won awards, and gained prominence.

Back then, Peter would routinely bring Dessa a bonbon after a hard day's work. "A good girl," he'd say, patting Dessa on the shoulder, "a responsible girl."

"Dessa, dear, go out this weekend and see a movie with your schoolmates," Tanya would sometimes suggest, but Dessa would always decline and stay home with Philip.

"Dessa discovered the nurse in herself," Peter would say with a wink, "and she likes it."

A good and responsible girl Dessa had been ever since, Tanya thought. Perhaps way too good. Far too responsible. A girl who Peter—and Tanya herself—taught that the right thing to do was to put her own needs last.

Peter got up, went to the cupboard, and pulled out a pack of cookies. He returned to his chair, stuffed his mouth, snorted, and turned to her, chewing.

"Think about it. This marriage is good for Dessa. It's good for all of us."

She stared with unseeing eyes at her husband. She wanted to believe him, to believe that everything was as it should be, that nothing terrible would happen to her daughter.

Her mind wanted to believe, but her heart couldn't.

After a few long seconds, a tear slid down her cheek and froze on her cheekbone. Her face twisted as a sob escaped, jarring her ribs, and she wept like a child struck out of nowhere, smearing tears with the back of her hands. Her husband swallowed his cookie, trying to grab her hand.

"Let me cry... I'll feel better afterward."

"Cry if you have to. Let it all out."

He bit another cookie. "Yet, as a woman, can't you fight worries with more pleasant techniques?"

"Well, yes... I can... with sex... but you never have time." She laughed through her tears, flopping back in her chair, and Peter laughed too.

She let out a breath, wiped her face with a napkin, and

stood up, stern and serious.

"You've had enough cookies! I'll make a real breakfast now... Moonstruck eggs! Cut two good slices of bread, and come keep me company."

After breakfast, Peter packed for the trip and helped Tanya pack too. He tossed their bags into the trunk, waited for Tanya to fix her hair in the visor mirror, and they headed for the airport.

The freeway was busy. All five lanes were filled with cars, people going to work. Taillights flashed, and the cars in front stopped now and again, just to set off slowly after a few seconds, giving him enough time to change lanes.

He spotted the I-5 interchange in the distance.

"Once we're past it, we'll be moving again."

Peter turned on the radio, and Louis Armstrong's gravelly voice filled the car. He unhooked his sunglasses from the visor, put them on, and sang along. But he didn't know the lyrics, so he just sang, *"dancing cheek to cheek."* Ella Fitzgerald joined in, and Tanya sang along too, her voice clear, vibrant, and plush, just like Ella's.

They reached the airport humming, parked, and headed to the tie-down area filled with small planes. Peter scanned the rows of aircraft, his mind already on the pre-flight checks.

The runway was congested, just like the freeway earlier. Peter drummed his fingers on the throttle, steering the Piper along the taxiway at a crawl. Tanya sat behind him, safely buckled in, as he watched the slow-moving line of planes ahead. He wished they were in the air already but could do nothing about it. He remembered the song, sang again, and glanced at Tanya as she joined in.

They fell silent for takeoff. He accelerated, the plane

picked up speed, and the wheels detached from the runway. They soared over the concrete, flew over a golf course, rose high above the flat waters of a nature preserve, and headed toward the beaches and the endless Pacific. They were going to make a U-turn over the ocean and head northeast toward Arizona.

It was a pleasant day, he thought, calm and sunny. The engine hummed steadily. The sky was hospitable. The Piper was rising. The Grand Canyon awaited. Life was good. He began crooning again, *"Heaven... I'm in heaven..."*

He spotted a pelican flapping its giant wings just a second before the collision shook the plane. Losing control for a moment, he gave full throttle and began stabilizing the aircraft. He tried to lift its nose, but the injured Piper was heading down. He called the tower.

"Mayday, Mayday, Mayday, Piper N939MB, we're going down."

"Where are you, and what can I do for you?"

"We're going down toward the ocean. Send somebody to pick us up. I think we will be fine, but we have struck a bird, and we've got to go down."

A minute later, he descended over the beach. The tide was low, and the strip of firm wet sand seemed good for touching down. A man and woman walking by the surf noticed the approaching plane and darted away.

All he had to do now was land.

Just then, a dachshund popped up on the strip. A little girl dashed down from the dune top to rescue the dog. Her mother rose from under her umbrella and froze with her mouth open in a silent scream. The plane was going to sweep over the little ones in an instant.

Peter swerved to the waves. In that final instant, he saw the child embrace the dachshund and rest her cheek on its head.

CHAPTER TWELVE

The Same Day, Washington

Dessa received the mission call before dawn. It was still pitch dark outside—but at least it wasn't two o'clock in the morning. As a rule, she kept her mission gear in her truck, so she threw on her clothes and took off. Ninety minutes later—after battling a bumpy, rooted forest road for the last four miles—she pulled into the deployment point by Barclay Lake.

She found the SAR food truck parked on the small lot, its tire chains glimmering in the snow. Jesse was in the cabin, working on a rescue plan, while Fred, she was sure, was cooking breakfast inside the truck. A dozen early-bird rescuers stood by the truck, eating sandwiches, drinking tea and coffee, and chatting. They had to wait for those coming from more remote parts of the county and for the search plan to be finalized, depending on the available personnel. Only after that, they'd go for the rescue itself.

The area was remote, and there was no cell coverage. Dessa locked her phone in the glove compartment, got out of the truck, and scanned the snowy ridges. Baring Mountain soared south of the lake, and to the north, its grim baby brother, Merchant Peak, jutted out. Though lower, Merchant Peak was inaccessible and dangerous, so climbers preferred the bigger sibling.

Last fall, on Blackout Wednesday, she'd set out from here up the climber's trail to search for Sheldon Bird after his ill-fated jump from Baring Mountain.

And now, she was back—for Sheldon once again.

The previous afternoon, Sheldon Bird had set out to try his new crampons. He'd told his mother he was just taking a stroll around Barclay Lake—but Dessa knew better. Climbers rarely went for casual strolls this far out in winter.

During last fall's search, his beacon had made the search easy, its pings guiding her team straight to him in the night. But this time, there were no signals from his device. "It's been sitting on the kitchen counter for a month," his mother explained over the phone. "He keeps saying he'll buy new batteries and never does."

Still, Dessa hoped to find him intact again —and get him out alive by nightfall.

Dessa chatted for a while with the guys and entered the food truck.

The truck was filled with the aroma of coffee and toast. Clifton was chewing on a sandwich and telling Fred a story. She listened, standing by the door.

"And then the hearse, instead of continuing to the cemetery, turned into the pub's parking lot, and the whole procession followed suit."

"Maybe the deceased wanted to have one last drink with everyone before the burial?" Fred winked.

"Ah, no... It turned out that the hearse had a flat tire, and at the same time, its oil was leaking. Just imagine—right on Christmas Eve! You can't make this stuff up."

"The dead guy was a big jinx." Fred turned to her. "Do you want a bagel and lox? The bagels are in the toaster. They'll be up in no time."

She nodded. Ever since Fred had treated her to his *Trout à la Dessa Sinich*, she was ready to eat whatever he cooked.

She watched him pull two crispy bagel halves from the toaster.

Fred set aside the upper bagel half, the one covered with sesame seeds, and smeared the bottom one with cream cheese while humming.

"A bagel with lox and a layer of cream,

Toasted up golden—it's a breakfast dream..."

Fred lined up slices of smoked salmon on top of the cheese, swaying to the rhythm.

"A bagel with lox and a layer of cream,

Topped with an onion slice, crisp and supreme..."

Fred wrapped the sandwich in wax paper and handed it to her along with a napkin.

"Thanks... I'm glad you managed to get the truck up this horrendous road."

"Horrendous road? Well, I didn't think about it. I just drove."

Fred gave her a wink, and she gave him a slight smile.

Fred was a great cook to have on SAR missions, she thought, and a good friend, too.

"Fred, listen... You have an extra toasted bagel, right?" Clifton asked. "Why don't you make one more sandwich for me? I'll pack it and eat it later."

Fred pulled two more bagel halves from the toaster and began making another sandwich. Dessa joined the others outside, eating her sandwich as fast as she could.

Half an hour later, with the plan finalized, Dessa walked with the rescue team to Sheldon's truck. She scanned the packed snow around it but found no crampon tracks.

He didn't need them here—he probably put them on later to hike up the slope.

The team split into pairs and set off to search the slopes around the lake.

Two hours later, Dessa and Clifton found boot and crampon prints at the base of a cliff. Sheldon must have paused here to put on his crampons, walked around the cliff, and climbed north toward Merchant Peak—ascending the treacherous mountainside.

She called the rest of the crew on the radio, and once together, they followed Sheldon's tracks, climbing snow and ice, roped in pairs.

She and her fellow rescuers proceeded with caution. They were trained for that, trained to never rush. Rushing would mean acting on impulse and taking shortcuts from established safety procedures. That could trigger an accident and cause injury—or even death—to a rescue partner or the rescue subject. Rushing meant making otherwise avoidable mistakes.

They proceeded as fast as possible but not faster. They were volunteers, but they weren't amateurs.

In the late afternoon, they found the spot where Sheldon had slipped, fallen, and slid down a steep snow chute, unable to stop.

It took them an entire hour to locate him a hundred yards down the chute because he was, for some inexplicable reason, dressed in snow-white camouflage clothing. He had crashed full speed into the trunk of a century-old fir. He lay beside it, motionless, with blood on his face.

Dessa took off Sheldon's glove and pulled up his sleeve. A tiny tattoo of an owl in flight appeared above his pale wrist.

"Hm... a flying owl." Clifton studied the mark. "A symbol of freedom and independence."

Dessa held Sheldon's wrist and checked for a pulse, but there was none. The man was dead.

Only four months ago, she had given Sheldon a second life after his ill-fated parachute jump from Baring Mountain. She wished she could once again extract him alive from the mountain, just as she had before, but this time he was dead.

Four years ago, when she was still a rookie rescuer,

she cried after witnessing the death of a young man she was supposed to rescue on the Pacific Crest Trail. "You must learn to balance reasonable compassion with staying detached enough to rescue anyone," Jesse had told her back then. "You must learn it, just as surgeons do."

It hadn't been easy, but mission by mission, she grew used to death as a part of her SAR life. She felt for the victims—but stayed composed.

Now, the corpse in front of her posed logistical problems. It could only be taken out by helicopter, but the day was nearly over, and it was too late to fly in the mountains. Besides, the SAR bird was grounded for maintenance, so the sheriff's office had to secure a helicopter from the King County SAR, the Navy, or the Air Force. In the end, the sheriff's office postponed the evacuation until the next morning.

Clifton volunteered to stay around the corpse overnight and help evacuate it by air the next day, and Dessa decided to join him. She liked sleeping outside anyway. The rest of the team had nothing more to do on the mountain. They said goodbye and headed downhill.

She and Clifton placed the corpse in a body bag. The zipper caught on the fabric, so she used her Swiss Army knife's tweezers to tug it loose. Clifton gave her a nod of thanks, zipped the bag closed, and together they secured it to the fir tree.

They climbed back up the slope, found a somewhat level spot, stomped down the snow, spread their bivy bags, and stuffed their sleeping bags inside. They had a quick meal, put on balaclavas, and slipped into their bags.

Within a minute, Dessa caught Clifton's muffled snores. Tired from the day, she soon drifted into the oblivion of sleep.

CHAPTER THIRTEEN

"We've overslept!" Dessa blurted, pushing herself partway out of her sleeping bag. A glow of dawn crept over the snow-covered slope. She nudged Clifton's shoulder through the fabric of his bivy bag. "Let's go! The helicopter could beat us to it!"

They checked with the SAR base, and the update came right away: an Air Force helicopter was expected in less than an hour.

The two descended the slope at speed, secured with a rope. Sheldon's corpse was still there, intact in the body bag. They decided to remain roped and eat while waiting. She munched on nuts and chips while Clifton pulled out his bagel and lox sandwich and took a bite.

Moments later, an Air Force helicopter appeared over the ridge, interrupting their breakfast. She and Clifton unroped right away, ready to hoist the body up.

"No need to hoist anybody down," she radioed. "We can handle it ourselves."

The helicopter crew lowered a Medevac litter. She and Clifton stuffed the dead man into the litter and tied him in. The crew hoisted the litter up, pulled it into the cabin, and headed for the city.

She and Clifton stood on the slope, watching the helicopter fly away. The metal bird swallowed Sheldon's body and took it to heaven, and there was no trace left of him.

Dessa thought of Sheldon's mother, who might have believed Sheldon was the best son in the universe. She now had to live in grief for the rest of her life. But at least she could take solace in knowing what had happened to her son, thanks to the efforts of the SAR team. When rescuers failed to locate a body, the lack of resolution left families in even greater anguish.

"As Seneca said, death is the desire of some, the relief of many, and the end of all," Clifton said, staring at the azure sky.

"Let's go; I'm still hungry!" It was a prosaic thing to say, but Dessa couldn't resist it.

They roped up again and headed back to their night camp.

"I forgot my sandwich!" Clifton stopped on the slope and looked back toward the fir tree. "I'll go back and get it."

"Don't sweat it. Fred will make you another."

"Fred probably went home." Clifton shifted his weight, the frozen snow crunching under his boots. "Besides, leaving the sandwich in the woods would be a sin. It's a real bagel and lox meal, not just nuts and chips."

"Well... umm... let's go down together. We're roped up anyway."

"No need. I'll only be a minute."

Dessa hesitated.

"Don't worry!" Clifton's laugh carried across the slope. "I've got an ice ax!"

She helped him untie from the rope, and he headed back down the slope. She leaned against her ice ax. Once they got back to the camp, they would pack up in no time, zip back to the lake, and drive home.

A bird's shriek—like a hungry croak—pierced the air, followed by Clifton's yell. She looked downhill just in time to see Clifton waving his ice ax toward a raven flying away with his sandwich—and gasped as Clifton lost his footing, tumbled, and slid feet first on his stomach down the steep snow chute from which they had just extracted Sheldon's body.

"Self-arrest with your ice axe!" Dessa shouted.

Clifton did not seem to react; he only screamed a few times. Within seconds, he was rolling faster than a bowling ball hurtling down the lane—heading straight for the fir tree that had already killed Sheldon. He hit the tree with his feet, ricocheted, dropped his ice ax, lost all control, and continued to bounce off trees and rocks until Dessa lost sight of him.

Blood surged in her muscles and brain, and in one tiny instant, she was ready to rush down the chute after Clifton. She managed to restrain the urge. Alone on the hostile mountain, she couldn't do much for him.

She pulled out the radio and called the SAR base for help. They said they would ask the Air Force crew, still on its way to the city, to make an emergency U-turn and come to search for Clifton.

Thank God, the helicopter was back in minutes, circling over the slope. A moment later, it hovered, and she realized the crew had probably spotted Clifton's bright-orange jacket somewhere down on the snow.

She watched as two pararescuers and a litter, looking like tiny specks in the distance, were hoist-inserted into what had to be a clearing—invisible to her but undoubtedly visible to them—down the hill.

Before long, the helicopter itself descended until she couldn't see it anymore, but she could hear the engine running at full throttle—and she knew they were making a one-skid hot landing on the hill, with the other skid remaining above the ground. She bowed her head, closed her eyes, and pictured the pararescuers loading the litter-packaged Clifton into the helicopter and slipping inside themselves.

The helicopter soared into the sky, and she watched it fly toward the city for the second time this morning. This time, it carried not only the dead Sheldon but also her rescue partner Clifton. Whether Clifton was dead or alive, she did not know.

The helicopter was gone, and she hung her head and moaned.

She had become used to injury and death as a part of her life as a rescuer, but what had happened now was different. Clifton wasn't a stranger but a teammate she knew well.

And it was all her fault. She'd taken a shortcut from a

standard SAR procedure and let Clifton go alone and unroped. She'd acted impatiently... *Let's go; I'm still hungry!* What a shame.

Yes, shame... With this single mistake, she had screwed it all up—her success in previous missions, her Medal of Valor, her colleagues' respect, everything.

The best she could hope for was that Clifton was only injured and not dead.

Her chest was tight, and her insides were quivering. She raised her hands, staring at her fingers, swollen from the cold. She twisted her engagement ring, and it hurt.

Exhaling, she dropped her arms to her sides. She had a treacherous solo return trip ahead of her and had to prepare for it. She meditated, anchoring her attention on the whisper of the wind in the trees.

In a few minutes, she was ready to go—as ready as the circumstances allowed. She adjusted her pack and headed back to Barclay Lake.

Just as Dessa emerged from the woods, striding across the lakeside parking lot, Fred's food truck arrived and parked beside her vehicle. Jesse's Explorer was already there. Together, they surrounded her icy truck in a metal-and-rubber embrace.

The men stepped out and walked toward her.

But what could she say? How could she explain that she'd lost Clifton?

Jesse pulled her into a bear hug, long and tight, while Fred shook her hand. His lips parted as if to speak, but he only licked them and stared at her, and Jesse stared too.

Their eyes shone with joy, which struck her as odd. A moment later, it dawned on her that they had worried for hours about how she'd make it back alone—descend alone from where the team had climbed together, everyone roped in pairs. The two men were happy to see that she had made it, and that she was well.

Perhaps Clifton was well too?

"How is Clifton?" she asked.

"He's alive but in a coma," Jesse said.

Jesse glanced at Clifton's lone Jeep. "No one knows when he's going to wake up or if he's going to wake up at all."

She bit her lip, stared at her boots, and in her mind's eye, saw Clifton sliding down the snow chute, pinballing off trees and rocks, and disappearing from her sight.

"Do you want something to eat?" Fred nodded toward his food truck. "I can make you a bagel and lox sandwich. I can also put—"

"No!" Dessa cut in. "As long as I'm alive, I will eat neither bagel nor lox. Never!"

Fred looked at her, perplexed.

"I let Clifton go down a slope for that stupid sandwich. I let him descend unroped."

She struggled to find the words—but pushed herself to tell the men the whole story.

"It's all my fault." Her voice cracked. "I should've gone with him."

"If you went with him, you might end up in a coma, too," Jesse said, "and neither of you would have been able to radio for help."

"If I were with him, I could have prevented it," she said, watching her breath dissipate in the icy air.

She would have descended behind Clifton, keeping the rope taut—yet with enough slack to allow for movement and flexibility. When Clifton lost his footing, she would have used her ice ax as an anchor in the snow to arrest his fall down the gully with the rope. If she had been with him, she would have provided an extra layer of safety.

If she had been with him—but she wasn't.

The mountain had taken Clifton, and she had played a part in that. Her chest tightened, her belly knotted—but she didn't care about herself anymore.

CHAPTER FOURTEEN

Dessa's truck cast shifting shadows on the walls as she pulled into the garage. She killed the engine, and for a minute, the only sound was the ticking of the cooling metal. She just sat, staring blankly, before dragging herself out of the cabin and heading inside.

Penelope and Archie played a board game on the kitchen table, while Chewbacca lay by the fireplace, watching them.

She tossed her keys in the tray, the sound flat and hollow.

Penelope stood, her steps halting as she moved toward Dessa. "How was the mission?"

"Bad. It couldn't have been worse."

Penelope smoothed her shirt, as if unsure what to do with her hands, and hugged her. "You know..."

Dessa pushed her back. "Let's not talk about it right now."

"I have to tell you something."

"Please, not now!"

Chewbacca rose and approached Dessa, wagging his tail, but she ignored him and went to the living room. She lay down on the couch, took out her contact lenses, and put in her ear plugs. Her Swiss Army knife slipped out of her pocket and fell into the couch, but she couldn't have cared less right now. She could retrieve it later.

Right now, she did not want to do, see, hear, or feel anything.

Penelope brought her a milkshake.

"Give it to Archie." She waved her hand, then drifted off.

Dessa wasn't sure how much time had passed when someone touched her shoulder. She opened her eyes and found Archie standing by the couch, holding the empty milkshake. She pulled out an ear plug.

"Are you dying now?"

"No." She pushed herself to give him a semblance of a smile.

"Because Grandma and Grandpa have already died."

"I'm not in the mood for April Fool's jokes right now."

Archie turned around and left the glass on the bookshelf. He grabbed a pencil and a plastic spoon, and started circling the room, doing his thing, his expression innocent.

She closed her eyes again, but before long, she caught Penelope's steps creeping toward the couch. She half-opened one eye and found Penelope kneeling by her side, gazing at her.

"I called you many times. I hoped you'd pick up."

"I was in the wilderness. No cell reception."

Now she remembered—her phone was still locked in her truck's glove compartment. It had rung a couple of times as she was driving back home, but she hadn't bothered to stop and see who had called.

Penelope reached for Dessa's hand and held it. "You know... someone called my number from the sheriff's office an hour ago... He said your mom and dad died yesterday."

Dessa's heart fluttered. *What? What was Penelope saying?*

"They attempted to make an emergency landing in the ocean, but their Piper overturned in the waves and sank." Penelope lowered her voice. "A couple of hours later, rescue swimmers pulled them out. They bore no injuries, but they had drowned."

"Oh, my God. No, no, no..."

Penelope reached to hold Dessa's hand, but Dessa lifted herself and hugged her knees, resting her head on them.

Gray spots swam in front of her eyes, and a soft light engulfed her mind. A flock of crows flew away from an autumn tree. A cloud of golden leaves broke off the tree and descended to the ground. Bare black branches jutted into the gray sky. The crows cawed in the distance.

"The man asked if you could go to California, identify the deceased, and receive them."

Dessa held her breath, pressed her fingers against her eyelids—and exhaled. Her body softened; her bones mellowed. An invisible tide swayed her, and she was as helpless as a jellyfish. She kept her eyes shut.

"Stop running!"

Penelope's shout silenced Archie's steps. The boy was likely frozen in place, as he usually was when Penelope yelled, his bewildered eyes staring at his mother.

Penelope spoke to her again.

"I know it's hard for you—but I can help you."

Penelope's voice sounded deep. It always did when Penelope tried to be nice to her.

"Take a break if you want. You don't have to do anything."

Dessa was glad Penelope stayed quiet for a moment.

"Yes, take a break. Ditch the tutoring. Drop the missions..."

Dessa didn't want to listen to Penelope anymore. Now she was trying hard to remember how her parents looked. She'd seen them on Thanksgiving, only four months ago, right here, in this room. Yet, the harder she tried to remember them, the more their faces melted away.

They melted away like fog.

They were gone.

She was left alone in the universe, and all she could do was sob convulsively.

◆ ◆ ◆

An hour later, Dessa wasn't sobbing anymore. She gripped her thighs, as if holding herself together, her nails pressing into her skin through the fabric.

She knew that everyone would die someday and had long ago accepted her own death, learning to live without dwelling on it. Her parents' deaths, however, blindsided her.

If they had been ill, she might have anticipated it. She would have been warned. Warned and prepared.

She looked around the room, her eyes unseeing.

Yet their death in a plane crash had a good side, sort of... Their passing was quick, and they did not endure prolonged suffering. She was thankful for that.

She dropped her feet to the floor, rested her hands on her thighs, clenched them into fists, released them, and clenched them again.

Everyone would die someday, she thought, and the best they could hope for was that it wouldn't hurt too much.

Yes... That was the best everyone could hope for: a quick, painless death.

She rose and walked to the bedroom.

Penelope and Archie trailed after her in silence. Chewbacca peered from behind the door.

Dessa pulled out a duffel bag and threw some clothes into it.

"Are you heading to California right away?"

She nodded.

"You're tired from the mission," Penelope said.

Right, she was tired.

"Stay the night with us. The three of us will cuddle, and we'll all feel better."

"I'd rather leave right now." Dessa carried the duffel bag out of the bedroom, and Penelope followed her. "There's less traffic at night. I need quiet roads."

"Don't go now. I'll buy tickets, and tomorrow we'll fly to California together."

Archie hovered around them, twisting his plastic spoon.

The spoon cracked, and Archie dropped it on the floor.

Penelope stood in front of her. "We'll fly to California together, the three of us."

Dessa zipped the bag and lifted it, ready to go.

"You should have told me about my parents the moment I walked in. No matter what."

Penelope's face flushed red. She stomped back to the bedroom, and the door rattled closed behind her.

Dessa couldn't believe she had just denied Penelope her wish. Yet, she had—for the first time since they had been together.

She headed to the garage, but Archie took her hand and pulled, harder and harder, forcing her to stop.

She looked at Archie and frowned. Why was he doing this? He was okay. He still had his mother, healthy and alive. But she had lost her parents, and now she had to take care of their bodies.

She had to take care of herself too—because nobody else would, as Fred had told her a few weeks ago in his trailer.

"Leave me alone." She forced her hand out of Archie's.

Archie burst into tears and ran to his room. Chewbacca tucked his tail and followed the boy. Dessa shouldered her bag and stepped into the garage.

Her heart ached, but she knew if she didn't leave now, she never would.

Dessa turned on the garage light and slid the duffel bag under her truck topper. As she struggled with the rear window latch, her engagement ring glimmered on her finger. Giving up on the latch, she stared at the ring.

With a faint nod of resolve, she stepped onto the stool, reached up, and slid a shoebox out from beneath a stack of weathered photo albums. She brushed the dust off the lid, cut the tape, and rummaged through the box. Her frayed penguin doll, her high school diary, a "Dessa" wood cutout, a broken heart card inscribed with *Wherever you are, whenever you need me, I'll be there. Your Tucker.*

She returned the card to the box, set the engagement ring beside it, closed the lid, and placed the box back on the stack.

Dessa started the engine and drove off. A minute later, she stopped in front of the abandoned house and got out of her truck. The night was just as cloudy and cold as it had been four months ago when she'd walked here after Penelope's proposal.

Except the engagement ring wasn't there to burn her finger.

Just as she had back then, she stepped up to the house and stood at the door, staring into the darkness. "Hi, brother."

A minute passed without a response.

"Hi, brother. Mom and Dad passed away."

She waited another minute in silence.

"I suppose you already know. The three of you should already be together in heaven now."

Silence again.

"Well... that was the news."

She walked to her truck, opened the door, but faltered and turned back toward the house.

"Oh, and I think I'm leaving Penelope," she whispered. "I hope you don't mind."

A gust of wind slammed the truck door shut.

She stared at the slammed door for a few seconds. It seemed her brother did mind.

Yet, she had to go to California, no matter what. Her parents' bodies waited for her there.

She jumped into her truck and drove off.

CHAPTER FIFTEEN

Dessa had never dealt with a coroner before. Today, though, she had to meet one—and identify the bodies of her mom and dad.

Her legs a bit stiff, she walked into the coroner's office.

"My name is Dale Brown." The silver-haired coroner's tone carried the practiced weight of sorrow. "I'm sorry we are meeting on such a sad occasion."

He pointed to a chair. She sat down, raised her eyes, and saw a giant poster on the opposite wall. The poster was full of hot air balloons floating in emerald skies.

She turned her gaze back to the coroner.

"Let me start by saying there's nothing to worry about regarding today's identification."

The man accentuated his words as if each one had an importance of its own.

"We are not going to the morgue, as they show it in the movies."

"Good to hear." Dessa feigned seriousness. "I had imagined that an unshaven orderly would take me to a gloomy basement and lift the top of the sheet while blowing bubblegum. I was concerned I'd scream 'Yes, that's them' before fainting and falling to the wet concrete."

The coroner raised his spectacles to his crown, glanced at her, and slid them back onto his nose.

She stared at her feet. Why had she said that? Was she just too nervous? Was she trying to control her mood with tasteless, dark humor? This elderly man seemed near retirement, and she had no reason to make his job harder. She had no reason to insult him.

"No, no wet concrete." The coroner sounded firm yet solemn. "We'll identify the bodies here, in this room, just the two of us—using photos."

The coroner reached into a drawer and pulled out a clipboard.

"Two photos are attached here, face down. One shows the face of a man, presumably your father, and the other shows your mother's face. We've already made a preliminary identification using their driver's licenses.

"Now, let me warn you so that you're prepared: your father's right eyebrow is bruised, as is your mother's lower lip. Both are small wounds. Otherwise, they both look good... good for people who spent time on the ocean floor."

She glanced at the coroner. No wonder her parents didn't look too bad—they had been underwater for only two hours.

As a search-and-rescue volunteer, she was no stranger to pulling bodies from the waters of the Pacific Northwest.

Every year, with the onset of summer heat, young and old rushed to the coolness of mountain lakes and rivers, still flooded by snowmelt. People enjoyed sailing in kayaks, small and large fishing boats, tubes, inflatable mattresses, or simply wading and swimming—and some died in the cold waters from rollovers or accidental slips.

Rivers often trapped victims underwater in the branches of fallen trees, held them in whirlpools, or pinned them to rocks. Finding the bodies was difficult, and recovering them was even harder. An unfortunate corpse could spend days or weeks underwater before being pulled to dry land.

Last spring, a skier slid into a hole in the snow above a hundred-foot-tall waterfall high in the mountains. At that time, a thick mantle of snow still covered the waterfall and everything around it. Rescuers knew where the body was, but they had to wait for the snow to melt.

It was fall by the time Dessa and her teammates recovered the body. The skier's face was unrecognizable, but the epidermal ridges on his fingers were well preserved, even though the epidermis had begun to slip away like a glove. At the morgue, the medical examiner cut the epidermis off, put her own hand inside that glove, and took the dead man's fingerprints. The prints turned out well, and she formally identified the deceased.

"You don't have to look at the pictures right away," the coroner continued. "No one expects you to see them immediately. Give yourself time; prepare mentally... I'll wait for you as long as needed."

"No worries. I've seen dead bodies. Plenty of them."

The man pushed his spectacles up on his nose and studied her.

"You have?"

"Yes. I do search and rescue up north."

"I understand... You've seen dead bodies plenty of times. But you won't be looking at strangers' dead bodies here. You'll be looking at your parents' bodies. I've seen quite a few tough souls collapse when they have to identify mom or dad."

The coroner placed the clipboard in front of Dessa and lowered his head.

Without giving herself time to think about it, she pulled out the photos and examined them.

Here were her parents, right in her hands.

Her mom—in her left hand. Her dad—in the right.

They always smiled in the pictures she took of them, so it seemed wrong that they weren't smiling in the photos she held now. Their eyes were closed, and their mouths were set in fine lines, giving them an oddly serious look.

She couldn't take her eyes off their faces. Did they think of death when they crashed? Did they think of Philip? Did they think of her?

There was no way to know.

But did it really matter? What mattered was that they had given her life, but they were gone, and now her own being was all that remained of them. She wasn't just herself anymore. She was also her mom and her dad, all in one, and because of that, she had to stop her false bravado. False bravado was not something her parents would have ever displayed.

She clipped the photos back and nudged the clipboard toward the coroner.

"Yes, it's them, my parents." Her voice shook.

"Thank you. We're done with the toughest part."

The coroner fell silent for a few seconds, pulled out a colored leaflet from the drawer, and opened it in front of her.

"Let's discuss the next step, choosing a funeral home..."

Ah... choosing a funeral home... Tears welled up in her eyes.

"...choosing a funeral home to arrange for the release of the bodies and assist you in..."

She brushed her eyes.

The coroner glanced at her, set the leaflet on the desk, and handed her a tissue.

"Listen, I know it's hard for you... but let me give you some personal advice. Personal advice that I'm not supposed to give."

She gave the man a slight nod.

"I think your parents wouldn't want you to be overcome with sorrow. If they see from heaven that you grieve too much, they will be truly sad—they will feel guilty because you suffer for them while they're powerless to help."

The man bowed his head.

"When my dad fell terminally ill, he asked my mom not to tell me. I was in college, and he didn't want me to stress over something that I could do nothing about."

He cleared his throat.

"I'm a father of three, and let me tell you, I wouldn't want them to mourn too much after my death. I'd like them to remember me and love me, yet I'd want them to carry on with their lives."

His gaze rested on her. "Believe me, no parent wants

their child to be devastated by grief."

She glanced at him. Perhaps he was right, this old coroner. Dale Brown was his name, wasn't it... Perhaps Dale was right. She knew her mom and dad loved her, albeit in their own ways. They loved her—and this was precisely why they wouldn't want her to be torn apart by grief.

A woman with a sad face and dark clothes appeared at the door. "I have an appointment." Dessa and Dale finished the formalities and said goodbye.

Outside, Dessa paused on the sidewalk and stared up at the blue sky.

"Mom, Dad," she whispered, "I'll never forget you."

She bowed her head.

"You'll always live in my heart, day and night, forever."

Dessa slid into her truck, the words she'd whispered still reverberating in her mind. Her parents were gone, yet somehow, they felt closer now, their presence woven into her very being. She tightened her grip on the steering wheel, ready to head home—to her mom and dad's house, to be precise—when her phone rang. Penelope's name flashed on the screen. For a moment, Dessa considered letting it ring—but answered, knowing the guilt of ignoring it would linger.

"How are you?" Penelope asked.

"Fine."

"Did you make it to California?"

"Yes, I did."

"Archie is missing you already. He's been browsing through your pictures for hours. He even wanted to see your old Bulgarian photos."

Archie didn't miss only her, Dessa was sure. He missed his dad and his grandparents too.

"You left your engagement ring. I found it when I was getting your old stuff for Archie."

Oh… Penelope had rummaged through her old shoebox!

"I'm going to mail you the ring right away."

Dessa took a moment before speaking. "I don't need it."

"You don't need your engagement ring?"

"Not right now. Right now, I'm dealing with my parents' passing."

"I called you three times." Penelope's voice rose. "You didn't pick up!"

"I silenced my phone because I was with—"

"Yes, I know you were with Tucker! Tucker, the '*Wherever you are, whenever you need me, I'll be there*' guy."

Here was Penelope, growing jealous again for no reason. Dessa had kept Tucker's 'broken heart' card in that old shoebox over the years, but she had no idea where Tucker lived now. All she knew was that he'd gone to college in Europe, landed a job there after graduation, and never returned to California.

"I know very well why a woman would silence her phone!"

Dessa heard a bang—as if Penelope had pounded against the garage door.

"It's pretty obvious what's going on when a woman doesn't wear her ring and doesn't answer her phone!"

"I silenced my phone because I was with—"

"You were with Tucker, of course! You prefer him to me." Penelope's shouts broke into sobs. "You prefer him to console you. That's why you didn't want us to fly together to California. That's why you went alone."

Oh, how Dessa wished Penelope was right! How she wished she was with Tucker… Tucker or anyone else—just someone who respected and loved her as an equal.

But Penelope was wrong, so terribly wrong. Dessa spent the morning with an old coroner, identifying her mom's and dad's bodies.

She shouldn't waste another moment indulging Penelope. She should just cut her off immediately.

She could do it! Yes… she could… Yet what would

Penelope do, deranged as she was?

Penelope would unload her anger on Archie, one way or another.

In the best case, she could shatter the boy by telling him —point blank—that Dessa had left them for another person. In the worst case, Penelope could harm him and herself. Like the man who drove into a river with his son strapped in the back of the car, after his wife said she was going to spend Christmas with her lover and wanted a divorce. The man murdered his child and himself to punish her.

Philip had once told her that Penelope had a dark side— she could be toxic.

Dessa closed her eyes. What had Philip done when Penelope was being toxic?

Philip just stopped talking to her. He ignored Penelope no matter what she said. He kept silent until Penelope cooled down.

This was exactly what Dessa was going to do now. She'd disconnect from Penelope for a while. She'd give Penelope all the time she needed to cool down—and realize she was wrong.

Dessa opened her eyes and hung up without a word. She leaned back, still for a moment, fired the engine and started the drive home.

CHAPTER SIXTEEN

April—May

Dessa didn't know what to do about her dead parents.

Was she supposed to bury them here in California, where they had no relatives? But who would visit their graves here? Maybe just a couple of colleagues and a few casual acquaintances who would soon forget them.

What about Washington?

Not only had her parents never lived there, but she was unsure how long she herself would stay in the state.

Not to mention, she couldn't cover the costs of a decent funeral out of her own pocket—she didn't have the money—nor could she wait until her father's life insurance paid out.

Eventually, she called the funeral home and asked them to cremate her parents and place their ashes in a family urn. She would decide later what to do with them.

She went on Facebook, posted a death announcement on her wall, and tagged her mother and father so their friends could see it.

Exhausted, she retreated to her old room. It was preserved just as it was when she'd left four years ago. The picture of the old village house in the Balkan Mountains was still pinned to the wall, and next to it still hung her favorite poster of a shrew-like animal crawling along a fern.

She turned off her phone, pulled a blanket over her head, and slept for two days. She got up only a couple of times, nibbled on pizza she found in the fridge, and drank milk straight from the bottle.

On the third day, she woke up rested. She spent an hour in the backyard pool before heading to the funeral home to pick up the urn. Back home, she set it on the living room table, sank down on the couch, and stared at the dark TV screen for a minute.

She turned her phone on and was flooded with notifications. There were sympathy messages from the SAR pilots, Jesse, a host of close friends, and acquaintances. The crew chief, Big Joe, told her that Clifton had come out of the coma and could soon message her himself. She closed her eyes for a moment. It seemed Clifton didn't hold her mistake against her.

Everyone was being nice, trying to comfort and encourage her.

Penelope's parents had written to her too, but there were no messages from Penelope.

She opened Penelope's contact card and stared at her picture.

Three days ago, Penelope had found Dessa's engagement ring hidden in a shoebox and accused her—so absurdly—of being involved once again with her high school sweetheart. Now feeling heartbroken but too proud to call, Penelope probably expected Dessa to call her. Call her, apologize as usual, and even beg for forgiveness. The idea that Penelope might have been wrong could not have found its way into Penelope's mind in just three days.

But Dessa wasn't going to call and apologize. Not this time.

A week later, Dessa received a call from Fred. He said he was planning to spend the summer in Paris and offered to show her around if she decided to clear her head and visit.

But she couldn't go to Paris now.

"My parents left no will. I'm trying to claim the inheritance, but it's an uphill battle." She hesitated. "I'm lost."

"Hire an attorney."

"An attorney?" She laughed. "I can't afford that."

"Well... you could try the library. They have manuals for everything."

She went to the city library, asked for help—and the librarian handed her a thick book on estate settlement. It was a do-it-yourself guide that she followed day after day, resisting the urge to rush or become frustrated. She filled out, signed, and filed all sorts of forms in public and private offices. Each completed form, however, seemed to take revenge on her, bringing forth two or three more that she also had to fill out, sign, and file.

There seemed to be no end to her ordeal until one evening in May when she found three letters in the mailbox that instantly changed her life. The insurance company was issuing her a check for her father's life insurance in the amount of two annual salaries; the bank was releasing her parents' deposits to her, and the pension company was doing the same with their retirement funds. With all that money, she could, if she wanted, live in ease for years without working at all.

The next day, she hired an attorney to handle the probate sale of the house. However, she still had to go to Bulgaria and deal with her parents' real estate there. She could only hope that her Bulgarian, which she hadn't used in a long time, was still good enough and not too rusty.

She bought a ticket for a Lufthansa flight to Sofia and secured a permit to carry the urn. It was in her parents' native land that she would decide what to do with their ashes.

As she waited to board her plane, Dessa called Penelope.

"Hi... I'm at the airport, about to fly to Sofia."

For a few moments, Dessa listened to Penelope's throaty breathing. "I thought it was fair to let you know."

"But when are you coming back home?"

Six weeks ago, Dessa thought, she had been with the coroner, identifying her parents' bodies, yet Penelope had yelled at her. Penelope had yelled at her—but now wanted her back.

"Why do you want me home?"

"I can't sleep. I can't eat or drink."

Penelope paused.

"Yesterday, I had a fever, and right now, I have heart palpitations."

Dessa had nothing to say. A few seconds passed in silence.

"I just need a little peace," Penelope uttered. "Only you can give it to me."

Six weeks ago, Penelope had sounded tough; now, she sounded heartbroken.

"Penelope, I don't know when I'm coming back."

"I love you..." Penelope whispered. "I need you."

Dessa pursed her lips. She should tell Penelope point-blank she didn't want to be with her anymore.

But she was away from Penelope anyway, wasn't she... and now she was going to Bulgaria for God knew how long.

Time healed all wounds, her grandma liked to say.

Yes, time could fix everything.

With time, Penelope would get used to the idea that they weren't together anymore. She would get used to it as days, weeks, and months passed. Archie would gradually get used to it too.

Time would resolve everything by itself, without Dessa hurting anyone. All she needed to do now was give Penelope more time.

"Listen, I've got to go; my flight is boarding. I'll call you later."

But she knew she wouldn't.

CHAPTER SEVENTEEN

Late May, Sofia, Bulgaria

Sunlight flooded through the window, blinding Dessa as she woke. Her body told her it was morning, yet to her confusion, the sun was setting—over a mountain that looked like Mount Si. Had she somehow found herself back in Washington, with Penelope? No, this couldn't be Penelope's house—her own father's guitar was hanging on the wall. That meant she was still in her parents' home in California, and the transatlantic flight had only been a dream. But why did the air here smell different from California's?

She rubbed her eyes and sat upright, assessing her body. No visible injuries, just stiffness from sleeping in her clothes. A sunbeam hit something reflective, sending a flash into her eyes. She turned and saw her family photo at former Lenin Boulevard, framed under glass on the wall.

Now, everything fell into place—her flight and late arrival, the taxi ride, and her trek up the dark stairs. She was back in her childhood home in Sofia—just as she had intended.

The events of the previous night unfolded in her mind.

Lufthansa crews had gone on a six-hour strike in Frankfurt, and Dessa landed in Sofia in the wee hours of the morning. The border officer asked for her Bulgarian ID, and she had to explain at length why she had only a U.S. passport, promising to acquire a Bulgarian one as soon as possible. He knew English but insisted she converse only in Bulgarian, and she managed pretty well, even giving him a smile in the end.

Walking out of the terminal, she took the first taxi from the long, sleepy queue. The young cabbie sped down the deserted night boulevards and dropped her in front of her family condo's low-rise on Yuri Gagarin Street in just ten minutes. She tipped the man, turned on her headlamp, and climbed the dark stairs to the top floor. Moments later, she was already dozing off, still in her clothes, on the living room sofa.

That had been last night, and now the day stretched before her. She rose, shook off the stiffness from her limbs, and stepped onto the balcony. Below, a young mother pushed a stroller along the silver-fir-lined alley between the buildings. A man with a dachshund approached her. They stopped to talk, and the dachshund played on the grass.

Dessa looked up above the trees to the green-gray silhouette of Vitosha Mountain, still dotted with snow beneath the ridge. She took a picture and shared it on Facebook. *Guess where I am,* she posted with a grin.

She returned to the living room and gazed at the family photo: herself, finishing her second ice cream on a sidewalk of Lenin Boulevard; her parents beaming beside her; and Philip lowering one eyelid while keeping the other open, practicing how to wink. They all looked young, innocent, and happy.

Her parents were gone now, and so was her brother. A lump grew in her throat, and she tried to swallow it, to no avail. Forlorn chimes rang in her ears. In a few seconds, the ringing began to fade, and she heard the old deputy coroner's voice murmur instead.

Believe me, no parent wants their child to be devastated by grief, he had said. *The child must carry on with their life.*

Dessa loosened her shoulders.

She unzipped her bag, pulled out the urn with her parents' ashes, and placed it on the shelf above the TV. She carried the rest of her belongings to the bedroom, piled them in the wardrobe, and slid the bag under the bed.

Her stomach grumbled. It was evening here in Sofia—but morning in California. She needed breakfast, a big one.

She went out, looked around the street, and spotted shoppers going in and out of an Aldi supermarket housed in a communist-era building that was once a cinema. Next to it, a few early-bird patrons were drinking, smoking, and chatting in the old neighborhood pub. Across the street, families with children and quiet young couples ate hamburgers and fries on the patio of a brand-new McDonald's.

She headed to the supermarket, humming a childhood song. A BMW, decked out with balloons, popped out of the intersection and honked festively. A curly-haired prom girl poked out of the window, her shoulders bare, and waved. Dessa waved back. The evening was setting in, violet-blue and full of promises.

Dessa brought home two bags packed with groceries and ate. She took off her bra, changed into sweatpants, sat on the couch, and got on her phone, making occasional runs to the fridge for yet another ice cream bonbon. All she wanted to do tonight was chat with friends and eat desserts.

Around midnight, Fred called her for a video chat, but she didn't answer, as she was busy texting with Clifton, asking him to repeat this and that. His replies trickled in, but they came—and that alone eased her.

Twenty minutes later, Fred rang again, and this time, she accepted the call.

"How was your trip?"

"It was okay. Everything went fine, except that..."

A soul-piercing scream came from the stairwell, echoing in the hallway outside the condo. A woman's voice yelled for help, fell silent for a moment, and screamed again. Dessa tossed her phone on the coffee table, ran out the front door, and dashed down the dark staircase.

"Freeze!" Dessa leaped down the steps, sliding her palm along the railing. "Stop! Stop, I'm talking to you!"

Heavy footsteps rattled in the darkness. Someone barged through the building's entry door, and the steps faded away along the concrete alley to the street.

A woman's whimpering drifted from the landing. In the glow filtering through the stairwell window, Dessa recognized Alma, her downstairs neighbor. A curly-haired brunette in her early forties, Alma was smearing her makeup with her fists, her elbows pressed firm against her purse.

The door to Alma's condo opened, spilling a patch of light onto the floor. Alma rushed inside, and the landing was dark again.

Dessa took a few steps upstairs but turned back; she needed to check if Alma was all right. In the old days, their families had spent time together, so Alma was a bit more than just a neighbor to her.

She walked to the door and pressed the doorbell. When she didn't hear it ring, she knocked. No one came to the door, but she caught some muffled chatter. It sounded like Alma was telling her husband and parents about her ordeal. Dessa knocked again, waited for a few more moments, and headed home, alone in the darkness of the stairwell.

Back in the living room, she heard Fred's voice from the phone.

"Dessa! What's wrong? Are you okay?"

"I'm fine... Just a second, okay?"

Dessa ran to the kitchen, grabbed an ice cream bonbon, and sank onto the couch, reaching for her phone.

"What are you doing?" Fred asked.

"I'm eating ice cream bonbons... Mm, delicious."

"But I heard shouts... You dropped your phone... What's going on?"

"Everything is fine. Except that..."

Her doorbell rang, fell silent for a second, and rang again. She went to the door and found Emilia and Simeon, Alma's parents, standing on the landing. Their flashlights cast shadows across their faces, making them look like aged vampires.

But Dessa knew they were harmless. Simeon, a tall doctor with a humpbacked nose, bowed to her, while Emilia stared at her with perplexed eyes and lips that couldn't decide whether to smile or droop. She had acquired this unsettled expression from teaching math in high school for decades.

"Welcome," Simeon said. "Welcome home after so many years."

The man spoke softly yet with aplomb, his voice carrying a sense of solemnity.

"We heard your parents passed away." Simeon took a moment to sigh before saying, "Please, accept our condolences."

Dessa didn't want to talk about her parents' deaths. She just nodded.

Simeon looked at her, frowning.

"We understand that Alma was attacked by a *tziganin* on the stairs and that you rescued her."

In Dessa's native Bulgaria, Romani people were called *tzigani*. In English, she'd refer to them as *Gypsies*, but it was not exactly the same, as the Bulgarian *tzigani* were not vagrants. They lived in their own homes, mostly segregated in unofficial ghettos. Many of them had useful professions. In fact, the best heart surgeon in the country was a *tziganin*. Yet, many Bulgarians treated the *tzigani* people with prejudice, subjected them to derogatory comments, and openly discriminated against them.

"I don't know if he was a *tziganin*," Dessa said. "He ran away before I could see him."

"Ah... a *tziganin*, of course, who else!" Simeon scoffed.

Emilia pointed her flashlight into Dessa's eyes. "The circuit-breaker box broke a month ago, so the stairs are dark. Or maybe that *tziganin* broke it on purpose, who knows?"

Dessa lowered her head, saying nothing, and Emilia fell silent.

"You know, tomorrow is Cyrillic Alphabet Day," Simeon

said. "We want to have you over for dinner and celebrate together. It's our Bulgarian alphabet after all!"

Dessa accepted the invitation with thanks, and the couple walked away, their slippers slapping on the steps.

She smiled to herself, thinking of Simeon's pride in the alphabet.

In fact, every Bulgarian she knew seized any opportunity to lecture a foreigner that the Cyrillic alphabet had originated eleven centuries ago in the First Bulgarian Kingdom. The Bulgarian would inevitably be offended, even angry, whenever the uninformed foreigner would call it the *Russian* alphabet.

"It's not a Russian alphabet," the Bulgarian would state. "The Russians took the alphabet from us."

They would go on to explain that Bulgarians used the alphabet to translate religious books from Greek to Old Slavic after Bulgaria adopted Christianity from Byzantium in the ninth century. When the Russians accepted Christianity a century later, they took the already translated holy books and the Cyrillic alphabet from Bulgaria. Thus, as Christianity spread north to Russia, the Cyrillic alphabet journeyed with it.

Yawning, Dessa returned to the living room and resumed the video chat with Fred. He wanted to know everything, but she decided she'd chatted enough for the night. She told him it was time for bed and disconnected.

CHAPTER EIGHTEEN

Dessa wished her parents could see her now—walking downstairs to her neighbors with a bouquet of white roses and a bottle of Pinot Grigio. Flowers for the hostess, wine for the host. It was what her parents had always done when visiting others. "That's the European way," they'd advise her time and again. She'd never listened—until now, after they were gone.

At the door, she paused for a moment, balancing the wine bottle against her arm to free a hand, and knocked.

"You shouldn't have brought anything." Emilia accepted the roses with a warm smile.

"It wasn't necessary." Simeon took the wine from her hands.

Her parents would have said the same. In Bulgaria, insisting *it wasn't necessary* was the Bulgarian way of saying *thank you.*

"We have plenty of food and drinks." Emilia led Dessa to the eat-in kitchen.

Dessa stared at the table, speechless. Around a golden-brown duck, still in the roasting pan, sat two bowls of salad and plates with pickles, grilled *kyufteta*—the Bulgarian version of meatballs—sheep and goat cheeses, zucchini baked with mozzarella, and a kind of blood sausage... what was it called? Ah, *bahur*! A basket of white bread was flanked by crystal cups filled with peanuts and almonds. There was also wine, beer, the local favorite fruit brandy called *rakia*, sparkling water, Schweppes, and Coca-Cola. A giant bottle of her once-favorite malt drink, *boza*, rested on the floor by the table's leg.

Alma and her husband, Danny, stood by the table,

waiting for her. She shook hands with them.

"Thank you for chasing away that damned *tziganin* last night," Danny said.

"Don't mention it." Dessa turned to Alma. "Are you okay?"

Alma shook her head.

Dessa remembered that in her native land, shaking one's head meant *yes* and nodding meant *no*.

"I'm glad," Dessa said with a smile. Her Bulgarian, though still rusty, was coming back faster than she had expected.

Emilia piled food on plates, Simeon poured drinks, and everyone sat down at the table.

Danny raised a glass of *rakia*. "Cheers to Cyrillic Alphabet Day!" He downed the liquor, chased it with a bite of cheese, and filled his glass again.

Dessa was a fast eater, just like her father, and she was hungry, so she finished her food in a few minutes and pushed the empty plate away. Emilia grabbed it and piled it high once more.

Dessa stared at the new portion, then resumed chewing. In her homeland, hospitality knew no bounds. Clearing her plate meant she wanted more. Her problem was that not eating everything would imply she didn't like the food, which would offend her hosts. Her only option now was to eat as slowly as possible until dinner was over.

So she chewed, taking breaks between bites, and clinked glasses, her glass filled with water.

"In June, we'll go on a weekend trip to Greece and stay in Thessaloniki's Astoria hotel," Danny said, turning to Dessa. "We took advantage of Astoria's Pentecost sale... Here's a video."

Danny held up his phone to show her a clip of the place.

"It's a four-star resort," he added as she watched.

"I'd never go to a three-star hotel," Alma muttered.

"It's just a few minutes' walk from the seafront

promenade," Danny continued, as if oblivious to his wife's interjection. "And the entertainment district is also close by."

Dessa googled *Pentecost* and found out it was a Christian festival celebrating the descent of the Holy Spirit on the disciples of Jesus, fifty days after Easter.

She gave Danny a wry smile. Going around to pubs in Thessaloniki would surely make for a joyful Pentecost.

Her countrymen, many of them pseudo-religious, loved to celebrate Christian holidays by traveling and partying rather than reading the Bible and praying.

After two hours of eating, drinking, and chatting, Dessa's stomach strained against her waistband. She hardly noticed Alma and Danny's son returning home, grabbing a plate, and retreating to his room without a word, a headset clamped over his ears.

Simeon sighed with satisfaction. "The time has come for dessert."

Oh God, no! No more food! Dessa wished she could unbutton her pants, but she didn't dare. She leaned back in her chair, trying to make herself look at ease.

Emilia hurried to the fridge. "The dessert is very special." She served Dessa a piece that could feed a small rescue team. "Orange with strawberries! You can make it yourself in America! I'll tell you how! First, cut off the top of the orange in a zigzag—"

"It is a very special dessert indeed," Alma interrupted her mother. "I'll put it on Facebook."

Alma snapped a picture and turned to Dessa. "Should I tag you?"

Dessa thought about it for a moment and agreed. Since it was needed for the tagging, the two connected on Facebook.

"Do you mind if I connect with some of your friends?" Alma asked.

"Sure... but that's not up to me... It's a matter between you and them."

Dessa wondered what kind of Facebook friend Alma would turn out to be. A harmless selfie narcissist? An oversharer? A spammer? A man-huntress?

Hopefully, she was just a harmless foodie.

Emilia pushed back her chair, the sudden scrape against tile announcing the dinner's end. As she began filling a giant plastic box with leftovers, her voice rose above the clatter of dishes.

"Did you all hear the news?" Emilia turned to Dessa. "We've been ranked as the poorest country in the European Union again... yes, the poorest! Once again!"

"We're the most corrupt country too," Simeon added. "In terms of corruption, we hold first place."

All Dessa could do was sit and nod politely, her stomach heavy, as the conversation whirled around her.

Emilia grabbed a duck's leg and waved it at Simeon. "But what can you expect when our prime minister is a former communist policeman turned shady bodyguard in the first years of democracy?" She dropped the duck's leg in the box. "Our president is a former communist too!"

"Both are generals, though," Alma chimed in. "We've become a NATO country, so the former commies are now NATO generals."

"Yes, we're ruled by former communists and their proxies," Simeon said. "They're everywhere. They own the political parties, both the left and the right ones, all of them. They own the media. They own the economy. They own law enforcement. They own the whole damn country. They are a mafia."

"Every normal country has a mafia," Alma said. "Here, the mafia has a country."

Dessa made an effort to give Alma a polite laugh.

Emilia glanced at Dessa, as if reminding her it wasn't a laughing matter. "Yes, it's all bandits, and that's why our country is shrinking faster than a deflating balloon. Two million people have already packed up and left, and plenty of the remaining six million want to do the same."

"Picture this," Emilia continued, now waving the duck tail, "you stroll into some fancy store, lurk in a corner, and before you know it, you'll spot a woman pretending to shop but actually on the prowl for foreign-looking dudes, classy gentlemen, you know? Once she spots one, she'll drop something on the floor, and of course, Mr. Foreign Gentleman will be chivalrous and pick it up for her. That's her opportunity to start chatting, score a date, tie the knot, and immigrate... and why the heck not? Why should she waste her life in a country infested with leeches and crooks?"

Emilia stared at the duck tail in surprise, as if only now realizing it was in her hand, and looked around. "Danny, do you want it?" Without waiting for an answer, she dropped the fat piece of meat onto Danny's plate, and—poor Danny!—he bit on it dejectedly.

"The European Union is giving us lots of money, but the mafiosi pocket most of it," Alma said. "They use it to build themselves mansions and buy expensive cars."

"And the West doesn't mind all that," Emilia added. "All that matters is that the West wants our country to stay away from Russia, and that's why it pours its money here."

"Emilia gave the plastic box a shake, causing the food to settle. Suddenly calm, she turned to Dessa. "I'll also give you zucchini, *kyufteta*, and sausages, so you will have food for a few days."

With the boxed leftovers in her hands, Dessa was eager to go. She said good night and walked to the foyer.

"Your parents did the right thing leaving the country," Simeon said, holding the door for Dessa.

Her face tightened, lips pulling downward. If her parents hadn't immigrated, they wouldn't have bought a plane —and crashed. They would still be alive.

The old man stared at her and leaned forward. "Why don't you come with us to Greece for Pentecost? We'll squeeze ourselves into the car somehow."

"I'll be in the Balkan Mountains at that time."

All she needed now was to leave this city's noisy consumerism and heal herself in the purity of the mountains.

"My parents' old house in Zarena awaits me."

Simeon gazed at her for a few moments.

"You know what, let me give you one special present before you leave."

Simeon went to the living room, came back a minute later, and handed her a black-and-white photo. "Here's all of us, almost thirty years ago."

Dessa held the photo with both hands. She, only a preschooler at the time, stood on a crowded street, gripping the hand of her brother, Philip, in front of their mom and dad. Simeon and Emilia were next to them, with Alma, a grinning big girl, holding a cardboard sign that read, "We Want Democracy!"

"We were together at the Million-Man March of Hope, remember? It was just a couple of days before the first free elections, and we were so convinced we would win that we celebrated victory before the elections themselves."

Of course, she remembered. How could she forget the sea of people raising banners and blue flags and chanting? There were singers and bands, and Art Garfunkel was there too, having arrived for the march all the way from America.

As Garfunkel sang, Dessa's mother, looking upset, spoke to her father nonstop: "Where is Simon? Why is Garfunkel singing alone? Why didn't Simon show up to sing too? They only gave us half of the duo... It's a bad omen."

Having spent their lives behind the Iron Curtain, none of them knew the duo had split up a long time ago.

Her mother cried a few days later when the communists claimed victory and the democratic forces conceded.

"All we wanted was to go from being trapped and unhappy to being free and happier," Simeon continued. "We dreamed of true democracy. But we missed our chance. We let the Reds use their bureaucratic machine to steal the elections and stay in power."

Dessa watched Simeon swallow, his Adam's apple rolling.

"Our flaw was that we wanted to be tolerant. The commies changed their name to *socialists* and said they'd change more. And we fell for it."

His eyes dropped to the floor.

"The truth is, we were scared to fight. Didn't want to shed blood. Shed their blood, and have our blood shed too. We were weak."

He raised his eyes, glanced at her, and lowered them again as if he were ashamed of what he'd said.

"So, we didn't fight, and naturally, we lost. The commies never left; they stayed entrenched, and we ended up with a phony democracy. Sure, we eat well, travel, and vote. But we're in a mess with a mafia, and we're still unhappy."

Dessa shook her head in understanding. Her countrymen had craved freedom and joy but couldn't leave their communist past behind. They didn't properly break with it. They didn't have the guts to boot out the Reds from public life.

She, too, wanted freedom and happiness. To get it, she had to purge Penelope from her private life, barring her completely and forever. She had to mute every thought of her past with Penelope and go after whatever her new days brought.

Unlike Simeon and the rest, she could see the light at the end of the tunnel.

She'd already left her engagement ring at Penelope's house, and Penelope had found it, so, in a way, she'd returned it.

Hence, even though she'd never spelled it out, with the ring already returned, the engagement was, in effect, broken. De facto broken—that's how she saw it. Sooner or later, Penelope—and Archie too—would see it that way as well. It was just a matter of time.

She was now an ocean away from Penelope, with no plans of turning back, engagement shattered... free to wander the globe.

She thanked Simeon for the picture and bid him good night.

CHAPTER NINETEEN

The Same Day, Paris, France

The scent of lemon polish lingered, mixed with the faint aroma of croissants. Fred sat in the lobby, his glass of grapefruit juice untouched on the table before him. The stillness of the late hour made the occasional creak of footsteps upstairs sound louder.

He hadn't set foot in Paris since his parents' deaths more than two decades ago. Now, he stayed in what used to be their home. The bistro where his mother had served *soupe à l'oignon* to the lunchtime crowd was gone, replaced by this sterile lobby with its reception desk and worn furniture. Upstairs, his childhood bedroom had been split in two. He slept in one half; the other half was storage.

His neighborhood, like the house, had changed. His old school, where he'd once played soccer with friends, was now a retirement home. The people he'd known had scattered, just as he had—and they'd slipped from his memory as he had from theirs.

He spent his days wandering around town, sipping wine and watching passers-by, and retreated to the hotel for the night. Before bedtime, he read the news, peeked at his social networks, and wrote emails. His room was small and uncomfortable, so he preferred sitting in the coffee lounge with his phone.

That night, leaning back in his chair, he opened Facebook, following the same routine.

Fred hesitated when a friend request appeared on Facebook—Alma from Sofia. A stranger. But not entirely. She was friends with Dessa.

Curious, he clicked her profile picture—a casual selfie, ordinary enough. Why would someone connected to Dessa want to add him?

He scrolled down her timeline. Photos of books, family gatherings, and Sofia landmarks filled the page. Nothing seemed alarming.

Fred shrugged. It seemed harmless enough. He clicked *Accept.*

Thanks for your friendship, Alma messaged him right away, in English.

He decided to chat in Bulgarian. Having finished his class at U-Dub, he knew just enough of the language to make using Google Translate fun.

Why do you need my friendship? he wrote back.

Ah, but you know Bulgarian! Alma replied and fell silent.

Are we going to chat anyway? he sent with a wink emoji.

Okay, Alma replied. *Do you like books?*

Fred typed back: *Are you asking if I like books?*

Decades ago, when he still worked at his family's Paris bistro, his parents had taught him to parrot back to customers whatever they said.

"When a customer starts chatting with you," his dad would tell him, "just repeat their words, as if you're reflecting on them. This will keep the conversation going while you still do the cooking."

"Don't talk much to people," his mom would add. "They don't really want to listen; they just want to talk and be listened to."

Parroting back was a mechanical process that he'd readily adopted, making people believe he cared about what they had to say. This worked miracles for business back then, but it also did him good later in life. His parroted responses made people—men, but especially women—feel they were talking to someone who understood them, encouraging them to talk more about themselves and—when he desired it—open up. His parroting back helped his love life, sometimes landing women in his bed without much effort on his part.

Are you asking if I like books? Fred repeated, switching to English.

Yes... that's what I'm asking... Because I love to read.

Alma's English seemed good enough for a chat.

What are you reading these days? Fred asked.

I'm reading Anna Karenina.

Oh, yeah? Interesting... I'm reading Anna Karenina *right now, just like you,* he lied.

He'd read it a decade ago but wanted to sound positive and help the conversation flow.

Ah! This is an interesting coincidence! Alma wrote.

Yes... I love Anna Karenina. *I've read it more than once or twice.*

I've read it many times too. Now I'm just rereading it. Actually, I know it almost by heart.

Fred sipped his grapefruit juice. *Tell me the first thing that comes to your mind from the novel.*

Well, "All happy families are alike, and every unhappy family is miserable in its own way."

I see, Fred said.

He and Alma continued to chat some more about *Anna Karenina* and then about *Madame Bovary.* Eventually, they switched to his favorite, *The Red and the Black.* All this took them an hour. They spent the next hour discussing *Lady Chatterley's Lover.*

Alma messaged she wanted to take a shower. That was fine with him. He replenished his grapefruit juice and sank into the chair, sipping and thinking about Alma. Alma, who was now in the shower.

Uh, actually, are you married? Alma's message popped up on the screen, the jingle breaking the silence.

Would you prefer it if I were single? He smiled to himself.

I don't know. I'm married.

I see. Do you enjoy being married?

I don't know.

Tell me about it.

Well, I'm not exactly married. My husband stopped being interested in sex right after his grandmother died.

After his grandmother died? I don't quite understand.

My husband lost his libido after his grandmother died. He started saying that sex was just a marital obligation. He promised he would do it for me as long as he could. However, he doesn't do it at all.

Fred chuckled to himself. Alma's husband might be the first man on earth to use his grandma's death as a coverup for his lack of interest in his wife.

I see... your husband says sex is just a marital obligation, he repeated. *How do you feel about it?*

For him, sex may be an obligation, but for me, it's a pleasure.

Aha, he typed, but Alma didn't react.

Come on, he thought. *Explain yourself.*

You see... I'm healthy, and I like it, Alma typed. *I feel like I could do it four or five times a day, maybe even more.*

Fred stirred in his chair.

Since when have you felt like you could do it four or five times a day?

Don't mock me.

I'm not mocking you. I'm just curious... Since when?

Since Danny's grandmother—my husband's—since she died.

Do you mean her death boosted your libido?

No... That's when my husband stopped making love to me. That's what boosted it.

Got it. But how do you manage if your husband doesn't do it?

I satisfy myself.

Ha! Tell me more about it.

Well...I take a hot shower, just enough to warm myself up and relieve the stress...and then I direct the jet...there.

Isn't that dangerous?

Dangerous? What's dangerous about a shower? Nothing, of course. It's very pleasant. You can see for yourself...

Oh! See for myself?

Yeah—to see for yourself on the web. I found some hands-on videos, and that's how I learned. I showed them to my girlfriends once, but they just laughed at me. I'm not like them. I'm open to everything.

Do you like not being like them?

Yeah, I like it.

I understand.

I'm glad you understand. That's nice... Because I'm like Anna Karenina. I can be anything to a man who understands me. I'm ready to give myself with all my heart.

What does that mean?

Well, everything—romantic love, physical love, and anything... Anything! My girlfriends, however—mention anything *to them, and they would scream. They're very old-fashioned. They won't even talk, let alone try. Yes, I am different.*

Like Anna Karenina?

Yeah, just like her. Like Anna, I'm not happy with my husband, and my name sounds like hers—she is Anna and I am Alma, and physically we look alike—hair, lips, and even breasts. Mine are just like hers.

What do you mean?

Wait, Alma wrote. *Let me run to the bathroom.*

A minute later, he received a selfie from her. The light in the photo was dim, but he could tell her blouse was pulled up against a foggy mirror. Her breasts were visible, and he examined them for a while.

They're nice. He sipped his grapefruit juice. *They remind me of grapefruits.*

Exactly! They're like grapefruits. Large, juicy grapefruits. Juicy but firm. A teenage bride's breasts wouldn't be any better."

That's beautiful.

Alma responded with a red heart emoji.

I'm back in the kitchen, she chatted on, *and I'm going to send you a picture of my son.*

Oh, a picture of your son?

A boy with a well-groomed haircut and already growing facial hair grinned at him from the photo, a tennis racket in hand.

Your son's very handsome, Fred wrote.

He's handsome, Alma agreed. *He's actually great. I love him very much, but I'm worried about him. I don't know if I can secure him a decent future. Hardly at all here in Bulgaria, that's for sure.*

Alma seemed to be fishing for an invitation to leave Bulgaria for the sake of her boy. Fred stared out the window at the dawn sky.

Isn't it time to go to bed?

Time to go to bed? Ah, you don't know me. I can spend all night here. And in the morning, I'll just jog around the park, shower, and be ready for work.

He sent her a red rose emoji.

Where are you now? Alma wrote. *Halfway around the world?*

Ah, no. I'm not halfway around the world. I'm in France. In Paris, to be precise.

Paris! I love Paris. If I could, I'd fly there right now.

You'd fly here right now?

Yeah, if I could. But I can't. I have to write a business report, and after that, we're going to Greece.

Greece?

Yes, to Thessaloniki. The whole family. Old and young.

Everyone. But I don't want to go. I wish I could skip this trip. Maybe I can tell them I can't go because of the report.

Reports are the worst.

Reports aren't so bad. I prefer doing them over going to Greece.

Why? Is Greece that bad?

Haven't you been there?

No, I haven't.

How about Bulgaria?

Never been to Bulgaria either.

If you fly, Sofia is a couple of hours from Paris. Just think about it.

Oh...fly to Sofia?

Yes...come visit for a few days, Alma wrote. *You'll love it.*

Interesting idea, he typed back, mulling it over.

Being a Frenchman, he wasn't bothered by Alma's marital status as much as his SAR colleagues in the States would have been. It didn't seem to bother Alma either. She was a mother, ready to love for her son's future. Not unheard of in Eastern Europe.

He didn't see marriage in his future, though. All he needed was a woman to hold him tight and make old age go away for a night or two. Alma appeared willing to do it, and that was the only thing that mattered.

It was time to say good night, but not before they agreed to meet again on Messenger. Tomorrow night, same time.

CHAPTER TWENTY

Early June, Balkan Mountains, Bulgaria

A drop of rainwater fell onto Dessa's cheek and rolled to her lips. She licked the water and pulled her sleeping bag hood over her head.

But the hood was soaked!

She shot up to a sitting position, striking the tent's sagging ceiling. The rainwater pooled above burst, drenching her in a cold deluge.

She awoke, blinking into the darkness. She wasn't in a tent at all but lying in her parents' bed in their old house in Zarena, deep in the Balkan Mountains.

Another drop struck her nose, and she rubbed it away. The next one brought her fully awake, washing the dream away.

Now she heard the rain drumming on the tin roof.

She groped under the pillow for her headlamp and switched it on, illuminating the whitewashed ceiling. A water droplet shimmered above her, in the middle of a wet spot. The droplet broke off and fell, and she caught it in her palm. She jumped out of bed, grabbed a rain jacket from the hook, and spread it on the bed under the dripping spot. She dashed into the hallway and illuminated the attic hatch.

The two-centuries-old hatch boards were the color of honey.

One distant summer day, her brother, Philip, still

healthy then, had climbed into the attic and pulled the ladder from under Dessa's nose. Dessa raised her face to Philip and begged to join him, but Philip only collected dusty chaff between the beams and threw it down on Dessa's head, laughing. Dessa sneezed, begged again, and everything repeated.

They enjoyed themselves until they heard a car humming up the steep hill and realized their parents were returning from the village market. Philip closed the hatch and hushed in the dark attic, waiting for the right moment to slip away unnoticed. Dessa sneaked into her bed and fell asleep, innocent as an angel.

Dessa's pillow was gray with dust and sprinkled with straw when her mom woke her and led her out. Her father had lit a fire in the backyard, as he did during power outages, and Philip was helping him. Water steamed in the old copper cauldron above the fire.

Their mom bathed her and Philip in a zinc tub and helped them into clean clothes. Their dad stowed the cauldron and tub in the basement, and the four of them sat around the fire. Their dad played his guitar while their mom sang. When Philip and she knew the lyrics, they sang along; otherwise, they just hummed.

An hour later, the outage ended, and their parents went inside. She and Philip stayed outside, playing with the dying fire, while the sounds of their dad clacking away on his typewriter upstairs and their mom clanging pots and pans downstairs drifted out to them.

Smiling at the memory, she tightened her headlamp strap. She had felt loved and cared for in this house. It was still her home, and she was going to tend to it. Tend to it for her parents' and her brother's memories, and for the sake of her soul.

She hurried downstairs and opened the front door. A lightning bolt cut through the darkness, illuminating the sprawling water splashes battering the old house. The whitewashed walls beneath the eaves flashed wet.

Barefoot, she ran around the corner and unlocked the basement door padlock. She grabbed the same ladder she and Philip had once played with, carried it to the second floor, climbed up, and inspected the roof decking. She found damp boards here and there, but water dripped only from one spot above the bedroom.

She returned to the basement and fetched the old copper cauldron, still tinned and shiny inside, blackened by countless fires outside. She took it to the attic and placed it under the drip. Still, she listened to the storm. It was subsiding, and she climbed down, humming.

She changed, went to bed, and dozed off under the fading chant of the rain.

The next morning Dessa walked onto the veranda with a mug of mountain tea, stood behind the railing, and looked into the distance. Ragged clouds drifted over the ridges in the cool, breezy morning. Sipping tea, she scanned the village houses, weathered with age, and newer summer cottages squatting along the ridge. She studied the bell tower of the two-hundred-year-old church in the village center, shifting her gaze east toward the red fortress walls built when the Bulgarian state had been founded thirteen centuries ago. She knew that south of the fortress ruins, somewhere in the forests beneath Mount Sinich, lay Devil's Cave, undisturbed by human footsteps.

She had spent her first week in the village sleeping, eating, and chatting with neighbors, so it was time for her to climb the mountain and find the cave.

Just as Dessa finished her tea, the gate of her widowed neighbor Lenka swung open with a creak. Bruno, the bloodhound, dashed outside, his nose to the ground as he circled a few times before licking the dripping street faucet. Lenka emerged after him, calling out, and Bruno trotted obediently back. Lenka glanced up the street and waved. Dessa flashed a grin, waving back, and walked down to Lenka's gate with her mug still in hand.

The two went into Lenka's house, sat down at the kitchen table, and talked, as they often had in the last few days.

"Eat some more baklava; I've made it with walnuts," Lenka said, pushing the tray toward Dessa. "Shall I refill your mug?"

Without waiting for an answer, Lenka picked up the milk jug and refilled Dessa's mug. "Here we go... Drink, eat... It's all homemade. It's good."

Dessa wasn't hungry but helped herself to another piece.

"Boris is coming home this Saturday," Lenka said. "He wants to take Bruno out and track foxes in the forest... You'll be here too, so you'll see each other."

Boris, a peer from Dessa's childhood, had once vowed to marry her at the end of their last summer together in Zarena. She hadn't seen him since.

Dessa drank her milk and stood up.

"Are you leaving already? You're not in a hurry, are you?"

"Well, I want to go to Devil's Cave."

"All alone?"

"If you give me Bruno for company," Dessa said, "I won't be alone."

Dessa clipped her satellite beacon to her day pack and headed up the forest road, with Bruno prancing alongside her.

In a few minutes, she walked past a dilapidated barn and into the open. Rolling green pastures were fenced by a dusky pine forest to the left, and the whitewashed Holy Trinity Chapel stood out against the dark backdrop of remote mountain ranges to the right. The chapel's rooftop cross was projected against the blue sky.

A slender man, his back to the road, stood with a brush in hand in front of an easel near the chapel. The man made a few quick, short brushstrokes, stared at the chapel and the mountain behind it, and continued to paint.

She paused and eyed the man, tilting her head. She had never seen an artist in Zarena before.

A honey buzzard with a larva in its beak appeared from a nearby growth of flowering oregano, eyed Bruno, and flew away with its loot. Bruno barked. The artist turned around, stood still with the brush in hand, relaxed his arm down, and gazed at her.

She gazed back.

Wavy coffee-colored hair framed his pale face, highlighting a straight nose. A trimmed mustache and delicate chin framed his slightly parted, inviting lips. Crisscrossing, multicolored splatters made his gray shirt look surprisingly elegant.

Bruno barked again, and she knew he was getting impatient. The man glanced at the dog, turned back to the canvas, and raised his brush. She pulled out her phone, checked the map, veered left off the road, and continued up through the meadows.

The trail to the cave was swallowed by the pine forest. She and Bruno bushwhacked through the undergrowth, still wet from last night's rain. Panting, they traversed a steep, slippery rock and reached the cave mouth.

Dessa stood on the edge and looked down into the shaft. The bottom was not visible, hidden far below in the darkness.

She was keen to go down but not before buying some climbing ropes.

Stepping away from the shaft, she took in the scenery, humming. It seemed no humans had visited here for quite a while. This was true wilderness, with nobody around.

Dessa loved to discover—all alone—solitary places like this.

She took off her backpack, pulled out a water bottle, sipped from it, and poured water for Bruno into a deep pothole by the shaft's edge. The dog lapped up the water quickly. She unwrapped a sandwich, took a bite, then tore off half and tossed it to Bruno.

Going back was easier because they already knew the way, and it was all downhill, so it took them only an hour to cross the forest and meadows and reach Holy Trinity.

The man was still there, still painting.

She passed him, slowing but not stopping. Bruno stopped briefly, casting a glance back at the artist before bounding after her. Five minutes later, they reached the old house.

"We'll go to the cave again, Bruno." She patted the bloodhound's side. "Sooner rather than later, we'll figure it out."

The mountains loomed in the distance, quiet and steadfast, as the evening light softened. Inside, the house greeted her with its familiar stillness and the lingering aroma of her family's memories. Dessa closed the door behind her, her thoughts still fixed on the cave and the adventures it promised.

CHAPTER TWENTY-ONE

The next day dawned crisp and clear, sparrows darting through the air as Dessa waited for the handyman she'd found in her dad's old address book. From the gate, she saw him park his hatchback in front of the gate, wedge stones behind the rear wheels, and approach with a tool bag slung over his shoulder.

They greeted each other and shook hands. The handyman circled the house, peeked into the basement, retrieved the extension ladder she had used to climb to the attic, leaned it against the gutter, and climbed onto the roof, lugging his tool bag.

Dessa watched from the yard as he walked around the roof, stomping on the tin sheets and examining the joints.

The man had thick, glossy hair, like an actor's, and piercing gray eyes.

"The roof is old, and the sheets have moved over the years," he said from above. "The storm last night blew rain into the gaps."

He pulled a pack of cigarettes from his pocket.

"I think I'll fix it by noon."

That was good news. If he finished by noon, she could use the afternoon for another hike to Devil's Cave.

Horse hooves pounded up the street. A moment later, a colt showed its head at the gate, neighed, and entered the yard. Its skin was golden like a deer, white on its forehead and above its hooves. A gray-eyed child, about ten years old, rode it. The child had a blond braid falling past the saddle, reaching the stirrups.

"Hi, I'm Jesus," the child said to Dessa. "My dad drove here to work on your roof, so I decided to take my horse out for a ride, but Dad beat us with the car."

"Hello and welcome, Jesus."

Jesus rubbed the back of his neck.

"You come from America, don't you?"

She shook her head—yes, she was from America.

"I like American movies."

He stared at her, as if unsure whether to continue, and she gave him an encouraging look.

"Last week, I watched *The Force Awakens,*" he said. "Too bad Harrison Ford died."

"I believe he's still very much alive."

"I know! He died only in the movie. But it's still sad."

He was silent for a few seconds before changing the subject.

"Yesterday, you hiked to Devil's Cave, didn't you?"

News traveled fast in the village.

"Yes, I did."

"Would you like to go to the cave together?"

She said nothing. Jesus seemed sympathetic, but she preferred to go to the cave alone—with only Bruno by her side.

"I can show you a shortcut from the village center," Jesus added.

A shortcut sounded intriguing, yet she preferred the route she'd found herself. The one via Holy Trinity Chapel... where that artist painted.

"If we go together," Jesus said, making a last-ditch effort, "I'll let you ride my horse."

"Oh, yeah, sure you will." She gave him a wink. "Your father won't let you."

"The horse is mine." The boy stood his ground. "My dad has nothing to do with it."

"It's his, indeed," his father called from the roof, crouched above the gutter with a cigarette.

The three of them talked a little longer. Then Jesus left with his colt, and the handyman finally started work.

Dessa stayed in the yard, staring at the roof. She could not see the handyman but could hear his steps and his tools' clatter. A minute later, she decided to move onto the veranda. All she could do now was wait for him to finish his job. Finish it by noon, as he had promised.

She lay in a hammock and wrapped herself in a blanket.

A breeze caressed the hammock and brought the scent of lilac. A dog barked far down in the village. Two butterflies played under the veranda roof near the eaves. The sky was cloudless and blue.

She closed her eyes and drifted off, the muffled noise from the roof reaching her as if in a dream.

In her dream, Dessa walked out to a seashore bluff and stopped by a cranberry bush. Ragged clouds raced over the churning sea, the waves rising and falling. The bay below formed a crescent moon, and the beach was deserted; only an abandoned fire fumed at the end of the sand, with a reindeer costume thrown beside it.

She stared at the bay—a tween boy struggled in the waves, trying to get to the beach and the smoking fire. He swam as hard as he could, legs kicking and arms flailing like windmills in the choppy waters, but the closer he got to shore, the feebler his movements became. Ten yards from the surf, the boy stopped swimming, lifted his head above the water, took a sorrowful look at her, and mellowed, motionless. His body tilted toward the bottom, and his head submerged, but he stayed afloat. His hair spread around the crown of his head like the veil of a jellyfish. Waves rolled around his head, lifting it up and down.

Dessa had to get to him, now!

The path to the beach blurred beneath her feet. She reached the smoking fire, but a branch snagged her steps. She fell forward, the cool sand rushing up to meet her palms.

She stood up and pulled the branch out of the fire, dashed to the surf and dipped the flaming end in the water. The hiss of the hot charcoal blended into the noise of crashing waves.

She waded out into the sea. The water lifted the branch to her chest, and she lay on it and embraced it, kicking as hard as she could to get into the deep before the next wave hit her.

When she reached the boy, he showed no signs of life. She moved behind him, grabbed him under the armpits, placed his head on the branch, and began swimming backward to shore.

Once on shore, she pulled the boy onto the wet sand. He was no longer breathing, and she had to revive him. She slowly knelt beside him, gazed at his pale face, and kissed his forehead.

"I miss you."

"I miss you too," he said, "but we have a problem."

Dessa stirred in the hammock, the boy's words still echoing in her mind: *We have a problem.*

She blinked up at the handyman, his silhouette framed against the veranda's eaves. He was lighting another cigarette.

"Sorry to wake you." He took a drag. "But we have a problem.

She rose from the hammock, staggered, and stood beside him.

"The gaps turned out to be rather large, and my silicone won't be enough. You need to buy more… before they close the store for lunch."

"Okay, I'll go right away."

"And the work is more than I thought." He shook the ashes off his cigarette. "It will cost more."

Dessa frowned and hurried to the village store for silicone.

Back from the store, she handed the handyman the silicone and lay in the hammock again.

She closed her eyes and saw the abandoned fire from her dream, smoldering on the beach, and the reindeer costume thrown beside it.

Archie had wanted to go to school dressed in that same costume last Halloween.

So, it was Archie struggling in the choppy waters of her dream. It was Archie taking a sad look at her before mellowing motionless in the waves.

Her heart sank. Did her dream mean that Archie was in trouble?

But if Archie had been in trouble, Penelope would've called her. Penelope would've nudged her to return, confident that she missed Archie. Penelope wouldn't have let slip such a chance to bring her back.

Yes, Dessa missed Archie—but she didn't miss Penelope.

Enough worrying—it was never worthwhile. Archie was likely okay, and she still loved him even though they were far apart.

Shadows stretched long across the yard as the handyman, done at last, descended from the roof. Dessa paid him, they exchanged goodbyes, and he walked toward his car, the tool bag swaying against his hip.

She eyed the sun and decided she could still reach Devil's Cave in daylight. If needed, she could use her headlamp on the way back.

CHAPTER TWENTY-TWO

For as long as Dessa could remember, there had been a bulletin board with obituaries on the streetside wall of Lenka's house. Elderly women liked to congregate there in the afternoon, sit on the bench beneath the board, and chat until evening.

Whenever one of them died, the others pinned her photo obituary on the board, and the deceased seemed to ascend, meekly and quietly, from the bench to the board above. Another woman, now old enough, would take the free place among the living on the bench.

This afternoon, three neighborhood women were already sitting on the bench. Dessa went down the street, still smelling the fumes of the handyman's car, and stood in front of them.

Lenka, Maria, Petya.

"Hi there," Dessa said. "How are you?"

Their faces lit up.

"We are fine," Lenka answered for all. "We're chatting about this and that."

"We're talking about an eighty-year-old granny who played piano in downtown Australia," Maria explained.

"Downtown Melbourne," Lenka corrected her.

Lenka was the youngest.

"Yeah, downtown Melbourne, still in Australia," Maria insisted.

"They showed her last night on TV," Petya chimed in.

Nobody said anything for a few seconds.

"We could play too," Maria said, "but we don't have money for a piano."

"If you had money, the three of you would play better than she does for sure," Dessa said.

"It's not just about money," Petya said. "That Mel... Melbur... that Melburnian woman never picked potatoes with her bare hands, and that's why she can play."

Petya raised gnarled hands, cackling. "I can't even turn on the TV, let alone play the piano."

The three elderly women laughed, and the afternoon sun flickered in their eyes.

Maria stood up, pulled a plastic bag full of beans from her apron pocket, and handed it to Dessa. "I've brought you pinto beans."

Another elderly woman, Mitra, approached the bench. She held a bouquet of peonies, their stems wrapped in old newspaper.

"Your mother loved peonies." Mitra's hands trembled as she handed Dessa the flowers. "I picked these especially for her and for your father. They're from my garden."

Dessa took the peonies, sniffed them, and they smelled sweet and rosy.

She gazed at the village women. They seemed happy with the little they had, free of empty wants, and eager to share whatever they had with her. They led a simple life, a life she wished for, too, a featherlight life, just like in childhood.

She was inching closer to this level of lightness she so admired. She had already decided to remove Penelope from her life. Besides, by leaving Penelope, she in effect had let go of her guilty promise to her brother. She had left SAR, too, a place she loved—but she knew she would return there one day.

"Is it true," she heard Maria ask, "that you brought your mother and father from America?"

"It's true." Dessa opened her eyes. "But not them... their ashes, actually."

"Yes, their ashes," Maria said. "But is it true that they're in a vase?"

"They're not in a vase; they're in an urn," Lenka said.

"Now, what are you going to do with them?" Maria asked. "Are you going to bury them or something?"

"I haven't decided yet," Dessa said. "I'm not in a hurry. I've got time. Besides, they're both just fine in their urn."

A few village cows appeared from the ridge on the forest road, with a man walking beside them.

Even from afar, Dessa could see the village herder was grumpy.

"Drunkard Pasko had been herding the herd the whole day long—and now he's thirsty." Petya winked.

"Be careful with Pasko," Lenka whispered. "A man disappeared a couple of months ago... People say that Pasko killed him and fed him to his cows."

The women fell silent, lowering their heads as Pasko and the herd came close.

The cows had huge udders so full of milk that they wobbled as they trudged downhill.

Petya got up, crossed the street, and opened her gate. A red cow mooed, separated from the herd, and plodded into Petya's yard. Pasko and the rest of the cows passed the women and continued down to the village center.

"Dess, tomorrow morning, I'll bring you fresh milk." Petya closed her gate, and followed her cow to the barn.

"Everyone gave you something, but I—nothing," Lenka said, looking around as if hoping to spot anything of value on the road.

"Give me Bruno. I'll take him out for a walk."

"Ah!... Going to the cave again?"

"Why not?" Dessa smiled. "I like it there."

Dessa and Bruno made it to the Holy Trinity Chapel in

five minutes. The man was there again, just like yesterday, standing in front of his canvas and painting.

She stepped closer, looked at the canvas, and found a dilapidated chapel with a tilted cross in the middle of a meadow strewn with plastic rubbish, a dark mountain looming in the background.

Bruno approached the easel and sniffed it. The man turned to her, his brush held midair.

"Do you like my painting?"

Dessa folded her arms. "No."

He turned the brush in his hand, studying it for a moment.

"Why? You don't like nature?"

"I love nature, but not painted... and preferably with no rubbish."

The man dropped his hand, looking down at the brush for a few seconds before raising his eyes to her and stepping closer.

"What's your name?"

He had a chant-like voice that bordered on singing. It could match her guitar tunes quite well.

"My name is Dessa Sinich, but I'm used to being called just Dessa. And you?"

"My name is Christo Millerov, but people call me Father Christo."

She looked at him in surprise.

"They also know me as the new priestling." Christo furrowed a brow. "I've only worked in Zarena for three years. You haven't visited in a decade, so you haven't seen me. Now you've come to sell your father's house."

"I can't sell it," Dessa said. "My lawyer said it had to go through court probate. It could take years... if I ever started it. But how do you know?"

"I'm a priest, and people tell me everything."

Christo must've asked around about her, but she didn't mind.

He pulled out a pack of cigarettes and lit up. His movements were soft and graceful.

"You're surprised I'm an artist, aren't you? You're probably wondering, how could a priest paint?"

He looked at her and continued in his measured, priestly tones.

"Here, too, everyone wondered, but they're getting used to it. Every time the villagers ask me, I tell them it's a special gift from God."

"And do they believe it?"

"Why wouldn't they?... They believe it, just like anything else I preach."

She shifted from foot to foot and glanced at him from under her eyelashes.

"And why shouldn't I paint?" Christo perked up. "So, what if I'm a priest? There's a Catholic priest in Chicago who's a jazz vocalist. His friends from the orchestra attend his church, play during the service, and he preaches and sings with them."

Christo took a drag and exhaled a cloud of smoke. "The arts make people better."

Bruno lay down next to Dessa, pointed his eyes at her, at Christo, back at her, and relaxed his head on his paws.

"My mother once bought a reproduction of a Matisse... an abstract paper collage of a boat," Dessa said. "Actually, it was just the sail and its reflection—without the boat. The water and the sky looked the same in the painting.

"Mom hung it in the living room, and it dangled there for two years until a colleague of hers visited and noticed that the painting was upside down—the sail underneath and the reflection on top. My father and I laughed so much..."

Her face tightened. Her parents now lay in an urn. They'd never laugh again.

Her eyes dampened.

In a moment, she shook her head and glanced at Christo. "What style do you paint in?"

"What style... what style do I paint in?" Christo drew

from the cigarette. "I believe... I'm an expressionist."

She had no idea what expressionists did.

"See, realists are like photo cameras," Christo said. "They paint what everybody sees."

Christo looked at her, and she wondered if he was checking whether she cared. She met his gaze with a light smile.

"We expressionists don't exactly paint reality. We express what we feel about it instead."

"That's interesting."

She was intrigued by whatever he had to say.

Christo fidgeted with his hair.

"For example, if I see two happy lovers on a boat, I'll paint two drowned bodies instead."

"So, you don't believe in love?"

"Why should I?" He looked her in the eye. "Romantic relationships are hugs and kisses for social networks—but broken hearts and disappointments are kept behind the scenes, aren't they?"

What could she say? She shook her head in agreement.

Christo finished his cigarette, dropped the butt into a small jar by the easel, and stared at the canvas.

"I don't like my painting either." Christo took the canvas off the easel and threw it on the grass.

He seemed so vulnerable... so vulnerable.

She watched him set a clean canvas. When he stepped close to her, warmth flooded her chest. She almost raised her hand to take his.

"I prefer to focus on people rather than landscapes." Christo's voice dropped to a whisper. "Would you pose for me?"

"Yes, I would."

She paused. "I can do it right now."

Bruno rose, barked, looked at her, and dashed around the meadow. He stopped for a moment, sniffed a flower, shook his head, ran in a zigzag, went back to the flower, sniffed it again, and wagged his tail.

◆ ◆ ◆

"I don't do preliminary sketches," Christo said, running a streak of paint across his thumb as if testing its depth. "I prefer to jump straight into the unknown."

Straight into the unknown? Dessa tipped her head. *That's brave.*

"Some make sketches, but not me. We're all different."

Christo began painting. Her eyes wandered to the woods behind his shoulder. Bruno lay down next to her again, and time passed in silence.

She flexed her fingers in and out and cleared her throat. She couldn't stay still for long, and when she had to, she'd soon grow restless.

She looked at Christo as if she wanted to say something, and he glanced at her, his gaze gentle, as if inviting her to speak.

"Your last name is unusual... Millerov. I like it."

"My grandfather was an Englishman, Christopher Miller. He was a painter who came to the Balkans to look for exotic subject matter. He met my grandmother in Sofia, got married, and even produced a baby boy. But he couldn't take the climate, fell ill, and when he ran out of money, he went back to London. My grandmother and the child remained in Sofia along with his name, which she refashioned in Cyrillic, and that's how we carry on to this day."

"So, your dad is Christopher Miller's son?"

"Yes."

"Is your father an artist too?"

"Yes... He was an art teacher in Sofia."

"You could've become an art teacher too."

"Well... I didn't. My father-in-law is a big shot at the Patriarchate. He nudged me to study theology... and it wasn't a bad idea because I was a strong graduate and landed a full-time ministry at a decent Sofia church."

"But you ended up moving from Sofia to this village."

"Yes, I ended up here because..."

"Because?"

Christo put the brush aside, wrapped his arms around his shoulders as if embracing himself, and looked away, his gaze lingering on the ridges.

"I fell in love with another man's wife."

If her parents could hear this, they would be shocked—a priest falling for another man's wife. She, however, imagined Christo's struggles with his feelings for a married woman—and wanted to hear more of his story.

He lowered his eyes. "It all happened after my father passed away four years ago... A bee stung him on a Sunday morning, he went into allergic shock, the ambulance was an hour late, and he died en route to the hospital while I was preaching at the church."

Christo had lost his father unexpectedly. Just like her.

"His death ruined me. I couldn't bear it. I lost my desire for life, stopped painting, and barely dragged my feet around."

He picked the brush back up and resumed his brushwork.

"My duties at church weren't a big deal, so I managed somehow, but at home... at home I wasn't good for anything. I started spending my days in a local coffee shop. It was where I'd worked when I was younger... and had pleasant memories."

She watched Christo paint, pause to utter a few sentences while gazing at the painting—but not her—and continue making brushstrokes in silence.

"One day, the coffee shop was packed, and she sat at my table. She looked at me, smiled, and said, 'You're as sad as someone who knows precisely when he's going to die.'

"She was nice, and she was interested in me.

"Then I said, 'Yes, I know exactly when I'm going to die, but I'm not going to tell you.'"

Christo lit another cigarette.

"Much later, she told me it was those words of mine that

made her fall in love with me. I personally think she felt sorry for me and decided she had to help me. Or maybe hers was pure curiosity, I don't know."

Dessa couldn't stop herself from cutting in. "Um... Do you really know exactly when you're going to die?"

"This winter, when I turn thirty-seven." His face remained emotionless. "Van Gogh died at thirty-seven... He was a priest, and I'm a priest. He was an artist, and I'm an artist. So, I shall die like him, at thirty-seven."

She chuckled at the joke, and Christo responded with a faint smile.

"Either way, had I kept quiet back then, things would've turned out differently. We wouldn't have started an affair, then been exposed—and they wouldn't have banished me from Sofia."

He'd been dishonored, she thought, because he'd been lonely—and fallen in love. But if he'd been lonely in Sofia, he'd be much lonelier in Zarena now.

She watched him work with the brush for a while before he spoke again, looking down at his palette.

"After the scandal, they sent me to Zarena, but my wife stayed in Sofia. That's where she takes care of our son. In fact, she and I are informally divorced, but I visit there for a few days each month to see my boy. I love him, and I can't abandon him."

Dessa went silent. Yes, she understood... Orthodox priests must be married. If Christo were to divorce, he'd lose his priesthood.

"I'm worried because she and her big-shot father don't know how to raise a child. They bought him a Nintendo, and he sits on the couch and plays Super Mario for hours, and when he gets bored, he turns on the TV and watches Cartoon Network till bedtime."

Christo gazed at the canvas, silent for a while.

"Enough talking about me. Tell me about yourself."

She told him about Penelope and Archie.

"Send me pictures of Archie and his mother. I may use them in the painting."

They swapped phone numbers.

Dessa barely noticed that two hours had flown by. The sun grew heavy and rolled down the mountain. Bruno trudged down the road, going home alone.

Christo began cleaning his brushes.

She wanted to see the painting and stepped toward the easel.

"Please, not today," Christo stepped between her and the easel. "I don't want you to see it before it's ready." He stored the canvas in the box. "I'll show it to you when I'm done."

The two walked down the forest road toward the village. Christo headed on to the village center, and she went home.

The sun hid behind the mountains, and the night set in. Dinner could wait, Dessa decided—it wasn't what she needed tonight. She wouldn't go to bed either—not this early. She hugged her father's guitar and sat outside, striking tunes in the darkness as the eternal stars shone in the sky and countless June fireflies danced around the yard.

CHAPTER TWENTY-THREE

Mid-June, Washington

Penelope drew a Swiss Army knife from her pocket, flicked it open one-handed, and held the blade still for a moment as it caught the sunlight. She snapped it shut, pocketed it, and pulled it out again. Open, close, pocket. Faster and faster, she repeated the motion, her movements sharp and practiced.

Her parents and Archie sat in silence on the garden chairs, their gazes steady, unreadable. Not that she cared.

Archie had found Dessa's Swiss Army knife stuck down the back of the couch a couple of days after her departure to California. Penelope let him play with it for a few minutes before taking it away from him. She had not parted with the knife since then.

"How do you manage to open it with just one hand?" her dad asked.

The other day, her dad, Tim, and her mom, Betty, flew in from Honolulu for a short visit with the apparent aim of cheering her up.

Penelope stepped toward her dad's chair. "Here's how you open it: the main blade has an oval hole. You stick your finger in, pull, and the blade opens."

She put the open knife in front of her dad's face. "It's very convenient."

He pulled back slightly. "Be careful!"

Penelope smiled at her dad. No, she'd never hurt *him.*

"This knife is small, but it's built like a battleship. The wood saw is long enough to be functional, not decorative, and is very sharp. There is a large-slotted screwdriver and a beefy Phillips screwdriver: both are cool. Here is the main blade; it cuts like the devil—dangerous and efficient."

As she spoke, she opened various parts of the knife, showing them to her dad.

"Scissors and tweezers are useful when traveling... and so is the bottle opener, which I'm going to use right now."

She hurried inside, grabbed a bottle of Warsteiner beer from the fridge, and returned to the yard.

"See how well this knife's opener works." She popped the beer open and tossed the cap into the grass.

She took a large gulp and placed the bottle in the chair's drink holder. She pulled out a pack of Marlboros, lit a cigarette, sat down, and started blowing smoke rings.

Her parents stared at her. Her dad touched his face wart, and her mom's jaw dropped, exposing her bare teeth for a couple of seconds.

They had never seen her drink or smoke before, so it was understandable for them to be *a little* surprised, she thought—but decided to give no explanation and just chugged the bottle.

Archie stood up, saying nothing, and dragged his feet toward the house, hunched over. A minute later, Penelope's mom also stood up and followed the boy.

Penelope took another gulp of beer. Warsteiner was all she needed today. Warsteiner—and Marlboros, as well.

Archie sat on the couch, alone in his thoughts.

That was what he wished for, being alone—but his grandma appeared at the door. She stopped for a moment before approaching and sitting next to him.

"How are you, Archie?"

He remained silent, staring out the window. Outside, three rings of tobacco smoke wafted toward the sky and melted away.

"Are you sick? Tell me, please. Grandpa and I worry about you."

"I'm not sick... Except..."

"Except?"

"Except I'm a little sad."

"Why are you sad?"

"Because Mother is sad. She even cries."

Grandma closed her eyes for a moment before gazing at him. "Um... right... yesterday, she was a little sad in the restaurant... but today she isn't sad anymore. Mommy isn't upset all the time, is she?" She reached out and held his hand.

"She's... She is not upset all the time," Archie agreed. "But when she is not upset, she is tense... annoyed... angry... and sometimes she's really mad."

Grandma said nothing, and he also kept quiet for a while.

He turned to Grandma and looked at her. "Grandma... have you ever drunk Perrier water?"

"Pe... Perrier?" Grandma laughed, shifting her gaze away. "I guess I haven't."

"How about San Pellegrino?"

"Neither San Pellegrino."

Grandma winked at him and even smiled, but it wasn't funny.

"Now, my turn to ask," Grandma asked. "Have you drunk Aquafina?"

He grunted and pulled his hand away.

"Dessa has drunk both Perrier and San Pellegrino. She even visited the actual sources in Europe. But Aquafina... well, who doesn't drink it in America?"

Thankfully, Grandma remained quiet. For a minute, only his mother's and grandpa's muffled voices came from outside. But then, she spoke again.

"Do you want to go for a walk?"

"Why?"

"To see trees, grass, clouds. To see nature."

"I see nature through the window." He moaned and looked at Grandma. "Can I play on my phone now?"

Grandma nodded, and he lay down on the couch to play. White rabbits and reddish greyhounds ran amid green bushes on his screen, and he shot at them. He'd hit rabbits, and they'd disappear as if they'd evaporated. Once in a while, he'd shoot a hound by mistake, and the hound would disappear too.

"Do you like bunnies and doggies dying?"

Grandma always wanted him to quit shooting games.

"Do you like them all dying?" Grandma insisted.

Grandma probed if he was sad and blue. But of course, he was—just like his mother.

"Dunno."

"In fact, you're going to die too," he muttered. "We're all going to die."

Grandma gasped and tried to reach out, but he pulled his hand away and continued to play, his eyes vacant, his mind lost in the game.

Penelope needed more beer, so she walked into the living room and hurried toward the kitchen, pretending not to notice her mom and Archie. She pulled a Warsteiner bottle out of the fridge and glided back to the yard.

At the patio door, she stopped, her reflection catching her attention. She pinched the tissue around her middle and tugged her T-shirt down to cover her belly.

Her eyes fell on the T-shirt's print: a scene of her and Dessa standing on the seats of a blue-green Ford Thunderbird, its soft top folded down, both facing the rear of the car. Penelope—in a commanding position—stood upright on the rear seat, her right foot planted high on the seat's back. Behind her, Dessa stood on the passenger seat, hands in her pockets, short-haired as always.

They'd had the picture taken three years ago at a classic car show in downtown Seattle. She'd had it printed on half a dozen T-shirts and used it as wallpaper on each of her devices.

At that time, Dessa's soul still belonged to Penelope.

But then, Dessa got involved in SAR, connected with all those people, and had fun with them. Penelope didn't desire her less for that; she actually wanted her more, especially when she was away from home.

Dessa, however, changed. She didn't smile while talking with her, not anymore. Dessa's attachment to her shrank like a shadow, a shadow that grew smaller and smaller as the sun rose in the sky.

SAR was Dessa's sun.

When Penelope decided to mend their relationship, it was too late. It was too late—even her engagement proposal couldn't hold Dessa at her side.

She bit her lip and walked out the door.

Out in the backyard again, she opened the new beer and sat opposite her dad.

Her dad stared at the picture on her T-shirt. "Has Dessa called you?"

Penelope shook her head and raised the bottle to her lips.

"She's still mourning," her dad said. "She's still overwhelmed by grief for her parents. Perhaps that's why she isn't calling you."

"No, she isn't overwhelmed by grief," Penelope said.

"How do you know?"

"I know from Facebook."

She checked Dessa's page every evening.

"Dessa isn't overwhelmed by grief. In fact, she travels and meets new people. She seems quite happy to me."

Her father rubbed his face wart, first with one finger and then with another. "You know, you can call her. Don't be too proud. Call her first."

"No, I won't call her. She doesn't want to talk to me right now," Penelope insisted.

"How do you know if you never call her?"

"I know." Penelope took a swig. "She tells me that every night."

"How so?"

She looked her dad in the eye. "As I sleep, her face pops up right in front of mine."

Dessa's face would appear so close that she could touch her lips. And her cheeks. Her neck too.

"I gaze at her and want to know when she is coming back home, but she's, like, 'I don't want to talk to you right now!'"

Penelope sipped her beer. "I ask her why, and she interrupts me with, 'Not now! I'll call you later.'"

"And after that?"

"I wake up."

Oh, she certainly wanted to call Dessa. She did.

She wanted to call Dessa and ask her to come back and marry her, but then she pictured Dessa rejecting her, and she didn't.

Her dad rubbed his wart again.

"You have this dream every night?"

"Yes, every night when I actually manage to fall asleep."

"You have insomnia. See a doctor. He'll give you some pills, and you'll feel better."

Her dad glanced at her.

"Because your mother and I worry about you. We worry about Archie too. A doctor will—"

"I don't need your concerns, Father!" Heat flushing through her body. "And I don't need your advice!" She pounded her fist against her knee. "I don't need your stupid doctor because I'm not ill!"

She sprang out of her chair and paced around her dad's.

"Dessa never rebelled, never said no, yet she abandoned me, and I don't know why! That torments me, but it can't be cured with pills!"

She thought of Dessa a hundred times a day, but Dessa probably didn't think of her even once a week.

She had no words to describe her pain.

The worst part was that she couldn't even imagine herself ever healing and moving on, feeling condemned to misery for life.

"Cheerily, cheer up, cheer up, cheerily," a robin sang on the rooftop. The song cut off as the robin flew over her head and slipped into the birdhouse in the tree.

"Have you ever been left, Father? Left by someone you were engaged to? Left by someone you wanted to spend your life with?"

Her father opened his mouth to reply, but she cut him off.

"You haven't! Let me tell you—it's demeaning and insulting. It's so painful that it makes you wonder why life even exists."

She paced again, chewing her cheek.

"To make my misery worse, nobody ever says anything nice to me. Management criticized my proposal, and my colleagues blame me for failing them... And you too, Father. You also criticize me!" she shouted. "You too! 'Don't be proud, call Dessa.' Bullshit!"

She pulled the knife out of her pocket, opened it lightning-fast, and threw it full force at the birdhouse. The blade struck the front an inch from the hole, and the knife shuddered with a quiet buzz. The robin shot out and away. After a moment, the knife loosened, tilted downward, slipped from the board, and fell to the ground. She picked it up, wiped it on her pants, folded it, and tucked it back into her pocket.

It was a good knife, a useful knife. Her knife. A knife that could be handy in the days to come.

CHAPTER TWENTY-FOUR

Balkan Mountains

Dessa had not posed for Christo since Wednesday—it had already been three days.

On Thursday, she took the bus to the city and picked up a few new things to wear. Nothing else happened. But on Friday morning the church bell tolled for a funeral: three strikes, a minute of silence, and three strikes again.

"It's for a man," Dessa's neighbor Lenka told her. Lenka was dressed in black and held a bouquet of garden flowers. "For a woman, it would strike twice instead of three times."

So, the bell tolled harder for men than for women.

"He was a rodbuster, a handsome man, and very capable, but he'd had cirrhosis."

Lenka looked up and down the street, then lowered her voice. "He didn't die from cirrhosis. He went missing, and when they found him, no one could say for sure if it was him, so they had to analyze his body in Sofia."

Dessa strained to hear Lenka's whispers.

"They found him below Mount Sinich, and Drunkard Pasko is the only man who roams there... grazing the cows. We knew Pasko killed him."

Lenka's eyes searched for a reaction, but Dessa only blinked. A few moments passed in silence.

"After the funeral, there will be a free lunch at the

restaurant," Lenka spoke, her voice turning upbeat. "Why don't you come along?"

A free lunch? Dessa wasn't interested. A funeral meant Christo would be busy, so she wouldn't be modeling for him today. She mumbled an excuse and went home.

On Saturday morning, Dessa went out on the veranda with her phone in hand, lay down in the hammock, and dozed off. Her phone rang; startled, she stumbled out of the hammock and caught herself on the railing to avoid falling.

It turned out that it was Fred calling from Paris for the second time this week. Not wanting to keep the line busy, she ended the conversation within a minute.

In the afternoon, Boris, Lenka's son, came carrying an old scythe, with Bruno—now in a harness—alongside him. She unleashed Bruno and played with him while Boris mowed the lawn. When Boris finished the job and stepped up to her, she glanced at him—stout, silent, silver chain glinting—and she had nothing to say. She just paid him, and he went away, pulling Bruno behind him.

She settled into bed early, turned off the light, and opened her phone, her thumbs gleaming in the screen's glow.

Jesse called her on Messenger from Washington, ten time zones away. "Your nose is shiny—rosy like a piglet's snout," he said, trying to cheer her up.

The joke fell flat. Dessa stared at the screen in silence. She wasn't in the mood, and they ended the chat soon after.

She scrolled through SAR news and commented on a few Northwest Hiker posts.

It was late, almost midnight, but she wasn't sleepy yet, so she went on Amazon and watched an entire season of a Canadian rescue TV show. She drifted off at last, the TV screen's glare lingering in the room like a ghost.

◆ ◆ ◆

Dessa got up late, the still Sunday morning stirring

an odd tension in her. She made breakfast but barely tasted it, then wandered downhill, gazing at houses and yards, as though waiting for something—or someone—to break the silence.

Older country houses, roofed with heavy slates, were deserted. Once a roof leaked, her dad had told her, the rafters beneath decayed until one day the weakest one broke under the tons of stone. Eventually, the entire roof would collapse, and soon everything in the open-to-the-sky house would rot. The stone walls, however, could stand firm for decades, engulfed by vines and white like skeletons.

New villas had sprouted among old houses like giant mutant mushrooms. City families would fill them up on Fridays and add life to the village. On Sundays, they would all drive back to the city, leaving the village in a sleeplike stillness, alone with the locals.

Dessa halted next to an unfinished three-story villa as a yellow concrete truck stopped in front of her and dropped its load on the pavement. Half-naked workers rushed to carry the mix in buckets to the backyard. She watched them for a moment, then stepped off the blocked street and took a shortcut trail across the gully.

The trail led her to Deaf Vera's shack on the opposite bank, where Vera stood in her front yard. Bent over a small tin stove, she stirred a saucepan, her flesh peeking through her shirt. She rose and grinned at Dessa, then said something in a loud, shrill voice and repeated it. Dessa couldn't grasp a word, ran her hand through her hair, and averted her eyes to the shack just in time to notice Drunkard Pasko peeking shirtless from behind a faded curtain. Their eyes met for a moment before he smirked and pulled back. Dessa hurried to wave goodbye to Vera and continued down the street as Vera's cackling echoed behind her.

Dessa approached a stone house with a tiny garden of beans and potatoes behind a wire fence. Three local men sat on a bench in front, staring at her in silence, their eyes vacant. A scruffy chicken pecked breadcrumbs at their feet.

Her phone kept silent.

"Excuse me, is there a church service today?"

The men seemed to wake up. "Yes, yes... there is. Of course. It's Sunday today."

She reached downtown, paused, and looked around. Local men and city people filled the coffee shop patio, drinking coffee and chatting as tobacco smoke drifted up toward the blossoming lindens. Folks walked in and out of the country store across the street. Several women skirted around a black Land Rover parked squarely on the crosswalk and headed toward the church. She hesitated for a few seconds, then followed at a distance.

The sun's rays bathed the church roof slates. She stepped into the arcade, opened the century-old door, and walked in. Daylight burst into the twilight of the nave, illuminating both the worshippers and the patinated paintings along the walls. Her neighbors Lenka and Petya waved to her: "Come join us." She nodded, murmuring "No, thanks," closed the door from the inside, and leaned against it.

She steadied herself and turned her gaze toward the altar.

Christo was there—his curls springing out from under his black kalimavkion and flowing toward his cassock-covered shoulders. He was reading something, almost singing, but she didn't catch his words, just their tune.

She stood still, and time seemed to stop.

His lips had a life of their own. What would they taste like?

His almond eyes didn't turn to her.

A car stopped outside with squeaking brakes, and footsteps approached, quick and heavy. The church door behind her opened, nearly knocking her down. A city man in a tracksuit burst into the church, pushing her out of his way, a golden cross swinging over his potbelly.

She snuck out through the open door, paused beside the

black Land Rover now parked in the alley, squinted for a few seconds—and headed home.

Dessa reclined in the hammock, phone in hand, scrolling through climbing gear on the Alpi store. Ropes, ascenders, descenders—she piled them all into her cart and paid. A week from now, they'd be delivered to Zarena, and she could descend into Devil's Cave. But what about today? She closed her eyes, listening to the blackbird in the cherry tree. Christo still hadn't called.

Late in the afternoon, she hiked to the Holy Trinity Chapel. Empty. No Christo. Back at the old house, she killed time online, ate dinner, and lay in bed. Finally, she dialed his number. Once. Twice.

Christo wasn't answering.

She squeezed her eyes shut.

It seemed as if Christo didn't want to talk to her.

He didn't want to talk to her. But why did it matter?

"You're growing infatuated with him, that's why," came Philip's voice.

Dessa met her brother's eyes, so similar to her own—a mix of brown and green with flecks of gold.

"Yes... It does seem as if I'm attracted to him. What's wrong with that?"

"Nothing is wrong. Except that the man you're attracted to is married with a child."

"His marriage is only pro forma. He's an Orthodox priest and isn't permitted to divorce, but he is separated from his wife... Besides, he's a good father who cares for his son."

"Yes, he cares for his son, while you left Archie behind."

Dessa opened her eyes, and Philip disappeared.

She scrolled through pictures on her phone... Philip feeding baby Archie, Philip hugging him, Philip teaching him to walk, Philip singing with him... Philip taking care of Archie while Penelope was busy with work... and now, in this picture, Dessa herself holding Archie in her lap.

Archie's hazel eyes stared at her from the picture, his lips slightly open as if he were about to say, "Do you love me, Auntie?"

Of course, she loved him. But she was only his aunt, not his parent. Archie had lost his dad, and Dessa couldn't do much to reverse that loss.

Dessa was already falling asleep when Christo called.

"I'll paint tomorrow. Will you come?"

He should have called earlier. She responded with silence.

"I need you to come."

His voice was steady, almost gentle.

"Will you?"

Dessa hesitated, her fingers curled around the edge of the blanket.

"Yes," she whispered.

CHAPTER TWENTY-FIVE

Gray clouds spilled across the mountains, their shadows creeping down the valley. Dessa smiled at the clouds, then glanced at Christo. He had already pitched the easel and was now examining his canvas, the breeze teasing his hair.

He turned to her. "We begin."

They got to work. Christo painted, while she tried her best to stay still.

Half an hour passed.

"Last night, I saw something on TV..." Christo paused mid-sentence and made a few brush strokes. "It was a film about the homeless in California."

She watched his hand dance over the palette as he stirred paint with a rhythmic grace.

"They had built themselves a tent city, but the police tore it down."

"Things like that happen," she agreed.

She took an extended pause, just like him.

"In California, I met a homeless artist, Cantalupi."

Christo froze, holding his brush near his chest, and she hurried to clarify. "Cantalupi is his name. He had lined his paintings up on three tables at a coffee shop."

"Did they kick him out?"

"Ah, no. Cantalupi may be slightly nuts, but he's harmless."

It would be fun, she thought, if she could take Christo to

California and introduce him to Cantalupi.

"During the day, Cantalupi works with crayons in the coffee shop; in the evening, he parties at the nearby club, and at night he sleeps in his old pickup truck."

Christo bit down on a cigarette and clicked the lighter. The wind extinguished it, and he clicked it again. Once it was lit, he took a deep drag, held it, and exhaled with a sigh.

"As a young man, Cantalupi had been a sailor," she said. "He'd even sailed the Black Sea and bathed on the beach in Varna."

"How do you know all this?"

"Well, we're friends on Facebook."

Christo dropped the brush and raised his head to the sky. She raised her head too.

The clouds were moving fast, spreading out and casting deep shadows on the slopes.

A lone thunderclap sputtered over the mountains like a child's firecracker.

"Cantalupi dreams of having his own condo," she said.

"Right... then he'll be able to keep dry when it rains." Christo flicked ash from his cigarette.

"No, he wouldn't live in it. He'd rent it out to have a steady income."

A gust of wind slapped the canvas, shook the easel, and stirred the tuft of oregano next to it.

She tilted her head toward Christo. "When a person moves into a house, Cantalupi says, that house settles into his soul."

She looked at Christo, but he kept quiet.

"But what kind of soul would you have if it were inhabited, for example, by a gloomy high-rise built of hundreds of precast concrete panels?"

A bolt of lightning flashed, and thunder boomed. Two startled magpies took off from a nearby walnut tree. Dessa looked at the sky just in time to see the sun sneak behind the clouds.

A second thunderclap boomed nearby.

"We have to take shelter somewhere." Christo scrambled to place the canvas in the box, somehow managed, then packed his brushes and paints into the briefcase.

They rushed down the road. Only fifty yards from her house, the downpour hit, leaving them soaked as they slipped inside.

Dessa glanced down at her red-and-black plaid dress and bare knees. "My mom wore this the day she met my dad." She handed him old hiking pants and a blue shirt. "They're my dad's. They'll fit you."

She returned to the room in five minutes and eyed Christo, standing by the sofa with a sullen look. Her dad's clothes hung on him like empty sacks. She chuckled, tried to be serious, and diverted her eyes to the window, struggling to hold back laughter.

The rain poured, and the gutter shot water like a fire hose.

"It's not going to stop anytime soon." Christo placed his hand on his lower back, grimaced, and stretched. "June is the month of storms and rains around here."

"While we wait, I can cook sausages for lunch." She looked at him, and he shook his head in agreement.

She rummaged in a kitchen drawer, retrieved her mom's handwritten recipe, and started reading it.

"I have to heat the oven first." She turned the dial and sat on a chair opposite him.

Christo watched her silently.

She went pensive for a while, recalling her walk across town yesterday: the pile of concrete on the street in front of that three-story villa, Deaf Vera's cooking in her front yard, and the potbellied city man with the golden cross who nearly knocked Dessa down when he stormed into the church.

"What kind of people come to your church?"

"All sorts. Both locals and weekenders, poor and rich."

"The rich give money to the church and build chapels." That's what the neighborhood women had shared with her.

"They build chapels because they have many sins."

As usual, Christo spoke in a measured low voice. He would fall silent from time to time, and she didn't know if he would continue.

"For the rich, religion is like money; they think they can use it to obtain whatever they want," Christo said, "power, status, the forgiveness of all sins."

It couldn't be easy being a priest in Zarena, she thought. City people like the potbellied man certainly gave him a hard time.

"Local people aren't wealthy," she said. "If they have riches, it's not money."

"I'm talking about the nouveau riche from the city, of course."

Christo clasped his hands together, and twisted his waist as if twirling an invisible hoop in slow motion.

"My back hurts. Every day, whether I paint or preach, I'm on my feet the whole time."

She bit her lips.

"Why don't you get some rest. You can lie down on the sofa until I finish cooking if you want."

Christo nodded and lay down.

She pulled a pack of sausages out of the fridge, arranged them on a baking tray, and glanced at the recipe, shifting her weight from one leg to the other. She made several cuts in each sausage, pushed the tray into the oven, and set the timer.

She turned to Christo, but he had dozed off. His left hand lay with fingers spread on his chest, and his right rested on the sofa along his slender body. The man breathed slowly and calmly.

She pulled a chair and sat at the edge. She gazed at him, her lips parting slightly, her muscles relaxing.

Ten minutes later, Dessa was still gazing at Christo when his phone rang in his pocket, jerking him out of his sleep. He blinked, pulled it out, and glanced at the screen.

"My wife..." he muttered, still sleepy. "My ex-wife."

He shoved the phone back into his pocket.

"I don't want to talk to her."

He remained stretched out on the sofa, silent for a minute or two.

Dessa gave him a small smile.

"I'll tell you everything about her." He stared at the ceiling. "She was a student when we first met."

Just as before, he would utter a sentence or two, pause, and then continue.

"I wanted to study painting, but I didn't have the money, so I began sneaking into art classes. That's where she befriended me.

"I had no right to be there—sometimes felt like a hunted animal—and she was being nice to me."

"One day, she invited me to a party. Everyone there was a student—everyone except me. Everyone seemed happy—dancing and laughing. I didn't know life could be so pleasant.

"And then she got pregnant."

Christo raised his head, turned to Dessa, and exclaimed, "I wasn't ready to be a father—not at all—but she wanted the baby no matter what."

Dessa remained motionless.

Christo rested his head on the pillow and stared at the ceiling again.

"So, I got hitched—and realized that, in fact, nobody was really happy. No one laughed, no one danced, no one loved."

He paused, his hand drifting to his chest, fingers brushing idly over his shirt.

"For years, I did everything mechanically and was lonely

to death."

He closed his eyes and fell silent, still.

She, too, had done everything mechanically. She had done it just because Penelope wanted it. She, too, had been lonely to death.

Now, however, *she* could choose what to do, not Penelope. Choose what to do—and do it for herself.

She leaned in, inching closer, unhurried, and kissed Christo.

His eyes opened wide, but only for an instant. Christo kissed her back, wrapped his arms around her, and they merged in an embrace.

She explored Christo's body and let him explore hers, until, at last, she lost herself for moments that stretched into eternity—a *little death* she hadn't known in years.

CHAPTER TWENTY-SIX

Early July, Washington

Penelope paced the living room in the twilight, muttering to herself as she had often done in the three weeks since her parents' visit.

She was waiting for Archie to return from a sleepover with his schoolmate Colton.

"Dessa... She's coming back?... But when?" Her words trailed off into indistinct murmurs, as she tried to catch thoughts that kept slipping away. "Dessa's odyssey... But when?"

When Archie returned home, Penelope stood by the wall without saying a word. Next to her, Chewbacca, the Afghan hound, snoozed on top of the living room beanbag.

Archie tossed his pack on the floor and dragged his feet toward the beanbag. "Don't sit on the beanbag!" Penelope yelled too late—Archie dropped himself right on top of Chewbacca. The dog squealed, Archie rolled to the side, and the dog bit him on the forearm. Archie screamed and then cried.

Penelope stepped up to Archie and scolded him, and her own grumbling merged into a sad trio with Archie's whining and Chewbacca's whimpering.

Her son's wound was turning red and swollen, and she sent him to the bathroom to wash it with cold water. She leaned over Chewbacca, and the dog tried to defecate. She hurried to slide the patio door open and urged him outside. But the dog wouldn't move, so she nudged him out with her foot, and he crawled a bit. She continued nudging Chewbacca until he dragged himself into the yard. Once there, the hound relieved himself, and there was blood in his stool. She nudged him back to the living room, and the hound lay down by the fireplace, rested his head on his paws, and closed his eyes. He would shake from time to time, open his eyes, whine, and drift off again.

Penelope applied antibacterial ointment and a Band-Aid to her son's wound before guiding him to bed. She turned his light off and moved to the kitchen.

She grabbed a carrot from the pile of vegetables on the table and, without washing it, bit into it.

The night was going to be sleepless, as usual.

Rocking in place, she glanced at her email, and there was nothing from Dessa. She tapped the cloud library, opened a Dostoevsky book, and began reading.

"I am a sick man... I am a spiteful man. I am an unattractive man."

She chewed her cheek.

Was *she* a sick and spiteful person?

Maybe she was, or maybe she was not.

But unattractive she was.

She stared at her reflection in the window, pressing her stomach with the phone. A potbelly. Hamster cheeks too.

Well, she had a potbelly because, over the years, while busy working for Dessa and Archie, she hadn't paid enough attention to herself. She didn't eat the right food and didn't exercise; she didn't have time for all that.

She bit into the carrot and chomped. Eating carrots instead of pizza should get her in shape soon.

True, she hadn't paid enough attention to herself, but perhaps she hadn't paid enough attention to Dessa and Archie either. She didn't spend enough time with them. But on the other hand, always keeping busy, working all she could for them was the way she loved them.

She loved them, and she expected them to love her back. Love her as a whole person, just the way she was, not the way they possibly wanted her to be.

Dessa once loved her like that, the way she was. But now she didn't know if Dessa still loved her even a tiny bit.

She didn't know, and not knowing hurt most.

She finished the carrot, tossed the stump on the heap of unwashed dishes in the sink—and Chewbacca whimpered from the living room.

She stared again at her reflection in the window, just in time to see a brown bat dash over the dark yard and perch on top of the window sash. A few seconds later, the bat grabbed the rail, hung upside down, and stared at her. Its black wings radiated from its tiny body like a sorcerer's mantle. The bat opened its mouth, baring its teeth at her—and she bared hers right back.

The kitchen door creaked open behind her. She swung around, ready to fight, and found Archie.

"I can't sleep because..." Archie began, his voice trailing off as if he had forgotten what he wanted to say. After a moment, he continued, "Will you make me golden milk the way Dessa makes it? It will help me fall asleep."

She glanced once again at the window, and the bat let go of the rail and flew off into the night.

Moving to the cupboard, she retrieved a jar of turmeric powder and heated milk with honey in a small saucepan. She pulled Dessa's Swiss Army knife from her pocket, scooped turmeric with its blade, and dropped it into the milk. Adding cinnamon for taste, she stirred for a while and strained the beverage into a glass. Archie drank it up without saying a word, left the glass by the sink, and went to his room.

Penelope turned the kitchen lights off and headed to the bedroom. She left the door open, didn't bother to undress, and went to bed in her jeans and shirt.

She lay in the dark, listening to Chewbacca's

whimpering for an hour. When Archie emerged from the gloom of the hallway and stood in the door frame, she turned on the light and called him to her bedside.

"Is the dog bothering you?"

Archie nodded.

"Lie down here and wait for me. I'll take care of him."

She went to Chewbacca and slid the patio door open.

"Come on, let's go out into the yard."

Chewbacca slipped outside, whining, crossed the patio, and lay on the grass. Trembling, he turned his head to her, to the open door, and back to her. He strained and defecated blood —again.

Penelope looked down at him and froze.

"I'm a sick person," she whispered. "I'm a spiteful person."

She pulled the knife from her pocket, opened it with one hand, and—caressing Chewbacca with the other—slit his throat in one swift motion. Blood splashed on her bare feet as the Afghan slumped, dead, on the grass.

"Yes... that's better," Penelope said to herself. "One thing less to worry about."

She hosed her feet down, rinsed the knife, dried it on her jeans, and dropped it back into her pocket. The dog's body went into a thick plastic bag, which she stuffed into the garden waste bin. She wheeled the bin out of the yard and left it by the curb. All the trash was to be collected tomorrow and ferried to a remote landfill, hundreds of miles away. Chewbacca would be buried there under heaps of waste, and no one would ever know what had happened to him.

Penelope returned to the master bedroom and found Archie in the big bed, holding her phone.

"You've put Dessa's birthday on your calendar..."

She lay down next to him.

"... with no end date."

Archie scrolled forward. "July 8, 2242, falls on a Friday."

He fell silent for a moment.

"This is Dessa's two hundred and fifty-eighth birthday."

Penelope pulled her phone out of his hands.

"On that day, we'll all be dead."

Penelope slipped her hand under the blanket, running it gently along Archie's back—and he turned his head toward her and gazed at her. She moved her hand upward, over the bump on his neck, and into his locks. Then, with both hands, she caressed him behind the ears.

"Do you miss Dessa?"

Archie's expression tightened for a moment—but then his lips curled into a small smile.

"Yes... I haven't seen her in ninety-two days."

An artery twitched in Penelope's neck.

Archie missed Dessa. And she missed her too.

Dessa had been away for ninety-two days—a whole three months—and hadn't bothered to call. Not since she left for Bulgaria.

It hurt—but what could Penelope do about it?

She could *stop waiting* for Dessa and *go see her,* have all her questions answered, and have the pain gone for good.

She had to check. Not knowing hurt the most. Not knowing was torture.

She waited for the twitching to stop, then forced herself to smile at Archie.

"Would you like to go to Bulgaria and see her?"

"I don't know... Would she like to see us?"

"She would if I told her that *you* wanted to see her."

Right, she must call Dessa for little Archie's sake, not her own.

"We can be there for her birthday."

That would likely be acceptable to Dessa. Acceptable to everyone.

"In Bulgaria?"

"Yes, in Bulgaria."

"Colton's father said they have a huge hamburger monument in Bulgaria. It's all made of concrete and sits on a mountaintop."

"We'll go see it."

"Colton and his father went to a Tacoma café that's actually a teapot. Colton said it was a two-story building with a red handle and a red spout on the sides, and it had a red lid instead of a roof. He drank tea there, and his father drank coffee."

Her son had not talked so animatedly in a long time.

"They spent the night at a motel that looked like a windmill, and the next day they went to a tulip festival. It would be nice if we could go there too."

"Maybe, but after we get back from Bulgaria."

"Why, when are we leaving?"

"As early as tomorrow."

"Tomorrow?... But Chewbacca? I hurt him when I sat down. What are we going to do with him?"

"Don't worry, I've already found a good place for him. He'll be fine."

Archie smiled.

"Our dog will be fine."

He yawned.

"You know, Mommy, Colton's dog knocked the gearshift of their car out of park, but it didn't crash because Colton's dad —"

"It's time for you to sleep," Penelope interrupted, "because if you don't..."

She halted mid-sentence. There was no need to be rude to her son, not right now.

Right now, Penelope had to behave herself.

"You can sleep in my bed," she added.

With that, she got up and went to the kitchen.

◆ ◆ ◆

Penelope tapped Facebook, opened Dessa's page, and looked at her profile picture. There Dessa was, holding two-year-old Archie in her lap, bowing her head toward him. Archie looked up at Dessa with his lips slightly open, as if he were about to ask, 'Do you love me, Auntie?' Dessa smiled back at him, about to say, 'Of course I love you.' She had actually said that when Penelope took the photo eight years ago.

The photo resembled a *Madonna and Child* Renaissance painting she'd seen in a Seattle cathedral.

She looked up at the ceiling, almost in prayer.

Then she called Dessa.

She exhaled as Dessa picked up.

"Archie wants to see you for your birthday," she said. "May we visit for a week?"

CHAPTER TWENTY-SEVEN

Early July, Sofia

Fred arrived in Sofia on the morning flight from Paris.

"There's free Wi-Fi in the taxi." The cabbie lit a cigarette, launching a pop-folk show on his air-vent-mounted phone—and accelerated his newish Ford onto the freeway toward the city.

Fred gaped at the screen. An elderly man lay in a hospital bed, unshaven—but when a young rapper appeared beside him, the old man jumped up, revived by the music's rhythm. He tossed aside his medications, raised a large bottle labeled Viagra, took a gulp, and danced. Around him, sparsely dressed girls joined cigar-smoking, champagne-sipping men, all bouncing with joy as the rapper chanted a mix of Bulgarian and English.

"Shall I say screw you? Or just say cheers?"

The taxi drove along a wooded parkway. A quaint TV tower came into sight and quickly disappeared behind the trees.

"Screw you! And thank you! And cheers!"

They drove out of the park, swerved down a tree-lined boulevard, and stopped outside a hotel with shiny glass doors. Fred stepped out of the car and looked around. The boulevard stretched up the foothills of a green-gray mountain, while the city lay below in the valley, shrouded in smog. He shrugged; his main priority was a bath, and he hoped the hotel suite would have one.

Fred dropped his bag by the wardrobe and looked around the bedroom. The huge bed was laden with pillows. A garish painting of a country house, nestled in a garden, hung above the headboard—poppies bigger than sunflowers surrounded a stone well with a bucket dangling under a wooden roof, and two big, mustached fellows drank brandy high on the second-floor porch.

A sofa ran along the entire wall in his suite's spacious living room, and a small TV hung far in the corner. A monumental top-freezer/refrigerator dominated the kitchenette. He could cook for the entire SAR team here! He peeked into the kitchen cabinets, but they were empty—no silverware, plates, or glasses—just a lone salad bowl.

He went into the bathroom, turned the taps to fill the tub, then moved to the bedroom, where he hung his shirts in the wardrobe and arranged his underwear on the shelves. He returned to the bathroom just in time to see that the water was about to spill over the tub. The overflow drain was underwater, likely clogged. He called the front desk, and they promised to fix it.

He stood by the window and glanced out to the street. A beautiful woman walked on the sidewalk with a frizzy poodle, and he stared after her. Her curly dark hair reminded him of Alma, and he winked to himself.

In recent weeks, he and Alma had messaged every day, and each time, she'd invite him to Sofia. Now, here he was, ready to meet her in person—and, fingers crossed, make love to her.

In just a few hours, after her workday, she was going to come to his hotel.

Sex is a great thing, Fred thought.

He undressed and luxuriated in the bathtub's hot water.

At lunchtime, Fred went to the hotel's restaurant. Folk costumes and strings of chilies adorned the walls, and wagon wheel chandeliers hung from the ceiling. A large brick grill smoked by the side wall. He settled at a table next to it and ordered grilled trout and greens.

He ate and sipped wine as he watched the chef, dressed all in white, grill meat and vegetables for the other patrons.

An hour later, he paid the bill with a huge tip and went to wash his hands. He collided with the chef at the restroom door, stepped back, and noticed a large wet spot around the man's crotch. Fred furrowed his forehead, stepped forward to the sink, and turned the tap just a little bit. The tap remained dry, so he turned it more—and a mighty jet of water hit the sink, squirted out of it, and splashed on his pants. Now, he, too, had a wet spot.

Should he change? Why bother? The day was warm, and his pants would dry quickly. Worrying about them wasn't worth the effort.

He went out into the street and walked down the sidewalk. The sun was shining, and the sky was blue. A woman gawked at him, smiled, and walked on.

He entered a park, passed a group of blind men and women out for a walk, and took a blacktopped path that seemed to slope downward forever. When he reached a pond, he settled himself on a bench.

In front of him, two boys in shorts and T-shirts squatted on the grassy shore, holding model yachts. On the far side of the pond, a man with a beer belly raised his phone. "One, two, three—start!"

The boys pushed the boats on the water. The breeze carried the yachts across the pond, and the boys followed them with shouts of joy along the shore.

A boxer bounded over, smearing slobber on Fred's pants. "Don't worry!" The dog's owner called from a distance. "Berta's just excited to meet you." Berta, tongue unfurled, looked at Fred and ran back to her master.

A big man on a motorized bicycle rode up the alley. The noisy engine filled the air with fumes, making Fred yearn for the calm of his hotel.

On his way back, he stopped by a supermarket and bought a bottle of Courvoisier, some Aero chocolate, and red bulbs for the hotel suite's lamps.

Alma walked into Fred's suite wearing black pants, a white uniform shirt, and a blue silk scarf tied at the neck. While he locked the door, she sat silently on the sofa.

He walked over and looked at her.

Alma's face, now frozen, bore little resemblance to the lively image he knew from the screen. The lamp cast red light on her left side, leaving her right side in shadow. She sat motionless, embodying both determination and suffering.

He sat beside her and held her hands. She kept silent, her body limp. He hugged her and pulled her closer, but she remained stiff, as if carved out of wood.

He stood up and looked around, puffing out his cheeks. Shuffling to the window, he pulled the curtain across it. He turned on the TV, muted it, and stared at the screen for a few seconds.

This rendezvous wasn't going as he'd imagined. Maybe it was his fault. He should've booked a luxury hotel, taken her to a fancy restaurant, bought her perfume. But it was too late for that. The question was: what could he do now?

He lifted his chin, stepped back to Alma, took her hands again, and pulled her up from the sofa. He embraced her shoulders, looked into her eyes, and kissed her.

"You have sweet lips."

"You too," she said.

He continued to kiss and touch her, undressing them both as he inhaled her unfamiliar scent.

Fred and Alma were already topless. "Wait." Her voice was strained. "I have a present for you."

She stepped away from him, leaned over the sofa, and rummaged in her purse. Standing beside her, he watched her skin gleam in the darkness, white like marble.

Alma hung a blue corded pouch around his neck. "This charm will bring you miraculous protection." "It's filled with camphor, iris root..." She paused, searching for the words in English. "... toadstool and jellyfish powder."

She hesitated. "Garlic was also in the recipe, but you wouldn't like the smell."

He raised the pouch in front of his eyes and examined it. "Thank you," he muttered, abashed.

Alma gave him a slight smile. "I made a present for myself too."

She pulled out another pouch, this time red, and hung it around her neck.

"It helps to prevent pregnancy and other incidents."

Other incidents? Did she mean STDs?

"So be it," he grumbled—and hugged her again.

Soon, they were stark naked, with only charms hanging on their necks.

Alma's face still looked stiff, though.

He pulled back a bit, still holding her hands. She kept her head lowered, as if interested only in his bare feet.

He observed her in silence, caressing her thumb with his.

In the past weeks, she had sent him flirtatious selfies and shared everything that seemed to come to her mind, often of an erotic nature. Honestly, he had done little to provoke it except for listening and occasionally asking questions. That was how it was; he didn't do anything. Alma seemed to take pleasure in revealing herself in a bold and attention-seeking way.

Decades ago, he and his schoolmates had been all about showing off. They would say all sorts of things, acting like experienced lovers, yet deep down, they were insecure and sometimes scared to death.

What they really wanted was to be liked, arouse interest, impress others, and ultimately, be loved.

Alma had been acting just like them. A Bulgarian woman of about forty, bluffing like a schoolboy, but terrified like a virgin.

She wasn't the liberated woman he knew from Messenger, and having sex with her wasn't going to be easy.

Right now, Alma was cold and unaroused, and he had to do something to distract her. He needed to distract himself as well, instead of getting anxious—and help them both relax, warm to each other, and let their instincts take over.

He could try the usual approach of kissing and petting—but how do you pet an ice block?

He'd rather play a game with her—a silly game.

A silly game he played with his wife Eva decades ago—a game they both enjoyed quite well back then.

Today, he was going to show *Alma* how to play and lead her in the game. Perhaps she would be curious and not just obedient, participating as Eva did.

"Do you know how making love and cooking food are alike?"

She raised her face to him, her eyes widening, her lips parting. It seemed she wanted to know.

"You can make love or cook food to make money. Also, you need sex and food to produce offspring. Of course, you can use either to give yourself pleasure."

He paused, stealing a glance at Alma.

"I, however, don't want sex for reproduction. It's not for

me; it's for family folks.

"I don't want sex for money; I may be a professional chef, but I'm not a gigolo.

"I don't want sex for pleasure... I abstain with the power of my will!"

He was pretending, of course. Sex for pleasure was all he wanted right now, but to lure Alma into playing with him, he had to act rather than tell the truth.

"Lust, just like gluttony, is a force that only diverts an ambitious man from his noble goals."

"Then what kind of sex do you want?"

"I want abstinence sex."

"Abstinence sex? Never heard of it... Uh, how do you have abstinence sex?"

"I'll show you. You'll sit on my lap, facing away, and hold a bowl—yes, a salad bowl—filled with alcohol."

He squinted at Alma.

"We'll sit naked and sip from the bowl now and then. Our goal will be to stay cold and passionless until we drink it all. Whoever has the willpower to resist lust will obtain a magical power that will free them from the depressing cycle of birth and death."

He cleared his throat.

"Hindus call this power *Siddhi*. Those who have it can rule life, nature, the universe, and everything."

He released Alma's hands and looked at her, struggling to keep a straight face.

"Remember, our goal is to remain cold and passionless. Touching is permitted, but penetration is not. That's why they call it abstinence sex, right? Shall we try it?"

Alma shook her head. *Yes.*

He poured half the Courvoisier bottle into the bowl and broke the chocolate into pieces, leaving them in the tin foil on the sofa. "Cognac goes well with chocolate," he said, handing the bowl to Alma.

Alma settled into his lap, sipped the Courvoisier, and

passed him the bowl. He took a sip, slid a piece of chocolate into her mouth, and then into his own. He savored the combination, ensuring she did too. Occasionally, he glanced at the TV.

The chocolate was gone soon, and the bowl was half empty.

As he tried to sip again, his hands trembled, and he dripped Courvoisier onto Alma's back instead of into his mouth. He put the bowl on the sofa and licked Alma's white skin. She remained still on his lap, dutifully bent and as passionless as a statue.

"I can't resist it." He moaned. "You've defeated me."

He enveloped her body.

"You won, and I failed. Now you have Siddhi, and you can control nature and everything."

He penetrated her, but she was cold and slippery like a dead fish.

The TV blared as he stared at the screen. A circus train raced across the prairie, a clown painted on the first car. Giraffes stuck their necks out from the roof of the second car, while a young Indiana Jones leaped between wagons, pursued by three burly men. One of the pursuers caught up, and the two began fighting. Below, an agitated rhino pierced the rooftop with mighty blows, its massive horn punctuating the struggle above.

Fred moved in rhythm with the rhino on the screen. Alma followed, her movements obedient but lifeless, like a marionette on strings.

A ringtone cut through from her purse. She pulled the phone out, and Fred caught a glimpse of her husband Danny's smiling photo on the screen.

Instantly aroused, Alma wiggled, waving her legs, kicking the sofa's side, and swirling her hips, her warmth flooding over Fred. Her phone was still ringing in her hand when she screamed in orgasm.

He lay on his back, breathing heavily, his eyes shut,

trying to figure out Alma's arousal in response to her husband Danny's phone call.

Was Danny the person Alma wished she could be sleeping with rather than Fred himself? Was it seeing Danny's picture that stirred her to orgasm, with Fred being only a warm body on which to take out her lust?

Fred smirked, dismissing the notion. From their chats, he knew well enough that her arousal was an adrenaline reaction to the excitement of the forbidden—cheating on her husband while he was trying to reach her.

Fifteen minutes later, Fred was coming out of the bathroom when the front door lock snapped. A maintenance man appeared in the doorway, and Fred grabbed a towel, fumbling to cover himself.

"I have to fix the bathtub overflow drain," the maintenance man said, stepping into the bathroom.

Alma hurried to get dressed, telling Fred she would come back for the whole weekend. She kissed him and slipped out.

CHAPTER TWENTY-EIGHT

Balkan Mountains

Penelope endured, with Archie in tow, a sixteen-hour flight from Seattle to Frankfurt and then a hop to Sofia. She called Dessa from Frankfurt to remind her they would be there that evening.

"I haven't forgotten," Dessa said. "I've already set up bedrooms for each of you."

Bedrooms for each of them? Penelope's mouth tightened. Dessa didn't sound like she was going to accept Penelope in her bedroom.

At Sofia airport, Penelope rented an Audi with a driver and headed to Dessa's village of Zarena, a hundred miles away in the Balkan Mountains.

"Don't put on the seat belt," the driver said. "Nobody checks anyway."

Unshaven, his voice was as gloomy as his appearance.

They left the city, cruising along the freeway through wooded hills, with distant, snow-patched mountains in the background. Silent, Penelope watched the scenery pass by. The car plunged into a tunnel under a ridge and descended onto a plain.

Archie spotted a McDonald's and insisted they stop.

After eating, they drove off again. Archie curled up beside Penelope in the back seat and soon fell asleep.

They pulled off the freeway, bypassed a sprawling city, and entered a mountain gorge. The road climbed with twists and turns along a rushing river. Penelope spotted eagles flying high above the cliffs.

"These are the Balkan Mountains," the driver said. He lowered his window and stretched his hand outside.

They got caught behind a bus, and diesel fumes filled the Audi through the open window. Penelope held her breath against the fumes.

The driver floored the accelerator to pass the bus. As the Audi entered a narrow curve alongside it, a red car popped in front, swerved, and sped along the shoulder. Loose gravel cracked and slipped under its tires. The cars passed each other in an instant, and the Audi pulled ahead of the bus.

"You dirty faggot!" the driver yelled in Bulgarian, still panting. "Some peasant with a broken Russian clunker!"

Penelope understood enough. She glanced at the driver, momentarily frightened, and raised her eyes to the sky in prayer. Instead of God, she saw the ruins of a fortress perched on the cliffs, high above a sea of bare rocks and islands of bushes.

Bare rocks and islands of bushes. Even if there had once been a forest here, people had cut it down.

She used her fingertips to massage her forehead, trying to ease the growing pain. Glancing at the roadside river, she noticed the water's foamy surface flickering with chemical hues. She raised her eyes again and saw the ruins disappear behind a bend. There could have been real greatness in these lands, but it was all gone.

"That moron made me nervous!" The driver lit a cigarette.

Archie coughed from the smoke, but Penelope didn't dare say anything. All she could do was hope that most Bulgarians were nicer than that.

They continued the trip in silence, arriving in Zarena at nightfall. Archie was still asleep when they stopped in front of a whitewashed house.

Dessa emerged, and Penelope, her heart thumping, extended her arms to embrace her and kiss her. Dessa recoiled a bit but allowed her to kiss her cheek.

"Welcome," Dessa said.

Penelope watched as Dessa hugged Archie and carried him toward the house, careful not to wake him. She hurried to pay the driver and walked through the gate, suitcase in hand, into a grassy yard, glancing around. To the left stood a spacious veranda; to the right, an open door led into the house. In front of the veranda gate, a bloodhound raised its head.

She stepped into the house. The first floor opened into a large living room with a kitchen. A single flight of wooden stairs led to the second floor.

She went upstairs, where Dessa met her in a small hallway.

She gazed at Dessa. "You've changed. You're growing your hair out... and you're wearing earrings."

She had never seen Dessa wear earrings before.

Dessa said nothing, just stared at her—and Penelope dropped her gaze.

A couple of moments later, she looked up at Dessa.

"You've gotten yourself a bloodhound."

"Yes, Bruno. But he isn't mine. A neighbor is visiting her son in the city, and I offered to take care of Bruno while she's away."

Penelope nodded. She was going to play with Bruno in the days to come.

Dessa half-turned toward an ajar door. "This is your bedroom." Dessa pointed to two closed doors. "That one is Archie's, and the other is mine."

Dessa opened the door to Penelope's bedroom and stepped back. "Do you need anything right now?"

Penelope needed her, of course, but she acted so distant,

so independent, that Penelope couldn't utter a word.

She walked in and left the suitcase on the floor.

Perhaps Dessa was tired from making up the bedrooms, tidying the whole two-story house, and shopping at the last minute for groceries?

Indeed, Dessa looked tired.

Penelope was tired too—exhausted from the red-eye flight and the ten-hour time difference. The long drive hadn't helped either.

Everyone was tired, Penelope thought, and getting a good night's sleep was the best thing for them to do tonight. Tomorrow was going to be a fresh day, and Dessa would be different. Dessa would warm up to her and talk to her. Talk to her just like before.

She turned back to the door to wish Dessa goodnight, but Dessa was already gone.

Penelope wanted to fall asleep right away but found herself rolling in bed instead. Occasionally, she paused, listening to the night, but heard only silence.

Just before dawn, she finally dozed off—and slept late.

Penelope woke late to the homey aroma of fried *mekitsi* wafting from behind the old plank door. She stretched, yawned, and caught Dessa's and Archie's muffled voices blending with music. She listened—were they singing?

She got dressed, opened the door, and sat on the top of the stairs.

From the kitchen, the Beatles' "All You Need Is Love" filled the air.

"That's what you need," Dessa's girlish voice joined in, improvising.

"Love, love, love," Archie followed Dessa, "that's what you need."

"Do you want to fry the last *mekitsa*?" Dessa asked.

The Beatles continued their "love" refrain, drowning out Archie's answer.

Penelope let her eyelids droop and tipped her head back, her fingers gliding along the railing. For a few timeless moments, she didn't want to be anywhere but here, on the wooden stairs of this old house, listening. Listening to Dessa and Archie singing along with the Beatles.

◆ ◆ ◆

The Beatles were still chanting as Penelope walked down the stairs and peered through the door to the big room. A frying pan of hot oil smoked on the stove. Archie held a ball of dough, staring at the oil. He stood poised to throw the ball in the pan and bolt.

"First, stretch the dough in your hands," Dessa instructed. "Turn the ball into something like a dough elephant ear."

"I can't," Archie said.

"Why not?"

"Elephant ears are huge, and this ball is tiny, so the dough won't be enough."

"Well, okay. You're right. Your dough ball is tiny, so make one tiny ear for an itsy-bitsy baby elephant."

Archie began to pull the dough, sticking out his tongue. "Here it is!" He dropped the dough into the pan, and the oil sizzled around it.

Dessa hugged him over his shoulder. "You're going to have to turn it over to brown the other side."

Penelope watched them, leaning on the doorframe. When they finished frying, Dessa noticed her, greeted her with a nod, and invited her to the table.

The three of them sat down to eat. The warm mekitsi were piled high on a porcelain platter, surrounded by a jar of jam, a plate of feta cubes, and three steamy cups of tea.

Miraculously, they were a family again, just like before—

and that was all Penelope needed for now.

They ate, knives and forks clanking on plates.

Penelope sipped her tea, and it tasted funny. She sniffed it and wrinkled her nose.

"It's yarrow tea, it grows wild in the mountains." Archie took a sip. "Dessa washed my dog bite with yarrow tea and put gauze on it."

Penelope turned to Dessa. Had she really treated her son's dog bite with a wild weed?

"Yarrow is not just tea—it's a medicinal herb." Dessa took a sip. "Men around here used to use yarrow to heal battle wounds, while their wives used it to ease menstrual bleeding."

Archie followed suit, sipping yarrow tea. "If we had yarrow back home, we could've healed Chewbacca with it."

Penelope pushed her cup aside. "Even without yarrow, the vet will heal Chewbacca just fine." She had already told everyone she'd left Chewbacca at the Puget Veterinary Hospital.

She remained still, watching as Archie mirrored Dessa's every move—sipping tea when she did, forking cheese when she did, and biting into the mekitsa as she did.

Her son adored Dessa, as always, but that was no reason to be jealous... or was it?

They were still eating breakfast when Dessa's phone rang.

Penelope overheard a man's deep, melodic voice.

Dessa stood and walked away from the table, pressing the phone to her ear. She approached the cupboard, opened the drawer, and pulled out a red hairbrush, as if unaware of the motion.

Penelope watched, transfixed, as Dessa spoke on the

phone, smoothing her hair in slow, soft strokes. Dessa's eyes, now blurred, wandered around the room without seeing.

Penelope swallowed, but the food scraped her throat, rough as sandpaper.

Dessa was smitten with the man on the other end of the line.

Dessa had chosen someone else over her... *A man!*

The world collapsed beneath Penelope, a flood of disgust, resentment, and anger surging through her.

Jealousy rose and fell in waves, but she had to get a grip.

She had to hold herself together long enough to figure out who he was.

Penelope watched Dessa slip on her sneakers, toss "I'm going out" over her shoulder, and slam the door. Left alone, she went to her bedroom and paced from corner to corner, her lips clamped together.

An hour later, she stopped, stood still for a few seconds —then stepped into the hallway and shouted down the stairway.

"Archie, what are you doing?"

No answer.

She yelled again. "Archie, what are you doing?"

"I'm watching Cartoon Network."

She slipped into Dessa's bedroom. The old plank door had a key on the inside. She turned the key in the lock—it worked. She turned it back.

She stepped into the room and looked around: a bed, table, chair, wardrobe... all spartan. Ropes and other climbing gear lay scattered around an open box on the floor.

The bed was unmade. She reached over and raised the pillow. Underneath, Dessa's parents grinned from a black-and-white wedding photo.

It struck Penelope as strange that Dessa kept a paper

photo under her pillow. She could have taken a picture of it and gazed at it on her phone all she wanted. Was that sentimental —or just foolish?

Penelope dropped the pillow, went to the wardrobe, and slid the door to one side. She looked at the underwear on the shelf and tucked her nose between two blouses on hangers, catching the scent of church incense. She stepped back, perplexed, then sniffed the blouses again and sensed the same aroma.

She closed the wardrobe, slipped out of Dessa's bedroom, and stomped down the stairway. After hesitating for a moment, she put her shoes on, dashed through the yard, shut the gate behind her, and looked around.

A crumbling asphalt street, lined with rural houses and villas, ran downhill to the village center.

A rough forest road led uphill, starting right from the house.

Where had Dessa gone?

Penelope looked down once again, toward the street and the village, then up, toward the steep forest road.

Dessa would prefer to ascend to nature rather than descend to the human anthill.

Penelope set out on the road uphill, toward the meadows and the forests.

When she reached an old barn, she jumped over the fence, circled the dilapidated building, peered through the broken door—and saw a snake hanging from the log rafters. She gasped, stepped back, and hurried onto the road, continuing toward the open ridge.

Soon, she stopped again. A lone easel with a canvas stood in the meadow to the right of the road. A small, whitewashed chapel rested several yards farther away.

A villager was herding a few cows far up the ridge.

Penelope walked over and looked at the canvas. In the foreground, a young woman stood amid a barren plain, holding an infant in her arms. A man with a halo around his head approached them from the left, and on the right, a dark female silhouette was heading away, going toward a giant bloody moon.

The young woman had Dessa's face, and the baby had Archie's.

Penelope chewed her cheek.

She crossed the meadow, hands in her pockets, and peered through the chapel window. In the dim light, an Orthodox icon lamp illuminated cheaply painted icons. There was Dessa, behind a rusty candlestick with dead candles, embracing the shoulders of a long-haired man, her face lifted in anticipation of a kiss.

The man put his arms around Dessa's waist, pinned her to himself, and kissed her—and Dessa kissed him back.

Penelope's face grew numb, but she pulled herself together and glowered.

What a pretentious movie kiss... *Gone with the Wind... Clark Gable kissing Vivien Leigh.*

The two in the chapel went on, oblivious and theatrical.

Penelope twisted her face into a grimace, heat flushing through her body. Approaching the chapel door, she drew the Swiss Army knife from her pocket and opened it. She paused at the door for a moment, then rushed toward the easel, glancing at the herdsman's silhouette in the distance. Without hesitation, she faced the canvas and stabbed the painted man in the head, dragging the blade down to the frame, splitting the figure in half. She spat at the torn painting, closed the knife, hid it in her pocket, and walked down the road to the old house, feeling strangely calm.

With the canvas destroyed, the painting session ended, and Dessa and Christo parted ways. When Dessa returned home, she found Penelope and Archie huddled on the sofa in the big room, watching Cartoon Network.

The three ate dinner in silence and went up to their bedrooms.

Dessa turned off the lamp, climbed into bed, opened her phone, and scrolled through Facebook. She was already feeling sleepy when Christo called.

They talked about his slashed painting.

"It was Drunkard Pasko who did it," Christo said. "Pasko, the man who herds the cows."

He cleared his throat and repeated, as if to convince himself, "It was Pasko who did it."

Indeed, Pasko had been around with the cows when they'd found the painting slashed.

"Yes, it must've been him. But please, don't worry too much. I'll pose for you again, and you can redo the painting."

"Thanks... Unfortunately, I won't be able to paint for a few days." Christo cleared his throat again. "My son's fallen ill, and I must leave for Sofia early tomorrow."

Christo had to go, and she had to stay here.

She was going to miss him—but she had no choice. She could do nothing about it.

CHAPTER TWENTY-NINE

Dessa was turning thirty-three today.

Still in bed, she unlocked her phone to a swarm of greetings popping up on the screen. She scrolled through, reacting and responding.

Happy birthday! Fred messaged her.

Thank you, she replied. *Aren't you up too early?*

I would've been if I were still in France, Fred responded with a grin and a wink emoji. *But I'm in Bulgaria now.*

Really? she typed, moving to the next message.

What are you going to do today? Fred asked. *Climb a mountain?*

Kind of... I'm going down a cave.

A cave? I love caves. I wish I could go with you.

She replied with a shrug emoji.

Are you going alone?

No, I'll take my parents' ashes with me.

Fred sent a care emoji. She replied with a thumbs-up and closed the chat.

Half an hour later, she got up, stretched, and stepped into the hallway. A greeting card lay waiting for her by the door. The front of the card bore a message in blood-red letters, framed by rainbow squares:

They will never find your body...

Dessa unfolded the card and discovered the inscription continued inside:

...as hot as i do!

The letter *i* had a little blood-red heart on top instead of a dot.

HBD, Penelope had added by hand.

Dessa tightened her lips, left the card where she'd found it, and stomped down the stairs to the first floor.

Dessa found Archie and Penelope at the table.

Archie sat next to a ketchup-smeared plate surrounded by eggshells, engrossed in his phone.

Dessa looked at Penelope, who remained silent, clenching her fists.

Dessa turned to Archie.

"What are you looking at?"

"An owl that's having a bad feather day."

Penelope glanced at Archie, let out a moan, pushed back her chair, paced the room, and sat down again. Archie only stared at his empty plate for a few seconds, then turned to Dessa.

"This owl is molting." The boy turned the screen to Dessa.

A cranky-looking owl stood on a windowsill, holding a feather in its beak.

"It's anxious because it's shedding its feathers," Archie said. "It doesn't know it'll grow better ones."

That owl worried for nothing, Dessa thought. It just needed to shed its old feathers, embrace change, and come out prettier and happier.

Her phone rang.

Penelope moaned again.

It was Christo calling, and Dessa picked up.

Christo greeted her for her birthday, and she asked how his ill son was doing. He replied that he would explain everything once he returned from Sofia, though he wasn't sure when that would be. After a moment, he ended the conversation.

It took her another minute to realize Penelope and Archie were watching her in silence.

She winked at the boy. "Your molting owl is nothing compared to the tree-climbing octopus… Let me show you… It only climbs down to lay eggs."

"That's not funny!" Penelope yelled. "It's not funny at all!"

Penelope jumped out of her chair, slammed the entry door behind her, and stepped onto the veranda.

Archie dragged himself to the sofa, lay down, and turned on Cartoon Network.

Dessa peered out the window. Penelope paced around the veranda, occasionally pausing in front of Bruno, petting him and talking to him.

Dessa shrugged, reheated four pieces of spanakopita, poured herself a glass of milk, and ate breakfast.

An hour later, Dessa stood in the doorway, her pack pressing on her back.

"Archie, I'm going out."

The boy didn't seem to hear her, drawn to the TV like a moth to a flame.

"Archie! I'm going out!"

This time Archie turned his head at her words and stared at her hiking shoes.

"Aren't we having a birthday party today?"

She pulled Archie in a quick hug. "We'll have a party when I get back."

"And after the party, we can go see the hamburger monument."

"Yes, we'll do that next week. I promise."

She went out onto the veranda, told Penelope she was

going down Devil's Cave to spread her parents' ashes, slipped Bruno in his harness—and he followed her outside, running up the forest road as if he knew they were going to the cave.

In no time, she backtracked to the house, led Bruno onto the veranda, and handed the leash to Penelope.

"Hold him for a moment."

Her father's guitar was hanging on a hook behind the door, packed in a soft black case. She strapped it to her pack, returned to the veranda, and reached for Bruno's leash.

"Why don't you leave the bloodhound here?" Penelope didn't hand over the leash. "He can't go into the cave with you."

"He'll be waiting for me outside, tied under a shady tree."

"Oh... That's why you leashed him. But you'll spend hours in the cave. Poor dog... He'll be worried, tied up alone in the woods."

True, Dessa thought, it would take her a while to rappel down into the cave, explore it, and leave her parents' ashes in a place to her liking. Climbing back up the rope with her guitar would be time-consuming as well.

"Leave the bloodhound here," Penelope insisted.

Bruno wagged his tail.

"I want to take Archie and Bruno out for a walk. Archie will feel safe with the dog and agree to come along."

Dessa nodded.

A minute later, she hiked up the winding forest road, now alone. The urn, stowed inside her pack, was pressing hard on her back, and she stopped at Saint Trinity to rearrange the load. She found her satellite beacon at the bottom of the pack, turned it on in tracking mode, and the beacon flashed green as she attached it to the pack's top.

Petite but muscular, she walked fast and only paused before the final ascent to catch her breath. She drank, looked around, and spotted Drunkard Pasko with his herd on the ridge above.

◆ ◆ ◆

Penelope sat down on the house's doorstep. The bloodhound pawed her, and Penelope stroked him. The bloodhound sniffed Dessa's sneakers by the door, nudging them with his nose. Penelope picked up one and tossed it toward the fence. The dog rushed over, grabbed the sneaker, and brought it back.

They continued playing with the sneaker. She would throw it farther and farther away, and the bloodhound would find it no matter how far. Eventually, she threw it with all her strength into the dense thicket at the gully's bottom, and the dog found it there too.

She led the bloodhound out of the gate, paused, and looked left and right. Not a soul was in sight. She let the dog sniff Dessa's sneaker again and then pressed his head toward a footprint of her shoe. The bloodhound lowered his nose to the ground, and the loose folds of skin around his head sagged forward, forming a scent-trapping cone.

"Tarsi!" Penelope commanded in Bulgarian. "Track it!"

The bloodhound picked up Dessa's scent and bounded forward. Penelope followed him up the hill, clutching the leash with her right hand and Dessa's sneaker with her left.

A couple of hours later, Penelope returned to the old house alone. She found Archie asleep on the sofa, the TV still on. She sat beside him and stared at the TV for an hour.

Her son cried out softly in his sleep, and she turned to him, watching the crimson shadows from the ongoing movie glow on his face and neck.

The villagers had told Dessa that Devil's Cave was a deep shaft leading to an underground chamber. They also admitted that none of them had actually gone down, and everything they knew was secondhand. So, Dessa wasn't sure what exactly to expect from the cave. But when she rappelled down its shaft today, landing on a pile of earth and collapsed stones, she was mesmerized by what she saw in the bright light of her headlamp.

The sparkling, airy, calcite-covered walls on both sides of the cave chamber were dry, while crystal-clear water trickled down the wall at the far end, dripping into a small lake.

Stalactites hung from the high vault, and stalagmites grew from the bottom, rising more prominently toward the far end, where they had finally met eons ago to form delicate columns around the lake, making it look like the stage of an ancient theater. A rimstone dam rose nearby, once filled with water but now dry, elegant as a court theater's royal box.

She moved to the center of the chamber. There, in a stone dish sculpted from countless water droplets, she discovered a giant cave pearl shining in an entourage of smaller ones. They had all been formed around grains of sand by dripping water that rotated them and uniformly coated them with calcite.

She approached *the royal box*. Yes, this was where she would bury her parents.

She took off her pack, unstrapped the guitar from it, and placed both on the ground. She pulled the urn out of the pack and unscrewed the lid. Stretching her hands out over the rimstone dam, she tilted the urn. Gray ashes, mixed with bone fragments as small as tiny mosaic tesserae, poured from the opening onto the ground.

She shook the urn to empty it completely, replaced the lid, and put it back in her pack.

Standing in front of the rimstone dam, she stared at the gray pile of ashes. That cone, right there, was her parents. That was all that was left of them... One gray cone.

She thought of it for a moment, then lowered her hand perpendicularly to the cone and divided it into two. She wiped her hand on her pants and looked at the two separate piles. "On the left is Mom," she whispered, "and on the right is Dad."

She pulled the guitar out of the black case, sat on the ground, leaning against the rimstone dam, and strummed the strings.

She played de Falla's *Homage.*

The acoustics in the cave were perfect.

She continued with Ravel's *Pavane for a Dead Princess.*

Her mom and dad would have loved it here... if they had not died.

For the finale, she played Bach's *Prelude in D Minor.*

The music made her feel better. The funeral had turned out well, and she had one less thing to worry about. All she had to do now was climb up the rope and go back to Zarena, which was easy. She shouldered her pack and the guitar, looked around the chamber one last time, and walked back to the shaft base. Her climbing rope hung right above the pile of earth and stones, just as she'd left it.

She began climbing up the debris.

Just then, a chilling yelp pierced the air above. She looked up and saw a body falling. The hairs on her arms stood up, and she sprang back.

But the body stopped falling with a jolt.

It turned out to be Bruno. Still in his harness, the bloodhound hung on the long leash, only two yards above the debris pile. Somebody up there cut the leash, and Bruno collapsed and rolled to Dessa's feet with a whimper. A moment later, her climbing rope, also cut, fell next to her. Bruno sniffed it and whimpered again.

The rope settled into silence.

The first thing she did was check Bruno for injuries. While groping and poking him, she wondered how on earth he could've ended up here, at the shaft bottom.

It was unimaginable that Penelope would have hiked with Bruno all the way to the cave. Penelope was a city person and didn't know the mountains. In fact, she detested them. She never hiked. It was more likely that Bruno had run away from her and come to the cave, looking for Dessa. That would be easy for the bloodhound, because he knew the route.

She understood the bloodhound could have tracked her, but she saw no reason for him to jump into the shaft. Jump and dangle on the leash like a hanged criminal.

Besides, who could have cut his leash? And her rope too? And why would they do that? She didn't know. But at least now she knew there were no visible wounds or fractures on Bruno's body. She patted him, and he lay down.

She needed to see how she could get herself and Bruno out of the cave.

There was no cell coverage. She turned her satellite beacon on, oriented it toward the narrow shaft opening above, and pressed the SOS button. The beacon's satellite connection light turned bloody red. The device was unable to connect to satellites and could not send an SOS.

That wasn't a surprise. She doubted anyone had ever managed to send an SOS from a cave before.

She turned the beacon off and scanned the shaft from its base up to the bright opening overhead. The shaft looked like an upside-down V, wide at the bottom and narrow at the opening above. Its walls were slanted, and winning the jackpot seemed more likely than climbing up with bare hands.

Yet, she had to try. The alternative was to spend the potentially short rest of her life here, and she didn't like that.

She tried to climb, grabbing ridges in the rock, pulling herself up, inevitably dropping down. Once, she reached three yards up the wall, but that was the highest she could climb.

An hour later, all her fingers bled, and she gave up.

She sat at the pyramid base, turned off her headlamp, and stared at the bright opening far overhead. Bruno dragged himself over to her.

Stuck at the cave bottom, all she could do was hope for help from outside.

But who could help her?

Earlier, hiking toward the cave, she'd spotted Drunkard

Pasko on the ridge, sensing he'd been watching her. He hadn't seen her return, so he might decide to descend to the cave mouth and check on her. When he did, he'd see her cut rope and sound the alarm.

Pasko could do all that, of course, unless he was the one who'd done the cutting. And who else could've done it? The cave was remote, and Pasko was the only man she'd ever seen nearby. If he was the one who'd cut her rope, he'd simply let her die at the bottom.

There was water in the cave, and she wouldn't dehydrate, but she had no food, so she'd starve to death.

She was a well-trained rescuer; she had dealt with people who'd starved to death, and she imagined what would happen to her as well. She'd gradually grow weak. She'd breathe slower and slower while her heart would beat faster. Her muscles would shrink, her eyes would sink. Her hair would grow colorless, her skin would flake, her legs and arms would swell, and her belly would bloat.

Toward the end, her body would be unable to produce enough energy to fight off bacteria, and she'd die from an infection.

But before she died, she would crawl to her parents' ashes, lie next to them, and only then would she take her last breath.

Her mouth was bitter. She swallowed and dropped her head. A tear rolled down her cheek. She brushed it away and moaned.

Another tear welled up in her eye. *This was the desolate pit that kept her prisoner in her dream*—Devil's Cave. She moaned again, deeply and long.

But wait!

Wait! There was hope!

Penelope was her hope.

When she was leaving, she'd told Penny she was going to Devil's Cave, so Penny knew where she was. Tonight, she would be late, and Penny would realize she was stuck in the cave.

So, it was actually a good thing that she hadn't said no when Penny had asked her a few days ago to visit her in Zarena. Penny was waiting for her in the old house, and tomorrow she was going to summon the rescuers. Dessa just had to wait for them to come and get her and Bruno out of the cave.

As time passed, the shaft's opening turned gray, darkened, and dissolved in the night; only Bruno's eyes glowered in the blackness of the cave. Dessa picked up her father's guitar and sang Bruno a lullaby.

She finished the song, set the guitar aside, and hugged Bruno, closing her eyes. She knew she had to sleep to conserve her strength. Bruno seemed to understand—and fell asleep before she did.

CHAPTER THIRTY

Sofia

"I feel most at home when I'm a stranger," Fred said.

He lay in bed, stretched out on his back, a sheet covering him up to his waist.

"How do you feel in the States?" Alma turned closer to him. "Like a stranger?"

"That's an interesting question." Fred reached out and held her hand. "At first, I felt like a stranger in the States, but it lasted only three or four years. It was only then that I was truly happy there—yes, only while I felt like an outsider. Then came a career, marriage, a mortgage, and voila, before I knew it, I became a local, no longer a visitor—fully committed and bound."

"In Bulgaria... where you're a foreigner... are you happy?"

"Well, yes. Here, my sense of being an outlander is perfect. Everything is foreign, everything is new, everything is unusual... A strange city, unfamiliar people, new cuisine," he said. "And yet, that's what makes it perfect."

New cuisine... and an exotic woman in my bed, he thought.

He looked at the chocolate curls that framed Alma's face. An exotic woman, whose ears tasted like Brazilian coconut truffles.

He turned to his side, brushed her hair away from her ear, took her earlobe in his mouth, and sucked on it for a few seconds as if he were a baby. Releasing it, he stretched on his back and gazed at the white ceiling.

"In Bulgaria, litter on the streets is a nonissue for me. Chaos everywhere is a nonissue. The graffiti, the broken sidewalks, the thoughtlessness, the negligence—it's all okay. All this is temporary and short-term because I'm here for only a couple of weeks."

He curled his lips.

"It's a foreign country where I'm just a traveler. I'm not involved, and that's why everything—both good and bad—is only a tourist attraction."

Alma's expression darkened a bit, but he was enjoying his eloquence, so he continued.

"See, with France, it's different. I'll never be a stranger there—but that's the problem, isn't it? Once you stop being a stranger, you stop being carefree. You start caring too much."

Had he read that somewhere, or had he come up with it himself? It didn't matter. The words were beautiful either way.

"An expat is never a true stranger in his native land, even after so many years. When I sojourn in France, I look at everything critically and become frustrated by even the slightest imperfection. For me, she is like a mother whom I idealize, expecting her to be flawless. Any imperfection in France annoys me."

"Really? Does Paris annoy you too?"

"Yeah, it does... Many things annoy me about Paris." He turned on his side to Alma again. "A candy wrapper tossed beneath a bench in the Luxembourg Gardens will disappoint me more than all the litter in Sofia piled together in a heap."

He touched Alma's nose with his forefinger as if it were a button, and chuckled.

"In Paris, the sight of a plump lady in leggings might put me off my meal, but in Sofia, a similar sight might whet my appetite."

Alma sat up and stared at her own body.

"Are my legs too fat?"

"Let me check."

He slid his hand between her knees, slowly trailing it

down to her feet, letting it linger there until she exhaled and turned onto her back. He shifted to caress one of her ears while kissing the other.

"I never suspected that a man with silver in his hair could have such a strong desire," Alma whispered.

Over the years, many things had shrunk, but desire wasn't one of them, he wanted to say.

But he didn't. He preferred licking Alma's earlobe to talking with her.

Fred had started his day early at the hotel restaurant, where he ate a croissant, sipped espresso, and messaged Dessa to greet her on her birthday. He returned to his suite, waiting for Alma to arrive.

She appeared dragging her suitcase behind her, as if unsure of what was meant to come. "I told them I was going on a two-day company retreat in the countryside."

He said nothing, just undressed her.

They stayed in bed for hours, their bodies' intimacy drawing their souls closer together. Their momentary fusion into a single creature, with two noses, four legs, and four arms—this unbound physical closeness—helped them grow accustomed to each other. Alma's initial anxiety visibly melted away. Their intimacy gave him not only physical satisfaction but also emotional reassurance and contentment. A much younger woman had accepted him, not just as a sexual partner but also as a potential stepfather to her son. This recognition of his health and vitality made him happy, at least for now.

He once wanted to kill himself, but he never wanted to grow old and sloppy.

Today, the sores and ulcers in his soul, opened by his wife Eva's pursuit of young men, vanished as if they'd never existed. Alma, with her healthy body—a quarter of a century younger than his—gave herself without reserve, unknowingly healing him in the process. She mended him, achieving what his shrink never had.

Now, after ten minutes of embrace, the bird of his excitement flew away for the third time, leaving him tranquil —but also strangely hollow, as if the satisfaction of the moment was slipping through his fingers.

When Alma headed to the bathroom, he grabbed his phone and browsed Dessa's satellite beacon web map. The beacon's signals dotted her route from the edge of her village up into the mountains. She was making good progress toward the cave, carrying her parents' ashes, as she had explained on Messenger.

Alma emerged from the bathroom and paused in front of him.

She raised her right leg, leaning it against the calf of her left, while holding a towel around her thighs. She stretched her free hand behind her neck and slipped her fingers into her wet curls. She remained motionless on one leg, her body rosy from the shower.

She reminded him of his favorite figure from a Picasso nude, one he had revisited a few months ago online.

"Let's not drink today—I don't want you to be a drunk like my husband."

Fred's hand tightened around the bottle neck—yet he put the Courvoisier back in the cupboard and dragged his feet to the sofa, where Alma, still naked but holding her purse, waited for him.

He sat beside Alma, who remained still for a few seconds before opening her purse. She pulled out a necklace of wooden beads, featuring a heart-shaped Orthodox icon in the middle, from which a small wooden cross dangled.

Holding the necklace with both hands, Alma slipped it over his head and arranged it around his neck. She pulled back, studying him with an approving gaze.

"You'd be better off with a crucifix—not alcohol."

What? A crucifix? He lifted the icon from his chest and looked it over.

"Who is this long-haired man in the picture?"

"This is the holy martyr Procopius, and today is his feast day. That's why I bought this necklace for you."

"Thanks." That was all he could master.

"St. Procopius is the patron saint of bees. On his feast day, honey should be eaten."

She sprang from the couch and fished a jar of honey and a spoon from her open suitcase. She sat back next to him, scooped a spoonful, and fed it to him.

"This honey is delicious." He swallowed. "However, I have to confess, I'm not religious." He licked his lips. "But you are, I can tell."

Alma reached into the honey jar and scooped some honey for herself.

"I'm religious, of course. Not that I go to church regularly, but I honor the holidays." She licked the spoon clean. "As you know, I went to Greece for Pentecost."

She scooped another spoonful, and he had to obey and open his mouth again.

"I'm aware I'm a sinner. But I also know there is a God who still loves me. He sent his only son, Jesus Christ, to die for all of us, and Jesus sacrificed himself to atone for our sins."

Alma ate more honey.

"He suffered terrible torments and died on the cross. But what can we do? We humans have no choice. We can't change our essence. We are all sinners by birth."

Fred leaned back. "I don't want any more honey."

"I feel good knowing there is a God, and I can count on Him." Alma put the honey jar on the table. "Yes, I know there is a God."

"No one *knows* there is a God." Fred kept his voice soft. "People just believe it. If they really knew, God would be indisputably one, one God for all. But He is not; every religion has its own version of God."

He paused for a moment, unsure whether to continue. He didn't want to offend Alma, but in the end, he looked her in the eye, smirked, and spoke again.

"You see, knowledge and faith are different. You know that six times four is twenty-four. And everyone else knows it, and that's why the result is the same—here, in India, or in Bora Bora. That's knowledge. It's not like this with faith because people freely choose to believe whatever pleases them."

"Don't talk like that." Alma licked her lips. "Faith in God is important. Everyone's life depends on it."

Choosing to say no more, he rose, walked to the cupboard, and pulled out the Courvoisier bottle. He took a swig, the cognac spreading warmth through his chest before settling in his stomach.

He sat next to Alma and hugged her bare shoulders, his other hand still holding the bottle.

"Every human life depends on three basic drives: to breathe, eat, and have sex. Three drives that live deep in the darkness of our subconscious."

He took a sip from the bottle.

"Breathing is a tireless, asexual worker, predictable and reliable."

He lifted the bottle to his nose, savoring the cognac's familiar bouquet of anise, fig cake, and praline.

"Eating is like a plump nanny, not necessarily noble but with a good character."

He took another sip, and this time he caught a tangy trace of dried citrus and cocoa.

"And sex is the bad boy in the group, a naughty Bacchus."

He rose, capped the bottle, and tucked it back in the cupboard.

"I live without a god—and at peace with my natural drives." He sat next to Alma. "I've lived this long without it, and I'll continue to. You understand, don't you?"

"Yes, I do." Alma looked down at her hands. After a few moments, she met his gaze and smiled. "I understand you. But I believe that one day, you'll find God too."

Alma pulled her phone out of her purse. Fred grabbed his phone, opened Dessa's beacon web map, and checked the dots marking her route. Clicking the last one, he reviewed its timestamp—the signal had been sent three hours ago from near the cave mouth. Dessa would soon pull herself out of the cave, he thought, and walk back to the village.

"Are you still in touch with your wife?" Alma turned her phone to him.

Eva's sparkling green eyes stared at him from Alma's Facebook app.

"No... We're already divorced." The lie came easily. "I'll have to unfriend her."

Alma tapped the screen a few times.

"Your ex-wife paints?"

"Yes, she does."

Alma stared at the screen, raising her eyebrows.

"This naked man here, is he a friend of yours?"

He glanced at the painting. Eva had posted a picture of some new guy seated on a motorbike in the backyard.

"No, he's just her friend."

Alma kept browsing through Eva's paintings.

"And the other men are her friends too?"

"Yep."

Fred, surprisingly, found himself getting aroused by the conversation. He set his phone next to the honey jar on the table, hugged Alma, and caressed her.

A few minutes later, he was making love to her again.

In front of him, Alma's body moved in rhythm with his thrusts. Bending forward, he grabbed her shoulders and continued moving, and all he could see were her curls.

The wooden necklace dangled from his neck, the icon and cross swinging back and forth across her back.

Alma giggled, and he froze.

She explained with laughter, “Saint Procopius tickles me.”

He stood up, pulled the necklace off his neck, and tossed it to the floor. Licking his lips, he leaned forward again and resumed his labor over her naked body.

Fred lay half-awake in bed, Alma dozing beside him.

The hum of an electric motor and the rattle of an elevator door broke the quiet. In the hallway, voices buzzed, a child screamed, and a quarrel erupted, all fading behind the adjacent suite door.

Startled by the noise, Fred rose and reached for his phone. Five hours had passed since Dessa’s last signal had appeared on her web map, with no new signals since.

Perhaps her beacon’s batteries had died.

He checked Messenger to see if she had been active, then opened Facebook, but found nothing new from her.

Alma stirred next to him and opened her eyes.

“What are you reading?”

“I’m reading the news,” Fred lied.

“What’s new...?” She yawned, stretching. “Ah... What’s the news?”

“Some mechanic stole an empty passenger plane from Seattle airport.” He chose a news story he had read a week ago. “The guy took off, flew over Puget Sound, but was soon intercepted by two fighter jets. Seeing them, he dove the plane, nose-first, full throttle into the ocean.”

Alma peeked at his screen.

“I was looking up that guy’s Facebook profile.” He flipped the phone cover shut. “I wanted to learn more about him.”

“Um... Did you learn anything?”

"Yes… His friends say his girlfriend left him for another guy, and he just couldn't get over it. They believe he planned to fly to the island where she lived, crash the plane into her house, and kill her—and himself too."

Fred suppressed a sigh, remembering his own suicide attempt.

"Once the fighter jets intercepted him, he faced a choice: return to the airport doubly disgraced or die. I think he chose death to end his misery."

"Twice disgraced? How come?"

"First, he was disgraced when his girlfriend hooked up with another man. Second, his attempt at revenge ended in a ridiculous failure."

"He had probably been depressed."

"People sometimes want to kill themselves without being really depressed, but to punish someone, or get revenge, or provoke compassion."

Alma just yawned.

"We all harbor, more or less, a subconscious death wish," he mused. "Paradoxically—our fear of death seems to drive us to seek and desire it."

"Oh, enough about death. I know I'll die one day, but that's for God to handle, not me. It's not something I have to take care of."

He looked at her, puzzled.

"Didn't you ever want to kill yourself, just a little bit?"

"Kill myself? No way. If I did, who would look after my son? The thought has never crossed my mind."

She rose from the bed and dressed.

"I'm going to order some pizza for dinner," he said.

"Don't waste your money. I brought homemade food." Alma opened her suitcase and unpacked several food containers. "I told the folks back home I'd need this for the retreat."

He watched her as she served the food onto plates. She was sweet, taking on the role of hostess in his hotel suite.

Yes, she seemed to enjoy being his hostess. And she surely wanted to avoid room service costs—and awkward explanations if seen dining with him after claiming she was at a company retreat out of town.

Fred woke up in the middle of the night and snuck into the bathroom with his phone. He checked the web map for new signals from Dessa's satellite beacon but found none. An ache forming in his chest, he hurried to text her a message, riddled with typos. He waited a while but did not get a reply. All he could do was return to bed and lay restless, imagining everything terrible that could have happened to her, compulsively rechecking for signals.

The night was dying when he stood at the window and gazed at the first light of dawn in the eastern sky.

Why hadn't Dessa signaled? Where was she? What could have happened to her?

He didn't expect anything from her, just that she was okay, healthy, and safe.

He left Alma sleeping in the hotel and took a taxi to the bus station to catch the first bus to Zarena, Dessa's village in the mountains.

Yes, he had left Alma behind in the hotel, but he planned to call her later, explain himself, and ask for her forgiveness.

CHAPTER THIRTY-ONE

Balkan Mountains

Fred, seated at the rear of a secondhand intercity bus adorned with German inscriptions, tracked his position on Google Maps. In the third hour, the app's blue dot traced a winding mountain road. It passed a spa resort squeezed into the canyon, and he realized he had to get off at the next stop.

Fifteen minutes later, the bus pulled into a rest area. The driver, without a word, wobbled toward a roadside kiosk with a green tin roof, his legs stiff. The passengers spilled out and followed the driver to the kiosk.

Fred was the last one to get off the bus. He noticed two fellow passengers—village women with bags in their hands—crossing the main road to take a side road along a mountain creek. That was the route to Zarena, so he hastened after the two women and even overtook them on the ascent. Panting, he passed old houses and crossed a narrow bridge over the creek. The road forked here, and he halted, unsure which way to go. To the left, a tree-lined street followed the creek, its sidewalks peppered with linden blossoms. To the right, a steep street loomed ahead, climbing a ridge lined with uniformly plain red-brick houses.

He continued left along the creek, where the sweet scent of linden blossoms filled the air. Moving at a steady pace, he took in the surroundings: a neglected kindergarten across the creek on the left, an old post office to the right, and a rusty, padlocked infirmary door on the left. Ahead, a new chapel stood on the right, just before a bend in the street. He passed a small park with a colt tied to a tree beside a war memorial and continued to an underground public toilet swarmed by flies. From there, he reached the village center, where the town hall, a café, and a general store stood.

He paused in the middle of the street and looked around.

The café patio was full, with patrons seated under brand-new advertising umbrellas. Each was emblazoned with *Kamenitza Beer—Men Know Why!*

Across the street, an elderly man in gray work clothes, seated on a shabby chair by the general store entrance, sipped from a half-liter *Kamenitza* bottle. A hunched-over woman wearing a black headscarf approached the man and spoke to him. He replied and then stared at Fred. The woman also turned to look at Fred. Probably a married couple, Fred decided and headed toward them.

"Good day. My name is Fred."

The elderly man extended his hand for a handshake. Fred shook it before extending his to the woman.

"I'm looking for one deep cave," Fred said in his broken Bulgarian.

A boy holding a Snickers milkshake walked out of the store. He glanced at Fred, stopped nearby, and sipped.

Fred gave the old man a slight bow. "My friend Dessa Sinich is in big trouble there."

The man took a sip from his beer. "Dessa Sinich?"

"Yes, Dessa Sinich... The only thing I know is that she has an old house which is on the edge of the village, near a small church in the field."

He paused, somewhat discouraged by his struggles with the Slavic language. Perhaps he could fare better with Google Translate?

"Well, our church may be old, but it is very nice," the elderly woman said. "Today, however, there is no service, and it's locked." She looked at her husband. "The new priestling hasn't returned from Sofia yet."

"I didn't have an old church in mind," Fred turned to the boy, gazing at his waist-long braid.

"English?" the boy asked.

Fred confirmed, pulled out his phone, and launched Google Translate in dialog mode.

"I'm Fred."

"I'm Jesus."

Fred conversed with Jesus quite well using his phone as a mediator. It turned out Jesus knew where the cave was and offered to take him there. Fred agreed with a handshake, and Jesus led him up the street along the creek.

The elderly man shouted something in Bulgarian after them. Jesus paused, shouted back, and turned to Fred.

"The old man told me to take my colt to the cave, but he doesn't know the route is too steep and overgrown for riding."

Jesus pointed toward the village park.

"My colt will be happy grazing until I return."

Jesus strode up the street, and Fred hurried to follow him.

Fred and Jesus made their way out of the village, reached a trailhead, and climbed up a wooded slope.

There was no one around, and Fred wondered if he should have trusted Jesus so easily—a strange boy with an odd name and a bizarre braid.

He looked at his phone and froze. "I'm afraid we're not on the actual cave route."

His mouth went dry in an instant.

Jesus glanced at him, eyebrows furrowed, but said nothing.

Fred licked his lips. "Here, look!" He turned his phone toward Jesus, showing Dessa's beacon web map, where her signals shaped an arc.

"Yes, we are." The boy shrugged. "We're just taking a shortcut. Up in the meadows, we'll join Dessa's path."

Fred felt his ears grow hot and tried to laugh. Lowering his chin, he followed Jesus up the trail.

He was glad the steep climb was over at last, and they emerged into the open meadows high above the village. It took them a while to cut across the tall, dense grass and reenter the forest.

As they pushed farther into the woods, Jesus's phone rang. "My mother." He picked up the call.

Fred stole a look at his own phone map and parted his lips in a slow smile. Indeed, they were already following Dessa's route.

Uttering a few words in Bulgarian, Jesus hung up. "I told my mother I wasn't going home for lunch." He slipped his phone into his pocket, and they headed onward.

It was still before noon when they traversed a steep, slippery rock and stopped at the cave mouth.

"This is the Devil's Cave," Jesus said.

Fred knelt on the edge. Below, the cave's shaft was pitch black.

"Dessa!" His voice echoed into the abyss.

A voiceless whiff of wind stirred the leaves.

"Dessa!" he shouted.

Again, only silence.

"Dessa, answer me!" Fred screamed.

Another moment passed in silence, until a dog barked somewhere below, muffled as if from Hades—and then Dessa's voice drifted up, weak and far away.

"Fred, is that you?... Sorry, I was asleep."

Still kneeling, he turned to Jesus, grinned, and raised his hand for a high-five. Jesus slapped his palm with all his strength. Fred pretended to stagger toward the shaft, and Jesus, stunned, jumped back. Fred laughed and bent over the edge again.

"Dessa, are you all right?"

"No, we're not! How could we be all right? The dog and I are terribly hungry... We're as hungry as wolves, but we have nothing to eat, and we can't get out to go to McDonald's before it closes."

He grinned. There was no McDonald's in the mountains. Dessa was joking already, and that was a good sign.

"I'm here with a friend, and we'll call for a rescue," Fred yelled. "Except I don't know if rescuers will bring food."

Jesus called 1-1-2, speaking briefly in Bulgarian. "The operator promised to tell the Mountain Rescue Service," the boy said in English, hanging up.

All Fred could do now was be patient and wait. He passed the time talking to Jesus.

He asked Jesus about his mother, but the boy avoided the question and pulled out his phone, showing him pictures of his colt instead. Then Fred asked Jesus what foods he'd like to eat —and told him in detail how he would cook them. Fred was hungry, just like Dessa, and suspected Jesus was starving too.

"Actually, I've brought some food," Jesus confessed.

He stood up and pulled a Snickers bar from his pocket.

Fred discussed the situation with Jesus, and the boy agreed that they should drop the Snickers bar to Dessa. After they did, they turned off their phones to conserve battery power and lay back on the grass, close to the rocky edge of the shaft.

Inhaling the aroma of grass and pines, Fred mellowed—and the weight of exhaustion hit him—worn out from his date with Alma, the sleepless night, the bus trip to Zarena, and now the hunger.

Next to him, Jesus stayed awake, his eyes wide open, watching the birds soar in the sky.

Fred turned his back to Jesus, closed his eyes, and drifted off to sleep.

◆ ◆ ◆

Fred awoke when the rescuers—five men and a young woman—arrived around four in the afternoon. He stood up, blinking, and stared at them.

The men wore a mix of T-shirts, all paired with red helmets. The young woman sported a pink T-shirt adorned with deer antlers and emblazoned with *Hunter Girl.* A towering man, shouting various commands, wore a helmet barely large enough for his big head. The helmet was marked in white with his last name, *Ivanov.*

Without much ado, the rescuers set to work preparing ropes for the descent, while Fred watched from the side. They knew their work—all the ropes were ready in twenty-five minutes. After one final check, Ivanov and the hunter girl disappeared down the shaft.

Fred crossed his fingers. It wasn't over until it was over. Anything could happen. He caught Jesus's eye and hid his hands behind his back.

But then, what could go wrong? The ropes were secured, rescuers descending, Dessa waiting unharmed below. Soon she'd climb out safely, and he would finally rejoice.

He was Dessa's savior, just as she had been his nearly a year ago in the North Cascades.

Standing tall with his legs spread, he waited for her.

Dessa's head popped out of the cave.

"Woo-hoo!" Fred pumped his fist in the air.

He clapped his hands together as two men in red helmets helped Dessa over the edge. He stepped closer when they began releasing her from the ropes.

At last, Dessa stood up in front of him. He hugged her, and she rested her head on his chest for a moment or two, before pushing him away.

"I'm glad you're here... but how come?"

He explained how he had traced her on her web map,

seen she was in trouble—and came to the rescue. He didn't mention anything about Alma, though.

Dessa thanked him, managing a strained smile. She glanced around, seemingly searching for someone, before puffing out her cheeks and exhaling.

Soon after, Ivanov and the hunter girl emerged from the vertical cave shaft, hauling up a dog and a guitar. Fred watched Dessa embrace the dog, just as she had embraced him minutes earlier.

"Is this your dog?"

"It's not just a dog. It's a bloodhound. His name is Bruno."

Bruno licked her, and she kissed him on the snout.

Oh well, Fred thought, *not just any dog—a bloodhound that got a kiss, while all he got was a lousy hug.*

He watched Bruno wag his tail and nuzzle into Dessa's hand. Then he smiled. It was all right. Everything was as it had to be, and he was happy.

They ate and drank what the rescuers had provided, then gathered the ropes and headed back to the village.

As the sun began to set, the group traversed slanted meadows, passed a countryside chapel, and descended the forest road toward the village's first houses.

Bruno barked, dashed in front of everyone, raised his bottom to the sky like a professional acrobat, and began to walk on his front paws along the roadside bushes while peeing on their top branches. He continued for ten yards, and, having relieved himself, dropped back to all fours, turned to the group, and barked again.

Fred and Jesus laughed, and everyone else joined in except for Dessa.

"Back to the veranda!" she yelled, and the animal sprinted down the road, disappearing behind the curve.

The group reached the first house in the village, a whitewashed, weathered abode. Everyone paused, and Ivanov spoke to Dessa. Fred listened, catching only snippets: "Report... tomorrow police... questions... the incident... the cut ropes...

the dog and everything."

"Take care." Ivanov switched to English, first turning to Fred, then to Dessa.

"Yeah, be careful," the other rescuers called.

Jesus shook Fred's hand. "Take care."

Everyone said their goodbyes. The red helmets headed toward the village center, with Jesus trailing them.

"They parked their SUV at the trailhead down by the creek," Dessa said, walking through the gate.

Fred followed her across a grassy yard into the old house. It had been a good day, and he hoped the evening would be just as good.

CHAPTER THIRTY-TWO

Archie sat at the table, playing *The Vanishing Hitchhiker* on his phone, while his mother watched TV at the other end. When he'd asked his mother half an hour ago what she was watching, she'd said she didn't know.

He caught muffled footsteps in the yard. The front door creaked open, and Dessa appeared in the vestibule, pausing at the room doorway. A man peeked over Dessa's shoulder, glancing at him.

Archie recognized the man. He'd seen him in Dessa's SAR pictures—images of people in uniforms. He tossed his phone on the table, leaned back in his chair, and smiled, then rocked back and forth. "Dessa, that's Fred, right?... Dessa, that's Fred..."

Dessa stepped closer and ran a hand through his hair. She turned to his mother, parting her lips as if to speak, but no words came. Instead, she looked back at him.

"Last night, I called you... But you didn't answer."

"I was in the wilderness and out of coverage."

"You like sleeping in the wilderness, don't you?"

"Yes, I do."

"Where did you sleep?"

"In a cave." Dessa turned to Fred, still standing in the doorway. "I got stuck inside, but Fred found me and called the rescuers."

Archie glanced at Fred, hoping for more details. Instead, Fred's stomach let out a loud growl, and Archie quickly shifted his gaze back to Dessa.

"I asked Mother if she could call the rescuers, but she said there was no need to panic because you often sleep in the open."

"Yes. I often sleep outside, and most times have no coverage to call."

Fred's stomach growled again, and Archie couldn't help but smile.

"My belly is a villain who quickly forgets past meals," Fred said. "He's hungry again. I have to cook dinner to calm him down."

"You're my guest and are not supposed to—"

"Today, you're the rescuee... Besides, I'm the search-and-rescue chef, remember? I should do the cooking, and you should rest."

Archie thought Fred had a good point.

Fred waved his arms. "Now, I'll need the table."

Archie's mother and Dessa settled on the sofa, so Archie dragged his chair next to the wall, allowing him to watch his mother, Dessa, and Fred without turning his head.

Fred peered into the fridge, then rummaged through the cupboard. He pulled out four eggs, a packet of rice, a can of tomatoes, an onion, a dusty bottle with two fingers of olive oil at the bottom, salt and pepper shakers, and a package of dry mint, lining them up on the table.

"There isn't much here." Fred turned first to Archie's mother, then to Dessa. "But I can cook sorrel with rice given what's available."

"There isn't sorrel here either." Archie's mother's voice scratched like when she had her morning cough.

"I saw sorrel in the meadow around the chapel." Fred gestured toward the door. "I'm going to forage there and pick some before it's too dark."

Fred stepped out. Archie's mother and Dessa talked in low voices, even whispered. Archie caught his mother telling Dessa, "Bruno ran away."

Not wanting to eavesdrop, Archie pulled out his phone and played *The Vanishing Hitchhiker*. He had waited for Dessa all day, playing *The Vanishing Hitchhiker*. If she hadn't come back tonight, he would have played it again tomorrow, finding her just like he found the hitchhiker girl so many times today.

When Fred returned and opened the squeaky front door, Archie's mother and Dessa stopped whispering, and Archie's mother clenched her teeth; her lips reddened, swelling as if inflated by a bike pump. Fred stood in the doorway, raising a bag full of sorrel over his head, and tried to smile, but his smile didn't come out well.

Fred set about cooking his sorrel. Archie didn't like sorrel, so he stopped watching Fred and switched to watching videos.

When Fred served the food, the four sat around the table. Each had a plate of sorrel with rice, topped with an egg. Fred pounced on the food, and Archie knew Fred's stomach wouldn't growl anymore. A bark came from the veranda—it was Bruno. Dessa hurried out to feed and water him. When she returned, she dove into her meal like Fred.

Archie's mother stared at her plate without eating, and Archie did the same.

"Archie, try it," Fred said. "It's delicious."

Fred's plate was already empty.

Archie took ketchup from the fridge and doused his egg with it. He plucked his fork into the mix, ate a bit, and pushed the dish away.

"Archie, eat your food," his mother said.

"I don't like sorrel," he muttered.

"You have to eat it anyway."

Archie looked at Dessa, and she was biting her lip.

"I don't like sorrel," he repeated.

"Fine—go to bed!" His mother's voice was louder now.

"But I want to stay," he whispered.

"Go to bed now!" His mother's fist hit the table with a thud.

Archie slid out of his chair and slunk toward the door, his breath hitching.

"March to your room!" his mother yelled behind him.

Archie dashed up the stairs, crying like a banshee. Footsteps pounded after him, and he feared his mother was coming, but it turned out to be Dessa. She hugged his shoulders and led him to his room. He kept whimpering, worried she might leave him alone and return downstairs. But Dessa didn't leave him alone and stayed with him until he fell asleep.

After Penelope retreated to her room, Fred sat in silence, the living room still saturated with the echoes of Archie's cries, watching as Dessa prepared the sofa for him.

"Thank you for dinner." Dessa headed upstairs.

At the door, she paused. "It's a pity the evening ended so badly."

"It could have been worse." He glanced at her. "You could still be in Devil's Cave."

True, it could have been much worse. He could have been in Sofia, making love to Alma while Dessa died alone in the cave. But he had arrived just in time to rescue her. She was safe here, and he couldn't ask for anything more.

Dessa entered her bedroom and reached for the lock, but the key was gone. She checked the other side of the door, shrugged, and stepped to the window.

Right now, she needed Christo.

She gazed at the village lights, still lit, not too late. She took out her phone and dialed his number.

Christo didn't pick up.

Five minutes later, he called her back. The first thing she heard was water running, as if he were filling a tub. His subdued "Hello" came next.

"How's your son?" Dessa asked.

"He is... he's okay... But I have to make a sacrifice for him."

Christo's sigh cut through the running water.

"What sacrifice?"

"My wife is pregnant."

So, it was over.

"I'll have to help her, because if I leave her alone, his life... my son's life... even though he is completely innocent... will be ruined."

"Who is the father?"

"Who is the father?"

A pause.

"I don't recall..."

"You don't recall who the father is?"

"I don't recall sleeping with my wife."

She straightened, a smirk tugging at her lips.

"It's not what you think!"

Christo had lied to her, and she was done with him for good.

"I have to go before the milk boils over."

"The milk will boil over... Um, who boils milk this late?"

She didn't answer.

"Wait, don't go!... Please!"

"The milk will boil over."

She hung up.

Christo had taught her body to feel passion again, and she was grateful. Yet he had also deceived her, and she couldn't forgive that.

She was done with his lies, done with him.

She turned her back to the window and found Penelope looming in the doorway.

"I heard everything—and I know everything."

Dessa stared at Penelope, who held the missing key, wagging it between her forefinger and thumb.

"But I forgive you. I'm not going to ask you anything about that man."

Dessa didn't want to stay in this room any longer. She glanced at the door, and Penelope rushed to close and lock it.

Clenching the key in her fist, Penelope stepped to her and kissed her on the cheek.

"We'll start a new life together." Penelope pressed the fist holding the key to her own chest. "We'll be happier than ever before."

She took a step back from Penelope. "You don't understand... We can't be happy together... I can't be... Please, let me go."

Penelope scowled, chewing her cheek for a few seconds.

"You're not getting out of here."

Penelope strode to the window. "I'll prove I'm not kidding." She threw the key out.

"What have you done!"

"I locked the cage." Penelope's eyes glinted. "The birdie can't fly away now."

Dessa looked out the window.

An owl perched on the ridge of the veranda roof, with the moon rising overhead. Her eyes wandered down the street, and she spotted the key shining among the cobblestones.

She could rappel down and retrieve the key in less than a minute.

"You're not walking away from me," Penelope said, raising her voice. "You promised your brother."

The next thing Dessa knew, pins and needles crept up her legs, covered her arms, and leapt to her face.

She closed her eyes and reached out to Philip. *Brother, I love you.* She squeezed her eyes tighter. *I love you, but I'm lost. Penelope wants to enslave me for life, and I don't know what to do.* A sob rose in her throat, but she forced it back down. *Please, help me find my way.*

A whiff of wind blew through the open window and ruffled her hair. She opened her eyes and looked out; the owl spread its wings over the veranda roof, rose, and disappeared like a good spirit into the night sky. A feather dropped from the bird and floated to the ground.

Her eyes followed the falling feather.

An owl shedding feathers to grow new ones meant change and rebirth, and the bird soaring in the air suggested freedom and independence. That's what she'd learned from little Archie, the dead Sheldon Bird, and her rescue partner, Clifton.

Yes—she was going to change. That's what Philip had just told her.

She was going to free herself from Penelope, now.

All the pins and needles in her face vanished with the bird, and she felt light as a feather.

"You're not leaving me," Penelope snarled.

"I've already left you, and you're a stranger to me," Dessa said, turning to Penelope. "You can't change anything."

"I'll prove to you that I can."

Dessa opened her mouth to object, but Penelope yanked a Swiss Army knife from her pocket and flicked it open.

Dessa gasped.

"That's my knife... Did you cut my rope with my own knife?"

"Yes, I did."

Penelope approached her, waving the knife in front of her face. The blade gleamed in the lamplight.

"Put that away," Dessa said.

Penelope didn't seem to hear her.

"You'll be mine. Yes, you'll be mine!"

She retreated to the door, arms raised in defense, and locked eyes with Penelope.

"No, Penelope!... No, I won't belong to you! Not anymore!"

Penelope dropped the knife to her side, stepped forward, and paused two steps away.

"You'll be mine forever!"

Penelope's mouth corners hung down, her eyebrows arching up, her eyes squinting. A mere two feet away from Dessa's eyes, Penelope's face transformed, resembling an ancient Greek tragedy mask.

"You'll never forget me..."

Penelope flung her head back and closed her eyes. Her hand shot up, and the knife's blade sank into her neck.

Penelope's blood splattered onto Dessa. Her palm opened, releasing the bloodied knife, which clattered to the floor. As if in slow motion, she slumped over it, wheezing, gurgling, and going slack. A pool of blood gathered on the carpet around her head.

Dessa squeezed her eyes shut for a moment. Then she stared at Penelope, and her muscles stiffened.

She knew she had to act fast to stop the bleeding without suffocating Penelope.

She yanked the blanket off her bed, knelt by Penelope's head, and pressed the fabric against the wound.

The cut was deep, and blood soaked through the blanket, staining her hands.

Penelope had severed her carotid artery, Dessa realized, hence the extensive bleeding. The strike had been powerful; the blade might've even reached Penelope's spine.

She gazed at Penelope's face, now devoid of any tension. Yet, there was no calmness either. It was immaculate but utterly expressionless, resembling a sculpture by a technically skilled but uninspired artist.

She stood up, stared at her bloody hands, and her knees gave way.

But she was a rescuer, a warrior—and on the search-and-rescue battlefield, she'd seen it all. Climbers, nearly frozen—brought back to life. Hikers, vanished without a trace—never found. Children, injured in ravines—saved. Bodies, bloated in rivers and lakes—recovered. Every time, she managed to quell her emotions, focusing on the rescue itself. There was time for feelings once the mission was done.

Now, too, she needed to stay cool, stay calm. Keep it together—like she had at Wallace Falls, on Baring Mountain, in Devil's Cave. Even Penelope's death—her ex's death—shouldn't throw her off-balance. It mustn't. It wouldn't.

She closed her eyes, drawing in a deep breath and holding it for a few heartbeats before exhaling steadily. She focused on the tip of her nose and inhaled again.

After a dozen breaths, her body softened. She glanced at her hands, now trembling less. She wiped them across her pants and dialed 9-1-1, but the call didn't go through.

Of course. She was in Europe—she needed to dial 1-1-2.

When the call connected, she reported what had happened, and emergency services said they would be there as soon as they could.

Hanging up, she stared at the door. Penelope had locked it and hurled the key out the window. Dessa was trapped here —with Penelope's body—unless someone helped her get out.

She dialed Fred, but her call went straight to voicemail. Fred was sleeping downstairs and might hear her if she shouted—though she didn't want to risk waking Archie next door.

She had no choice but to rappel out of the locked room.

After rummaging through her climbing gear, she pulled out a rope and secured it to the bed frame. With one last tug to test its hold, she climbed over the windowsill, swung outside, and rappelled down the wall to a downstairs window. She knocked on the glass, and Fred stirred, rising from the couch in the dark.

He opened the window and gazed at her. "Dessa!"

The rope bit into her hands.

"The moonlight around your head... You look like a saint."

"I'm no saint."

Fred's eyes widened. "Is that blood?"

"Yes, it is. Now back up."

She swung onto the windowsill, landing in a squat, and

jumped into the room.

"Can you help me wash up?"

CHAPTER THIRTY-THREE

Fred stood at the window, staring into the night. "Why haven't the cops arrived yet?"

Dessa stirred in her chair, her throat raw. "Zarena is a tiny village." Deep in the Balkan Mountains, they were far from the services they'd taken for granted in Washington State. "There's no law enforcement here. The police have to drive all the way up the mountain from the county seat."

Fred left his post at the window and sat opposite her. "You haven't had your tea."

"I tried… I couldn't swallow."

She bowed her head.

"Do you want anything else?"

She raised her eyes to meet his, her chin quivering. "I want to reverse time and handle everything differently." She let out a sob. "I'm a rescuer, not a murderer."

"You're not a murderer—not even indirectly. It was Penelope who wanted to murder… murder *you*—didn't she?"

"Yes… but that was because Penny was sick. I should've been patient with her. I should've taken care of her—instead of thinking of myself."

"Taking care of others but forgetting about yourself," Fred said. "Do you know what that is?"

She just stared at him.

"I call it rescuer's syndrome. It's like a drug; it gives you pleasure, but in the end, you end up devastated."

She knew he was right. Taking care of her brother made her happy, giving her a place in her family. Rescuing strangers brought joy too, earning her a top spot in the SAR community. But sacrificing herself for Penelope had been a trap.

Dessa brushed her tears away and peered at Fred.

"Remember the last time you visited me in my trailer?" he said. "When you told me you were nothing—but a speck of dust in the universe? You were so blue."

"I had no confidence back then."

"Exactly. After four years serving Penelope, you lost all belief in yourself."

She nodded.

"You had no confidence—even though you're such a sharp rescuer."

She couldn't help but agree. She was a fine rescuer, and she saved many strangers. But in the end, she had to save herself too.

Police sirens wailed in the distance, their shrill tone slicing through the silence. She glanced at Fred, and he offered a reassuring smile.

She swallowed her tears.

Who would have thought, after the way they'd met a year ago—when she'd hoisted him off a cliff face and carried him to safety—that Fred would be her only support in this surreal moment?

CHAPTER THIRTY-FOUR

Two Years Later

After Penelope's suicide, Dessa left Bulgaria and moved to Seattle, resetting her life. Every now and then, she would talk over the phone with Lenka, her Bulgarian neighbor in the mountain village of Zarena.

It was Saturday, and Dessa called to check the village news.

"A horrible rainstorm hit us the other night," Lenka said. "All the roofs in the neighborhood leaked, but yours didn't."

Dessa wasn't sure if that was good or bad news.

"I went in, and the house looked good. The house looks nice inside and out, but nobody wants to buy it." Lenka lowered her voice to a whisper. "People say your dead spouse's soul still lives in there."

"Penelope was not my spouse."

"Um... yes... She was only your fiancée."

As far as Dessa was concerned, Penelope wasn't her fiancée either, but it didn't really matter. Penelope haunted Dessa's old Bulgarian house, just as her shadow haunted Dessa's soul, but Dessa knew she had to live with it.

Living with Penelope's ghost was the price Dessa paid for her freedom.

She decided to change the subject.

"What else is news?"

"Drunkard Pasko isn't herding our cows anymore."

Dessa didn't ask why; Lenka would tell her anyway.

"The doctor said he has cirrhosis and must not work."

Apart from Fred, Pasko was her only witness in Zarena two years ago.

"The doctor said Pasko is a good man and only looks evil because of his cirrhosis."

Two years ago, Pasko had told the cops that while he was herding cows near Devil's Cave, he spotted a foreign-looking woman go to the cave with Bruno and return without him. His testimony, alongside Fred's, confirmed Dessa's account of Penelope's visit and suicide and helped her avoid a murder charge.

Pasko was indeed a good man, and cirrhosis was a terrible disease to happen to a good man.

Dessa stayed silent for a few seconds.

"Who's herding your cows now?"

"We take turns herding them ourselves." Lenka chuckled. "When you come to visit us, we'll let you take turns too."

The line hummed for a moment.

"Because you love to hike, don't you? So, you could hike with the cows."

Lenka laughed, and Dessa laughed along with her.

Two years after his mother's death, Archie was living in Honolulu with his grandparents, who treated him well. They gave him a weekly allowance. They let him take his phone to school, just as his mother and Dessa had before. They also bought him an iPad for his homework.

He chatted with Dessa on Messenger every day, except when she was busy with her job. Chatting with her made him feel good, but he wished they could be in the same room. But that wasn't possible since she lived far away in Seattle, not in

Honolulu.

He feared their separation would last forever unless he somehow moved in with her. He wanted it more and more, so he started making plans—but told no one. He didn't even tell Dessa. His plans were a secret that nobody in the whole universe knew. Nobody but him.

As usual, he found everything he cared about on YouTube. Depending on how he felt on any specific day, he'd watch videos of insects, different countries' flags, toilet fixtures, or fireworks. He used to watch videos on ceiling fans too, but he wasn't interested in them anymore.

He also watched one video that was not about insects, flags, toilets, or fireworks, not to mention ceiling fans. It was a news clip about a boy who walked out of his home in Georgia and took a bus to the airport.

He watched that newsclip every day and knew it by heart. He remembered everything the newsman and the newswoman said.

"The boy really wanted to board a plane and fly away," the newswoman would say, "but he had neither a boarding pass nor an ID."

"His desire seemed impossible in today's world," the newsman would add, "given how seriously American airports have taken air travel security since 9/11."

It was the newswoman's turn to talk. 'Yes, it seemed impossible, but the boy found a way to pass through security and board the plane,' she would conclude.

What that boy did was slip into a large family, blending in as they cleared airport checks and boarded the plane together.

However, the boy was unlucky. That particular flight was fully booked. He couldn't find a free seat and wandered around the plane. A flight attendant caught him, and he was escorted back home by the police.

Yes, that boy was unlucky. One always needed a bit of luck to achieve something big.

Archie's school year began in early August. One morning, he walked out on the street with a backpack to catch the school bus. But that day, instead of boarding the bus, he hailed a taxicab and soon found himself at the airport.

He browsed the flight board and walked to the Seattle flight's check-in counter. A family with five children was just leaving the counter. The father hurried ahead with his three boys. "C'mon, we're going to miss the plane," the father said. Carrying a crying baby in a car seat and a bag, the mother somehow managed to follow them. One of the kids, a blue-eyed, blonde-haired girl with a Disneyland bag, trailed behind, swinging her arms and humming.

The girl seemed nice. Archie approached her and walked beside her.

"Hello," he said.

"Hello," she replied.

"My name is Archie."

"I'm Anna."

"Where are you going?"

"Seattle," Anna said.

"I'm going to Seattle too."

Anna smiled at him.

"Will you let me carry your bag?" he asked.

"But it's pink!" Anna said. "Not good for a boy; it's too girly."

"No problem. I'm a gentleman."

Anna pulled out a doll and handed him the bag.

The baby was still crying when they reached the security checkpoint. As they stood in front of the security agent, the agent's mouth slid into a brief grimace, and for two seconds, he looked like someone who really disliked crying babies. The father handed the agent a bundle of IDs and boarding passes. The agent grabbed them, processed them in about twenty seconds, handed them to the father, and waved his hand, and the whole group proceeded to the X-ray machine.

Archie, still holding Anna's pink bag, kept chatting with her as they walked. He told her about the monarch butterfly's migration to faraway lands, and she told him about her family's Disneyland vacation a year ago. He liked it when, occasionally, they would fall silent for a moment and look into each other's eyes before talking again.

Before long, he revealed to Anna that he had run away from home and was going to see his Aunt Dessa, who had bought a new home near Seattle. See her and her new puppy too.

Anna said nothing, just gazed at him. But her eyes were glowing, and he knew she was going to help him.

When Anna's family was about to board, the baby wasn't crying anymore, and Archie wondered what would happen now. Then Anna took him by the hand, and her touch was warm and soft. Together, they watched the gate agent count the boarding passes, and there were seven. The agent counted the heads: the father, the three boys, the mother, Anna, and Archie himself. She should've counted the baby too, but she missed it, probably because it was quiet at that moment.

They all passed through the gate like a cloud of butterflies.

Anna's father had reserved seven seats in two middle rows of the Boeing jumbo jet. The eighth seat was vacant, so Archie took it.

Archie knew this was his lucky day.

The baby wanted to eat, so Anna's mom had to feed it. The boys argued about Nintendo, and Anna's dad joined in. Once the plane took off, there was some peace and quiet, and Anna's parents checked on the kids. Anna's mom exchanged words with Anna's dad and turned back to Archie.

"Where are your parents?"

He did not know what to say, so he only glanced at Anna.

"They're in the back," Anna chirped. "We'll go see them."

The two went to the back of the plane, took two free seats by the window, and watched the clouds pass by. After a while, Anna told him she had to return to her parents, and he had to stay put where he was.

Before Anna left, she kissed him on the left cheek and hugged him, then kissed him on the right cheek. His cheeks were still red-hot when the plane descended for landing, but they were only slightly warm by the time he boarded the light rail to the city.

Dessa was at home when Chewbacca Junior barked and rushed to the door. Someone knocked; she opened the door and found Archie with a school backpack. The little Afghan jumped up, resting his front paws on Archie's thighs, trying to lick his face as he leaned down to pet him. She pulled the puppy away and turned to Archie.

"What are you doing here?"

"I came to live with you."

She phoned Archie's grandfather, Tim, in Honolulu immediately.

Tim thanked her for calling and said he and Betty weren't surprised that Archie had traveled alone all the way to Seattle and was now with her.

"Not surprised at all," Betty said. "He set a bunch of your pictures as his tablet's wallpaper, so he would see a different picture of you every time he used it."

"Betty and I understand everything, you know," Tim added. "We had actually talked several times about you and him."

"And we think that two parents are, on average, better than one..." Betty said.

"...but just one good parent is better than two not-so-good ones," Tim finished her thought.

A few seconds dragged on in silence.

"We are old, and we will pass away sooner rather than later, and Archie will be left all alone in the world," Betty said. "Unless he is with you."

Right. Tim and Betty were old, and she was young. If she didn't crash with the helicopter, she'd live long enough to raise him. She could be Archie's family, and he could be hers.

Her brother wanted her to be with Archie too. She glanced at the boy—kneeling on the floor, hugging Chewbacca junior, gazing at her.

But of course—she'd be happy to raise him!

However, she didn't intend to be his caretaker for life, endlessly catering to his needs while neglecting her own. She would teach him to provide for himself and meet his own needs.

She said goodbye to Tim and Betty—then embraced Archie, kissing his temple as he leaned against her.

Penelope, or more precisely what remained of her body after cremation, had spent the last two years in an urn at the New Hope Columbarium in Honolulu. Her ashes rested in a double granite niche in a four-foot wall of blue Brazilian marble with onyx ornaments. She was conveniently located at eye level next to the ashes of important citizens. Her parents had provided her with the best.

She knew they would come every Sunday after church, sit on a bench covered in snow-white enamel, and gaze at her—gaze at her picture, to be precise—and torment her with their feelings and thoughts.

Her dad would listen to the murmur of the solar fountain, wondering what in the world had led her to attempt to take Dessa's life and then take her own. The old man usually blamed himself. He thought he had not been a good father, though he did not know what he had done wrong.

Her mom would take in the exotic scents of the flower

garden without thinking much. "This is how it had to be," she would say to her dad, "because God always does the best He can, even when He punishes us... Yes, the best for everyone—for Dessa, Archie, you and me, and our dear Penny."

Penelope wished she could tell her parents how it all was. Tell them that not only had Dessa gone to California by herself, leaving her alone with Archie, but she had also gotten rid of her engagement ring. Tell them she couldn't get over it and developed depression. Tell them she suffered outbursts of jealousy and rage, outbursts that led her to kill Chewbacca and—after learning Dessa preferred another person to her—destroy a painting of Dessa's lover and twice attempt to murder her.

Tell them that it was easy to cut Dessa's rope while she was in that cave, but it turned out to be impossible to slit her throat in Dessa's old house as Dessa looked her in the eye.

She wished she could tell them how disgraced she felt back then. Disgraced not only when Dessa dumped her for that painter but also when she failed in her revenge attempts. Tell them that, in the end, all she wanted was to kill herself and end her misery.

After an hour on the bench, her parents would walk away, taking small steps with their shoulders slumped. Walk away and leave her in peace. At peace, at last.

Fred was getting married in the morning.

It had all begun a couple of years ago, when he met Alma online and later slept with her in Sofia. At the time, he'd thought it was just a fling—and for him, it was. He'd enjoyed his time with Alma and flown home satisfied.

Back in Washington, he did his SAR duties, cooking for the team during rescue missions and cleaning the food truck afterward.

Rescue missions, however, weren't that frequent, and

most of the time, being a recent retiree, he didn't know what to do with himself. So he thought a lot. He thought of Dessa's cave ordeal and Penelope's suicide. He also thought of his fling with Alma.

A couple of months later, he realized that Alma was the first thing he thought of when he woke up in the morning. She was also the last thing he thought of before falling asleep at night.

Was he falling in love? Falling for a married woman who was ten time zones away, probably cooking dinner for her husband right now? Wasn't that a bit too silly?

He tried to resist his heart by thinking of Alma's flaws. Alma's hands were too big. Alma had freckles on her back. Alma laughed too loudly. Alma wanted him to quit drinking and go to church.

Thinking of Alma's flaws didn't work, though, because the more he thought of them, the sweeter they seemed.

The more he thought of her, the more he desired her.

He didn't want to surrender to his heart, so he decided to stop messaging her forever. Yes, forever!

He managed not to get in touch with her for two weeks, and just as he thought his brain had won over his heart, he surprised himself by writing her a long message, asking her if he could revisit her in Sofia.

She agreed, and he flew to Sofia to meet her. After a few months, he did it again, and then again.

A year later, Alma divorced her husband. Fred traveled to Sofia once again, and they spent every hour she had free from work together.

Just before he departed, he proposed.

"Will you marry me?"

Alma glanced at him, seemingly hesitating.

"If you marry me, I'll buy us a home next to Seattle's Russian church."

"Why the Russian church?"

"Because there's no Bulgarian church in Seattle."

"I know, but there is a Greek one, and I like it better than the Russian."

He took a deep breath.

"If you marry me," he proposed again, "I will buy us a home next to the Greek church."

"Will there be a room for my son?"

"Yes, there will be. Besides, we'll buy him his own car."

"Why would he need a car?"

"He must have a car so we can send him to play tennis anytime we want to be alone and make love."

She laughed and sealed the deal with a kiss.

"You're so romantic," she said, kissing him again.

True, he was romantic now, and Alma had always been practical. They were so different. But they were going to complement each other, just as cognac and dark chocolate did. Being different and complementing each other was why they were going to be happy.

Tonight, he had embraced her as a lover one last time. Come tomorrow, they would hug each other as husband and wife.

Still breathing heavily, he turned to his side and gazed at Alma. He touched her forehead and drew his forefinger along her face, down to her nose, paused for a moment at her lips, went down her chin and neck, and stopped at her chest.

Next, he caressed Alma's left eyebrow, then her right one.

Alma closed her eyes and turned her head to the side. He leaned over her, kissing her neck, and gazed at her until she opened her eyes and turned her head toward him.

"You've changed," she whispered.

"How have I changed?" he whispered back.

Alma closed her eyes again and remained silent.

He held her hand and waited.

"When we first met," Alma whispered again, "you only played with me before sex. But now, you play with me after sex too."

He nodded and rested on his back.

He had changed, indeed.

When he'd met Alma for the first time two years ago, sex was just a way for him to prove his masculinity. Now, sex was a way for him to show how much he loved her. That was how he had changed.

Should he tell Alma how much he loved her?

No, he'd show her instead.

When it came to love, showing was always better than telling.

He embraced Alma and began showing her his love once again.

Dessa wanted Archie to help her cook Seattle-style hot dogs for dinner.

"Put them on the grill," she said, handing him a pack of bratwursts.

She set buns, cream cheese, and sauerkraut on the table, then opened a can of pink lemonade concentrate, poured it into a pitcher, added water, and stirred it.

When the bratwursts were cooked, she had Archie plate them. They started eating and talking about the future while Chewbacca Junior, who'd had an early dinner, snoozed in his corner.

"When I grow up, I'll have a hot dog and pink lemonade stand." Food bulged in Archie's cheeks.

He got out of his chair, turned it so the backrest was to the side, knelt on the seat with his legs stretched back, and took another bite, stuffing the food in with his fingers.

"Why are you eating like that?"

Food bulged in Archie's cheeks. He chewed and washed it down with pink lemonade.

"I'm practicing for hot-dog-eating contests."

"But why on your knees?"

"On your knees, you can reach and grab whatever you have to eat for the contest a lot easier. Also, you can move and shake to help wiggle the food down faster."

She opened her phone's camera and pointed it at Archie.

"Wait!" Archie sprang from the chair and sat back down. "Now, take a shot at table level."

She kneeled on the opposite side of the table and took a close-up shot, just the plate and the boy's face.

"The picture turned out so nice because I'm sitting, not kneeling or standing," Archie said.

They finished dinner and cleared the table.

Half an hour later, Archie went to bed.

"Now tell me the story of Baba Yaga."

She told him that same story every night, a tale from her native country. Twisting and changing it was their bedtime ritual.

"Once upon a time, there lived a witch, Baba Yaga," she began. "People thought she was weird just because she liked to dwell in the forest in a hut standing on chicken legs. But she only seemed weird. She was good-natured and kind, and she actually helped everyone. Santa Claus was flippant and irresponsible once and did not want to deliver presents to the children. Baba Yaga took the bag of presents and delivered them for him."

"Except nobody knew it was her," Archie added. "She also helped children with their homework. And she cooked many delicious hot dogs for the king."

"But she loves to fly her broom to and fro," Dessa continued. "That's why everyone thinks she's a bit weird when in fact, she's nice."

"She likes to fly her helicopter as well," Archie said.

"Yeah, the helicopter too." Desa smiled.

Archie smiled back at her. He stayed silent for a few seconds, then yawned and fell asleep.

Her phone buzzed with a message.

It was a new mission call.

She donned her uniform and headed out into the night.

SEVEN SHORT STORIES

SCENE FROM POMPEII

"Where's Fred?" Jaden stretched and yawned. "I haven't seen him since yesterday."

Irritation flared through Eva at the mention of Fred, but she forced a smile. Fred often vanished, complicating things. "He's a grown man," she chirped. "He'll manage."

She tightened her short kimono and bent down to open the oven door, the hem brushing against her bare legs. "Forget about Fred—I cooked you a meal while you slept!" She pulled out a tray with four fish. "Baked trout wrapped in grape leaves!"

Jaden didn't even look at her. He yawned again, walked to the fridge, grabbed a bottle of orange juice, and reached for a glass.

"Don't!" She sprang up. "Don't drink that juice. I'll peel you a real orange—a big one, just like you."

"Whatever... Juice is orange too. I want juice."

"Juice isn't an orange—it's liquid sugar. No pulp, no fiber, no vitamin C. Trust me, I'm a professional."

When Eva was a culinary arts student, she had worked at Starbucks. After their wedding, Fred got her a job as a waitress at the college faculty club. She graduated, had twin boys, and returned to work at the club. For the past ten years, she'd been the proud manager of the place.

"Well, if juice is so bad, why do you buy it?" Jaden asked.

"I didn't buy it." Standing by the table, she was peeling an orange. "That fool of a husband did."

Jaden stepped closer, towering over her by a full head. She rose on her toes to slip a slice of orange into his mouth, then wrapped her arms around him, imagining his milk-chocolate skin beneath Fred's black bathrobe. A moment later, she sensed Jaden swallow, his throat catching as he breathed in the scent of her hair. She was glad she'd dyed it first thing that morning—coppery red with an herbal-based dye.

Eva had found Jaden online, on the Cougar Life dating site. The young men she'd met before him would spend a night or two with her and then disappear, but Jaden stayed. At first, he visited during the day, sitting still for hours, his eyes following her brushstrokes, but in the evenings, he'd return to his mother, a Seattle woman who had raised him alone. For the past week, though, Jaden had started spending both days and nights with Eva. She'd managed to keep him from dwelling on Fred, who often wandered around with a hangdog expression—in the hallways, the kitchen, or out on the porch of the family house.

An hour later, Eva and Jaden finished lunch. She cleared the table, started the dishwasher, and, with a glance, invited him into the living room. Sunlight streamed through the picture windows. It was her favorite time to paint.

Jaden, still in Fred's black robe, lay on his stomach on the couch, dutifully turning his face toward her. She perched on a stool in the middle of the room, lifted her bare legs onto the easel's crossbar, and began working with her brush.

The next hour dragged on in silence. Bored, the Labrador

flopped down by the fireplace and dozed off.

Painting was dull without music. Eva jumped up and started looking for the remote. She spotted it behind the couch —so that's where it was—along with a pocket edition of the Kama Sutra.

She aimed the remote at the family TV and scrolled through her favorites. As the song streamed, she grabbed her palette and settled back behind the canvas. Raising her voice to sing along with the music, she danced across the canvas, brush in hand.

"*Come on, baby, hop on the truck, hey; let's ride, honk honk.*"

Jaden stirred. He sat up, cross-legged on the couch, facing Eva as she straddled the easel. He grinned and joined in the song.

"*We'll be rocking, oh yeah, just jump on board, baby.*"

Eva swayed her hips back and forth.

"*I'm ready to ride, honk-honk! I'm ready to ride!*"

It was Jaden's turn again.

"*Stop pretending and come along! Come along!*"

Eva beamed.

"*I'm not pretending, and hey, I love coming along with you!*"

Just then, her phone rang.

"Please, keep singing, don't stop!" She answered the call.

Two minutes later, the song and the conversation both came to an end.

"My sister." Eva tossed her phone under the easel and turned to Jaden, speaking through gritted teeth. "Yesterday, Fred tried to hang himself on a tree near Pilchuck—but the branch broke, and he tumbled down some rocks. The rescuers airlifted him, and my sister picked him up at the hospital. Now, she and her husband are coming to get his things. Fred's going to stay with them for a while. Can you imagine? The two of them are going to take care of him."

"Damn..." Jaden muttered.

Eva paced back and forth.

Jaden watched her, his eyes flicking left and right. She could tell the boy was worried, but at the same time, she knew he couldn't be serious for long. To him, everything was a joke in the end.

Calming down some, she stopped next to Jaden.

Jaden rubbed his armpit. "What do we do now?"

"What do we do? We'll just keep working. There's not much left. I'll finish the painting before they get here."

◆ ◆ ◆

Eight years ago, during a family trip to Anacortes, Eva had no idea that the day would change her life forever. They were simply browsing galleries, enjoying a quiet Sunday outing—but everything shifted when Fred became captivated by the watercolors at the Magic Arts Gallery and struck up a conversation with Maggy, the Bulgarian expat who owned it.

"I graduated from the Academy of Arts in Sofia and worked as a model in Germany, in Kaiserslautern," Maggy explained. In Kaiserslautern, she met Kevin, an American Air Force pilot stationed nearby. They got married, and 42-year-old Kevin retired. For five years, they traveled the world before eventually settling in Anacortes. There, they bought the gallery, and now, while Kevin played golf, Maggy painted and ran the business selling her artwork.

Eva's gaze dropped as Maggy finished her story. "Oh, how I wish I could travel someday... paint... live an interesting life..."

"Why someday?" Maggy smiled at her. "You could start this August."

It turned out that the Magic Arts Foundation was organizing a summer workshop in Bulgaria, on the Black Sea coast. The trip was supposed to mix cultural adventure with creative freedom, Maggy said, explaining how being in a new, welcoming place would spark inspiration. There was still one open spot at the time, though Maggy wasn't sure how long it would last.

Fred, of course, hemmed and hawed, arguing it was too expensive. But when Maggy told him that all the foundation's proceeds supported a home for Bulgarian orphans, and he gave in.

That was how Eva ended up spending two weeks by the Black Sea. She painted in the mornings, swam in the afternoons, and in the evenings, she went out to taverns with the group. Toward the end of the workshop, she met Vitaly at the hotel bar. The young associate professor from Moscow was in Bulgaria for a conference on Eastern European history. They spent the next three nights together.

As they parted, Eva invited Vitaly to visit her in the States. It was her first time with someone other than her husband, and she didn't want to forget him. But at that time, their twins lived with them, and besides, Fred wasn't quite used to such things yet. So, Eva talked to her sister, Laura, who was single back then, and Laura agreed to arrange an invitation for Vitaly and host him at her house.

Vitaly arrived in Washington State from Moscow for a two-month visit. Laura, a real estate broker with flexible hours, took it upon herself to show him the West Coast.

Eva asked her sister to send pictures from the trip every day—and Laura did—so Eva knew what the two were doing: in Snohomish County, they hiked through the moss-covered trails of Lord Hill Regional Park and visited a salmon hatchery, where Vitaly marveled at the size of the fish. In Seattle, they rode the ferry to Bainbridge Island, ate clam chowder at Pike

Place Market, and took in the view of the city from the Space Needle. Continuing south into Oregon, they explored the Columbia River Gorge, stopping at Multnomah Falls, and crossed into California, where they had fun navigating the theme parks at Disneyland.

But then the stream of photos Eva had been receiving from her sister dried up. And that wasn't all—Laura and Vitaly stopped answering her calls.

When the two returned to Washington, Laura informed Eva that she and Vitaly had grown close and decided to get married—brazenly justifying it by saying that Eva's extramarital affair with Vitaly had been harmful to her family. Moreover, Laura claimed, showing no shame, that by marrying Vitaly, she was doing Fred and Eva a favor, as well as their twins—and even Vitaly himself.

Furious at the betrayal, Eva boycotted the wedding and cut off her sister for a year—leaving Fred bewildered. In time, though, the sisters made peace. Vitaly got his U.S. green card and became an associate professor at Snohomish College. During the school year, he regularly lunched at the faculty club and exchanged a few words with Eva now and then.

Eva had left the door open, not wanting to deal with the awkwardness of a greeting. The crunch of gravel signaled her sister's car pulling in—and Laura and Vitaly walked straight in, Eva's Labrador bouncing around them in excitement. Jaden stood, pulling the robe tight around himself. He glanced at Eva, waiting for what would come next.

"This is my favorite model." Eva looked into her sister's eyes, standing tall—her back straight and her chin neither raised nor lowered. It wasn't difficult; she was calm and at peace with herself. After a moment of silence, she shifted her eyes to Vitaly, then to the easel, parting her lips.

"I'd better head outside." Jaden went off to look for his clothes.

Eva watched him leave through half-closed eyes, pleased that her sister was staring at her.

"I'd like to take a look at the painting," Laura said.

Eva nodded and stepped around the easel, with Laura and Vitaly following behind. She waved a hand toward the canvas, where a beefy black bull mated with a bronze heifer. Beneath the heifer's thrown-back mechanical head was Eva's own face, her mouth wide open in ecstasy. The bull had a mask resembling Jaden's face. In the background, a herd of cows grazed peacefully, and among them slouched an old ox—Fred.

"My God!" Laura's lips parted, but no other words came.

"Oh, that... I know that story. I've even seen something like this painted in Pompeii." Vitaly launched into the tale.

Eva smirked. She'd learned *that story* in a hotel bed far away in Bulgaria. Vitaly himself, holding her in his arms, told her more than once about how Poseidon gave King Minos a divine bull, and how Minos's wife, Pasiphaë, fell in love with the animal. Consumed with desire, Pasiphaë went to Daedalus, the master craftsman, and had him build a hollow wooden heifer she could hide in so she could approach the bull. Daedalus built it so expertly that the bull was fooled—and eagerly mounted it.

"And that's how the queen got to experience the pleasures of beasts and her own secret desires." Vitaly said, his tone betraying excitement over his little lecture.

Jaden appeared from the hallway, wearing baggy jeans and a black hoodie. He nodded to Eva and made his way to the door.

"Where are you going?"

"I don't know."

"Better not catch you playing Angry Birds at the arcade again."

"You won't catch me," Jaden said, slamming the door. Outside, he turned toward the window, puckered his lips in a fish face, stuck his tongue out, and wiggled it up and down. Eva wagged her finger at him, just like she would at a child—and Jaden winked at her, hopped on his bike, and disappeared.

"Does his mother know he's in the painting?" Vitaly smirked.

Laura snapped at him. "Go collect Fred's clothes!"

The two sisters were now alone—and Eva knew that practical, composed Laura expected explanations.

Fine, she'd give them—not because she had to, but because she wanted to.

She sat on the high stool in front of the painting and stretched out her bare feet.

"I don't love Fred anymore. Not at all.

"You see, in the beginning, I actually enjoyed sex with him. I was just an innocent student, and he—as you know—was a professor, a French one at that. I found him fascinating. When I got married, I thought it would always be like that."

Out of habit, Eva lifted her feet onto the easel's crossbar.

"But things didn't turn out the way I'd imagined. I expected him to have ambitions, to achieve more, but all he cared about was French food and wine..." She hesitated, "...and lazy sex. He must've thought we were dinosaurs with spikes on our backs because he never tried anything other than belly-to-belly. You see, until recently, I slept with him regularly—but I didn't enjoy it at all because I was disappointed."

"And now with Jaden, aren't you afraid you'll be disappointed again?"

"I don't care. I'm taking all the risks!"

Laura closed her eyes and rubbed her temples. Eva suppressed a smile. Laura now worried about her and Jaden, but she had once taken her own risky chances—with Vitaly.

A few seconds later, Laura opened her eyes and looked at her. "What does Jaden do for a living?"

"He's a plumbing specialist, but right now, he's in a transitional phase—and between jobs. He wants to start a design studio—luxury bathrooms, high-tech toilets, kitchens, things like that. I'll help him."

Eva had no doubt and didn't hesitate. "Jaden's very capable, very artistic. He can go far."

Vitaly appeared, holding a plastic bag.

"Fred has a lot of socks with holes. Should I take them?"

He rummaged through the bag and pulled out a purple sock, embroidered with a red heart beneath a red trim. A hole gaped next to the heart. Vitaly waved the sock around, grinning, but Eva barely reacted—it was time for the couple to leave.

Eva closed the door behind them and walked over to the window. She watched as the two piled Fred's things into the back seat before settling into the front.

In the car, Vitaly suppressed an urge to pull away when Laura reached out, took his hand, and squeezed it. The two remained still and silent.

Laura freed his hand. "Let's go buy Fred some socks!"

As Laura backed down the driveway, Vitaly glanced up at Eva's window for just an instant—and met her cat-green eyes.

THREE GRAY MICE

A month ago, Fred tried to hang himself on a tree near Mount Pilchuck. The branch snapped, and he slid toward the abyss, the rope still looped around his neck, until he came to a stop on a ledge. An hour later, a young rescuer in an orange jumpsuit hoisted him up into a helicopter. She brought him back to civilization, alive and unharmed—but his heart kept bleeding.

Since then, Fred had been living in a camping trailer, courtesy of his sister-in-law Laura and her learned Russian husband, Vitaly. Heartbroken, Fred preferred to be alone, cooking for himself and avoiding the couple next door. Today, however, they took the day off and convoyed him to Seattle to see a French movie together. He knew they wanted to cheer him up.

The film turned out to have no English subtitles. He realized his hosts would grow—sooner rather than later—bored with movie dialogue they could not understand.

"Who thinks they are ugly?" Madame Gagnebin asked from the movie screen, her gaze sweeping across the room. No one in the auditorium raised their hand. Everyone was silent. And strangely enough, he felt he was the one who was supposed to respond.

"Since no one admits they are ugly..." continued the professor from the film, "since no one admits..."

Laura's phone vibrated, and she fumbled through her purse. The screen shone and lit her face. She rose, and the thud of her seat silenced Madame Gagnebin's words. She sneaked past him and walked out of the cinema.

"So now I want you to take a piece of paper and list several things that you see as ugly," Gagnebin ordered and waited, her back turned to the students.

Everything is ugly for me right now, Fred responded in his mind.

Marriage. His wife's infidelity. His age. Being old, useless, unloved—and unable even to kill himself. Everything was just so ugly.

Laura came back, slipped into her seat, and whispered to Vitaly. Fred realized she was talking about his wife, Eva—and it pained him every time he caught her name in the darkness.

He tapped Laura on the shoulder. "Let's leave and have some coffee." She whispered to her husband and nodded back to Fred in agreement.

Fred and the couple exited the cinema and crossed the alley. As they settled into a local café, Fred sipped his coffee, jotting notes on a napkin. Opposite him, Vitaly launched into a Russian joke, his loud voice shattering the quiet. Laura's laughter echoed around the table, but Fred barely noticed.

Vitaly turned to him. "What are you scribbling?"

"Everything is ugly for me right now," Fred recited from the napkin. "Marriage, infidelity, suicide, old age. Everything is so ugly."

"Infidelity and suicide are ugly." Vitaly grinned. "Except when some genius describes them as beautiful."

"What are you talking about?" The Russian was already getting under his skin.

"Obviously, I'm talking about Anna Karenina." Vitaly's voice carried a touch of unwarranted cheer. "In life, being abandoned by your lover and run over by a train is quite disgusting, but in the novel, it is beautifully described. My countryman Tolstoy turned an ugly story into a masterpiece."

Vitaly sipped his coffee and raised his index finger, as if speaking to a pupil. "The true artist can make a masterpiece out of anything!"

He seemed to contemplate it for a while.

"To distill premium cognac from sour wine, that's true art," he said, winking at Fred, and continued, smirking at Laura, "and to cook an insipid borscht out of fine vegetables, that's kitsch par excellence."

The Russian sniffed his coffee cup, sipped again, and wrinkled his nose.

"This coffee is quite bland. It would be much better with a bit of cognac and whipped cream." He gazed at Fred. "French coffee has both, but they don't serve it here."

Fred lifted a shoulder, offering no comment.

"We can stop by O'Hara," Laura said. "It's on the way to the parking lot anyway. They have a promotion, free chips with each pitcher of beer."

She glanced at Fred, and he nodded. She turned to Vitaly. "But the French coffee there is Irish."

Vitaly grinned. "Oh, that's all right. I will put up with Irish coffee."

He'd put up with anything, Fred thought, as long as it had enough alcohol in it.

Fred trailed behind as the three of them made their way

down Mercer Street. The city's noise was distant, as if muffled by the twilight.

They passed a martial arts school, its windows flooding the street with light. Slowing down, Fred glanced inside: a dozen students in white jackets, black pants, and yellow belts stood like soldiers in a row, mimicking the instructor as she stretched her arms forward.

Fred caught the patter of hurried feet behind him and turned around. A petite brunette in a martial arts uniform nodded at him before slipping through the entrance.

The young woman had the same face and bright eyes as his rescuer! Could it really be her? Had she recognized him—and nodded in acknowledgment?

He couldn't be sure, and there was no way to find out. Vitaly and Laura, who had stopped ahead, were waiting for him. Vitaly waved, urging him to catch up.

A short walk later, they reached O'Hara. The pub was empty, with the TV flickering untended on the wall. The barmaid was scrolling her phone, one leg on the floor and the other leg bent against the door of the beverage fridge. Her short, tight dress—black with red and white vertical stripes on the sides—accentuated her young figure quite well.

He followed Vitaly and Laura inside. The barmaid slid her phone under the counter and straightened up.

"Hi, I'm Christine. Welcome!"

Fred sat at the bar and let the other two order the drinks. Silent, he listened to the coffee grinder whirl and the espresso machine gurgle. He watched Christine pour the brewed coffee into a tall glass, add brown sugar, and blend in a shot of Tullamore Dew whiskey, then fulfill Vitaly's request and pour two more shots of the whiskey.

In the end, the tall glass was packed, with no room for cream, so she only decorated it with a cinnamon stick before serving it to Vitaly. She filled a pitcher of beer and placed it in front of Fred and Laura, along with clean beer mugs and a bag of chips.

"Christine, may I have a plate for the chips?" Fred tried to hide his dismay.

He was a Frenchman, after all, so he preferred the finesse of porcelain.

Christine slid a plate in front of him. "I like your accent. Where are you from?"

"Paris."

"Paris!... But do you like it here?"

"It's okay. I got married and stayed... I stayed here for love."

"Oh, that's so beautiful, so romantic... I don't think it's gonna happen to me, though."

"You don't need it," he said, then muttered, more to himself than to her, "A man marries for pure love, only to find out that his wife is Messalina."

Christine raised her eyebrows as if the name Messalina meant nothing to her. Just then, Vitaly, done with his Irish coffee, reached for the pitcher—and poured beer into his coffee glass before Christine could offer him a clean mug.

"Messalina was a Roman empress," Vitaly said, raising his glass to the barmaid, "who had a long string of lovers." He took a gulp. "A very long one, indeed." He gave Christine a knowing smirk. "But what can you expect from a young and beautiful woman married to a docile old man?"

Fred's chest grew cold as he watched the Russian gulp again and shake his head.

"Her hubby Claudius was nearly three decades older than Messalina."

Fred frowned. True, Eva had been twenty-one—just like Messalina—when they married, but he had been only forty-three. Claudius, by contrast, was five years older at his wedding.

Fred massaged his temple. Vitaly was giving him a headache. Why was he dropping hints and making comparisons?

"Of course, Fred was happy with the enormous age gap —" The Russian hiccupped. "Excuse me… I mean Claudius."

Fred bit on a chip and sipped from his mug. Was Vitaly trying to insult him? Or was he just getting drunk, the Russian way?

Keeping his eyes closed for a few seconds, he listened to the Russian refilling his beer and slurping the foam.

"He was certainly happy with the enormous age gap, but Messalina became unsatisfied with the marriage quickly, and she—"

Fred caught Laura giving her husband a funny look.

"Never mind… All those stories about Empress Messalina working as a prostitute and sleeping with twenty-five men in one night are political slander," Vitaly said, glancing at Laura and then at Christine. "They were made up by Tacitus and a couple of other brown-nosed historians like him, simply because the powers at the time were enemies of Messalina's clan." Vitaly drained his glass and wiped his mouth with the back of his hand. "In reality, Eva was always a sweet, lovely woman."

It took Fred a few seconds to realize that Vitaly had said Eva instead of Messalina.

Laura stared blankly at the bag of chips, and Christine lowered her head, confused.

The silence stretched, prickling Fred with discomfort.

He broke it, turning to Christine and trying to catch her eyes.

"May I ask you where you're from?"

"Flagstaff, Arizona... I grew up near the Grand Canyon."

"How do you like it here?"

"Well... it's not bad, but I can't feel completely at home... among all these millions of people with millions of cars." Christine shook her head and laughed. "I feel like a mermaid in a sea of cars."

Two women in matching leather jackets walked into the pub and sat at the opposite end of the bar. Christine approached them, and the three began an animated conversation. Laura used the pause to step down from her barstool and head to the restroom.

Vitaly emptied the pitcher into his glass.

"You are lucky." He smirked at Fred. "The mermaid likes you."

Fred glanced toward Christine before lowering his gaze to his mug.

Nobody likes me, he thought.

Fred's head throbbed, each beat in sync with the muffled bass from the TV's speakers. Vitaly let out a burp that filled the room and, with nothing better to do, stared at the screen, where a melancholic rapper swayed, singing about his loneliness. The Russian began humming along, his notes slurred and uneven.

Fred disliked rap. His head was about to burst, so he closed his eyes yet again, pointed his face towards the floor, and rubbed his temples. The wretched rapper continued with the hook.

"I'm feeling lower than ever before, down, down, down, sinking to the floor."

When Fred's headache softened somewhat, he opened his eyes and found, right between his shoes, a little gray mouse sniffing a piece of chip. The mouse bit down on the morsel and scampered off. Fred followed it with his eyes until it hid behind a column.

He had never heard of a mouse in a pub before.

He dropped a chip crumb between his legs. The mouse ran back, its eyes glinting, grabbed the piece, and darted away.

He picked a few fresh chips and munched one while crushing the others as softly as he could and dropping them under Laura's barstool.

The singer—and Vitaly—went on.

"I've been working to fix my ego, but it's broken, broken, broken, shattered like a whiskey glass."

Fred looked at the floor and found three gray mice scurrying among the chips. He fixed his eyes upon them and froze in silence. Vitaly noticed his lowered head and traced his gaze down to the mice.

"Mice! Do you see them?!"

"Oh, that down there? That's chips. There are no mice," Fred said, making a poker face as he watched the three rodents huddle around the chip crumbs on the floor.

Laura came back, slamming the door, and the mice skittered away. She climbed on her barstool and crunched on a chip.

"What's wrong with you two?" Laura looked at Fred and Vitaly, both mum. "Did something happen here?"

"Vitaly saw mice under your barstool."

"Just mice? If he doesn't stop drinking right now, he'll be

seeing flying blue elephants pretty soon."

Vitaly flushed, his temple vein pulsing. He jumped from the barstool, knocking it down, and stumbled towards the door. Fred, pretending to be concerned, stood up, watching him disappear into the night.

Laura ran a hand through her hair. "I don't know what's wrong with him."

She waved to Christine.

"Don't worry, Fred." Laura waved to the barmaid again. "Vitaly will get home by train. He can do it on autopilot."

Fred wasn't worried.

Three little mice kicking the devil out of the Russian. An act of priceless revenge.

He glanced at the chip crumbs on the floor and smirked.

Fred rushed after Laura as she bolted out of the bar, his breath catching in the cool night air. He and Laura paused on the sidewalk and looked around, but Vitaly was nowhere to be seen. They hurried to the parking lot, pulled out of downtown and headed north along I-5.

The traffic was slow, people commuting from work to their suburban homes all alone. As far as Fred could see, red lights shone ahead like strings of rubies in the darkness; on his left, garlands of diamonds floated back towards the city.

An accident happened a hundred yards in front of them, and Laura jumped on the brakes.

An hour passed before the traffic started moving again.

The kitchen lights were on when they got home, Vitaly nodding off at the bare table.

The Russian glanced at Laura, a bubble of saliva

glistening at the corner of his lips. "Everything's fine." He turned to Fred, his gaze unfocused. "I simply dropped the reins, and my horse brought me straight here."

Fred bid the couple goodnight and headed for his trailer. Out on the porch, he overheard them already bickering.

He chuckled to himself. Bickering was a family trait. His wife Eva, Laura's sister, thrived on it.

Anyhow... He was going to divorce Eva. Divorce her, live free as a bird—and do whatever he wanted.

Do whatever he wanted, like going to bed without brushing his teeth, just like when he was a boy.

He undressed and slid under the covers. He closed his eyes, envisioning Christine the barmaid in her tight dress, its vertical red and white stripes outlining the curves of her body.

A minute later, he pulled the cover over his head.

The warmth of his breath spread over his eyelids. Two angel wings unfurled from Christine's shoulders as her dress transformed into an all-orange jumpsuit. Her face morphed into that of his rescuer—the young woman who had hoisted him from the cliff into the helicopter a month ago. His orange angel.

Fred's lips curled into a faint smile before he fell asleep.

THE BIGGEST INJUSTICE

Vitaly stepped into the faculty club and scanned the room. It was nearly empty, save for a whispering pair in the corner —Mei Chang, the junior art instructor, and Kip Mott, the slouching sculpture professor—and Roberto, a waiter in black ironed trousers and a spotless white shirt, who was picking up spilled salad from under the buffet.

Eva sat alone at her desk near the buffet, behind a *Manager* sign and a laptop. Beside her, a twisted metal sculpture of Romeo and Juliet gleamed—Kip's gift, Vitaly remembered. The lovers were made from dessert forks and tea balls, polished to a glow like fake silver.

He'd never liked this sculpture.

Eva raised her head, her cat-green eyes locking onto his —and stood, as if she'd been waiting. Without a word, she gestured in the direction of the buffet, but something in the way she moved made Vitaly pause. Was it her familiar motherly attitude, or something else?

All he needed was lunch, nothing else.

"We have vegan barbecue and roasted salmon with herbs and lemon," Eva said. "I'd recommend the salmon. It's packed with vitamins, sulfur, selenium, antioxidants... It's good for your heart." She paused, waiting for his response.

"Fine."

Eva, her posture rigid, moved ahead, glancing back at him. He followed.

She motioned toward the dessert stand, sweeping her arm like a conductor showing off an orchestra. "We've got oatmeal cookies and little pastries, but today we also have some artistic desserts. Look at this sailboat." She pointed at the plate, watching him. "The sea is made of blueberries, the boat's a slice of melon, and the sail's a tiny triangle of watermelon."

Eva kept talking, but Vitaly just nodded. He'd heard enough.

"These were made by the culinary students." Eva spun on her heel—and her skirt flared briefly as she headed back to her desk.

Vitaly loaded his plate and sat down. Chewing without feeling the food, he flipped through a book.

At two o'clock, Kip and Mei left. Vitaly watched Roberto clear their table, his hands darting to gather plates and wipe the surface, as if he'd done it a thousand times. (He had.) The dining room grew quieter, emptier. Vitaly tossed a handful of blueberries into his mouth, closed his book, and stood up to leave. Just as he slung his bag over his shoulder, Eva appeared at his side.

"No need to rush." Eva's smile was somehow rehearsed.

He hesitated.

"Stay. I'll bring you some coffee and cookies."

Vitaly nodded and sat back down.

He reopened his book, sipping coffee and chewing on a cookie. Across the room, Eva busied herself, helping Roberto clear the buffet with the same energy she always displayed.

It didn't take long before Roberto left. Eva returned to Vitaly's table with a cup of coffee and sat across from him.

A minute passed in silence—and Vitaly stirred in his chair.

"What are you doing for Columbus Day?"

"Nothing. I'm an individualist; I don't follow official holidays. Spontaneous ones are much better... And you?"

"We'll be together, Laura and I, as usual. She wants us to go to a nursery outside of town to buy more bushes and trees. She also wants to plant garlic in the garden... says homegrown garlic makes everything taste better... you know your sister. We'll spend the day working in the yard, and in the evening, we're going to a ballroom dance class."

"Romantic."

"I don't know... it could be annoying. Sometimes it's better to be by yourself." He rubbed his neck. "And you? How did you end up alone? Laura told me you were happy with Jaden."

Vitaly caught a spark in Eva's eye.

"Jaden dreamed too much. Like a child."

"Tell me about it."

"It happened one night. At three in the morning, Jaden woke up, sweaty and anxious."

Vitaly studied Eva's face, waiting.

"Jaden had dreamed he was in this high-tech bathroom at the top of the Space Needle. He really had to go—but couldn't figure out how anything worked. He found the faucet and all that... but no toilet itself. He randomly hit a big yellow button, and a woman's voice told him to use the tub. But there wasn't a tub! Just as he started wetting himself, he woke up."

"Ha! Pretty nasty dream."

"It's just a dream! What's the big deal?... Jaden was supposed to be a man, right? Yet there he was, sweaty and trembling like a child. I did everything to calm him down. I held him tight and stroked him... even played around a bit, hoping to turn him on, because I know from experience—*that* helps with nerves. It didn't work, but he eventually dozed off. Then he started dreaming again."

Eva stood up, slipped into the service room, and returned with an open bottle of cognac and two glasses.

"A sip of cognac improves the mood." She poured the burnished liquor into the glasses.

"And two sips are a cure for excessive decency."

The liquor burned slightly in his throat as it went down, but it was a welcome warmth. He loved cognac, so he held his glass out to her.

"Excessive decency is sterilizing!" Eva topped his glass.

Leaning back in his chair, he raised it. "Go on, tell me more."

Eva took a sip and ran her tongue over her upper lip. She gazed at Vitaly, her tongue brushing her lower lip.

"Jaden soon started dreaming again. This time he was standing in front of a Nazi officer. The officer had pulled out a pistol and pointed it at him. Terrified, Jaden started trembling, whimpering like a puppy and begging for his life, but the officer shot him right in the heart."

Eva's gaze dropped for a moment.

"Jaden woke up and couldn't fall back asleep. He got up and made himself some coffee. I went to work, and when I came back, he was gone. He'd packed his bags and left."

"Well, that's quite a story," Vitaly said.

Eva shook her head, her face darkening, her eyes closing for a moment. She touched the corners of her eyes with a finger, running it under her nose as if drawing a bow across a violin, trying to coax out a sad song.

"Life screwed me over again today," Eva said, her voice catching.

Vitaly watched her, holding his glass.

"Do you know, right when Jaden left—damn him!—that very same day, the administration opened a new position... General Manager of all food services at the college... in charge of both the faculty club and the student cafeteria. It was the perfect job for me. I applied immediately—"

Eva stopped mid-sentence and swallowed hard. A second later, tears streamed from her eyes.

"Marissa, the manager of the student cafeteria, applied too, but I wasn't worried at all. She's way less experienced than me... I was so sure of myself. But today, she told me they gave her the job."

Eva sobbed again, choking on her tears. Vitaly handed her a napkin, and she blew her nose. He passed her another, and she wiped her eyes.

He was glad when her crying finally stopped.

"Bitch!" Eva's voice turned metallic. "She spends every evening at the gym, riding a bike for hours, shaking her ass in front of men, and in the end, she satisfies herself with the bike seat. A young, heartless bitch!"

"Uh-huh... I can imagine." Vitaly sipped his cognac.

Eva fixed her eyes on him.

"Tell me, please—why is life so unfair to me?" she cried, her voice full of anguish. "It's not just about Jaden and the jerks here at the college... You know I was forced to live for years with a husband I didn't love!... I've never seen a man with uglier ears than his... I hate him! And the man I was truly in love with... he was taken from me—by my own sister. Injustice after injustice, how can anyone live like this?"

Vitaly stared into his empty cup and gave it a shake. "Life is unfair by nature, that's just how it is." He looked up at Eva. "We start out as innocent babies and grow into overconfident fools wandering through gardens of dreams. Then we wither, wrinkle, and die."

Eva stared at him, eyes wide.

"Death is the greatest injustice of all," Vitaly said, meeting her gaze. "Think about it—everyone around us, even the most successful, will be dead in just a few decades. Our most beloved people... including us... yes, even our dearest loved ones will rot in the ground, eaten by worms, and vanish without a trace, forever. Innocent, completely innocent! It's the most terrible injustice anyone can imagine, isn't it? The worst injustice there is—and yet we all find a way to live with it."

Vitaly lowered his head for a few seconds, then lifted his eyes to Eva with a faint smile.

"If we can live with this mega-injustice, we can live with any of them. A cheating lover, an unfair boss, a lousy husband, or a crazy president—you name it—those are minor annoyances."

Vitaly watched as Eva held her breath, then let it out sharply—*puf*! Her face softened, and she seemed calmer now.

They sat in silence for a moment.

"You're so smart, Vitaly," Eva whispered.

She rested her hands on the table.

"I'd forgotten how good I felt with you... how good it used to be. You always spoke so tenderly to me... But after we broke up, I grew used to never being told nice things, not anymore."

"Yeah... I see," Vitaly said.

He didn't feel like talking much about it.

"I don't think anyone has loved me after you," Eva continued, "because no one else ever said it the right way."

Vitaly nudged his glass aside.

"I've always felt like a target, a means to fulfill someone's desires, a step to boost someone's ego—and never really loved. No other man ever told me he loved me in a way I could believe. You were the first—and the last—to say it right."

Eva reached across the table and squeezed Vitaly's hand, her eyes glistening. She held on tight for a few seconds before letting go.

"You know what... let's go to my place in Lynnwood. I'll make some coffee."

"Haven't we already had coffee?"

"Yeah, but the coffee here isn't good, to be honest. I'll make real Turkish coffee, like we had that summer on the Black Sea, only mine will be even better, with cardamom!"

"Are we just having coffee, or are we doing something else?"

"Well, we could play Folklore. I know you love that game."

Vitaly hesitated.

"When we played back then, you wouldn't let me blow on the dice."

"I'll let you do it now!... But it's chilly outside. Won't you be cold in that light jacket? I'll give you a sweater—I have one here."

Vitaly glanced at the sculpture on Eva's desk—Romeo kneeling at the bottom of a frying pan, Juliet stretching her hands towards him from the top of the handle.

"As you like."

He turned on his inner autopilot and trailed Eva out the door.

SEQUENCE OF INCIDENTAL EVENTS

Eva and Vitaly returned from the Magic Arts Christmas party in Anacortes in the early hours of the morning. Having met new people and still tipsy, the desire to make love hit her as soon as they entered the living room—right there, without delay, on the carpet.

They woke up late and made love again, this time in bed. Satisfied, Eva left Vitaly to fall back asleep.

Now, lying on her side, head resting on her hand, she watched him. His face was expressionless, as if something had left his soul with the pleasure of their embrace. But his breaths were light like those of a child, and she knew he was contented.

Staring at him, Eva remembered her twins. She had breastfed them as babies, and they would sink into the same serene calm after nursing. She smirked—too bad Vitaly didn't have a twin.

◆ ◆ ◆

Feeling Eva's gaze on him, Vitaly opened his eyes, and Eva gave him a quick kiss. She licked her lips and kissed him again, this time lingering. At last, she pulled away, only to rest her head on his arm, while stroking the hair on his chest.

He remained still, staring up at the ceiling. Then he yawned, but Eva continued to caress him. Soon, she reached down under the covers. "Let's see if there's a nice ripe zucchini ready to be picked..." But he knew there was nothing there this time.

Eva sat up, kissed him again, and stared into his eyes.

"What do you like most about me, baby?"

He shifted his gaze toward her chest.

"I like sucking on you the most," he said, his own voice sounding robotic.

Eva knelt, and the mattress rocked gently. She turned toward him and started inspecting her breasts.

"Which one attracts you more?" she asked, lifting them with her hands.

"The left one."

"Why?"

Why, for God's sake? What was he supposed to say?

"Because it's bigger."

"Bad boy!" Eva said with a laugh. "I want you to be a good boy and suck on the right one, too!"

"Alright," he even managed to joke, "big or small, I like them all."

Eva giggled and gave him a light slap before lying on her back. He leaned over her and took the nipple of her right breast into his mouth. As he kissed her, he diligently stroked the left one with his hand. Eva lay there with her eyes half-closed, her breathing growing faster.

"What do you feel when you enter me?" she whispered.

He hesitated, unsure of what to say.

"I feel like I'm returning to the warm cave I came from."

"And what else?"

"Well... I feel like we become one."

He stopped stroking her and rolled onto his back.

Eva's glazed eyes lingered on him.

"It's not going to happen. I'm too tired."

An awkward silence stretched.

"Ah-ah, he's tired," Eva said. "Poor thing."

Vitaly remained quiet.

"Since you're too tired, let's try teabagging."

"Teabagging? What's that?"

"You seriously don't know? Have you never played Halo?"

"I haven't."

"I'll lie down on the floor," Eva said, "and you'll kneel over my head, serving me eggs for breakfast."

She winked at him.

"That's teabagging. It's easy, even if you're tired. You'll enjoy it."

"How exactly are we supposed to do this? Like this, naked?"

He was already thinking about getting dressed.

"Not completely naked," Eva teased. "I'll wear my locket."

Eva tapped her phone, and Barber's *Adagio* in its electronic arrangement streamed from the open door of the living room. He lowered his head and followed her there.

Swaying to the rhythm, Eva placed a pillow on the carpet before lying down on her back. He hesitated for a moment, then knelt over her head, watching as she adjusted herself underneath him. In a moment, Eva's locket began to shimmer on her chest: a pair of silver waves framing two crystal hearts —one pink, one blue, with her name engraved on the upper wave and his on the lower one. The *Adagio* flowed from the speakers, and the crystals cast pink and blue glints in time with its rhythm.

A whimper drifted from the entrance. A moment later, Eva's Labrador started scratching at the door. They had left him outside the night before so he could relieve himself in the morning without bothering them too early.

"Ignore him," Eva whispered. "Let him whine."

It was as if the Labrador had heard her and decided to act out of spite, turning his whimpering into sorrowful sobs—but Vitaly knew it was hunger driving the dog. The sobs swelled into a heartbreaking howl, shifted to barking, and returned to howling. The animal pounded at the door with its paws, and Vitaly pictured it upright on its hind legs.

Vitaly stood—leaving Eva on the carpet—and cracked the door open. The Labrador darted into the living room, made two quick laps around Eva, and began licking her with gusto. Petting him as she rose, Eva headed to the pantry for some food, the Labrador trotting behind, tongue hanging out.

Meanwhile, Vitaly slipped into the bathroom.

Vitaly spent an entire hour alone under the shower, savoring the caresses of the whispering water. Finally, he put on a black bathrobe and headed to the kitchen. There, he found Eva, her damp hair wrapped in a towel, bare legs peeking from beneath her kimono. She must have showered in the en-suite.

"I made a Tsar Nicholas tea for you," Eva said, her eyes inviting his reaction, "and an espresso for myself."

Vitaly remained silent. He was hungry, so he approached the refrigerator, pulled out a pack of Polish sausage, and reached for a plate.

"Oh, not that... I bought it specifically for the dog!" Eva took the package from his hands. "Wait a minute, I'll make an omelet with tofu and plenty of vegetables."

Vitaly shrugged and sat down at the table, sipping his tea.

By the time Vitaly and Eva finished their late breakfast, it was nearing noon. She started loading the dishes into the dishwasher while he stared out the window. The sun filtered through a haze. To the northwest, a wave of cold, dark clouds loomed.

"I'm heading out before the rain starts," Vitaly said.

"Are you going to Mukilteo again? Huh? Make sure to dress warmly!"

Vitaly stepped outside and inhaled the damp wind. A dry twig broke off the old apple tree and rattled against the roof of his Honda. He slipped into the car, drove down the deserted street, and turned right onto 35th Avenue. In five minutes, he reached Mukilteo Speedway and headed north.

He would catch the ferry to Whidbey Island, as usual.

He loved crossing the strait, spending a couple of hours on the island, and then returning home. Bad weather never scared him. This time, he planned to take a walk along the beach, scattered with driftwood polished by the waves. Afterwards, tired and hungry, he'd stop by Whidbey Bakery, order a spinach bagel with feta, and warm up with a large coffee. He'd check the Russian news on his phone before taking the ferry shuttle home through the waves and wind.

Vitaly glanced to the right toward Pizza Hut. Right here, the road cut through the southwest corner of Paine Field. A small Cessna was lining up for takeoff, as if from the restaurant's backyard. Far beyond the runway, the Boeing factories loomed. Dreamliners sat parked in front, awaiting the day when, freshly painted, they would roll onto the same runway for their first test flight.

The first raindrops splattered against the windshield, and Vitaly turned on the wipers. The Cessna lifted off the concrete, its lights flashing, and he watched it through the rhythmic squeaking of the wiper blades. A flock of birds took off, startled, from the grove beyond the runway. The small plane veered left and wobbled, on the verge of falling, before stabilizing, correcting its course, and continuing to climb.

It was raining in Mukilteo. The Christmas garlands on the lighthouse gleamed with wetness, still unlit. The park was deserted. The gray crests of the waves rolled in an endless rhythm toward the pier. The clouds, in rows of dark and gray stripes, making their way toward the shore like celestial reflections of the waves, slowed to a crawl.

The waiting lanes at the ferry terminal were full, and

police were directing cars to the overflow parking. One of the three ferries had broken down, it turned out. With sixty thousand people living on the island, some would be waiting for hours in their cars before finally getting home later that evening.

Vitaly waited for the oncoming traffic to pass, made a U-turn, and headed back before the swift women in uniform could funnel him into the waiting lot. Today, he'd go without a walk, without a bagel, and without coffee. He pressed the gas, sinking into thought, imagining how a tiny accident—perhaps a loose screw—might have fallen into the engine, damaged it, and caused the ferry to halt suddenly, ruining people's holiday plans.

Life is a series of accidents, some good, some bad. Whether it's a ferry, wives, or girlfriends—everything comes down to chance.

Take me, for example—I'm Russian, driving a Japanese car in America... I'm married to an American, but living with her sister, whom I fell in love with in Bulgaria...

Lost in thought, he slipped into autopilot.

My life began with the chance encounter of an egg and a random sperm, one out of a hundred million. He smiled faintly. *What else brought me here, if not a string of coincidences?*

Deep in reflection, Vitaly missed the turn onto 35th Avenue toward Lynnwood and Eva, continuing straight down Route 99 toward Edmonds. This route was also well known to him, as he had driven it for years. He only realized his mistake when, out of habit, he found himself heading toward Laura's house.

Once headed toward Laura's, Vitaly decided to keep going. The street was a dead-end, and it would be easier to make a U-turn at the cul-de-sac before heading back.

He continued, savoring the neighbors' Christmas decorations. Electric garlands twinkled under the eaves, wreaths hung over the doors, and the yards were filled with inflatable reindeer, sleighs, and elves. And there it was—Laura's house, also decorated.

In the front yard, a nativity scene caught his eye. He slowed to a crawl, staring at the display. It was made entirely of flat white plastic—a silhouette of baby Jesus in the manger, with Joseph and the Virgin Mary bowed in prayer, a white barn in front of them topped by a star, and the figure of a donkey off to the side.

A gust of wind shook the figures. They were going to fall, Vitaly thought. The wind seemed to read his mind—and blew again, even harder. The plastic display wobbled, then collapsed and scattered across the grass. The white donkey, caught by the gust, tumbled playfully across the wet lawn.

Vitaly parked the car by the curb, got out, and looked around. There were no people on the street. Relieved, he stepped onto the grass, gathered the plastic panels, and inspected them. The pieces fit together like a puzzle, and he began to reassemble them. First, he attached the door and the walls. Then, he positioned the manger with the three figures at the back and secured it with two metal stakes he found, muddied, in the grass. The soil was damp, and the stakes didn't hold well. He decided to weigh them down with a couple of bricks. The bricks would remain hidden behind the manger, invisible from the street.

He knew there were bricks in the garage, so he entered the old code—and the door creaked open. The bricks were still there, piled up along the wall behind Laura's Mercedes. He carried a few to the yard and placed them over the stakes. The wind blew in from the street, the tall barn door swayed, but the display held firm.

"Blow as much as you want."

"Do you want to wash up?" Laura asked.

He turned around. She was watching him from the frame of the massive front door. Behind her, his cat Zina was peeking out.

The cat meowed. Vitaly hesitated, glancing toward the house. Through the dim light inside, he spotted a decorated Christmas tree. Zina meowed again, a long and mournful cry, and Vitaly bowed his head and moved toward the entrance.

Seven years ago, Laura brought home a three-week-old kitten as a birthday present for Vitaly. "It's a girl," she told him, and he named her Zina. He called the kitten by name, and soon she learned to respond, just like a puppy. Six months later, the vet revealed that Zina was actually a boy. By then, the cat was already used to the name and almost always came when called, so Vitaly decided not to rename him, simply adding "Mr." in front of Zina.

Vitaly would introduce his cat to guests as Mr. Zina, and the cat never objected. For those unfamiliar with the backstory, he explained that the cat was highly intelligent, bilingual—understanding both English and Russian—and even had an MBA. He'd point to the wall, where two diplomas hung side by side in solid mahogany frames: his own from Moscow University, and, next to it, the cat's diploma from Goldcrest College in Texas, issued in the name of Mr. Zina Zucchini, complete with an official signature and seal. Then, he'd recount how he personally applied on the cat's behalf for an experience-based bachelor's degree in business administration, all for the reasonable fee of $299.

In the application, he stated that Mr. Zina Zucchini had taken business courses at a two-year college, worked at a fast-food restaurant, served as an occasional babysitter with hourly pay, and interned at a rodent control company. In response, the college informed the cat that its accumulated work experience not only qualified it for a bachelor's degree but also for a master's, for just an additional $100. He sent the check and promptly received the diploma. The formal transcript accompanying it listed the cat's GPA as 3.50 out of 4.00—a solid distinction.

His story always ended with laughter and jokes. Amused, both guests and hosts would head to the kitchen, where Laura would invite them to start the party the Russian way—with vodka and herring.

Vitaly stepped through the threshold, walked past Laura —avoiding her shadowed eyes—and headed for the bathroom. Mr. Zina followed at his heels, waiting by the door while Vitaly washed. When he came out, Zina meowed, rubbed against his leg, and led him to the living room, glancing back every so often.

Zina reached the Christmas tree and lay on his side on the carpet. Vitaly knelt, grabbed him by the scruff, and spun him in a circle. He did it again, and then once more, spinning faster and harder each time, while Laura watched from the kitchen. It was a ritual they had shared for years. Vitaly stood, and the cat stretched, front paws extended forward, and rear end lifted high, before rubbing against his legs.

"Would you like some vodka with herring?" Laura said, staring at the floor. "You must've gotten chilled out there in the rain and wind, dealing with my clumsy decorations."

Vitaly straightened up. "Your decorations are beautiful."

"You like them, don't you!" A smile crept across Laura's face. "The plastic is super sturdy—marine grade, with a fifty-year warranty. And the reviews are all positive."

She pursed her lips.

"I wonder if I should've bought extras... They had magi, and even sheep... everything was on sale."

"You don't need sheep or magi—your donkey is more than enough."

Laura didn't seem to hear him.

"In the evening, when the lights are on outside, the shadows of Joseph and the Virgin Mary fall across the blinds," she murmured dreamily. "I turn off the lights inside, sit on the couch, and watch the two shadows on the window, and I think of us."

She swallowed hard, tears welling in her eyes.

Vitaly disliked women's tears. "Is the vodka cold?"

"Yes, everything's ready. But today... not in the kitchen. Let's stay here, by the Christmas tree."

He nodded—and Laura wasted no time serving everything.

They settled onto the couch behind the coffee table. Vitaly sipped from the thimble-sized glass and took a bite of his snack.

"You've decorated a beautiful tree."

"The little package under the tree is for Zina."

He took another sip and glanced at Zina. The cat lay next to the tree in a sphinxlike pose, its paws tucked under its belly. Zina gazed at them, ears perked, listening to their conversation.

"I bought him scented ear-cleaning wipes and a cat toothbrush—the kind that fits on your finger. Hopefully, he'll be pleased."

"Hmm... A cat toothbrush, huh..." Vitaly finished his vodka and eyed the tall glass of green juice in Laura's hands. "And what are you drinking today?"

"Today, I'm having zucchini juice... It's low-calorie." Laura patted her belly. "Plus, it helps with hemorrhoids and constipation."

Silence followed. Vitaly sank into thought, twirling the empty cup in his hands.

"*Nu, znaesh shto, Larunya*?" he said in Russian. Her surprise made him catch himself. He cleared his throat and switched to English. "You know, Laurie, the ancient Romans believed that the first cup was necessary to quench your thirst, the second for your health, and the third for your pleasure. After that, you stop drinking because the fourth cup is for rudeness and insults, for fights, and for breaking furniture."

Laura stared at her glass.

"You see, Laurie, it turns out that only the fourth cup is harmful."

Without a word, she stood and headed to the kitchen. A

minute later—which looked like eternity to him—she returned with two water glasses and a bottle of vodka. She set them on the table, her movements unsteady. The bottle tipped—but his hand shot out and caught it before it fell. *Quick reflexes,* he thought.

He opened the bottle, sniffed its mouth, and poured drinks for both of them. Picking up his glass, he looked at Laura, beckoning her to join him. Laura stared at him for a few moments, her face looking tense, but then raised her glass, drained it in one gulp, and chased it with a sip of zucchini juice. Her face relaxed—*of course!*—and her eyes softened. He offered her a grin—and downed his vodka in one go as well.

He got up and walked to the window. The rain had turned to snow, falling in large, wet flakes. The roof of his car was already white, and icy slush coated the street. He lowered the blind and returned to his seat.

"I wonder if Fred is in his trailer." He chewed on a herring. "I'd like to stop by, catch up... He's a good guy."

"Fred's in his trailer, but I'm not sure it's the best time to bother him."

He raised his eyebrows.

"Fred's got a young visitor. It's the woman who saved him with the helicopter when he tried to hang himself. He asked her over for tea and homemade cookies to say thanks."

"Fred does make good tea."

Laura reached for the green juice but paused for a moment, then poured vodka for both of them, and took a sip herself.

"Do you know why older men want to date younger women?" Laura fixed her gaze on him.

He thought about it, sipping, forking herring, and chewing.

"Isn't it because young women are cheerful, open-minded, and uncritical?" He stopped chewing and stared at his wife, then washed down the herring with a gulp of vodka. "They don't have a long list of demands for their partner or a rigid set of career goals."

He cleared his throat.

"Maybe that's why they're friendly and always in a good mood. Their carefree attitude toward life is refreshing."

"It's their backsides that are refreshing." Laura swayed her rounded figure. "But that uncritical carefreeness... or should I say... carefree uncriticalness... whatever—that could easily make some old men hang themselves."

"If you're hinting at Fred," Vitaly said, "let me tell you, he'd had a big red birthmark on his forehead as a kid. Not a big deal—but he thought he was ugly and that girls didn't like him because of it. The birthmark faded as he got older, but the shame stuck with him. He told me once, after a few drinks. That's probably why he started chasing after young women later—to make up for that."

Vitaly took another bite of herring, about to continue—but then Laura burst in.

"No, that's not Fred's problem!" she snapped. "The problem with guys like him is they don't age well! They're already old men, yet they deny that their time has passed. That's why they chase after young women, trying to prove they're some kind of exception—that age doesn't affect them. And it's less about proving it to others—it's more about proving it to themselves."

Laura's eyes flashed at him.

"They are men trying—even if they don't realize it—to prove their masculinity; men for whom success as men is everything! But aging makes them insecure—so insecure that they need to draw from the energy of youth just to feel alive."

Vitaly listened, nodding his head. After every few nods, he took a small sip of vodka.

"What do you think about that?"

"Ninety-nine percent of questions have simple answers." The phrase had worked miracles for him in the classroom. "And my answer is simple: older men chase young women because they look sweeter than the rest. It's basic instinct:

biologically, they're best suited for sex and having children. That's just how things are."

"Ah, there it is again—sex... Men, especially the younger ones, think it's the most important thing in the world!"

"They do when they're young... and when they get older, they realize it's absolutely true."

He smirked.

"But seriously—you men are like animals! Why isn't it enough for you to have a loving wife and a peaceful family?" Laura lifted her glass of juice, emptied it in one gulp, and set it down on the table with a thud. "But no, you stay deaf to the music of pure feelings... blind to the beauty of platonic love..."

"Yes, yes, you're right... but think about it... platonic love is like a dish with too little salt—it's healthy, but it doesn't satisfy."

Laura stood up and looked down at him.

"Tell me... Tell me! Do you love my sister? Huh?! Did you go to her out of pure feelings and love, or just for sex?!" Her voice grew sharp, cutting through the haze of vodka.

"Only for sex, only for sex." He lowered his eyes to the table. His glass was empty again and he reached for the bottle, muttering, "I didn't need love... What good is love... just a silly complication of a simple pleasure."

"No! Love is a pleasant complication of foolish natural instincts! And by the way, I'm taking this!" Laura snatched the bottle from his hands. "You've already had three glasses... one for thirst, the second for mood, and the third for pleasure, right? But no fourth for madness. That's enough for you!"

Eyes welling with tears, Laura carried the vodka bottle to the kitchen. The cat stood up, its tail tapping on the floor.

Vitaly dragged his feet to the door and left.

◆ ◆ ◆

Laura returned from the kitchen and peeked through the blinds. Vitaly stood in the slush on the street, clearing snow from the roof of his car. She watched him struggle to reach a strip of snow on the far side of the roof.

He jumped up, swiping his outstretched hand across the roof like a windshield wiper, managing to push off half the snow. He jumped again, but slipped—his legs flew into the air, and he landed on his backside in the slush.

Vitaly lay there, stretched out on his back, arms spread, not moving.

She rushed outside, circled the car, and bent down toward her husband.

"Are you okay?" She grabbed him by the shoulders from behind and tried to lift him. "Sweetheart, are you okay?!"

"I'm fine." Vitaly groaned, turned over, and with a grunt, managed to get up, pressing his palms against the asphalt. "It's just my backside—hurts like hell. I think I hit my tailbone."

"Let's hope it's only bruised and not broken." She wrapped her arm around Vitaly's waist, her other hand supporting his arm slung over her shoulders. "Move slowly," she whispered, guiding him toward the house.

Fifteen minutes later, Vitaly lay in the old marital bed, dressed in pajamas and propped up on high pillows. Laura placed a steaming cup of tea on the nightstand next to a plate of Russian cookies. She watched as Mr. Zina leaped onto the bed, his tail swaying back and forth. A smile tugged at her lips as the cat, just like in the good old days, snuggled under Vitaly's arm and buried his snout in his pajamas, purring with half-closed eyes.

"I'm going to re-wrap Mr. Zina's presents in two separate boxes. It wouldn't feel right if, tomorrow, on Christmas, I gave him two gifts and you gave him nothing."

She left, easing the door shut behind her. Five minutes later, she returned, cracking it open and slipping her head through the gap.

"Which gift do you want to give him? The toothbrush or the scented ear wipes?"

But Vitaly didn't respond. He was already asleep, with

the cat cuddled under his arm.

PLATONIC AFFAIRS

"You have pretty awful handwriting," Dessa told him.

"It's because I wrote in bed," Fred said. "What matters is that the sonnet is beautiful."

"Why do you have to write with a pencil? Can't you just dictate it into your phone like everyone else?"

"But my best sonnets... I've written by hand, lying in bed... That's when I'm most productive."

The corners of Dessa's lips curled into what looked to him like a restrained smirk.

"I'm like Brahms," he said. "Brahms was at his most creative lying down, too. Once, his friend Chef Carême visited him and found him composing under the covers. When a sheet of music slipped out and fell to the floor, Carême stayed in his chair. Instead of getting up to fetch it, Brahms simply wrote a new duet."

He winced, realizing he'd misspoken—it was actually Rossini, not Brahms, who composed in bed.

Stone-faced, Dessa raised her Dr. Pepper and finished it in a few gulps. The empty can clattered onto the table.

He shifted his weight. "Do you like Brahms?"

"Who?... Brahms? I don't think I'm into his music."

He got up and wandered to the counter. A gust of wind hurled raindrops against the kitchen window. He glanced at them, then returned to stand by the table.

“Actually, I don’t care much for his symphonies either.”

Dessa said nothing.

“Honestly, I’m more intrigued by his platonic love for Clara Schumann... It was that love that made him a great composer.”

Fred lowered himself onto the edge of the chair.

‘Yes, a love that was platonic and pure... even though, when Robert Schumann was admitted to the asylum, the young Brahms moved into the family home to stay close to Clara and help her—a convenient proximity, no doubt, offering him plenty of opportunities for sex, which he never took advantage of but... on the contrary, well, not exactly...”

Fred rattled on, but with every sentence, he grew more confused, while Dessa watched him, her eyes narrowing. Sweat pricked at his forehead, but he swallowed—and pressed on. To save himself, he needed to explain everything.

“The fact that Brahms didn’t sleep with Clara doesn’t mean he was impotent. It’s well known he was a regular at brothels and couldn’t get enough of the prostitutes. But not with Clara... She wasn’t a prostitute, of course. To him, she was pure and innocent, like a saint. Not that she wasn’t interested in sex— she’d had eight children with Robert by then. Yes, sex, but not with Brahms, who had no need for physical intimacy with her. He loved her only through his music.”

Dessa pulled her phone from her pocket as if Fred wasn’t there, scrolling through her messages like she was completely alone. Fred fell silent and waited. When Dessa looked up from the screen, he began speaking in fits and starts.

“It’s called the Madonna-whore complex.” His mouth went dry, and he licked his lips, trying to swallow. “To him, Clara was so wonderful... virtuous... innocent... pure and forever virginal...”

Fred lowered his gaze. “...And I’m like him.”

Without another word, he jumped toward the shelf, pulled out *Trio*, and held the book out to Dessa.

"You can read it if you want. It'll make everything clear."

"Thank you, but I don't have time for reading." Dessa stood, slung her backpack over her shoulder, and added, "I've got to go now."

Fred wanted to stop her but didn't know how. He set *Trio* down on the table—just as someone knocked on the front door.

The knock on the door sounded again, more insistent this time, and Fred hurried to open it. At the foot of the trailer steps stood Vitaly.

Fred stared at the Russian—unshaven, with a coffee stain the size of a saucer on his knee.

"What's up?"

Vitaly scratched his unshaven jaw but didn't reply. For all his fresh face, Fred felt just as grim as the man before him.

"Why are you knocking on the door?"

"I don't know," Vitaly muttered. "I just let go of the reins, and my horse brought me to you."

Vitaly looked pale—his pupils dilated.

"You don't look well. Are you sick?"

"I'm not sick, but I really don't feel right."

"Seems like everyone who visits me today isn't feeling right." Fred narrowed his eyes. "Spit it out!"

"Laura hid all the booze. She won't let me have even a teensy drink."

Fred thought for a moment. Was fate sending Vitaly to his aid? The Russian was a quarter-century younger than him, and when he drank—but only in moderation!—he became a *charmant compagnon,* capable of brightening even the gloomiest atmosphere.

"Too bad you're not sick." Fred leaned against the doorframe. "Sometimes a few sips help, especially when someone's unwell. Like with a cold, for example."

"Oh, yes!" Vitaly brightened. "I'd forgotten I have a cold!"

"How long have you had this cold?"

"Well, since now." Vitaly raised his eyebrows. "Look how long you've had me out here in the wind and rain."

Fred smirked and stepped aside. "Come in, then."

They entered, and Vitaly paused in front of Dessa.

"I feel like I've seen you somewhere before."

"Probably on Facebook—Fred is our mutual friend."

"Nice to meet you in person." Vitaly extended a hand, and Dessa shook it.

Fred drew a breath and exhaled quietly. He placed two saucers with petits fours on the table. "Sit down, please, while I prepare a remedy for Vitaly."

He opened the cupboard and pulled out a bottle of plum brandy, lifting it high like a sports trophy. Imitating a TV commercial, he announced, "Mulled brandy with honey—the secret Bulgarian super-weapon against all kinds of colds and other ailments!"

Turning his back to his guests, he grabbed a kettle and busied himself with the brandy and honey by the stove.

◆ ◆ ◆

Vitaly settled behind the table, waving his hand for Dessa to sit. Dessa hesitated for a moment before seating herself opposite him and pulling the saucer with the petits fours closer.

A quarter of an hour ago, the idea that she could be the object of romantic aspirations from a man thirty-five years her senior had shocked her. But now, as she nibbled on the pastries and inhaled the cloud of plum brandy vapors rising from the kettle, she realized her irritation was fading.

She was no longer sure her anger was justified. Fred writing her a sonnet wasn't such a big deal after all. What really mattered was that she had always seen him only as an older friend—and nothing more... a good friend with a kindred spirit, whose life experience was richer than hers. Conversations with him were pleasant, perhaps because, like her, he was a foreigner in America. And was there anything inappropriate about that?

Fred served cheese, yet another Dr. Pepper for Dessa, mulled brandy for Vitaly, and wine for himself, and took a seat behind the table next to the Russian.

They drank, ate, and talked. Dessa told Vitaly about her work as a helicopter rescuer. He asked to see the base and the helicopter, and she agreed to take him there someday. Then Vitaly told her about his cat, Mr. Zina, and Dessa, in turn, informed him about her dog, Chewbacca. Reassured by Dessa's smile, Fred preferred to remain silent.

"Since you were born in Sofia, you're almost a Muscovite to me." The Russian took a hefty sip from his third glass of plum brandy. "And Muscovite girls... Ah, Muscovite girls..."

"Let me top you off!" Fred pulled the glass from Vitaly's grasp. Left with empty hands, Vitaly glanced around until his eyes landed on the copy of *Trio* lying on the table. He picked up the book and flipped through it.

"Is this a novel?"

"Yes," Fred said.

Vitaly gave him an inquiring look.

"*Trio* isn't anything special." Fred weighed his words. "Just a fictionalized biography of three composers... It's not particularly authentic."

Vitaly tilted the book closer, scanning the back cover. "Ah, I see now—Clara and Brahms. Actually, their affair has long been known to me. A telling story! Brahms loved Clara so much that he neither wanted to nor could sleep with her."

Fred lowered his head, feeling his face blush. Vitaly drained his glass and held it out for more.

"To Clara and Brahms." Vitaly raised his glass. "To the two lovers who have proven with their lives that true love is puritan love. Cheers!"

Vitaly took a good sip of the plum brandy, leaned closer to Fred with a sly smile, and winked.

"Keep in mind, only the rational ones, the indifferent ones, can truly enjoy erotic pleasure. Not the ones consumed by love! That's the mistake some young couples make—"

"Look at that rain pouring down out there!" Fred cut him off.

The three of them looked toward the window. Just then, Laura's Mercedes turned onto the street.

Fred jumped up. "I'm going to invite her in!"

Laura slipped into the trailer, shaking the rain from her hair and telling Fred, with sighs and gasps, how the storm caught her in the mall parking lot and how the wind blew her hat away. She paused, sniffed the plum brandy vapors, cast a glare at Vitaly, and gave Fred reproachful glances before her eyes met Dessa's. With an expression of tentative acceptance, she sat next to Dessa and reached for a can of Dr. Pepper.

"The mistake some young couples make—" Vitaly

started again, but Laura cut him off.

"Enough with this youth fixation! What's so great about it?"

She sipped, frowned, and tapped the can on the table. "Young people are like flowers in a fresh bouquet. At first, they're all beautiful. Change their water regularly, and they'll stay that way a little longer. But eventually, they wrinkle and even start to stink. Same with the young!"

"I envy the young." Fred let the silence stretch. "Old age stinks."

To him, life was a river, like the Amazon. As a young man, he had imagined himself gliding in the middle of the current. But the passing years had pushed him toward the shore, where the water had slowed and turned stagnant. In the end, he could end up tangled in fallen trees, surrounded by trash, or even find himself in a foul-smelling swamp. That, he thought, was old age.

He finished his wine, stood up, and, without saying a word, began piling the dishes into the sink. The day was short, and it was already getting dark outside.

Dessa got up. "It's time for me to go."

"Look at that downpour—I'll drive you!" Vitaly rose, swaying.

"Ah, no!... Only my Mercedes has adaptive brake assist." Laura turned to Dessa. "You don't mind, do you, dear?"

A minute later, Fred walked them to the door. The two women dashed into the rain. Before slipping into Laura's car, Dessa looked back at him.

He returned her gaze with an invisible smile. He already knew she would let him remain in her life—though always at a distance.

AGE GAP

On Wednesdays, Eva expected Alex to come and work in her garden, and on Thursdays, to stop by and make love to her. "Just come straight through the garage," she'd remind him. "If a neighbor sees you, you can always say you're here to tune up the lawn mower."

Today was Thursday, and she was expecting him.

Alex's chat bubble popped up on her phone: *Done with school. Want me to come?*

Yes, as always. I'll be waiting for you on the Euclidean couch.

Don't forget to call your mother.

Alex's mother had grown suspicious that he was seeing someone after school, so Eva coached him to tell her he was staying late in the math club, solving problems with his classmates.

Okay. Be with you in ten min.

Eva lowered the blinds, opened the garage door, and shooed her Labrador out into the yard. She went to the bedroom, undressed, and slipped into a skin-tight minidress. Back in the living room, she spread a white sheet over the couch and arranged pillows in the center.

She'd bought this couch especially for the two of them—a sleek, modern version of the Freudian analytical divan, crafted from angular pieces of cherry wood. Because of its geometric design, the manufacturer had branded it as the Euclid Analytical Couch. "Alex, it doesn't matter much whether you're in the math club or lying here on the couch," she would laugh. "It's a Euclid couch, therefore it counts as math."

They would make love on the couch, and once they grew tired, they would play psychoanalyst and patient. The game would excite them again, and they would make love once more.

Eva lit four Crazy Girl massage candles around the couch, then knelt on it, resting her stomach on the cushions. She propped her bent elbows on the headrest and stretched her legs toward the ceiling, her toes pointed like a ballerina's. With her pink dress pulled up, she was ready to welcome the boy.

Eva heard Alex's footsteps in the garage, followed by the rattle of the closing door.

I'm here.

Come in. Door's unlocked.

The door from the garage opened, but instead of Alex, two women in jeans and sport shirts stepped into the living room. One was a brunette, the other a blonde, both about Eva's age. They introduced themselves with a casual lightness, revealing they were detectives.

Eva rose from the couch, smoothing her pink dress. She extinguished the candles, walked to the window, and lifted the blinds, squinting against the daylight. Turning to the women who had followed her, she straightened her back and offered a faint smile.

"Alex's mother is nervous about you two screwing," the brunette said.

The brunette had started the conversation informally, as if it were a neighborly chat, almost as though the three women were girlfriends. It was a tactic—her goal was to get Eva to relax and open up. Both she and the blonde maintained a chummy, casual tone, as if their questions were harmless. But the two detectives were experts at extracting incriminating information, and anyone who talked to them usually ended up in jail.

"We're not screwing." Eva lifted her chin. "We're making love. That's entirely different. It's so much more beautiful."

"His mother is worried about the age gap," the blonde said. "She thinks you're quite old—and he's still just a child."

"I'm well aware of our age gap—but I'm not embarrassed by it. I actually see it as a plus."

The blonde glanced at the brunette.

"Alex's mother felt sidelined," the brunette said. "So she checked his phone and found you."

A smirk tugged at Eva's lips. *The texts. Of course.*

"She came up with this idea for us to text you as if we were him. I hope you understand—we couldn't say no to her."

"It's okay. Nothing to fuss about. You're just doing your job."

"Alex doesn't know anything about the phone," the blonde said. "He thinks he lost it."

The brunette unlocked Alex's phone and showed it to Eva.

"There's a picture of you in a bikini." The brunette nodded. You look lovely."

"I sent it to him after our first time together. Almost six months ago."

"So, do you have, like, any nice photos of him?" the

blonde asked.

"Well, yes." Eva smiled. "Here, look!"

She tapped on her phone.

"Take a look at this and tell me—does he look like a child to you, or a man?"

She watched their faces as they examined the photo of Alex's equipment. "He sent me this on his own," she explained. "I didn't ask him for anything."

Eva chatted with the blonde and the brunette a little longer, their conversation staying amiable and even sprinkled with laughter. But then the detectives grew serious and informed her that they had to arrest her.

Eva took the news with a nod of understanding. She asked if she could change into something more appropriate, but the brunette said it wasn't necessary—she'd be given special clothes once in custody anyway.

The blonde took Eva's phone away, checked her for weapons, and the two detectives led her out.

Eva was glad the three of them got along well enough not to handcuff her. Still, she wouldn't have minded if they did. It wouldn't make a difference.

Nothing really mattered—not anymore.

Fred, her old husband, had squandered her youth. Vitaly, her unfaithful lover, had shattered her heart. Her adventure with Alex had been a rebellion, but that, too, had failed her. Now, with her life in pieces, she let herself sink into the absurdity of it all with tender indifference.

The two women who arrested her were like her sisters. The blonde could be married to a bore like Fred. The brunette could be in love with a cheater like Vitaly. The detectives were women just like her; she felt for them and wanted to believe they felt for her too.

A uniformed sergeant took charge of Eva at the police station. He was a likable man with African features and, with some reluctance, admitted that his roots were in Ethiopia.

The Ethiopian recorded her personal information, photographed her, and took her fingerprints. After handing her a set of jail clothes, which she put on with a shrug, he informed her she'd be taken to court for arraignment in just a couple of days.

"Do you need anything before I lock you in a cell?"

Eva hesitated. Her Labrador was still out in the yard, and before long, the poor thing would grow thirsty and hungry. But could she sway an Ethiopian man with a story about a thirsty Labrador? She had no idea.

"I've developed thyroid disease after a miscarriage, so I must take a special pill every morning, at 5 a.m. exactly," she lied. "If I don't, I'll fall ill, and I may die."

The man gave a brief chuckle—and then something in his face softened.

"Do you have someone you can ask to bring the medication?"

"Yes, my sister... It's been a while since we spoke, but I think she won't say no to me now."

The Ethiopian led Eva to the facility phone and stepped aside as she dialed her sister.

After a few "ahs" and "ohs" from her sister, she promised to take care of the Labrador, and that was all Eva needed for now.

CAT ON A LEASH

Vitaly hadn't had a drink in two days, and all he could do was sit on the couch, lost in the gathering twilight, and replay his memories of last Christmas Eve, when he had just returned from Eva to Laura. He'd sat here, at the same coffee table, and Laura had so kindly served him vodka with pickled herring.

Now Laura was out, still at work, showing log homes to a wealthy Indian family, both programmers at Microsoft.

There was no vodka for Vitaly, either. Just yesterday, Laura had thrown out all the alcohol from their home and made him swear never to drink again. Caught off guard and way too emotional, he not only promised to quit drinking for good but also handed over all the cash he had on him. From then on, he'd pay for everything with the joint credit card, which Laura could monitor through her phone to catch him if he was tempted to buy anything stronger than Coca-Cola.

Today, the couple had planned to go out for dinner together. "I want to take you to Organilux," Laura had said. "They cook everything with organic flaxseed oil, and they serve forty-two types of mineral water. The place is pricey, but it's worth it." And here he was, waiting for her to come home so they could go to Organilux together. But, in truth, he wasn't hungry at all—his head ached, and he was nauseous. Meanwhile, Laura was running late, busy with the Indians.

Vitaly stared for a minute at the movies scattered on the coffee table. He had borrowed them earlier in the week from the Russian Store. With trembling hands, he began picking them up and examining the titles. Not in the mood to take chances with something new, he decided to rewatch *White Sun of the Desert* for the umpteenth time.

He started the movie, and the screen filled with the image of a dreamy man wearing a hat with a red star. Reclining on the sand, he drifted into memories of a Russian beauty with a red headscarf tied under her chin. She appeared as he began talking to her, smiling silently back at him.

Vitaly's phone rang, and he paused the movie. The headscarfed beauty froze on-screen.

"The Indians decided to make an offer," Laura said. "I have to draft it and then play ball with the seller. I'm sorry, but you'll have to eat by yourself."

"Oh, that's not a problem. Don't worry about me."

They ended the call, and Vitaly hurried out, slid behind the wheel, and drove to the Russian Store.

The store was quiet, just as Vitaly expected on this Monday evening. The owner's wife stood at the register, while the owner waited at the meat counter, his blood-streaked gloves resting on the edge of the display case. Vitaly approached him and struck up a conversation, his eyes sweeping the room. He spotted Natasha arranging Russian beer on the back shelf, her braid cascading to her waist, and nodded to her. She nodded back, and for a moment, he felt like a blue balloon—light and carefree, floating above it all.

Over the past few weeks, Vitaly had found excuses to visit the store often, and whenever Natasha was on duty, didn't miss a chance to exchange a few words with her.

The owner enjoyed chatting with Vitaly. Today, he had received a new shipment of *krovyanaya kolbasa*, which he not only sold but also shared at home with his wife. The old man became engrossed in the conversation, reminiscing about how, as a child in Russia, he helped his father slaughter pigs and boil homemade *krovyanka.*

As the butcher spoke, clasping his bloodied hands together, Vitaly's gaze shifted to Natasha—she had just finished stocking the beer and slipped into the back room, her face set in a somber expression.

He wandered away from the counter and lingered in the store, hoping Natasha would reappear—but she didn't. Disappointed, he left without buying anything.

He took a few steps along the sidewalk, stopped in front of the "Teriyaki Chicken" window, and forced himself to examine the menu.

"*Dobryy vecher,*" Natasha called from behind him. "Good evening." He spun around, meeting her gray eyes.

"I'm on a break and heading to dinner," Natasha said.

"I'm on my way to dinner too." He nodded toward the restaurant. "Want to grab a bite together?"

"Actually, I have homemade *pelmeni* at my place." She glanced at him. "They're delicious, if you'd like... but it'll have to be quick—I need to be back at the store in an hour."

He remained silent, taken aback.

"My place is five minutes away, and my car is right here," Natasha added.

He surveyed the battered black Chevy parked by the curb—it looked like it had been around for a couple of decades. An oval sticker on the bumper caught his eye: "I love my sexy husband!"

Perhaps, a previous owner had put that sticker there, he thought.

They got into the car, and Natasha inserted the key

into the ignition. The CD player, left on, sprang to life, filling the car with Scheherazade. For a moment, it seemed to him as if the silhouettes of the young princess danced across the windshield to Rimsky-Korsakov's music.

With the engine rumbling, Natasha pulled onto the boulevard, turned left a couple of minutes later, and stopped at a complex of neat three-story apartment buildings.

"Our blackberries will ripen in August," Natasha said, pointing to the darkened hedge. "They grow big and are delicious."

On the asphalt, a pigtailed girl hopped across a chalk-drawn hopscotch grid, kicking an empty shoe polish tin from square to square and skipping over the lines.

From the walkway, he followed Natasha into her apartment—straight into a tiny living room. His eyes went to a poster above the sofa: Ivan Tsarevich riding a gray wolf through an enchanted forest, with Vasilisa the Beautiful resting her head on his shoulder. He had loved that painting since kindergarten.

Natasha headed to the kitchenette, and he trailed behind. Her sink gleamed with cleanliness and order—except that a drill with a worn-out brush attached to its end sat at the edge of the counter. "I use it to clean the sink and tiles," Natasha said as she pulled a bag of *pelmeni* (Russian dumplings) from the freezer.

Standing next to her, Vitaly watched as she scalded the pelmeni in a pot of boiling, salted water. One by one, the pelmeni floated to the surface, fully cooked, and Natasha transferred them into a ceramic pot decorated with red poppies. She carried the pot to the table and served the pelmeni in bowls, each adorned with a red poppy at the bottom.

The two had just sat down at the table and stuck their forks into the pelmeni when Natasha sprang up. She dashed to the fridge, pulled out a bottle of vodka, grabbed a glass, and poured him a drink. Vitaly thanked her with a grin and took a sip.

They polished off their meal in silence, and she cleared the table as soon as they finished. It was time to head back to the Russian Store.

Just before they left, Natasha handed him the bottle.

"A real *muzhik*—a true Russian man—doesn't stop at just one glass."

Vitaly gave her a grateful look. The bottle was nearly full, and he hugged it with both arms.

Returning home with Natasha's bottle of vodka, he hesitated, deliberating whether to hide it or drink it. Eventually, he decided it would be wiser to finish it before Laura returned from work.

The beauty from the paused movie was still there in the living room, frozen in her smile, waiting for him on the screen. He pressed play and sat on the couch with the bottle in hand. In twenty minutes, he finished the vodka, flung the bottle to the floor, lay down beside it, and started singing at the top of his lungs in a duet with a mustachioed man from the film:

Your Royal Highness, Madame Foreigner

I recall your warm embrace—yet love was never there

Do not ensnare me in your golden nets

In death, I am cursed, but in love, I am spared.

His singing faltered and stopped when he noticed Laura standing in the doorway, staring at him. He gave her a drunken smile, but Laura, finding her voice, let out a scream.

"You broke my heart!"

He looked at her, startled; he had never seen her like this before.

"Yes, you broke my heart," she cried, "not because of your dalliances with Eva, but because of your drinking!"

Tears streamed from her eyes, and he was at a loss for words as she ran to the kitchen, collapsed onto the floor, and curled into a ball, sobbing.

From time to time, he went to Laura, circling her like a puppy, attempting to console her. Then he'd drag his feet back through the open door, sink onto the couch, and stare at the darkened TV. After a while, he'd wander back to the kitchen again.

As the first light of dawn crept in, Laura's sobs subsided at last. She forgave him, and the two made up before going to bed.

The next day, leaving Vitaly to oversleep, Laura stormed into the Russian Store and confronted the owner in the back room. She told him about Natasha who gave Vitaly a full bottle of vodka the night before—he downed it in no time, and after a long day at work, Laura came home to find him dead drunk on the floor. She insisted that Vitaly was turning into a full-blown alcoholic—and that the only way to help him was to prevent Natasha from giving him any kind of alcohol.

The owner dismissed her concerns at first—but she threatened him with a lawsuit, and he promised Natasha wouldn't do it again.

It was Friday, and Vitaly had nothing better to do but wander the lobby of the Culinary Arts Department. He paced back and forth, pausing to peer down the empty hallway before setting off again. At the main door, the panels slid open, letting in the evening air. Instead of stepping outside, he turned toward the elevator as the door sighed shut behind him.

His palms trembled, as they often had lately, so he stopped and stretched them out, staring as if he could steady them with his gaze. The trembling worsened, and he resumed walking, swinging his arms. Before he knew it, he was back at the main door, which slid open once more, as if by habit. He stopped, touching his forehead. Did he have a fever? A wave of nausea hit, and he rushed to the bathroom to vomit.

Five minutes later, he returned to the lobby, feeling a bit better, and resumed wandering.

It was hard to believe that four days and nights had passed since he last saw Natasha.

After making up with Laura, Vitaly no longer went to the Russian Store or saw Natasha. He had stopped drinking again, but the devilish pain of alcohol withdrawal tortured him. The only thing that could save him was a single glass of vodka—yes, even a small one—a priceless glass that would revive him, heal him, if only he could get his hands on it.

It was this desperate hope of encountering a colleague who might offer him a drink that kept him lingering in the Culinary Arts Department.

The elevator clicked, beginning its ascent. A minute later, it descended back to Vitaly. The doors slid open, revealing Roger Armstrong. The Tsinoy instructor of Pastry Arts held a white, semi-spherical cake in both hands. Shaped like the moon, the cake was dotted with craters and topped with a chocolate model of a lunar lander in the middle. Beside the lander, a plastic astronaut planted an American flag, while another busied himself collecting moon samples.

Roger Armstrong, a Filipino of Chinese descent, was born near Manila as Ronk Mao. He had managed to emigrate to the United States through his marriage to Patricia Armstrong, a tall, gaunt American woman who proudly claimed to be related to the first man to walk on the moon. For his part, Ronk Mao wanted nothing to do with being Tsinoy, so he changed his first name to Roger and took his wife's surname.

Even so, Vitaly thought, Roger could never pass for a true Armstrong—his lineage was plain in his face.

Perhaps that's why Roger acted like a pushover, eager to please everyone. He was known for bowing to all; for senior faculty and administrators, he even extended his left foot backward in a gesture of exaggerated deference. He not only arrived ten minutes late to department meetings—signaling he didn't want to interfere with the plans of the higher-ups—but also brought his own stool and sat in a corner, even when plenty of seats were free around the table. He never spoke up on his own but nodded incessantly in agreement as others talked.

In the fall, Roger was set to apply for tenure and promotion, so he made sure to stay on good terms with everyone.

As he stepped out of the elevator, Roger smiled at Vitaly, greeted him, and bowed, drawing his left leg back.

The two men began talking about the cake.

"Such a beautiful cake," Vitaly said, trying to sound polite.

"I made it for Patricia in the office kitchen," Roger admitted. "I promised her weeks ago."

"The cake is nice, but why did you cover it with whipped cream?"

Roger's smile vanished.

"The whipped cream is perishable," Vitaly said, raising his voice, "and you shouldn't have put it on the cake. You should have added it to each slice right before serving!"

"I don't... I don't have cream at home right now." The cake wobbled in Roger's hands. "I had to put it on here before heading back."

"Stop making excuses!" Vitaly barked.

Roger's gaze darted toward the empty corridor. Vitaly glanced too. Not a soul in sight—no one to see or hear them.

"Sorry, I have a migraine." He made his voice sound weary. "Can you treat me to some ginger tea? I've heard they use it in Manila to cure headaches."

"I don't have ginger tea," Roger lied. "But I can take you to a place that serves ginger vodka."

The two stepped into the parking lot and headed toward Roger's car. The front passenger seat was piled with a jumble of women's clothing: a pink ballet tutu, green leggings, and a blue-and-white striped blouse.

"I picked up Patricia's things from the dry cleaners this morning," Roger said, adjusting the cake behind the driver's seat. "Would it be too much trouble for you to sit in the back?"

As Roger drove off, he started a video on the headrest monitor. Vitaly fixed his eyes on it: *Schlagobers (Whipped Cream)—A Ballet in Two Acts.* Children pirouetted in a Viennese pastry shop, cakes bouncing merrily alongside them. He watched as if in a trance until Roger pulled up in front of the bar.

They sat on the barstools, and Vitaly ordered a cocktail.

The bartender dropped ice into the shaker and poured in vodka.

"Add more!" Vitaly said—and watched as the bartender poured an extra stream of liquor. "You're a good man."

The bartender gave a slight nod, added lemon juice and honey syrup, and shook the mixture.

"There are only two races of people in this world," Vitaly said. "The race of good people and the race of bad people. That's all."

The bartender strained Vitaly's drink over ice in a Collins glass. "How do you decide if someone is good or bad?"

"It's simple. First, I imagine I'm in a Nazi concentration camp. Then I recall everything I know about the person and ask myself: Would I want them as my guard? If the answer is yes, they're good; if not, they're bad. It's quick, intuitive, and accurate. After all, no one wants a bad person as their guard in a concentration camp, right?"

The bartender nodded, added a splash of ginger syrup, garnished the glass with a slice of lemon and a sprig of mint, and handed it to him.

"I'd gladly endure a concentration camp under a guard like you," he said, raising his cocktail with a grin.

The cocktail hit him fast. After the second, he was drunk enough—but toying with the idea of a third. He was about to order it when Roger stood firm. It was getting late, and Patricia would be upset.

"Why do you need to get drunk?" Roger asked.

"To forget."

"Forget what?"

"Forget my parents."

"Why would you want to forget them?"

"Because they were drunks."

Roger fell silent, but Vitaly wanted to explain.

"I was still a student in Moscow. Every day, when I came home, I'd find them rolling on the floor, completely naked and completely drunk. Truly naked, truly drunk—every single day."

He bowed his head.

"I'll wait for you in the car." Roger paid the bill and walked out.

Vitaly stopped in front of the car and leaned both hands on the hood.

Roger rolled down the window. "Come on, please, get in."

Vitaly shook his head, spread his legs, and pushed off the hood to stand upright.

"Siberian women... ah, Siberian women!" he shouted. "Do you have any idea how hot Siberian women are when they bare themselves in the Siberian cold?"

He flung open his shirt and locked eyes with Roger.

"Outside—a bitter winter, but they're bare and warm, like it's Crimea!"

He staggered, lost his balance—and fell.

Roger got out of the car, helped Vitaly to his feet, settled him in the back seat, and drove off.

"Siberian women... Siberian women..." Vitaly kept mumbling, but when the ballet playing on the screen caught his attention, he fell silent, mesmerized. Princess Pralinée danced with Mariana Chartreuse, Vladislav Slivovitz, and Boris Vodka. Ignored by the princess and her companions, the small cakes rebelled, but their uprising was swiftly quelled with beer.

A voice broke through his daze. “Good night.”

Roger had stopped in front of Laura’s house, opened the car door, and was waiting for him to step out.

Vitaly stepped out and looked around. From beneath a pile of boards stacked near the trailer, a spotted black-and-orange salamander stared at him, its eyes wide open. In the darkness, a jet roared overhead, freshly airborne from Paine Field, and the salamander darted away. Vitaly lifted his face to the sky, watching as the plane’s lights vanished into the low-hanging clouds.

Vitaly stood facing the house.

“This is the home of the lonely clouds,” he mumbled.

He turned to Roger and added, “I don’t live here anymore.”

“Where do you live, then?” Roger whimpered.

Vitaly gave him Eva’s address.

Eva’s house was sunk in darkness. Vitaly climbed out, leaving the car door open behind him. A battered copy of *Iron Horse* magazine lay in the driveway. A gust of wind flipped it open, revealing a woman in a bikini astride a Harley-Davidson.

“This is the home of stormy winds,” Vitaly whispered. He nudged the magazine with his foot and added aloud, “I definitely don’t live here.”

He gave Roger the address of the Russian Store and, for the fourth time that evening, settled into the back seat.

It was late, and the Russian Store was closed. The window display was lit, and Vitaly peered through the glass, but spotted no one inside.

“Come on, get back in the back seat,” Roger called. “I’ll take you to sleep at my place.”

Vitaly nodded, obeying, and headed toward the back door.

A gust of wind splashed a few cold raindrops onto his forehead.

Vitaly stopped, sobering up all of a sudden.

"Why do I always sit in the back seat?" he murmured. "Why do others always do the driving and take me wherever they want?"

He glanced at Roger, waiting for him in the driver's seat with a dumb look on his face.

"When it comes to me, I have to be sitting in the front, right? I have to choose the direction, I have to make the turns... and yes, I have to decide which ballets to watch."

Vitaly peered into the car. Behind Roger's seat, the cake sat, looking pompous.

"No, I definitely shouldn't be in the back seat. But what keeps me there every time? Isn't it fear? Fear that I'll fail? That I won't be good enough?

"Yes, it's fear that holds me back—and unnecessary pride too.

"This malign pride that keeps me from admitting I've made some big mistakes—but I mustn't break my promises—even the ones destined to ruin me over time."

He opened the driver's door and locked eyes with the Tsinoy.

"Roger, what's the point of life if not to change?"

"Yes, yes... life is given to us so we can change... so we can change."

"Thank you." Vitaly nodded. "I think so too. Now, move over!"

Before Roger could protest, Vitaly grabbed him by the

shoulders and pulled him out of the car. Sliding into the driver's seat, he revved the engine as Roger scrambled into the back seat.

Five minutes later, Vitaly stopped at Natasha's place and, without turning off the engine, leapt onto the wet asphalt. The rain lashed his face. He stood tall and shouted into the darkness at full volume:

"This is the home of sunshine!"

His voice rang out across the sleepy courtyard.

He grabbed Roger's cake, dashed to the apartment's front door, and rang the bell.

Natasha opened the door, the familiar drill in her hand.

Vitaly met her gaze and blurted, "Will you marry me?"

Natasha lowered her head, gripping the drill with both hands.

Five seconds stretched out, the idling car pulsing in the silence.

"Say something!"

"Well, my washing machine broke down. I need to fix it."

"If you marry me, I'll buy you a new washing machine!"

Natasha looked at him, biting her lip.

"It'll be a premium model... Voice-controlled!"

Tears streamed from Natasha's eyes. She burst into sobs, threw her arms around Vitaly's waist, and clung to him with all her strength. Vitaly wrapped his arms around her shoulders and held her tightly. The two stopped breathing.

Stepping out of the car, Roger gawked in amazement. He watched as Natasha dropped the drill, which landed on Vitaly's big toe, and the cosmic cake, crushed between their chests, smeared itself during their embrace. The two didn't seem to notice. They disappeared inside, leaving the drill and the two plastic astronauts amid the smashed pieces of cake on the concrete landing.

Roger slid into the driver's seat and drove off, ten miles below the speed limit. He had no idea how he would explain himself at home—late, smelling of a bar, and without the cake.

Two Years Later

The apartment complex bordered a busy boulevard to the east, but to the south, west, and north, it was enclosed by a thicket of wild blackberry bushes. The blackberries were ripening, magpies perched in the trees, and wild rabbits hopped along the bramble.

A young woman took her boy out for a Sunday afternoon walk. The two circled the pool and strolled along the blackberry thicket, stopping here and there to taste the berries, snacking as they went. The boulevard's noise faded far behind them as they wandered.

"I've never seen a cat on a leash before," the boy said.

The woman turned and found Vitaly approaching, hand in hand with a mother-to-be. In his free hand, Vitaly held an empty plastic container, while she clutched the leash of a smart-looking cat.

"Hello, Dessa," Vitaly said to the young woman. "I didn't know you lived here."

"Hello, Vitaly," Dessa replied and turned to the mother-to-be.

"This is my wife Natasha," Vitaly said.

Natasha gave a measured smile, cradling her baby bump.

"We're going to pick blackberries for homemade jam." Vitaly raised the empty container in front of his chest.

He wore a weathered T-shirt that read: "I won the three-legged race." Below the slogan, two men holding beer mugs struggled to run side by side. They gave it their all, even though the right leg of one man was tied to the left leg of the other with a thick rubber band.

"I really did win." Vitaly grinned, tapping the drawing with the empty container. "The prize was unlimited free beer for a whole year."

"He's joking," Natasha said. "He didn't compete. I bought him the T-shirt at a yard sale."

Dessa gave a polite nod.

"Vitaly doesn't booze at all because of the baby," Natasha said, her serious eyes meeting Dessa's. "I tell him to have a sip if he's unhappy, but he just won't."

"The mother of the Elephant Man saw elephants and ended up giving birth to a child with an elephant's head," Vitaly said, winking at Dessa. "If I keep Natasha staring at bottles, she might just give me a baby with a bottle-shaped head."

They continued chatting and laughing, then began picking blackberries and dropping them into the container. The cat stretched out on the grass and started grooming itself, and the boy sat down next to it.

"In the afternoon, I'll make blackberry jam," Natasha said, turning to Dessa. "And I'll send Vitaly with a jar for the two of you."

And so she did—later that afternoon.

THANK YOU FOR READING

If you enjoyed *Dessa's Crossing: A Novel and Other Stories,* I would be deeply grateful if you shared your thoughts in a short review or rating on Amazon or Goodreads. Even a sentence or two helps other readers discover the book.

ACKNOWLEDGMENTS

I am deeply grateful to the following people for their invaluable support in writing this book:

Bruce McAlister, my literary consultant, for his critical review of the first draft, which led me to streamline my story.

Emily Ohanjanians, my developmental editor, for her evaluations of the second and third revisions and her insightful comments and suggestions, which encouraged me to make the story more complete and emotionally engaging.

Melissa Prideaux and Angela Bojinov, my line editors, and Ellen Tarlin, my copy editor, for their assistance in polishing the manuscript.

My dedicated test readers—Anita Storck, William Chernoff, Yana Radenska, Jim Carmichael, Boyana Norris, Claudia Horn, Christian Burris, Jill Carraway, Douglas Harms, Denna and Arthur Holland, and Kirsten Morton—who provided invaluable feedback at different stages, helping to enhance characters, fix plot issues, and refine dialogue.

My daughter, Yana Radenska, an experienced search-and-rescue consultant, for ensuring that my search-and-rescue scenes were as authentic as possible.

My wife, Roumi Radenski, an avid reader and top-class librarian, for her unwavering support throughout the five years I worked on this manuscript. Her tireless reading of countless scene and chapter versions, along with her zillions of insightful comments and suggestions, was instrumental in refining the story.

My Bulgarian publisher, Plamen Totev, for his steady encouragement while I worked on this manuscript, and cover designer, Stefan Totev, for his thoughtful consultation during the development of the cover. Both have supported my previous fiction in Bulgarian, and their belief in my work over the years has been a lasting source of motivation.

Dr. Kathleen Glaspy, whose kindness, confidence, and spirit have encouraged me not only to persevere with this book over the years, but also to experience life to the fullest—with courage and joy.

My friends, colleagues, and acquaintances—Julie Jenner, Violeta Gidulska, Joanne Kim, Zeynep Ataman, Frederic Murer, Federico Pacchioni, Kalina Sirakova, Tanya Vassilevska—each of whom contributed in their own unique way.

CREDITS

I gratefully acknowledge the following resources that I used or adapted in the creation of this book.

A private post on Facebook by Yana Radenska, which inspired me to craft the "Having a Dessa is like having a Swiss Army knife" scene in Chapter Five.

The twin talk idea by Kaleb Banning Kellum in the Writers Helping Writers Facebook group, which led me to the development of my twin talk scene in Chapter Six.

The engagement scene from the *Crocodile Dundee* film, which stimulated me to develop Penelope and Dessa's engagement scene in Chapter Nine.

The "Breathe & Relax" clip in the Let's Meditate app, which I adapted to develop Dessa's meditation after Clifton's debacle in Chapter Thirteen.

The article "Why Men Kill Their Children" from independent.co.uk, which I used in justifying Dessa's decisions in Chapter Fifteen. (https://www.independent.co.uk/news/why-men-kill-their-children-1289967.html)

The "Moving to Bulgaria—Culture Shock?" article from inyourpocket.com, which provided me examples of the cultural changes in Bulgaria, as described in Chapter Eighteen. (https://www.inyourpocket.com/sofia/moving-to-bulgaria-culture-shock_77171f)

The "Don Corleone is a noob" thread from Reddit.com, which provided me examples of the political culture in Bulgaria, as described in Chapter Eighteen. (https://www.reddit.com/r/bulgaria/comments/hzdgp0/don_corleone_is_a_noob_this_mafia_boss_has_a/)

The "26 Honest Steps to Let Go of Someone You Love and Move On & Find Peace" article from lovepanky.com, which helped me develop Penelope's reasoning in Chapter Twenty-Six. (https://www.lovepanky.com/love-couch/broken-heart/how-to-let-go-of-someone-you-love)

The "They will never find your body... as hot as i do" Valentine's Day card by Noble Works, which I adapted as a birthday card in Chapter Twenty-Nine. (https://www.nobleworkscards.com/c2151vdg-c3x1-never-find-your-body-hysterical-valentines-day-greeting-card-nobleworks.html)

The "Starvation" article from Wikipedia, which I used to describe the symptoms of Dessa's expected starvation, as she imagined it while trapped in Devil's Cave in Chapter Twenty-Nine. (https://en.wikipedia.org/wiki/Starvation)

The suicide scene from the *Un Chambre en Ville* film stimulated me to develop Penelope's suicide scene in Chapter Thirty-Two.

The "Baba Yaga" story written by my talented daughter, Yana Radenska, in her childhood, which I adapted for the last scene in Chapter Thirty-Four.

ABOUT THE AUTHOR

Atanas Radenski, professor emeritus at Chapman University in Orange County, California, is passionate about both the arts and the outdoors. His literary work transforms unusual yet real-life events, people, and places into compelling fiction. *Dessa's Crossing: A Novel* is inspired by his daughter's extensive experience as a helicopter rescue technician in the Pacific Northwest.

Made in the USA
Coppell, TX
17 January 2026